where the rivers meet

BY DANNY GILLIS

MacIntyre Purcell Publishing Inc.
194 Hospital Rd.
Lunenburg, Nova Scotia
B0J 2C0
(902) 640-3350

www.macintyrepurcell.com
info@macintyrepurcell.com

Printed and bound in Canada by Marquis

Design and layout: Channel Communications and Alex Hickey

Library and Archives Canada Cataloguing in Publication

Gillis, Danny, 1955-, author
Where the rivers meet / Danny Gillis.

Issued in print and electronic formats.
ISBN 978-1-77276-002-6 (paperback).--ISBN 978-1-77276-003-3 (html)

I. Title.
PS8613.I494F56 2016 C813'.6
C2016-902193-9
C2016-902194-7

MacIntyre Purcell Publishing Inc. would like to acknowledge the financial support of the Government of Canada and the Nova Scotia Department of Tourism, Culture and Heritage.

Funded by the Government of Canada | Canada

For Kathy, my Katarina

Thank you, Kathy, for your insights, for your editing, and for our love.

Thank you to my brothers and sisters and all our family.

Thank you, Donna Morrissey, for your tips on point-of-view and setting.

Thank you, Sam, for *Geronimo's Story of His Life.*

Thank you to the Antigonish library for having every other book I needed including all three volumes of *One Canada: Memoirs of the Right Honourable John G. Diefenbaker.*

Thank you to Father Joy Pelino and the field workers at the Social Justice Centre of the Roman Catholic Diocese of Marbel, the Philippines, and to Erita Capion for telling truth to power.

Thank you to Development and Peace and Scarboro Missions for teaching me about solidarity. Happy 50th! Happy 100th!

I would like to acknowledge the inspiration of James Joyce. If I could but touch the brim of his hat. I thank Mr. Joyce for his genius and for Tommy, Jacky, and Cissy Caffrey, for Nosey Flynn, and for Cunningham, McCoy, and Power. I include in this book three fully poached e.g.s of his genius, one from *Portrait of the Artist as a Young Man* (integrated into the last full paragraph on p. 144), one from *Dubliners* (last paragraph of "The Dead", p. 184), and one from *Ulysses* (Molly Bloom's thoughts in the last paragraph of an episode of "Bonanza," p. 210).

If I could not have started without Joyce, I could never have finished without John. Thank you, Doctor MacIntyre, for your dazzling first review and your good last push. We got 'er done.

—Danny Gillis

If you were only there to explain the meaning, best of men, and talk to her nice of guldensilver. The lips would moisten once again. As when you drove with her to Findrinny Fair. What with reins here and ribbons there all your hands were employed so she never knew was she on land or at sea or swooped through the blue like Airwinger's bride.

James Joyce, *Finnegan's Wake*

PART ONE

A LOT AFOOT IN THE LITTLE VATICAN

AN ENCOUNTER

It was Joe Dillon who introduced the woodies to the Wild West. For three summers they lazed in his screened-in sunporch amid a library of comic books. They savoured the adventures of Kid Colt, Rawhide, and the Two-Gun Kid. They imagined themselves brave. These sun porch sessions led always to war whoops, a dash through field and wood, and a choosing of sides.

Seven were in the wood that day. The Caffrey twins and their brother Archie, their cousin James Dunphy a.k.a. Jimmy Dog, Joe and Lyin' Leo Dillon from across the street, and Bart Cartwright who couldn't fart right. Six cowboys. One Indian.

"I-I'm Chris," said the biggest boy. Jimmy Dog had a too-much look. Eyes too black, lips too wide, stub for a neck, thick hair overly orange. He stammered his part then waited to hear the say so or no. The characters kept coming, cowboy name by cowboy name. Jimmy Dog relaxed. He would be the leader today. Blackhatted Chris, leader of The Magnificent Seven.

"I'm Billy the Kid."

"I'm Wide Earp."

"I'm Kid Colt."

"I'm the Rifleman."

"I'm Geronimo."

"I'm Rawhide."

"N-N-No you're not. Yer ah Indian," said the leader.

"You're ah idiot," answered little Leo Dillon. Lyin' Leo they called him for his indolence.

The leader leered and lorded it over him: "Shut yer yap. If I say yer ah Indian, yer ah Indian. Anyways, w-we can't all of us be cowboys. Y-Y-You and Geronimo'll be the Indians. Me, Kid Colt, Rifleman, Billy the Kid, and W-W-Wyatt Earp will be the cowboys. Pick yourself a name."

"Sucks!"

"Well suck it, dear Leo. Pick a name! Pick a f-friggin' name you retard."

"Ya yaka yaka yaka!" hollered Tommy Caffrey. The look of him! His hair in a scalplock, his feet in moccasins, a breechcloth wrapped tight to his groin. He could pass for a Pawnee brave, but today he was playing a Chiricahua Apache.

Rubbed clean of dirt and war paint, Tommy and his twin were the spit of their mother. Same lazy curled brown hair, same gold-green apple eyes, same ruddy hide under the same freckle spray. Thin lips. Weak chins. Skinny as whips. The only way people told the two apart was by their height. They said it was the fire. It stunted Jacky, they claimed. Slowed him down. After Jacky caught fire, people said, he had to become like a baby again. Learn to crawl. Only after that could he learn to walk. What every other kid did once, Jacky Caffrey did twice. That's what some blamed it on anyway. But not their mother. She swore to God Tommy and Jacky were genetically programmed to grow at different rates. According to Mrs. Caffrey her twins weren't identical. They just looked that way.

The twins had been barberbuzzed that very morning. Tommy had argued hard for the scalplock. Long on the back and piled on top. "No way," said his father. "You're not going to church tomorrow wearing a gee-dee coontail." They kept at it all the way to the barber. Tommy won a compromise, grudging, time limited, and vindictive. He could keep it for the day, but off it would come the next morning, razor to the scalp right before church. And no complaining.

Tommy put knee to ground and from under brush drew forth a weapon so formidable that little Lyin' Leo Dillon's buggy eyes bulged. A war club slashed through air.

"Narsty. Where'd ya get the tommyhawk?"

"Made it." Tommy turned the club over in his palm. The stone was a stumble-upon. But in another way it was no accident. The wedge and the hole were too perfect. It took him like a half a second to know it was the head of an honest-to-God Micmac tomahawk. Then the hunt was on for a shaft. Rock maple would be the preference. He found one laced into a dam up the brook. Polished and beaver-chewed. Perfect. He lacquered it, drilled it, and strung it with feathered rawhide. He jammed it hard into the hole. Tight. They were perfect together.

"You made that? It sure looks real."

"It is real. It was easy to make. Lookit, the tomahawk head I found had the perfect hole right through her."

The boys argued whether it could or couldn't be.

"It's phony," Jimmy Dog said. "It's just the head off'n a rusty old hatchet that Tommy banged up to look like it was lost by some hundred-year-old drunken screechin' wailin' wagonburner."

"I will be a Indian after all," said Leo.

"Yeah, *now* you will."

The tall twin, Geronimo, upheld a hand of peace. "Problem solved, boys. I'll be the only Indian today."

"Like hell you will," said the leader for all. "N-N-N-No way we're chasin' you down and you runnin' along with a friggin' hatchet waiting to fire it at us. You must think we're m-m-more retarded than you are."

"That's true, I do." Geronimo caught himself. *Be cunning and aggressive in the face of danger.* "What are you worried about? It's not like I'm going to throw it. Are you crazy? You think I'd do that? What if I missed? Then *you'd* get it and God knows what *you'd* do with it. Anyway, okay then, I'll bury it when I get to my hiding place. It'll stay there until we finish fighting. Promise."

The leader knew his cousin had the conscience of a martyr. But there was always a first time. He glared him down. "Okay, this is how it's going to work. All of us are cowboys, 'cept you. But you're gonna bury that thing before we get to you."

"I just said I would, didn't I? Just you gotta give me a longer head start so I can do it."

" I-If I had a B-BB gun, it w-w-would be different," the leader chirped.

His elders now in agreement, Archie Caffrey, a.k.a. the Rifleman, chipped in with saucy threats. "You better run far 'n fast Geronimo 'cause there's six against one and we're the six and you're the one. We're gonna blast you to Tim Buck Two."

Seven-year-old Archie took after his father's side. A little towhead he was, with chubby cheeks and a baby's beady blue-eyed stare. Gramma Caffrey said he was going to have the big hands too. Meaty, beaty, big, and bouncy. Looked nothing like the twins. That pair of apples dropped right off the Dunphy tree.

"Better run fast redskin," Archie jabbed again.

Tommy drawled, "There's a fine line between being funny and being annoying and your big brother will let you know when you cross it."

"Now *that* was narsty."

"What trail are ya takin'?"

"The brook."

"Okay. Run then. G-Get going. Twenty... nineteen... eighteen..." Jimmy Dog yelled. And as Geronimo ran, six woodsboys chimed in apace, "Seventeen... sixteen..."

They ran through the briars and they ran through the brambles
They ran through the rushes where a rabbit couldn't go
Ran so fast that the hounds couldn't catch 'em
Down the Mississippi to the Gulf of Mexico.

"Fifteen... fourteen... thirteen..."

Geronimo scampered down the brook trail, skidding behind a dogwood tree. The guitar song stroked and stoked his brain. "Apache!" Dust leapt about his legs and moccasins, but in the count of one he was on his knees, hands fumbling for the tripline. The trap. On the eve had he set the plan to mind and in the morning, even before the barber, it was hatched. At this spot where the path veered near the brook he would make his stand. There! There was the rope. He tugged, saw earth move, and looked ahead to where it strapped the tree opposite. He saw himself pull tight and pictured a posse tumble like pins in a bowling alley.

The Babblebrook Woods they called it and there were battle sites and trails and camps and bridges with names they all knew. Bullfrog Swamp. The Beaver Trail. The Hemlock Grove. Fox Run. Manysticks. Babble for the sound that was always near. Brook for its continuous presence in their woods. Babble among the slippery elm and red maple and white and yellow birch, among the water willow, trembling aspen, pine and spruce, hemlocks too tall to see the top, gnarly hawthorn, and alder near the water. Yellow leaves in the fall. Yellowthroats in spring. And in summer, green, green, green with boy-browned trails, zigging and zagging through paths of least resistance. Eden.

The opposite bank was an asphalt and gravel parking lot that buckled with each spring freshet, no match for the brown churning torrent that tore up the banks and menaced the storebacks of Main Street. From their pinetop perches, the woodies would cheer on the upriver detritus that smashed marooned vehicles and brought forth firemen with their pumps and sandbags. But with everything closed on a Saturday afternoon, the parking lot stood deserted as a clearcut save for the weeds sprouting through cracks and waving stiffly like wooden crosses.

From there came the walker. Tommy heard its guttural groan and growl over the babble before he saw the creature trekking the hardrock wasteland, lurching dull-eyed towards him, all burn and sinew, its clothes torn, its feet bare and wide as bearpaws. Black greasy hair blurred its burnt face. Groaning and growling the walker came, weaving, heaving, and retching. Six lengths from where Tommy lay, it stopped and cast a dull ear to the sound of the water. Burn and spatter let's get at 'er and the creature fell chestward and heaved and gushed a caustic cauldron of reek.

In the distance the chase cry went up. Just a make-believe posse, blackhatted Chris, Billy the Kid, the Rifleman, Wyatt Earp, Kid Colt, and Rawhide taking up the rear, just six boys, but it stirred the creature into instant attention. With savage intent its eyes roved the opposite bank and settled in fury on the boy. Roaring and rising, it flung one brookstone and another and careened towards its quarry, one arm hung low, one leg adrag. Midstream now and closing in, red ooze dripping from its toothy maw. Tommy snatched a thrown stone and fixed his gaze on one evil eye, saw it throb as the monster neared. Saw it stare raw, red, dull hate. He threw, but his aim was low and struck his attacker centrechest. It gave a wildcat snarl.

Shifting his weapon to his right hand, Tommy set his gaze upon the deadeye.

Old Hick'ry said we could take 'em by surprise
If we didn't fire our muskets 'til we looked 'em in the eye...

He'd wait till the distance was too short to miss. The tomahawk wouldn't have to leave his hand. But fear took over. He threw. He saw the man's head snap back, saw a deep red slice from forehead to high cheekbone and saw too his tomahawk flipping and turning, then yelling and howling the posse appeared.

"There he is! Get him! Fire! Fire!"

Tommy sprang.

"Stop," the leader hollered. "After him!"

"Get the redskin! Get him! Get him! Get him! Bang bang bang BANG!"

"Die, you frigging cheat. We got you already!"

"You're dead, Geronimo. You're supposed to die when you get shot. No fair."

"You'd better stop, you little prick!"

Along the boy-browned paths, over the fallen logs and manysticks, over the running stones of Bullfrog Swamp, guns blazing, they chased and leapt and demanded him to die, but their prey didn't stop until the Babblebrook Woods were far behind him.

Down the Mississippi to the Gulf of Mexicoooo.

He burst into sunlight, and ran, ran, ran, ran, ran, ran across field and street for the sanctuary of home. At St. Columba Street, the posse held their fire and their leader snorted like a bull. "That jerk. He's not supposed to run all the way home. That ruins it. Jacky, go in and get the little prick."

Jacky refused. "He's dead anyway. The game's over."

Jimmy Dog insisted. "Look. I'm the leader here. Tommy's a chickenshit. Just argue with him until he gives up. He always gives up. You just have to keep at the little prick."

From the darkness of the upstairs window, Tommy ignored them. Mangy bunch of phony cowboys. Over their heads and further he peered, over the field and through the greenwood that hid his babblebrook, that hid his crime. Dead or dying. It was one or the other, that was for sure. What should he do? He would stay where he was safe. But what of his tomahawk? What of the evidence?

Out there Jimmy Dog raged. Joey D bored, slunk away. Jacky bolted across the street for home, Archie on his heels. And to the remnant, the leader of The Magnificent Few yelled his orders signifying nothing, and nothing, absolutely nothing he yelled or did or thought could change what had happened. Nothing would erase the memory of the man falling like a timbered tree, dropping backward without breakfall. Nothing could erase the sickening crack like axe on wood. Nothing could resurrect that hatchet-sliced head agash, agush, and awash in the malignant water of the Findrinny Brook.

Katie Beaton ran through a sunshower in red cape and hood and rapped at the back door of her best friend's new home. A sallow beanpole of a man in full-length apron, blood-streaked and grease-splattered, appeared at the door. Mr. Samwell Hung crinkled his eyes and bade her to follow.

The aromas assaulted her. Sharp vinegar, frying oil, ginger, garlic, onion, soy, fish and guts. They hit her stomach like a swarm of eels. Everywhere were skinny men in stained smocks stirring steel pots, chopping carcasses, cackling and yakking in words she couldn't fathom. She stuck close to Mr. Hung and kept her red hood up. She near ran up the back of him when he halted, bowed obsequiously, and threw open the swinging leather doors to reveal the brand spanking new Brigadoon Restaurant. She had never seen anything so orange.

At the cash register, a dark-haired girl was concentrating on the act of money counting. Quarters and dimes and nickels gathered, rolled, and folded into paper sleeves. Seeing Katie, she gasped and gushed and dashed for a hug. They hadn't seen each other in a whole momentous month. But Katie held her at arm's length, scolding.

"Joyce, you can't be in a dress at the Findrinny Fair. You have to wear slacks. We're going on rides. Kids will see your underwear."

"Mama says I have to."

"Have to what? Let them see your underwear?"

"Ha-ha. You so fun-nee, Kay-tee. No, I mean she says I have to wear a dress. And didn't you know you're not supposed to wear shorts when you come in here?"

"Your Mom said I can until I'm thirteen. That's still four months away."

Joyce followed Katie's assessing green eyes on their first tour of the new Hung's. The golden potbellied laughing Buddha, all the other smiling, crying, staring slackbellies, the eternal flame, the stale cake offering, the lanterns, the long dragon head aflame, the blue tartans in the window. Nothing erased the original impression. Too orange! Way too orange.

"You like it?"

Katie pulled band from ponytail and shook her hair to its fullest blonde and golden and let it fall halfway to her waist. "I love it."

Joyce smiled. The dimples that grew within Mistress Hung's cheeks were fantastic to imagine, like big and brassy additional smiles on a round dumpling face. On that face they fit.

"I would never wear that dress to the Findrinny Fair, but I do declare you look very pretty, Miss Hung. Very pretty and very puffy."

Joyce gave permission for her cheeks to doubledimple—smiles four and five.

A waitress, Rose by her name tag, set down a tea set. A not-so-pretty girl made less so by an ochre uniform replete with sewn-in straps and checkered apron. She was bursting out of it.

"Hey, girlie, I seen you coming."

"Rose!"

"Well, well, well, it's Katie the Pretty. Nice to see you back from the mainland. First time here, right? How do you like the new place?"

"Lovely. Except... Lovely. A little too one-colour though, if you know what I mean. The decorations are amazing, your uniform is pretty cool. It's just that I feel a bit like Linus in the pumpkin patch."

"Yeah, a bit too much, eh? You should see it when the sun's shining. The glare will kill ya. But never mind that. Look how many booths there are, and tables, and the big picture window. The Brigadoon is the best restaurant in town. Better'n the Dirty O. Way better'n the

Rose Bowl. And what about the uniform? Don't you like the fit-to-form look? Sexy as shit, I think." She pulled a lighter and pack of Players from her pocket. "Jesus I have to remind myself that Sam won't let us smoke in here anymore, even when there's no customers. We have to go to a side table. Sweet Jesus," she interrupted herself. "Whaddya suppose dem two old birds'd be gawkin' at."

The girls turned to see a pair of faces peering through the plate glass window, palms over peepers.

"Checking the new joint out," guessed Katie.

"How rude," said Joyce. "You'd think that we weren't even sitting here the way they're looking."

"I hope they don't come in. Look at them. Is that wise or otherwise?"

The women swept into the diner, all feathered hats on blue hair, old as Methuselah. Tourists most likely. Purses stuffed with greenbacks. They plunked their ample posteriors upon a pair of plush seats, removed hatpins, plucked their chapeaus, and laid them on the table. A pair of peahens preening.

Katie and Joyce looked away. It wasn't polite to stare.

"Did they have to sit in that very booth?" Katie complained. But smelling her tea, she affected a Holly Golightly air. "Hmmm. Thank you oh so very much for pouring, Miss Hung."

"You're very welcome, Miss Beaton."

"Last weekend before school starts. Are you looking forward to starting back at your creepazoid school?"

Joyce held her cup close to her chin. Her face was flat, round, clear, and open, expectant of the fun the two would have at the fair. She didn't like to give her answers straight off, especially to Katie. For Katie it was always worth thinking them through, steeping them. Breathing sweet teaheat helped her ponder life's great mysteries, not the least being Katie's provocations. She closed her eyes, sighed, and smiled mildly. There they were again. Even the most imperceptible of simpers aroused those ever-ready dimples.

"I'm glad I'm going back to my school. I'm quite content not to have to go to Bishop Fraser with all those nunny bunnies running around. Now, they are creepy. Creee-Pee. I'm glad they don't get to strap me anymore for not knowing the rosary. Good luck with that."

Katie fake gasped. "Joyce Hung, I've never known you to speak with such intolerance."

"Me! You told me what Sister Dot said about Protestants."

"Sister Dorothea you mean. What's it to you if she speaks ill of Protestants? You're not a Protestant."

"You know what I mean. Don't make fun. You tease me enough by making me eat fish every Friday. Why is that again?"

Katie Beaton was never stumped for an answer. If she didn't have one, she would invent and expound. Joyce was her perfect foil, a girl who liked to get lost in the voice of a trusted companion. If she was engrossing, like Katie always was, it was "go ahead, don't stop, tell me a story." Getting a word in edgewise? Didn't matter.

Katie began. "Why do we eat fish on Friday? Well it all goes back to the alphabet. F is the perfect letter because it comes in the middle of perfect. Double f is double perfect. It's purfffffect. That's why Catholics have fish on Friday. It's true. In catechism we learn rhymes where we put lots of f-words together. Sometimes the same f-word over and over again.

"Like what?"

"Like the one about Friar Fred and Fair ____." Katie never said that name aloud. Mouthing her cousin Fiona's name barely made it tolerable.

Joyce requested the poem. Katie sipped and silently savoured sounds. She rehearsed them thrice in her mind. Then with confidence she rhymed a twenty-one word salute.

Friar Fred was left for dead
Beneath the mighty oak
'Til Fair ____ luscious lass
Licked him and up he woke

Joyce snorted and answered like an accelerated machine gun, slowly gathering speed, ending rat-a-tat fast, and breaking into laughter. "Yes, I remember now, you fun-nee Kay-tee. But not near so funny as five year of Flishy Flyday. Hahahaha." Joyce said it that way to make fun. You so fun-nee. It was how she talked when they first arrived from Hong Kong. But not now.

When they were forced into separate schools in Grade One, Katie and Joyce resolved to turn religion to their advantage. After the trauma of segregation, they ciphered how religion could bring them syncretically together. Katie asked questions about the Buddha. She meditated on the immeasurables: equanimity, kindness, compassion, and joy. She learned the Four Noble Truths and the Eightfold Path. She celebrated the forty-nine days between death and rebirth. They tackled metempsychosis. *Met him pike hoses,* hahaha.

For her part, Joyce accompanied Katie to benediction. She memorized the Our Father, the Hail Mary, and the Glory Be, learned about the seven sacraments, did the fish thing. Together they studied the lives of saints orient and occident. They made elaborate dolls with the help of Mrs. Hung who taught them to sew, and Mrs. Beaton who showed them how to stuff the feet of runny nylon stockings with cotton balls to make saintheads, bodies, and limbs, and dress them up with nylon, cotton, wool, velvet, satin, silk, denim, lace, crepe, Joycehair and Katiehair, and equip them with crucifixes, mitres, pallets, arrows, oranges, keys, pens, and books.

What wasn't there to admire about some saints? Saint Theresa of Lisieux, the Little Flower of Jesus. The humble nun who sought anonymity but was instead raised to the status of star of the pontificate of Pius XI. Protector of missionaries. Patron of aviators for seeing visions of elevators rising to the heavens. Friend to the sick for having suffered so much herself. Dead of tuberculosis at twenty-four. And so, for her versatility and for a life lived in humble service to the priests who came to her, they made her.

What wasn't there to pity about Santa Fina? The little Tuscan *ragazza* who lay on a pallet in the city of towers till she became one with the wood, her skin melding with the boards upon which she lay. Suffering Santa Fina, guilt-ridden for handing a juicy orange to a handsome soldier. And so she lay in mean estate while rats came nightly to nibble her. And so, for a life of saintly insanity, they made her.

They dressed Princess Mandarava in beggar's wear and Kuan Yin, the Bodhisattva of Compassion, in flowing white robes. Yogi Milarepa was clad in clothes of cotton. They coloured his skin with green food dye and had him wander the Far East drinking prodigious quantities of nettle tea and resting on pedlars' beds.

Peter, upon your rock I will build my church. Brother Andrew for whom kilts are worn. Christopher who carried Christ. Doubting Thomas. James the Great. James the Less. Jude, the Miraculous One, patron of hopeless, desperate, and lost causes. When a cause is despaired of and all other paths are stopped, when life itself hangs by the thinnest of threads, you call on Jude and his help often comes at the penultimate moment. The Saint of Brinkmanship. And so, for them and for their lives spent in the company of Jesus, they made them.

For Katie and Joyce, the foundational benefit of harmonizing their religions was the unheard-of arrangement that the girls had foisted on three levels of authority—parental, academic, and ecclesiastical. For five years in a row they conspired successfully to attend the same school. In primary, they both attended the Protestant school because Bishop Fraser was bursting at the seams with little Catholics. The overflow argument didn't hold in the second year. On the first day of school, for God's sake, Katie was informed she'd been enrolled at Bishop Fraser. "Different from Joyce!" she wailed. Their parents would not hear the last of it. Joyce offered to convert to the Holy Roman Church if it might restore them to the same orbit. Katie attended mass every day to dispel Mommy's fear of apostasy. They kept it up and after a year of finagling, the little Buddhist who wanted to learn all about Catholicism was allowed to attend Grade Two at Bishop Fraser alongside her equally ecumenical best friend Katie Beaton. The arrangement continued to switch back and forth between Bishop Fraser School for budding Catholics and the St. Columba Street School for Anglicans, Protestants, and the five little Buddhists named Hung or Ming.

In Grade Seven, the three levels of authority deemed the unorthodox practice could continue no longer. The new rector of St. Columba Cathedral had gotten wind of the arrangement and parents and principals fell quickly in line. The girls could manage apart for the one year before Findrinny High School unified them again. A full twelve years old now, they took it stoically.

In the garish gourd adjacent to the booth occupied by Misses Hung and Beaton, one bluehair remarked to the other and pointed a gloved hand to one corner then the other corner of the enormous picture window. "Oh look, Helen, at the wonderful window decorations."

"What, Aggie? Where? I can't see anything without my glasses."

Aggie indicated the swatches of bright tartan that hung in either corner of the plate glass.

"Oh, aren't they beautiful. Let's ask the girl about it."

"Oh yeees, Helen. They are nice. It's not often you see a blue tartan. Oh so blue. Blue, blue, blue."

"By the way, dear," Aggie raised her voice to the waitress. "Rose, is it?"

"Yeah."

"Like the Rose of Tralee."

She'd heard them all. A rose between two thorns. The Yellow Rose of Texas. A rose by any other name. Come up smelling like roses. The bloom is off the rose. They got old real quick. The best was Sam Hung last Highland Games weekend. Rose and her friend Violet had whooped it up with the whole gang from high school. She showed up to work the next morning with a hangover like a church bell. Violet, on the contrary, was fresh as the north wind. Samwell Hung looked from one to the other and droned, "It's your eyes what give you away. Rose's are red, Violet's are blue."

"Ha-ha. Rose of Tralee. Never heard that one before. What can I get ya?"

They ordered the new Friday combination, sweet and sour fish, broccoli chow mein, and mushroom fried rice. The old doll with the glasses pointed toward the window. "We see you have some tartan hung in the window. How nice. Very Scotch indeed. What tartan is it?"

Rose gave the table a wipe and turned in the direction of the Main Street glass. "Yeah, well, Sam put it up for the Highland Games. There's been lotsa compliments. So, you want anything to drink with your fishballs? Coffees? Milk and sugar?

"Yes, yes. But what tartan is it, please?"

"Pardon?"

"I asked, do you know what tartan it is? I don't believe I've seen it before. The blue is very bright."

"Yeah. Nice."

"But do you know what clan it represents?"

"Clan?"

"It does represent a clan, doesn't it? Don't they all?"

"Oh, I don't know. Maybe it's the McHung tartan and it represents the McHung clan." She snorted. "Get it? McHung in the windows." The tourists failed to see the humour. The waitress persisted. "Violet! Valerie! Hey Valerie! Do you know what kind of tartan Sam's got hung in the window? No? Not a clue? Violet? No? Sorry. So, fishball special and two coffees. Coming right up."

"They sure didn't like that," Katie whispered to the young Hung with her. "Look at that one sucking in her cheeks like she just swilled a whole gallon of pickle juice."

"That would be Helen," whispered Joyce.

The two ladies had indeed turned ugly. They snorted like warthogs, muttered, clamped purses, and fastened hats. They and their greenbacks bustled from the Brigadoon. They stormed down Main Street, beads rolling from their foreheads, and halted four doors east where they were cornered by a man in a bright red kilt standing in front of a gaudy display of tartan clad mannequins.

"Good day, good day. Ma'am. Ma'am. You're new to town, aren't you? Can I interest you in some souvenirs to take home? Here, take this postcard, no charge. Where are you from? Boston, I suppose. I'm sorry, are you okay? You seem flustered. Can I help you?"

The women read the sign above his head: "Wilkie's Celtic Court, Tartan and Findruine Galore." A novelist couldn't have planned it any better.

The women had come upon an authority with impeccable credentials and the gall to match. This was Mr. Wilkie Cunningham the Third, the district's chief importer and exporter of Scottish and Irish paraphernalia. Based on the evidence presented by the victims, Cunningham judged that both a dearth of knowledge and a paucity of propriety had been exhibited in the Brigadoon Chinese Restaurant that afternoon. He immediately offered to represent the plaintiffs.

"You've come to the right man," he said. Indeed they had. Cunningham was not a simple purveyor of plaid. He was a veritable tartan crusader. For years he had petitioned the Town Fathers to hang tartan from lampposts and telephone poles during Highland Games week and harangued his fellow shopkeepers to dress every window in a sea of plaid. He petitioned for a sign to be erected on every entrance to town. Every town in Nova Scotia had a moniker and soon the Town Fathers would decide on theirs. If Wilkie Cunningham had his way, everyone entering town would be welcomed to "Findrinny, The Tartan Heart of Nova Scotia."

The Cunningham name had always been associated with the Fair, the Games, and Main Street. The current scion was one of the town's leading citizens. Head of the Main Street Merchants Association, vice-president of the Findrinny Highland Society, secretary of the Ancient Order of Oddfellows, cantor in the St. James Choir, every Sunday morning in white shirt and Cunningham tie, surrounded by a brigade of rotund, ruddy-faced Presbyterians, their harmonized voices lifted in manly praise to their hoary headed Jehovah. On every morn besides the Sabbath, he wore the uniform of his Celtic emporium: ghillie brogues, tartan socks covering the whitest calves in the Quad County area, red flashed garters to match his flaming red kilt and tartan tie. He was gird with a chrome-buckled wide leather belt and a sporran of lynx pelt with the dead animal's head still attached, glossy-eyed, furry as ever, teeth bared, tongue curled like it was ready to leap off its flap. Over his stout torso Wilkie displayed an open collared white shirt, full and loose as a pirate's. And how fitting was that, for he was a modern class of corsair. Not of the sea, nor armed with flintlock and cutlass, but a sassenach buccaneer with a *skean dhu* stuck down one of his Shetland wool socks, a cash register for booty, and an iron vault to hold it fast. The richest of the three Jersey merchants who cornered the market on findruine after the Strike of '51. Though his name was always listed last when the triumvirate was spoken of, Cunningham had long surpassed Robin and Jones in personal wealth.

"Surely to God," he complained, "you'd think a waitress at a restaurant called the Brigadoon could learn the name of the tartan hanging in her employer's window. To think that a MacDougall could fail so miserably, and them always feeling so high and mighty and Gaelic and all. But I suppose the employer didn't take the time to teach her. Chinamen are like that. It's Sam Hung we have to blame. You can be sure I will have words with him this very day."

"Mr. Cunningham, we can't thank you e—"

"Call me Wilkie, please. Tut, tut, my dear ladies. Not only have you poor dears been ill-treated, but for heaven's sake, you still have not been informed of the identity of the tartan in question! Come with me. Perhaps together we can pinpoint it."

The owner-operator of Wilkie's Celtic Court knew as well as anyone what tartan hung in Hung's. It was he who'd sold it. As he often harangued his weary wife, "I am first and furthermost a businessman. Sam Hung can give me money anytime he wants. Yes, I sold him two swatches for his Grand Opening. I even watched Sally hang them in the corners. I had no problem with that. Then he stole my name, the cheeky little chink. I told him months before if I ever opened a restaurant in town I would call it the Brigadoon. He just out and out stole it. I never knew until two days before the Grand Opening when he hung that grotesque gigantic neon sign of a Highland dancer over the sidewalk and under it in big bold letters, Brigadoon Chinese Restaurant. Jesus, I was mad. Why couldn't he call it Hungs or Wongs or Wings like every other chink restaurant in the province? No, Sam Hung has to steal my name and embarrass our culture."

Wilkie cultivated the ladies. "And where might you be visiting from? Where in Massachusetts? Oh, Melrose. I see. And you? You're from where? Braintree, is it? How lovely. Lovely name, Braintree. A lot of intelligent people there, no doubt. Hahaha. Home for the fair, I suppose? Yes, but of course you might have relatives here? What's your faaather's name, as they say. I hope you don't think I'm nosy. Boyd, is it. And you? Oh, your husband is a Boyd. You're sisters-in-law then? So I see, you're now a Boyd and you're not now. You were, but you aren't anymore. You are, but you weren't. How will I get that straight?" And in this way he pried open purses like John Pettipas.

"Angus D. MacGillivray. He'd be your mother's father's brother, am I right? From the Point. He was a piper. Did you know he bought your great-grandmother's diamond ring from this very emporium? Set in finest findruine. And she left it for your grandmother and she left it for your mother. You know this history, of course. Yes, of course. Look at this, would you?"

The ladies were suddenly confronted with a showcase with but one inhabitant—a glittering piece of high-heeled footware, a silver satin cage sandal with crystal applications, mirrored leather straps, and double heel. Under it was a dateplate claiming the shoe was made in 1358.

"Do you know what this is?"

"Oh," gasped Mrs. Boyd.

The Sandal of Findrinny, like Strazza's Veiled Virgin of St. John's, was an artifact that escaped notice for a century under the noses of its unwitting protectors. Just as the little novices dusted and fussed over the marble head of the Mother of God, solemn-faced on her open column but just an elbow away from destruction, so had the Irish bumpkin who smuggled the most prized specimen of findruine from the Old Country to the New remained blissfully ignorant of its true value. Shoe Number Two, the *Toronto Star* called it when the story broke in '05. But by then it was already in the hands of the Cunninghams.

As with the Veiled Virgin, the Sandal fully arrested the first-time viewer. You stepped back, then you desired to caress and see if it could be true. So delicate and ethereal and yet so solid. It wasn't for sale, of course. He knew tourists would be so dazzled by it that none would leave without buying at least one piece of findruine, if only so they could legitimately speak of a personal relationship to Shoe Number Two.

He led the ladies gently to the next showcase, sparkling with silver and coppery red bands and bracelets and watches and rings. They gasped at the glitter and retreated. "Oh no, we can't afford that."

The reaction was not unknown to him. He blocked their passage. "Here you go," handing them a faded postcard of the Canso Causeway, something familiar to settle the nerves while he took them in another direction.

"Does your husband have a kilt, Mrs. Braintree? I mean, Mrs. Boyd."

Immediately they were surrounded on all sides by mahogany laying tables and floor-to-ceiling cubbies stocked high with tartan folds. The entire accoutrement for Highland dress stood to the mirrored end of the room: brogues, spats, buckles, socks of eight colours, flashes, sporrans of horsehair and leather, silky cummerbunds for the dandy, pipe band jackets, Prince Charlie jackets, button waistcoats, kilt pins and cufflinks, balmorals, glengarries, and tartan tams.

The twenty top-selling tartans wound around carousels made of bird's eye maple. Wilkie pulled the bolt of Cameron of Lochiel briefly areel and held it like a maitre d'. With a flick of the wrist, the cloth rewound obediently and stilled itself upon its sturdy carousel. Reverently, Wilkie showed in turn the MacNeil of Barra, the MacPherson and the MacGillivray, the MacDonald of Clanranald, the hunting and the dress, the ancient and the modern, allowing his fingers to idle on each presentation, looking the ladies in the eye and murmuring, "Uh-huh? Uh-huh?"

"It was a blue tartan," said Helen Bryant, meaning to speed him along.

"And here is the Boyd, your husband's tartan, Mrs. Boyd. We can have a kilt ready in two months. You could give it to him for Christmas."

"No, I'm sorry, Mr. Cunningham. He's not much interested. I couldn't get him in a kilt if the Queen Mum came for tea."

"A tie then. We have quality Shetland wool ties at the counter. You can get one before you leave. I'm sure he'll wear a tie. They're good for any occasion. And a findruine clip. Quite inexpensive. Good then. What colour did you say that tartan was? Ah, blue. Well, here we are now." He signalled to the right and with quick steps moved about the room, showing the options, intoning their names—Anderson, Ramsay, Smith, Thompson.

"That's it!" cried a matron pointing at the next one he yanked.

"Are you sure this is the tartan? Are you sure?"

"Yes," they agreed. "That's it. Absolutely."

"Well, Holy Hannigan, this is the one tartan for which there can be absolutely no excuse for ignorance. Every Main Street tinker, tailor, or teller should know this is Nova Scotia's very own and newly minted tartan. The woven emblem of all Bluenosers, first used to represent the province in 1955, registered at the Court of the Lord Lyon in 1956, and soon to be adopted by the Provincial legislature as our official tartan. I can assure you ladies that I will take up this matter with Sam Hung myself, and if nothing is done, the incident will be brought to the Highland Society for sanction. I myself commit to personally pursuing recompense!"

Back at the Brigadoon, Rose MacDougall laid down two plates of fried fishballs, doughy and dripping in fluorescent red sauce. "What a roast, huh? Most people do it the other way. They dine before they dash. Those old crooks must be on a diet. Turns out they didn't want nuttin'. You girls interested in somethin' deeff-ernt? On the house?"

From then on, Katie and Joyce talked only of the Findrinny Fair. Joyce wanted to see the dragons. For Katie it was the Ferris wheel because you could see so far. They would eat swirls of cottony pink candy. They would do the fun house. They would ride the carousel. They would enjoy the last week of summer, the last days before their sundering.

Old farts in nice kilts. These were the men of the Findrinny Highland Society. Not so old, though, since the Legion took an interest in the Society's mission and mandate. On St. Andrew's Day, 1955, forty members of Scotia Branch 59 joined the Highland Society en masse. Sergeant Major Ronald Atlas MacDonald led the charge. Without appearing too eager, Big Ran'l installed an executive of cronies, and when it suited him, assumed the presidency. A long-dormant gift of oratory sprung forth from him like a geyser. Every Tory in town said he should run for office.

MacDonald became chief of the clans during the Society's centenary year. He would be both *consigliere* and celebrant. Relieved of piddling matters and worries of the office of president, he could now do what suited him. The first thing he did was to invite Wing Commander Jack Allan of the Royal Canadian Air Force to bring his Golden Hawks to the Games. To see Big Ran'l stand tall among his townspeople, his large white head turned heavenward, ooohing and ahhhing, was to see a man in the prime of life, blood rushing through his dilated veins, chest heaving, his huge heart absorbing the firestorm of excitement that coursed through his people. And high above the multitude, the eight Golden Hawks wheeling like gods. Then came Bill "The Thrill" Stewart. Everyone knew what had befallen the solo stunter just that April. Flight Officer Stewart's engine had sputtered and failed and like a deadwing bird hurtled earthward where the "**Onlookers Watch in Horror**" and the "**Crowd Stampedes at Airshow**" and the "**Pilot Parachutes to Safety**." But The Thrill was on that day.

The entire week was a triumph for the Society. More bands than ever, more athletes, more dancers, more fiddlers. Five thousand showed up for the Concert Under the Stars. Even the university stepped up. Among its administrators and professors, Big Ran'l had collaborators aplenty. The result was like the Oscars. A summertime homecoming for alumni. Check. The granting of honorary degrees to three auspicious Scots. Check. The erection of a cairn to honour Malcolm H. Gillis, the famed Bard of Findrinny. Check. The Golden Hawks Airshow was just the cherry on top of a creamy Highland Games sundae.

People marvelled at how big Ran'l was getting. Involved in so much and still able to tend his many business interests. By the age of forty-five, MacDonald, farmer, war hero, lumberman, mine owner, land speculator, had become a very wealthy man. What he aspired to now was power and recognition. He could pay people to do the day-to-day. To endear himself to the populace, he joined a variety of service clubs, appeared at hockey games, and gave generously to all kinds of beggars. A reformed millionaire, what could be more endearing than that?

Next he pursued influence. A boatload of money to the Stanfield and Diefenbaker campaigns guaranteed him a seat at two tables. He wasn't ready to run in '58 so he installed a folksy puppet as his proxy. Cape Breton Highlands went Tory for the first time in three decades. A slim margin, but they always were, whoever came out on top. The morning after her election, Mrs. O'Leary opened her front door to see Ronald Atlas standing there hat in hand. No matter his riches, he was not above reaping the benefits of patronage. Big Ran'l had witnessed the Liberals when they were in power and was intent on evening things up. "Clemmie," he said, "to the victor go the spoils. Let's get spoiled."

Since the Diefenbaker landslide of '58, Big Ran'l had met the Prime Minister of Canada on three occasions. The most recent was at his official residence. Inflicted as they were with their Cape Bretonisms,

Mr. and Mrs. MacDonald showed up a good six hours early for dinner.

"Dinner," said Ran'l. "Where I come from, dinner's what you eat in the middle of the day." And this was just such a marvel that Ran'l would fixate on this detail with every retelling of the visit to Sussex Drive. But, he would always add, out of a transmutation of meal names came instant friendship. As was usual with his good wife, fortune followed foible. Yolanda kept Mrs. Diefenbaker (Call me Olive, dear. Okay, olive deer, what a beautiful shade of green doeskin you're wearing.) laughing the entire afternoon. A reciprocal invitation was made and the Diefenbakers promised they'd see them next year in Findrinny Fair.

It was the day before the Highland Society's monthly meeting that Big Ran'l, in his capacity as chief of the clans of that all-male cultural citadel, caught wind of what would become known in their annals as The Cunningham Motion. The news of the motion came through the Society president, Clansman Hector Caffrey, who had been lobbied by the mover, a conniving merchant of tartans and findruine, just that afternoon.

"Cunningham's on the warpath," said Hector. "He'll have us make fools of the Society and a failure out of poor Sam Hung. He's told Sam he has to either reprimand the waitress or take down the tartan. Sam flat-out refused. Now our illustrious vice-president is wanting the Society to put a letter in *The Crypt* telling people to stay clear of the Brigadoon. Sam's worried as hell but ticked off too. He kept waving his arms and saying, "He got no light. He got no light." Made me nervous there for a bit with all those big shiny blades hanging around the kitchen. I told him, "Don't even think about taking that tartan down. We'll figure something out."

"The son of a *whoo-er,*" said MacDonald. "Who does he have?"

"This morning when he talked to me he already had Ogilvy, MacNaughton, Gower, and Roddy Bec. Wilkie couldn't help but brag. He figures to have eight votes by the time we meet."

"At least he told you what he was planning, the runt. Sooo, he figures eight will do it. We need to turn out the troops. Let me see that list." Big Ran'l held it as far from his eyes as possible. When he straightened his back to read it, his sloopy gut hardened like bombshell.

He chewed and spit his way through the names.

"Cunningham only told me because it's me who makes up the agenda," Hector explained. "He knew I would rule out the motion if he made it from the floor. And I would have. So far he's called his sure bets. I'd say there's maybe three but not four others who would side with him. Johnny Tulloch could be convinced either way. I'm sure he's being offered a reward as we speak."

"Okay, say Wilkie has eight votes. We need that many and then you can break the tie vote. Who do we have?"

"There's you, Al Graham, Charlie, that's three. Blaise Cameron, four."

"Angus R?"

"They've got company in from the States. Angus wasn't planning on coming, but—"

"He'll come. Five. I suppose Judge Hughie is down in Port Hood this week, probably not planning on coming back for a six o'clock meeting. Get on the horn to him anyway. What about the rest?"

"The Major's away in Scotland till university starts up next week, so forget him. And I talked to the Venerable Bede. Saw him at the track. He's running a practice tonight. Says he has to stay with the kids. Nosey Flynn's so far back of Bornish he may as well be on the moon. Little chance he'll make it. It would be entertaining if he did, though."

"I'll talk to Bede. Je-esus, Nosey Flynn. Why do we even let people from Bornish on the board?" Ran'l screwed his face into a terrible corkscrew grimace until he looked three weeks constipated.

"Nosey's our honorary fiddler. We've got to have one of them. There's hardly a fiddler to be had in Findrinny. It's a sad situation. It's like they are vanishing all over Cape Breton. Flynn's the best we got."

"Any way to get him in here?"

"Maybe if I drive out an hour there and an hour back."

"Do it. What about Lucky? Any chance our mutual albatross will show up?"

"On a bender since Saturday," Hector said.

"Go find him, will you. See if you can sober him up at least for the vote." Big Ran'l paused while he bit off a new chaw then horked a dismissive stream of brown tobacco six feet from the stoop. "He's not a very serious man, our Lucky, is he?"

Hector ignored the understatement. "Alternatively, we could tell everyone to stay away. You included. If we don't get a quorum of eleven, Cunningham can't force a vote." Hector let it go at that. Best to let Big Ran'l puzzle it out on his own now that he was well-informed. If there was a strategy, the *consigliere* would devise it.

"Telling people to stay away?" Ran'l spit. "That would be the coward's way out. I'd rather fuck Wilkie Cunningham standing up. Fuck him real good."

With her usual zeal, sunny Cissy Caffrey prepared the noontime meal. She cooked the beef and barley soup and their go-with fluffy biscuits. She meted out the chores and the discipline too. The little scamps had better be at their best when Cissy Caffrey was on the nut. She counted four around the table this day. Just two amiss. One with Mommy being nappied for stinkybum. And number six banished to the Stool of Repentance. Already! Even before he sat for dinner.

The Stool had been Tommy's noontime perch since the murder, far away from the cacophony and an arm's length from the radio. He rested his cheek on the counter. At his back, out of sight but not out of mind, stood the dreaded wringer washer, bane of his nightmares. He'd heard of an evil pair of twins who jammed their little sister's hand into wringers just like those, breaking every bone in the girl's arm. In his own dark dreams the rollers grabbed tender fingertips and pulled him nails, knuckles, hands, wrists, arms, shoulders, and head toward its unforgiving maw, his dumb mouth shrieking into the tub's churning grey water until head and body, flattened like a flounder, flopped in the basket among the stiffened towels and petrified pajamas. "Tommy, turn up the radio, will you, since you're sitting right beside it." It was his father, for whom the noontime news was a ritual on par with the rosary.

Freed of the washing machine's magnetism, Tommy rearranged his focus on the newscast, the point of his self-banishment. What would CJFF sputter today? What would it say about a dead-drunk drunk found dead, dead, dead in the Findrinny Brook, tomahawk slice to the head. It was only a matter of time before the investigation traced to him, for surely the cowboys would talk, and then what? Every day his mind entered the cruel courtroom and the dark confessional. The DA accusing. The judge sentencing. Hang by your neck until dead, dead, dead. It didn't have to be that way. Tommy would put his salvation not in The Law but in The Lord. Tomorrow he would push through the burgundy velvet and enter the Tall and Small. He would kneel in the darkened space where his weight would trip the light that warned the other penitents that a sinner was preparing to unburden his invisible but immortal soul. The priest would draw back the wooden slide. The boy would confess and repent and gain escape from the grinding, gut-wrenching guilt that held him hostage.

If there was no news on the news (and there wasn't), Tommy would wait at his station another ten minutes, through the weather, through the sports, and unto the time they pronounced the recent dead. For distraction, there was the dining din. Molly spoonbanging. Jacky slurping. Archie with a buss on. Daisy's new words. Cissy regaling her father with the endless mindless minutiae of her mundane existence. Her A in Arithmetic. Edy Boardman's new balloon-tired bicycle. Oh my God, you should see it. Gertie MacDowell's new dress. Oh my God, you should see it.

Father's voice rose above the humdrum. "Tommy! Turn that up for the sports, will you! Let's hear if Maris or Mantle hit another one last night."

Cissy had a news flash. "Daddy, Bobo says he can't eat the soup 'cause he's allergic."

"I am lergic," Archie begged.

"You're allergic to soup? To all soup? Did you hear that, Daddy? Bobo is allergic to all soup."

"I am."

"Well, you can go hungry then."

"Good! I will."

"Look at that apple pie on the windowsill, Bobo. Doesn't that look good? Vanilla ice cream to go with it. Oh, I'm sorry. I forgot. You can't eat your pie if you don't eat your soup. Too bad for Bobo." And she bent over Daisy-in-the-highchair to tease her fat little plucks and the dainty dimple in her chin. "Now, baby," Cissy Caffrey said, "say out big big. I want a drink of water."

"How about a dink a DOOCE!" demanded Daisy.

"Woo-hoo!" cheered Hector Caffrey. "Another one for Mantle. See, Jacky, I only go for winners. The Yankees, the Habs, and the X-Men. All winners. You hear that? Go,Yanks!"

Into the kitchen swept Mrs. Caffrey, an infant slung in swaddling clothes from her hip. She kissed her husband, laughed, and hugged Daisy-in-the-highchair, laughed again at the buss on Archie and spotting a twin on the stool said, "Tommy! What's this? Day four?"

"Five," said Cissy. "He cursed again."

"Yeah, he said shit right out loud. Everybody heard him."

"Shush, Bobo. It's just as bad for you to say it." And to conceal a grin, Mrs. Caffrey brushed away a strand that had fallen from her unruly brown hair.

"Just telling is okay. It's not cursing."

"Still a bad word," Cissy ruled.

"Is not when I'm just telling a story. Daddy does it."

Hector and Tommy Caffrey shushed them for the obituaries.

"We regret to announce the death of John Johnny Willie Sandy MacDonald of Glenville, Inverness County. The death occurred at St. Mary's Hospital in Shean on Sunday, August 26. Remains of the late John Johnny Willie Sandy MacDonald will be resting at the Shean Funeral Home from..."

Tommy hiked up the volume. For five days, as much as he dreaded what he might hear, he had wangled the Stool of Repentance. All his powers were at play to hear and to discern the person behind the death notification. Johnny Willie Sandy was easy. Tommy's victim didn't die in Shean. That was twenty miles away.

"We regret to announce the death of Joseph 'Fiddler' Campbell

of Portree, Inverness County. The death occurred Wednesday at St. Martha's Hospital in Findrinny Fair."

"Do you know that man, Daddy?"

"Fiddler? Yes I do."

"Does he live near here?"

"He's from up the valley. Now shhhh."

"Did you go to the funeral?"

"Yes."

"Did he have anything wrong with his right eye?"

"Other than he can't see out of it anymore. No, nothing was wrong with his right eye."

"Are you sure? When did you see him last? Did he have long black hair? Was he old or—"

"Tommy! Be quiet until the news is over and you can ask all the questions you want."

"Just tell me how old."

"Please, Tommy, shut it."

When the daily internments had ended, the questions began anew, his father answering as best he could, his mother demanding to know why all of a sudden this interest in the dearly departed and did his cursing every day have anything to do with this newfound fascination with funeral announcements, just like his father. But Tommy had no patience for such questions. He knew his obligations. Confession was between him and the priest.

Jimmy Dog did not call on his cousins all week, a fact commented on by Mrs. Caffrey. "Jimmy is here every day during the summer, right at the crack, in the kitchen eating porridge and gone all day with you lot. And now he doesn't show up for six days. Why wouldn't I think something's up?" She stared them down. "Something's going on. Something *is* going on. I am going to call Aunt Mary if you don't tell me."

The twins weren't saying dick to their mother. But among themselves they discussed. They knew Jimmy Dog had to be mad, all of them cutting out like they did. But what was he going to do about it? That was the question. They decided to launch an investigation of their own. They didn't have to look far. Leo Dillon had the dirt if you could believe him.

"When you guys got away, Jimmy Dog was superpissed. He looked like his head was going to explode. Then he thought that you weren't carrying your tommyhawk when you ran out of the woods on us. He goes, 'T-T-T-Tommy wasn't carrying that o-o-old hatchet, was he? So he musta b-b-b-b-b-b-b-buried it like I told him to.' So me and him go back to that spot where you were hiding and dig up around there, but we only found some stupid trap you set for us. You were going to try to trip us with that rope, weren't you? Good plan. Too bad for you you got killed before you could do it."

"Yeah, and?" asked Tommy.

"Yeah and nothing."

"Didn't you see anything strange?"

"Whadya mean strange?"

"You didn't see anything in the river?"

"Besides polio slime?"

"Did Jimmy Dog find anything?"

"Like what. How am I supposed to know if he found anything? I wasn't watching him like a hawk."

Jimmy Dog was taking shots. Puck after puck slammed against the barn wall, each just adding to the black marks and missing shingles. He was shirtless, the late summer rays beating hot off his spotted back. He spotted Tommy entering his yard and hollered, "Are you retarded? You were dead and you ran home. You're not allowed to do that. It's against the rules. When you get shot yer s'pose 'ta die."

"Yeah, yeah, yeah, yeah. I'm sorry, okay. Did you find anything at the brook the other day?"

"Like what?"

“Like my tomahawk.”

“Your hatchet, you mean. Why would I want that piece of crap.”

“You went lookin’ for it.”

Jimmy Dog wound up with a cannonading drive at the red rectangle smeared on the teethmissing grey wall. BANG. “And the Rocket puts it in the top shelf! What a shot! You still here? Get off my property!”

He could hear shouting inside the house. The Dog’s parents were at it again. Maybe that’s why Jimmy Dog wanted him gone. He slunk to the property line. No dispute was ever easy with Jimmy Dog Dunphy. He had seen teachers pull Jimmy Dog screaming and flailing from enemies so foolish as not to back down. He had seen him tied up with ropes.

“So the fall fair starts tomorrow.” Tommy started. “D’ya wanna go?”

“Fuck off my property.”

“Why are you mad at me? Just because I ran home and wouldn’t fall down and act dead.”

Jimmy Dog cranked a bullet that caught low glove side. BANG.

“What makes you think I’m mad at you? Why would I be mad at you, ya yellabelly. You worry too much. You’re thinking too much, yellabelly. I just want you off my property, that’s all.” BANG. “You know what you are?” BANG. “You’re like the last thing the boy said before his head got sucked down under Bullfrog Swamp, the last words out of his mouth before the quicksand stuffed up his lungs.”

“What did he say?”

“Think about it.” BANG. “Look at me! LOOK AT ME!”

When he did look, Tommy saw vindictiveness shining through a veneer of vicious composure. He accepted face and fate as a criminal accepts ball and chain. There would be vengeance (Jimmy’s), but when would it come? There would be suppressed anger (his), but when would it end? For the sake of resolution, he would abide. For the sake of the oldest memory in his twelve-year-old head, he would always abide.

“Too deep, Tommy, too deep,” said Jimmy Dog. “You’re just too deep.”

By the end of August, Mrs. Caffrey felt that their social lives were fully controlled by the Findrinny Highland Society. *Ìosa,* they were busy. Hogmanay, Robbie Burns, the Culloden Commemoration, St. Columba's Day, the Highland Ball, the University President's Dinner, the Findrinny Highland Games, the Findrinny Fair. She had them all red-circled. And the last one double-circled: The Feast of St. Andrew, November 30. On that night Hector would relinquish the mantle of president and slide into the purely ceremonial, or so they say, role of chief of the clans. Nothing to do but wear his kilt and show off his new teeth.

Chief of the Clans. Just thinking of the title made her want to salute. And after a year of that, he could go back to being just an ordinary member in his pantheon of clubs: the Royal Canadian Legion, the Knights of Columbus, the Third Order of St. Augustine, the Findrinny Irish Society, The Cape Breton Fiddlers Associaaaaation. That's how they pronounce it here. Can you bear it? The long loopy low "ayyyyyyyyy" stretching out beyond credulity. Like what Wilfred Gillis said so authoritatively to that waitress at the Brigadoon, "Charge it to the Cape Breton Fiddlers Associaaaaation." But Hector's not out of it yet. Far from it. He's up to his eyeballs again, plotting and scheming with heavy hitters in tow. I exaggerate. One heavy hitter in tow but a very heavy one at that.

Thinking she had heard something in the yard, Mrs. Caffrey hastened to peer through a windowglass. "Darn," she whispered. "The grotto." Hector's damn grotto was in the way. She couldn't see a thing. He'd begun working on it their first summer on St. Columba Street. He dug up a truckload of loam and dumped it beside the house. Someone was throwing out a bathtub so he scavenged that. Clawfooted, all chipped porcelain, and rusted around the iron. Hector painted the great ugly thing and submerged one end two feet into the earth and then proceeded to build up an entire perimeter of big beach rocks, whitewashed to match the veil of the virgin. He planted roses to climb the rocks and welcome the statue when it did arrive. Sure enough, one afternoon he landed home with the Blessed Virgin Mary laid out like a sleeping child in the back seat of the car, her head on a pillow. The nuns gave it to him. When Bridget saw the pillow, she said, "My God, what do you think her capable of, waking up and assumpting away?" But she had to admit, Mary looked right at home in her tub. Our Lady of the Porcelain Throne. Look at herself. A regular bathing beauty.

Then she really did hear something. A crunch of gravel and a car pulling to a stop and idling. She couldn't see through the grotto, but she knew damn well what to expect—Hector and a carful of clansmen. She heard something upstairs as well. Three sets of flying feet. The little Christers were awake all this time. Now she had them to deal with too. She intercepted them in the porch.

"Get back to bed you three, there's nothing to see here. Who has Hector got with him tonight? I hope to God Lucky isn't in the car. *Ìosa,* there's Nosey Flynn. This should be wise."

A spindly-legged scarecrow of a man in Irish tam and baggy church trousers dislodged from the back seat. He was often seen fiddle in hand, trailing like a caboose a group of clansmen or comrades or university students out for a spree. Flynn's ferret eyes scanned the yard and took in the shining spectacle in the garden. It was even more spectacular at night, the grotto. Hector had planted six rosebushes that grew like gangbusters but produced not a single rose. Not one red bud. To compensate, he built an entire latticework enclosure, painted it blue and white, and strung it with a zillion Christmas lights.

"Jesus Christ, Hector! That's a bee-yuuuu-tiful shrine you have there!"

Then Nosey spotted the three Masters Caffrey standing in front of their mother. He screwed up his face in wonder and lurched forward to investigate. When the bag of bones was handy enough, Mrs. Caffrey observed two translucent drips coalescing at the reddened nares. Dewdrops they were, drips of clear snot. He halted and glared hard through the screen door, his eyes blinking, his lips moving across his face like a runaway canoe. "Dying Jesus," he croaked, "Am I seeing double or thripple?"

From the other side of his new Strato-Chief, her husband appeared, head bobbing and smiling above the car roof. Mrs. Caffrey did not return the smile. She hoped her glare caught him like a slap.

From the back seat slid another man in fits and starts. He stood briefly before pitching further toward the rear of the vehicle. He braced himself on legs spread wide for greater balance and slid partway down until he had reached the appropriate centre of gravity and remained there about ten degrees off plumb. He indicated by hand signals that he was alright. Bridget recognized the most elegant pompadour north of Elvis Presley. It belonged to her brother Lucky.

"Now, that's attractive," said Mrs. Caffrey.

He hollered, "Just need to recover my ekeyibrium, my ekeylibruum."

Archie said, "It's Uncalucky. And he's paloothered."

"Doesn't have a leg under him," said one of the twins.

"He was short and he got shorter," said the other.

"Dth. Dth. Dth," she scolded from behind them. "Get back to bed you fellows. Get."

From the shotgun seat—for that was the only place Ronald Atlas MacDonald ever occupied—the slow-moving giant extricated himself stiffly, one flesh leg, one steel leg at a time.

"C'mon, Lucky. See if you can move away from the car."

Dunphy failed to advance. Too risky, he indicated.

"C'mon. You don't expect me to carry you like I did at Monte Cassino," MacDonald boomed like a cannon. Without even trying, Big Ran'l had the most thunderous voice in Cape Breton. Louder than Billy Joe MacLean. More deafening than Jim the Rooster.

"By God, I think he does. Grab him, Hector, and hoist him on my back."

Indoors, they plunked Lucky alongside the kitchen table where one elbow at least could be supported. The fiddler Flynn sat on the daybed, waiting quietly to be served his whiskey. Big Ran'l liked the greater height afforded by the Stool of Repentance. But what a sight he was. Spread wide open, knees akimbo, ample stomach distended, a *cromach* erect between his legs, his large arse spread like flattened dough over the round stool seat. An avuncular Buddha surveying the populace.

Bridget pulled Hector aside. If there was one stance that scared him, it was her hands on her hips. It alerted him to the potential for the endless harangue, the nag, though it was a word she hated. But it didn't lead to that, thank God. "Please tell me. Why would you bring them back here? And Lucky to boot. You put the run to him last time, remember. Didn't we agree to never give him a drink in our house?"

"Well, Nosey is sleeping on the couch anyway. The boys are picking Ran'l up and Lucky's going with him. I won't give him a drink, don't worry. Ran'l will take him out to Sugarloaf until he sobers up."

"*Ìosa,* what's he got into him."

"I don't know. He seemed not bad when he got to the meeting, but Nosey says he put away half a bottle of Scotch afterward."

"You'd better not give him anything. I told him when he showed up last night that he's not getting one drink from us. *Ìosa,* will you look at him. What a go-ahead. You should have just laid him on the daybed. Look at him snoring at the ceiling."

"I can move him."

"Are you foolish? Don't you touch him, he might wake up."

"We won a great victory tonight, darlin'. Wait till you hear." It was Big Ran'l at his charming best, making her feel like the belle of the ball. "C'mon, we'll tell you all about it. Then we'll have a tune on the fiddle, won't we, Nosey. Then we'll get Lucky home."

"Didn't Hector tell you? Mary put the run to him. Hector says he's staying at your place."

Meanwhile, in the kitchen, the three Masters Caffrey regarded in silent fascination their Uncalucky. His mouth was slightly open and jerked violently and spasmodically at one corner. His face contorted and blushed a deep purple and the flesh of his neck grew thicker until suddenly he exploded into a high raw exorcism of coughing. The hack attack continued unrelentingly as their mother worked on him, until the boys didn't know if they should laugh or call a doctor. Uncalucky only stopped when he was spent of even the energy to spit. He keeled over in his chair.

"Is he dead?" asked Master Archie.

"Shush," said Bridget Caffrey, struggling to open her brother's collar.

"Is he dead?" repeated Archie, leaning over his mother.

"Shush, Bobo. Get away from here, you little *gommach*. All three of you get back to bed!"

"Check his pulse. See if he took a heart attack," said Cissy Caffrey, now on the scene and rubbing her tired blue eyes.

"Ìosa, are you up too?"

The lads retreated to the side of Big Ran'l. Owing to his gigantic size, his deformities, and his big-hearted bluster, Big Ran'l was a figure of intrigue and affection for the boys. Every haymaking he allowed them a tractor turn round the hayfield. In his lap they learned to steer, to work the gears and pedals, to ease the throttle, to open and close the choke. For the Masters Caffrey, Big Ran'l brought to mind juicy pork sandwiches named after the pig they came from. Belinda sandwiches. Peter sandwiches. He brought to mind rabbit pie, tall cold glasses of buttermilk, jingle bell horses, a deer dripping blood on the threshing floor, and the smell of fresh bullshit.

Once Lucky was breathing normally, Nosey Flynn piped up. "Well, that was a thing of beauty if I do say so myself. We should call up Sam Hung and get him over here for a *dileag*."

"I've already called him. He can't come up, but he thanks us. And we can still toast him." Hector handed glasses to Ran'l, Nosey, and the wife, and raised his own. *"Slainte!"* he said. "Here's to Sam Hung, honorary member of the Findrinny Highland Society."

"Slainte!" they repeated. "To Clansman Hung."

Nosey tasted the spirit and smiled in the afterglow. To the others, he recalled Wilkie Cunningham's speech earlier that evening, imitating the cackling condescension of the merchant. "Thwarted," Nosey chirped, "thwarted in their attempt to learn the name of the tartan that hung in Hung's restaurant. Thwarted, I might add, by a young woman who goes by the name of MACDOUGALL."

"Did you see how he looked at Charlie when he said that? He knows full well that the girl is Charlie's niece." Hector grabbed a tea towel and waved it above his head like a lariat. "This! This is the tartan in question. I am sure you all know its pedigree and would agree that anyone calling himself a true Nova Scotian should recognize it IMMEDIATELY."

Big Ran'l said, "Do you still have the motions, Hector? Read Wilkie's, will you. It's a doozy, Bridget, a regular manifesto."

Hector had already explained the whole saga to his wife. How Wilkie had indeed gone to Sam Hung and demanded, in the name of the Highland Society, that he reprimand, or better yet, fire the waitress, or failing that, immediately remove the two tartan swatches from his windows. Sam would agree to neither demand. Hector imitated Wilkie: "'Oh,' says Mr. Hung, 'it was all in fun.' Well! I say the incident is neither humorous nor inconsiderable. It is a cultural challenge and I say the Highland Society should address it forthwith."

Hector unfolded a sheet and read in the voice of the enemy: "Whereas disrespect for the Nova Scotia flag is a scandalous offence, so too is the offence of denigrating the tartan that will, in all likelihood, be officially recognized as our provincial tartan within the coming year. And whereas it has been reported that a waitress working at Sam Hung's Chinese restaurant did so denigrate the as-near-to-official-as-you-can-get tartan of Nova Scotia in front of two tourists, thereby thwarting their tartanry education, be it so moved that the Highland Society accept into the minutes of this meeting my report stating date and time of offence, a succinct account of the incident, an update on the status of our soon-to-be official tartan, and publicly reprimand Mr. Hung with a letter in *The Crypt* and request once more that he remove the two tartan swatches from his front windows."

Mrs. Caffrey shook her head and made the sound of a snake. "What a pompous ass. And he's going to be president next year? God help us."

Hector said, "When Wilkie started reading his motion he was pretty confident. There was a quorum in the room and he had locked up seven of the votes with only five against him."

"Then," said a self-satisfied Nosey Flynn, "I and Lucky and Johnny Tulloch and the Venerable Bede all made our entrance."

"So the vote went badly for Wilkie?"

"Indeed it did. And not only that but our chief of the clans submitted a motion designed to give an extra twist of the dagger." Hector handed the sheet to Big Ran'l. "You composed it Ran'l. You read it."

The big man held the sheet in his steel claw so as to gesture the better with the other. His rumble and roar disturbed the teacups: "In recognition that Mr. Samwell Hung, proprietor of the Brigadoon Restaurant, by virtue of being the first restaurateur in Findrinny Fair to display the Nova Scotia tartan; and because Mr. Hung is the first Chinaman to register for the Society's Gaelic lessons and in so doing has shown his support for the aims and objectives of our one-hundred-year-old

Society, I therefore move that Sam Hung be granted honorary membership in the Findrinny Highland Society."

"Is there such an animal?" asked Bridget.

"There is now," said Big Ran'l, laughing to show his crooked teeth.

Hector explained for her benefit. "Honorary membership had been in the Society by-laws for decades but was rarely invoked. It was a status reserved for those who failed to meet the parameters of regular membership: to own property in the district of Findrinny and to be of Highland Scottish descent."

"The Weasel Cunningham barely qualified for membership himself," said the big man from his stool. "His people were Jerseymen and Sassenachs. He was only let in the Society because he had a Campbell for a grandmother."

Lucky Dunphy uttered his first words since entering the house. "I'll not shake hands with a Campbell!" He reared as if to stand, but the body was weak. Rather than stand, he spent the spurt of energy in rubbing together his hands in brisk wringing movements.

Hector said, "After a lot of hullabaloo and crying from the other side, so much so I wondered if we still had enough votes to win, I cut off debate. I said, 'The Venerable Bede is wanting to get back to the track. The children are waiting. Let's have the vote.' Then just before we voted, Big Ran'l added something on a point-of-information to sweeten the pot."

"I just said I hope all of you will come to the Brigadoon for the Chinese smorgasbord Sam is putting on the Sunday of the fair—half price for all Highland Society members. Chop suey, chow mein, garlic spareribs, egg rolls, General MacTsao's chicken. All you can eat."

"You should've heard Wilkie wail," snorted Nosey Flynn. "Bribe! Bribe! Bribe! You can't do that!"

"Passed nine to seven, same as the first motion," said Hector, and raised his glass. *"Slainte!* Sam Hung, honorary member!"

Lucky Dunphy raised an empty hand in triumph. *"Slainte*. I'll not shake hands with a Campbell."

"Boooys," Big Ran'l drawled. "I think your Uncle Lucky needs a little *dileag* to help him settle in. Look in that cupboard there, Jacky, and see what you can find. Nooo… Noooo… Noooo... Yes! That'll do. Bring it here. Tommy, now you go and get some ice cubes and put them in a glass. That's a gooood boy." Ran'l clasped the bottle in his hook, unscrewed the lid with the heavy mitt of his good hand, and keeping a practiced eye to the whiskey, poured an even shot. "Now put just as much cold water into that and give it to your Uncle Lucky."

The acolyte obeyed.

Rubbing one hand vigorously across his mouth Lucky Dunphy's eyes rolled in the direction of Big Ran'l's voice then back to the table on which he still negotiated an uneven hold.

"Uncalucky. Here's the jillick for you."

Dunphy, his jaw and eyelids drooping in unison, stared blankly at the offering. It seemed to Tommy as though his uncle was waiting for the *dileag* to speak to him. Perhaps it did. When his eyes beheld the amber bead it was as if he had heard a kind word said with a welcoming voice. He grasped the vessel, admired it briefly, and drew half its contents in a breath. Revived, he set the glass upon the table, stretched his backbone, straightened his neck, and with a tremendous flick of his jaw, tossed the jet black hair from his eyes. You could hear vertebrae cracking clear to the mainland.

Within seconds, Lucky was pounding a fist on the kitchen table and roaring.

Well, I saw the Cape Breton Highlanders as they marched through a foreign land
And I saw the Cape Breton Highlanders
fal-ya-li-oh-fal-ya-lo

The whiskey rattled toward the table's edge so that Tommy was forced to rescue it. Appreciatively, Lucky seized the glass and held it on-high to his non-performing companions. He threw his head back, emptied the vessel, and launched once more into verse.

Old MacDonald got a letter from his folks way back home
Said the crops are in hell this season and the roof is off the barn
fal-ya-li-oh-fal-ya-looooooh

Lucky Dunphy waved the three boys forward and commanded firmly.

"Name, rank, and outfit."

"John Hector Caffrey," answered Master Jacky, saluting. It was not a new drill. "Private, Cape Breton Highlanders."

"Thomas Leander Caffrey, Private, North Nova Scotia Highlanders."

"Archibald Gordon Caffrey, Private, Cameron Highlanders."

Uncalucky saluted smartly. Slapping a hand to his rear pocket he produced a thin wallet and gravely handed each boy a bill, ones to Jacky and Archie, and a fin to Tommy. The twins dumbly held the ill-begotten booty while Archie shoved his bill quickly into his pocket. Their mother demanded all three return it. There was a commotion until she had her way.

"Too much, eh, lads? Well, too much of anything is bad," said Lucky, "but too much of good whiskey is barely enough," and he briefly examined his glass prior to making the final drain on it. He grew pensive then and the Masters Caffrey backed away.

"Ronald!" said Hector, officiously using the big man's given name. Will you have another *dileag* yourself?"

"No, no, Hector, I'm good. I'm good. It will soon be time for Lucky and me to be off, now that he's revived."

"What about you, Nosey? You'll stay for the night."

"I believe I will," wheedled Flynn.

Tommy leaned over to Jacky, "Look at his mouth. Could whistle in his own ear. Flap ears to match."

"Nose like a dill pickle."

Uncalucky spied Big Ran'l on the Stool of Repentance. He slapped his knee and coughed and sputtered and laughed. "Well, you goddam potlicker. N-N-Now you give us one, ya old cripple. You're the potlicker that can do it. Let's hear ya. Come back onto 'er. *Mademoiselle from Armatiers, Paaarley-voooo... It's a long way to Tipperareeee... Pack up your troubles in your old kit-bag and smile, smile, smile."* With this last one he was off again, waving his arms like a maestro, in full sideways attack on another ditty.

"...Smile, boys, that's the style.
What's the use of worrying?
It never was worthwhile, So!

Pack up your troubles in your old kit-bag,
And smile, smile, smile..."

Lucky saw the fiddler and hollered, "Let's have a tune, Nosey. 'King George the Fourth.' Give 'er hell. *Suas ahhhhh!*"

With the first note from the violin, Lucky's toes and heels were clicking and clacking. Hector grabbed his bagpipes and whispered in the fiddler's ear. When the strathspey flew into a reel, the pipes blasted to life and such inspiration filled Lucky Dunphy that he was up dancing before his sister could restrain him. He struck his hard black heels into the oilcloth and paused like a bull readying a charge. Like lightning, his feet flashed forward three times apiece. It wasn't long before they were stomping like twin pistons, the supramingling of fiddle music and Canadian rye whiskey boiling his Cape Breton red blood. He let out that little Gaelic hoot he did so well, and grinning like a hyena, set to dancing heel-toe round the kitchen on one foot, then the other, and without looking at Bridget, held high a hand to add her to his dance card.

She took it laughing, doing the Mabou shuffle. *"Suas ah!"* he whooped. "Yip," said she and kept her dainties away from the two jackhammers ramming the dance floor. With Flynn's final flourish of bow to strings, Lucky abruptly ended his performance, clicked his heels, and came deftly to attention. He saluted smartly to Big Ran'l MacDonald. "Private First Class Lauchlan Dunphy reporting for duty, Sergeant Major, SIR!"

"At ease, Private," said the superior officer.

Bridget put a hand on her brother. "Good, good, you can sit down now, Lucky. Right here. You're spent. Sit down and stay put. Will you look at him. Doesn't know the war's over." And licking his lips the man passed into the quiet aftermath of the fiddle frenzy and soon forgot what the commotion was about. His sister relaxed. "You're cut off, Lucky. You're on the tea now."

"Good boy, Lucky," wheedled Nosey Flynn. "Good boy yourself. You've still got the steps, boy. Ach, aye. You've still got the steps."

Little Archie Caffrey looked at his brothers and said, "I guess he wasn't dead after all."

The woods smelled like attempted murder. The brook flowed slow and sour, inflicted with a chartreuse algal bloom that had materialized during the polio days, before the Hela cells cured the scourge. Tommy was not afraid. He wasn't afraid when at the age of seven he stood in this brook and broke the spell. By his confessional example he proved that fluorescent green riverslime was not an agent of disease. He couldn't feel his feet till four hours later, but a sin was forgiven and the myth of polio was dispelled.

Like two spoonbills up and down the Findrinny Brook the twins swept in search of a lost tomahawk. Tommy dropped his eyes and trained them to submarine depths, sweeping one side to the other, the current pushing him gently downstream. Maybe it was true that the drunk got up and stumbled away. Good whack in the head did him good. He searched for a sign of him, a shoe he was wearing or an eyeball. Could he really have risen? Impossible. Too out of it. Too brain dead. Too much of a hole in his head. But it had to be.

Tommy's mood morphed from morose to angry. He had wasted a whole week in the embrace of an incubus named guilt. There was no dead man lying in the Findrinny Brook. That drunk wasn't dead. He was just dead drunk. He had jived, dived, and revived. Lived to drink in another day. Good. Tommy was well once more with his immortal self. No pit. No pendulum. He would move on from it. What did Sister Dot call it? The indestructibility of the soul.

"Ha hah!" yelled Jacky. "There it is! Your tomahawk!" He held it as though that's all it was.

Tommy, both fearful and joyful, laid the tomahawk aside and sought solace with his twin. They toyed with their fun sacks. Near a place they called the Little Bighorn, a place of plenty pebbles, a trickle of water, and heapbig high ground, they would do battle. Fifty, sixty bottle caps came a-tumbling from each fun sack. The twins scattered them carefully among the weeds and pebbles and through the ridges and valleys, face up, divided into opposing armies. Jacky's beer caps were the Seventh Cavalry riding into the valley of death. Mooseheads, Schooners, Red Caps, Ten Pennies, Keiths. Led by Captain Benteen, Major Reno, General Custer. Surrounding them on all hilltops, a war party of pop cap Cheyenne and Sioux. 7-Up, Sussex Cream Soda, MacLean's Lime Rickey, Hire's Root Beer, Nesbitt's Orange,

Canada Dry Ginger Ale.

"For your entertainment this afternoon, at the Babblebrook Theatre, we offer you the Battle of the Little Bighorn. Tommy Caffrey, known as Tommyhawk, the greatest cavalry killer of all time, will be providing stage direction, sound effects, gunshot, and battle cry. John Caffrey known as Jacky Jerkoff will provide bugle blasts and sound of baleful death."

As the tomahawk watched, the twins crouched like Manobos over their theatre, tossing pebbles at the other's caps, flipping them dead and dying. Two boys by their babblebrookbank with no one around to see them till the last warwhoop of victory and the culling of Custer's yellow scalp. Then they filled up their funsacks and tossed off their clothes and ran, silent as Indians and free, two identical dicks naked before Creation.

FINDRINNY FAIR

Tommy felt like hot baloney in a soggy sandwich. His father was behind the hoop. Ronald Atlas MacDonald, Big Ran'l, was riding shotgun, his farmer-tanned and muscled right arm resting on the Strato-Chief's open window. Those two seemed fine. Lots of room up there. The backseat was a sweatbox. On one side of the boy was a fatass bureaucrat from Ottawa, on the other a hairy-headed geologist from Down Under. The bureaucrat smelled like onion soup and bad aftershave, the geologist like money. They were motoring inland from Findrinny, up the Ani G'nish Valley, three times crossing the big river. A buzz of crickets racketed through the century farms and those of immigrant Dutch fresh off the boat. Every few miles along the trail, the Strato-Chief slowed and rumbled through a clutch of dwellings. At each roadsign Big Ran'l loudly announced the name of the village and asked, "Anyone need a piss?"

"Where'd they get it, the findrinny?"

"Findruine," his father corrected the bureaucrat. He was good with the facts, his father. He sounded just like a teacher when he got going. "The Little Smithy, Dan Maroon, brought the recipe with him from the Old Country. That was 1815. Seems Dan was the last one in Ireland with the know-how to make it. They say he left Ireland because the materials he needed were so scarce he was out of work. And he only taught the recipe to one Indian family, the Snakes, a clan of the Micmac. They know how to make it, but they don't have the materials to make it. There's another tribe up there that mines the copper and whatnot. They're called the B'laan. Just think, for a hundred and fifty years the Snakes and the B'laan had to work together to get 'er done, the B'laan doing the mining and the Snakes cooking up all that findruine."

"Why do you pronounce it like that?" asked the geologist.

"Like what?"

"Feen-drroo-inny."

"You're close. *FYIN-drwi-nee*. It's Gaelic. Findrinny is the best the English could do with it. So Findrinny is the name of our town and anything else we care to stick it to. Findruine is just used for the alloy that miraculously, and until not so long ago, was our biggest export."

"So," said the deputy minister in a careful and h-less accent, "You have had none for how many years?"

"Last time they came here was what, Ran'l?"

"I'm after forgetting. 1951? 1950? Yup," Ran'l sucked. The way he inhaled his Yups was no more explicit than all Cape Bretoners. Just louder. "Yup. That was it. 1950. Last time we saw them coming down the river. Things were going great. Then they just stopped coming. Cut us off like it was no great mischief. So much for partnership."

"Had they ever done it before? Just cut off the supply like that?"

"Of course we shut 'er all down for the war years. Shut down the whole industry by mutual agreement. Made full sense. Nobody was buying any frills. Every cent was going to the war effort. Jewelry and adornment and fine wire weren't fetching top dollar and the labour was needed for other business. But as soon as the war was over, boom, we were building up the trade again. In 1949, we put nearly two hundred tons on boats to Cork and Dublin. More than two million dollars' worth, all coming to the pockets of Indians and Findrinnians. Then them crazy fuckers just stopped making it altogether. No parlaying—just took their stock to Cheticamp, sold it for half what it was worth, and dropped out of sight. Not an ounce produced since, so we hear. Not that they will ever speak to us about it. Made no sense. We were all in it together. Findrinny people were employed in transportation, communications, power generation. The Indians were busy as fucking beavers. We had a whole class of managers and bookies. Business was booming. Money for public works. Money for some frills. Jewelry stores. Beauty salons. The papers and radio were booming with all the ads coming in. Nice houses being built. What was it made Findrinny Fair? It wasn't the university, Deputy Minister. It wasn't the church. It wasn't my lumberyard. It was findruine. We'd buy all that the Indians can bring us, but they ain't bringing any, Deputy Minister, and we can't make them."

"So there's no more?"

MacDonald turned to his backseat audience, paused, and growled for full attention. His jowls shook like jello. "Oh, there's more all right. There's more in the hands of the wanking fucking merchants. Not much, but they're still finding ways to profit. Look at that shyster Jones. Selling a purefin necklace for five hundred bucks. Those sons of whoo-ers aren't hurting. Meanwhile everyone else in the industry is twiddling their thumbs. What's in the merchant's vaults and on their shelves is the last in the district, except for what people are hiding away for a rainy day. A few years back that weasel Cunningham conjured to buy every reel and sheet people had stored in their barns and cellars and bedrooms. Boom. A quick bidding war erupted among the merchants. Robin outbid Jones, Cunningham outbid Robin, and boom, the entire world supply of findruine was in their vaults. In a matter of months they controlled the goddam world market. By the time they started meting it out to the smiths and jewellers, the price had tripled. That was 1955. It's gone up ten percent a year since. You know that two hundred tons we sent to Cork a decade ago, what that would fetch today? Ten million dollars, minimum. Minimum."

Tommy had enough of the blather and dribbling black juice that accompanied it. He leaned into the smell of French onion soup.

"If the price held," said the bureaucrat.

"If what?"

"If the price held you'd have made that."

Big Ran'l seemed not to compute the simple remark. His cud chew slowed and his expression went blank around the eyes.

Sensing the bureaucrat's ill ease, Hector broke in, "Yes, that's correct, Mr. Roy, but then you know we aren't talking about findruine anymore. We have to accept that those days are gone."

"That's what we are telling you," agreed the geologist. "It doesn't matter if it's worth a hundred dollars a ton or a thousand dollars a ton. What we do know is the price of copper. And what we do know is the price of gold."

The bureaucrat produced a coiled notebook. "What about the Indians who live there? What is it? In the entire reservation, fourteen thousand B'laan and eight thousand Micmac? And I understand four thousand-plus B'laan live in the territory to be mined."

"Four thousand," snorted the geologist. "Where we're mining, six hundred, tops. We'll be building a model village for them just outside the perimeter. Most of them can't wait to get going. They'll have decent homes instead of the shacks they live in now."

"Four thousand one hundred and forty is what my notes say."

Big Ran'l broke his dead stare and chew and turned his back on the bureaucrat. "The last census puts the number at, what is it, Hector? Five hundred and ninety-six? Someone's feeding you a load a—'ow do you say in Quawbec, Mister Roy, a load of *merde?*"

"When I arrived at the airport I was met by a spokesperson for the diocese. I'd asked your Bishop Power, an old friend from Montreal, if I could have a situationer. He sent this Pere McCoy. You may know him?"

Even Tommy noticed how the question hung. He saw Big Ran'l turn two oyster eyes on the bureaucrat.

"Theese Pair McCoy," the big man mimicked. Then he turned clear around to hawk a loogie at a passing signpost. "Cape Clear. Anyone need a piss?"

Hector Caffrey's 1960 Strato-Chief was a wide-track tiger. It had the new split-grille look that Pontiac invented in '59 and was powered by a 235-horsepower Tempest V-8 engine. But for Big Ran'l's purposes, it was neither looks nor power that mattered. What mattered was that the big Pontiac provided plenty of leg room for him and a high clearance for the rutty road to Cape Clear. That and a dutiful driver. Hector owed him a favour for escaping The Cunningham Motion.

The first stretch of dirt took them through flat fields of potatoes, corn, oats, and hay. Along the roadside, goldfinches undulated among bouquets of goldenrod, purple and white wild aster, and elegant Queen Anne's lace. The boy could see none of it. He felt doubly trapped by fatasses and bluster. He had never known Big Ran'l to smell so much of buttermilk and tobacco. Any other time he had been marooned with him, there had been an escape hatch. Another room. A radio. The great outdoors. Perhaps if the rumbling blabbering motormouth would stop turning around and making you look at him, he could be ignored.

"You look pretty squashed there, Tom. Are you able to breathe? Haha. Yeah? That's good. Breathe some more. You look like you're deflating. I can hardly see you between the two of them porkers." Ran'l laughed to indicate he meant solidarity not disrespect.

"You know what I think?" said Hector. "I think they're dead."

"Who's dead?" asked the deputy minister.

"The ones who used to make it. The Snakes. They're dead now and the other Indians don't know the recipe. That's the only excuse I can think of. And if the recipe died with them, she's all over. We missed our chance to get it and the world missed its chance."

"I say forget the goddam findruine. Forget it and move on. Remember what the Corkmen used to say, Hector? 'Of course the Indians aren't going to admit there's gold in their mountains. You think they're stupid? Why would they expose the ingredients of their secret recipe?'"

"I remember. They laughed at us. 'You Cape Bretoners are either blind or you're sly like foxes,' they'd say."

"How's that? Sly?"

"They'd say, 'Maybe you're just in league with your red brothers. Just keeping the booty away from the rest of the world. Stretching it out. Well, keep it that way,' they'd say. 'We're happy with our take if you and your Indians are happy with yours. Whatever else doesn't matter.'"

"Yup," Big Ran'l gulped. "Turns out the Irish were right. We seen it with our own eyes. Gold. We always knew there was copper in the Tampakan, now we know there's gold in there too. A regular fucking bonanza. Tell him how much Mr. Aussie."

The figures tripped off his geologist lips. "We completed eighty-five diamond drill holes for a total of thirty-one thousand, four hundred and seventy-four metres. We found gold and copper seams in every one. What we discovered indicates an incredible resource. We estimate there's two point two billion tons of copper ore, making the Tampakan Ridge Discovery one of the largest deposits in the world. As for gold, in the same range there are eighteen million ounces. Putting together the two, we value the deposit at two and a half billion dollars."

The bureaucrat whistled despite himself.

"Think of the money that will flow into Cape Breton, Mr. Roy. Think of the royalties the government will get on two and a half billion dollars."

Hector said, "It's not just the money. We want jobs for our kids so they can stay here where they belong, not go down the road like they're doing now."

"Archer-Atlas will hire Indians too," said Mr. Aussie. "There will be plenty of manual labour positions to be filled, hundreds of man-years. Depending on how quickly we exhaust the vein, it could mean thirty years of employment. We're talking the 1990s before all the copper and gold is pulled out of there."

"Long time to have full employment in an area. Could really help the whole island get on its feet," Hector pointed out.

Big Ran'l said, "I've got a state-of-the-art copper smelter. I've got road crews cutlining through the forest. I've got a new technology lined up to burn wood and coal mix. I'll use those old growth trees I'm cutting off the Tampakan for the wood chips. And I'll reopen the coal mines in Shean and Port Hood. More jobs. More money staying in Cape Breton. All we need is your government's approval."

"And what about the gold?"

"We sell that raw to the highest bidder. There will be plenty of interest, you can be sure."

"So it says here that if you get government approval by the end of the year, then by September '62, you could be ready to start taking out all that copper and gold."

"That's right," said Big Ran'l, his crooked teeth showing. "Only first we'll get the gold. Then we'll get the copper."

The Strato-Chief reached the end of cultivation. From there the car wound up four miles of twisting climbs and turns until it came to a clearing. In the middle stood a television tower.

"They only widened up to here for the CJCB tower," Hector apologized. "From now on it will be climb and level, climb and level, climb and level. We'll climb a thousand feet in two miles. In three or four months, the first good snowfall, you won't get through here. Not in this car. Not in any car."

The dark spruce closed in on them as they climbed. Conversation became more difficult with the jerking bodies. His father snapped on the radio. Johnny Preston crooned about Running Bear and the Little White Dove. Sappy as syrup, but it didn't matter, the loud voice had ceased. The boy snuck a peek under his father's seat. He had hid something there. Its dark cloth covering he could see but not what was hidden inside. He closed his eyes and mused on the promised sights that had convinced him to make this odyssey. Mount Kitanglad. The Three Sisters of the Tampakan. The Dream Valley of the Indians. Oblivious now to the dusty air and his stinking sidekicks, he dreamed of a hoary headed eagle-boy soaring over a valley of tall trees and clearings and gorges, spying from on-high through his eagle eyes moose, bear, lynx, bobcat, otter, marten, fisher, and deer. Tommy woke only when the motor stopped and all four doors sprung open at once. He could breathe again.

Big Ran'l stood his ground. "This is close enough for me. Way too close, in fact. Get down on your goddam bellies. Hup to it." He was wearing a short-sleeved checked shirt soaked in sweat from the thirty-mile pilgrimage. He flexed his strong right arm, windmilled it, and shook out his good leg. His iron side rested on his *cromach*.

"You don't have to tell me twice, Sarge," agreed the boy's father. "It's a sheer drop from the edge of this cliff, five hundred feet down to the Dream Valley. So stay on your bellies and move as slow as you need to. What you are about to see you'll never forget."

Between his father to his left and the two visitors, the boy edged toward the precipice then inched his eyes into a deep scintillating ocean of green. With blinking amazement the birds appeared, floating below him, and he thought, I am supposed to be looking at the bellies not the backs of eagles. Into a vertical drop his sight went far below to where a river snaked its path through green, yellow, and orange forests that swept up the far side of the valley to the highlands, to the mountain peaks, to the world beyond. The whole panorama swirled its majesty of colour and he was spinning with it.

"Hold on, Tommy," his father squeezed his arm. "The dizziness will pass. Just breathe. Let your eyes focus on the big river. That's the Ani G'nish. You too, Deputy Minister. Now follow it back that way to the northeast, to the tallest mountain in that chain. Mount Kitanglad. That's where the river rises, to the rear of that range. It picks up water from all through the highlands and spills out over the falls you see in that direction. Here, take my binoculars."

"Ani G'nish. Ani G'nish. What does it mean?"

"Damned if I know," boomed Big Ran'l from behind. "But I will tell you what I do know. There's gold in dem der hills, Mr. Roy. You see those three tallest peaks on the left? We call them the Three Sisters. The Indians have been mining copper outta them for centuries. Unbeknowingly to us, until two years ago, we found out they were digging gold outta there too. Good businessmen, I'll give them that. Kept it hidden. Just slipped what they needed into the findruine pot and didn't say a word about it."

"So why are we looking at this land from above and we're not down there talking with the Indians about it? What have your dealings been with them?"

"We have had grand dealings with them." Big Ran'l spit.

"Would you care to elaborate? I do happen to know we are not way up here just because the view is better."

"The point is, we'd been dealing with their chief, a big, brick-red stud named Enuffathem. And then there's this other tribe comes along calling themselves something different than the first and they have a chief too. It's all fucked up. Then this renegade band of Indians comes in there and shoots up the mine office. Kills a manager and two security guards. It's all under control now, of course. Now we have the constabulary patrolling the perimeter. It's all under control. But until Colonel Bravo gives us the say so, we decided we would best show you our territory from up here."

Mr. Aussie added, "We dealt with Enuffathem in good faith. He was the government-recognized band chief. Basically he told us that the Indians want what Archer-Atlas can give them—jobs, help when they get sick, decent houses instead of the shacks they live in. That's why they agreed to let us mine their mountains."

"We got all the government permissions to go in there and dig the drill holes. We got the tribe's consent. We've been legit every step of the way.

"I can see the pit you're talking about. *C'est enorme!*"

"Fucking right it's big. We're lining up all the equipment. We've got a new rail spur in from Findrinny to the Tampakan. We already have the smelter built. All we need is a piece of paper, then BOOM! Boats full of gold ore and processed copper will be leaving the docks. BOOM! Job's for everyone. We'll take down the side of that mountain, Mr. Roy. Peel her right back and get at the gold and copper."

"I see."

The boy's dizziness returned. He broke free of his father's grasp and shimmied backward and away from the precipice.

"I'm going back to the car, Daddy."

"Okay, stay there. Don't wander off. You hear me!"

Under the front seat, away from prying adult eyes, his tomahawk hid. He rubbed the shaft and caressed the grey stone, once dripping red, scrubbed clean now but the blood never forgotten. He remembered the sickening thud, the mangled socket, the body that disappeared. He nodded gravely. His tomahawk had saved his life.

Tommy wandered off. Paths through the Acadian Forest were of no concern. What led him one way would lead him back. The trees on this plateau grew evenly spaced and huge, maples two hundred years old, beech two yards around. It was noontime and the sun would be hot on his head except for their canopy casting a dappled sundrift down to the lower story where fields of flowers and great seas of ferns swayed among hardwood seedlings and saplings that reached toward the sun and bided their turn to replace a fallen giant.

A gravelly voice broke the silence. "Why are you here, you? Why have you people come to Mi'kmaw land?"

Tommy gripped his tomahawk behind his back.

"Those four overfed men. Who are they and what do they want?"

Long grey hair reached the old man's shoulders. With a bandana wound round his head and a patch covering one eye, the stranger looked more like a pirate than an Indian. But the moccasins left no doubt. Those and the lively black eye like obsidian marble and the redbrown skin stretching over cheekbones high and proud. The stranger opened his vest and strummed fingers on the hilt of a large hunting knife.

"You have a weapon behind your back. Let me see it."

Tommy listened for the Indian's breath and lowered his hatchet to his side.

"Where did you get this stone?"

The Indian ran a rough finger over the blade. "Dull as me arse! It's a shame. See how chipped it's become. How rusty. You may keep it. Tell me, why are your companions looking greedily at the Three Sisters? Should I go there now and throw them over the cliff and listen for the earth to receive them? What are they saying about my brothers the B'laan? Are they telling lies? You're not good at answering questions are you white boy? Would you like to ask me some instead? How do you track a moose? Why do salmon no longer swim in the Findrinny Brook? Why do we not bring findruine to your people? Good questions for an Indian."

"Why?"

"Oh, he can speak. Why what?"

"Why do you not bring findruine to my people?"

The Indian produced a rattle and dancing, shook it over Tommy's brow. He got in Tommy's grill so the boy could smell his breath. "Iron Claw. He knows. He has smoked sweetgrass with us. He has come into our sweatlodges. But now he tells fables. He speaks with forked tongue and crooked teeth. He does not tell his people what he knows. Can you guess why that might be? Something for you to think about."

"I do know. He says findruine doesn't matter anymore. You don't make it anymore so everybody should just move on."

"NO. He says it doesn't matter because gold is what he is after. He doesn't care about salmon in the brook. But we do and that is why we fight you. Iron Claw thinks he can get away with murder. The only trouble is our friendship with your people does not allow him to come and take the gold. I have heard and I have seen. In other places, the white man has taken all that belonged to the Indian. He has plenty of everything, but we are told that the White Man wants more."

"Is that true?"

The wind creaked in the boughs above and the screech of the eagle heralded a new comprehension. He looked the man over, unafraid, and said, "I have another question. The big river, the Ani G'nish. Why do we call it that?"

The answer to that and all other questions was not what he expected, but until the horn sounded, he stood enthralled by this encounter.

A joyous noise was raised above the town. The Caffrey twins and their bigger, rooster-headed cousin dashed along St. Columba Street, led on by a commotion that reached their entrails. Just yesterday they had gawked at carnies erecting an enormous whirring wheel that reached as high as the crosses on the cathedral. Just the night before, from bedroom windows, they had watched the wheel turn to screams and the flashing of a thousand lights.

"All right, there's the castle!"

They crossed the Wheelers Bridge and ran hearts-bursting toward Castle Fina. On either side of the gas station's square frame stood a tower topped by a turret rising toward bright blue sky. From one, the whitewashed one, a tricolour pennant flew majestically. The other, the neglected one, loomed drear and loathsome, its broken glass and stained tower oozing malignance. Surely Rapunzel or Juliet or lovely Hero dwelt in one of Castle Fina's two towers. God help she who languished in the other.

Past the Fina, the fairgrounds stretched for a half-mile along their brook. At one end, the pony barns and the stations for the breeders and owners, in from the country in their dungarees and tweeds. The corral was next, where the animals swung and jumped as weather beaten faces watched over white plank fences, smoking pipes and bantering in the language of ponymen. Beyond the corral came the hurleypitch, the humble game being played as they passed. Then, as far from the ponies as could be, the midway mayhem. Everywhere noise, smells, and spinning machines assaulted them, dizzied them, cast spells upon them. A red, sticky-faced child wailed over a lurid apple bleeding on the trampled grass between Tommy's feet. Yelping, shrieking children scrunched in buckets that tilted and wheeled and swirled around and around and around and around. A black man in stripes barked and whirred a great click-click-clacking wheel.

The wheel buzzed around sounding like frenzied hornets, its features blurred beyond recognition till it slowed with a click-click-click-click and the fates stopped to stare. Hearts and diamonds, spades and clubs, crowns and anchors.

"Two hearts! We have a winner!" the carnie called and thumbed across the table a spray of coins.

"Let 'er go again," the winner said. "We're lucky with the hearts today."

"What's taking you guys? Vamoose. Let's go. Let's try that one." Jimmy Dog pointed at the Ferris wheel.

"Are you crazy?" Tommy shot back. "Why don't we start with an easy one and work our way up to the fast ones. There! That one." He pointed to the wee jockeys revolving mildly to the sound of piano music.

"You're kidding, right? The carousel? That's kid stuff. You are kidding, right?"

"Gully Balls!" and they were off, the gullible one taking the hindmost.

From the apex of the Ferris wheel's journey, the twins made faces at friends far below and words came back that faded before they reached their great height. So high, so high, Tommy became dizzily and instantly drunk. Straight ahead, over the flat roofs of Main Street, under the soft blue sky, he saw a white wooden spire topped by a wrought iron rooster. Cock-a-doodle-do. This temple of Presbyterianism was not without its admirers. The fondest of these was the Great Elm that since the time of Confederation grew up in the face of its partner until it was as tall as the rooster's comb. Tommy could feel, though not see, the creepy boneyard behind the church where they scared kids on Halloween. On the next pass of the wheel, Tommy swung his view to the right where his house should be. He glimpsed CJFF, the radio station that dominated the hill behind his home, 5-80 on your dial, and below it the Protestant school. Another pass at ground level, staring children and a flash of strobing sunbeams. And in the next pass, Mount St. Joseph, motherhouse of the Congregation of Notre Dame, with window frames shaped like the peaked wimples the sisters wore when educating all the Marys and Kittys and Annies for their life of service to God and family. To the right of the Mount, stood the majestic cathedral, its lower half hidden behind a gauntlet of pine trees, and above the tree line, growing in righteous twin symmetry, its great twin towers, its sandy domes, its cupolas, and its crosses. The carved nameplate flashed in the sun. *Tigh Dhe*. The House of God.

Tommy knew what was hidden behind the pines—three sets of blonde doors: two smaller side doors heavy as bales of hay and a great pair of centre doors. It was through this central portal that the Grade Twos of Bishop Fraser School five years ago had trooped to make their first reckoning with priest and Lord. From his Ferris seat he was transported back memory and soul to this time, to the preparation that predated First Confession. The culmination of a spiritual pilgrimage to learn wrong from right.

"When the priest gives you your penance," said Sister Dot, "you must remember that what he gives you is minimum retribution. You need to examine your conscience before and after confession—before to recall your sins and after to determine the extent of your guilt. Sometimes, more often than not, you will find it necessary to add supplemental penance to what the priest has given you."

Cowboys and Indians is not a sin, she claimed. If you fight with your brothers and sisters, *that* is a sin. If you're not really sick and you tell your parents you are, just so you don't have to go to church, that is a lie—a sin of *com*mission. But more importantly, it would be a sin to miss mass. That is a sin of *o*mission. A mortal sin in fact. A kind of spiritual fornication. You would be putting false gods ahead of our Lord. You would have to kill someone to top that. Another example of putting false gods ahead of God is if you go into a Protestant church. Protestants are inferior because they do not believe in the Blessed Virgin Mary. Worse, they make fun of Her. In the playground, the boys wondered if simply saying the word "Protestant" might warrant a trip to the Tall and Small. But they had reached the age of reason and should surely know this.

The Ferris wheel had stalled the boys at the apex of its orbit as another bucket of brats was let off. Tommy looked away from the cathedral and upon the Findrinny Brook flowing sinewy silver below them. The boy could see neither its source in the faraway Indian hills nor its mouth yawning into the Ani G'nish a mile downstream. What he saw in his mind's eye was an image of himself, four years previous, a half hour after his First Confession, standing shoeless and penitent in the leprous brook.

Tommy had confessed a fiery sin in that first visit to the Tall and Small. A sin so terrible that memory blurred it behind a smoky film. He began as small as possible. He had hurt his brother. "How many times?" the priest boomed. And when the rest of the story had been squeezed from his gut, the confessor prescribed a stiff admonishment, perhaps the maximum allowable considering the age of the offender and delivered in a voice so loud that Tommy was sure the whole class heard.

The three left the cathedral together that grey day. Jacky content. Jimmy Dog gagging over the experience—imagine Jimmy Dog Dunphy being forced to admit a wrongdoing. Tommy ponderous with guilt. "Let's go to the woods," he said. The boys expected a hunt and chase, but when they reached the brook, Tommy said he and Jimmy Dog should stand in the water for what happened to Jacky. Only then would their souls be spotless.

"Like hell," said Jimmy Dog, "and get polio from that green shit."

But Tommy walked in, praying that he be made worthy of the promises of Christ.

Jimmy Dog said he wasn't going to stand in any freezing cold water for something that wasn't his fault. He said supple mental acts of penance were for fools. He said he didn't remember it the same as Tommy. Nobody double-dared Jacky to step into the fire. Especially not him. There had been no taunting or teasing. Tommy was retarded. He needed a new brain.

Tommy ignored the ivory whiteness of his bare feet and shins. He ignored the gnawing riverbite. He ignored his partner in crime, his threats and denials. He ignored his brother's pleading too. He tried to remember further into the ghost of sin, back to the burning season when neighbours set fire to yellowed dead grass and curious boys watched them turn to tufts of amber dancing flame. They were six at the time.

Something had happened that day at school. Tommy couldn't recall. It didn't seem important at the time so he let it go. But it was important to Jimmy Dog. He got in Jacky's face like he always did and for once Jacky pushed back. They fought like rat and terrier. Jimmy Dog had motive, that was clear.

They were walking among the amber tufts. As usual, Jimmy Dog was annoyed with the way the twins were with one another. “You guys got one brain or something?”

“No, we’ve just got twinstincts!” Jacky said.

“Tommy, your twin stinks alright. Get lost, Jacky. We don’t need you. I don’t need two Tommys. Yeah, that’s right. Waw waw waw. Go home to your maw-mee. Either that or show us your dick.”

It was hard to forget what happened next, after the teasing, daring, and double-daring. Tommy remembered his culpability. “Yeah, go home, Jacky,” he had said. But Jacky wouldn’t and this made Jimmy Dog turn red with anger.

“How brave are you, Jacky?”

Such moments can be forever burned in memory and only released with pain and confession. Tommy remembered the flames licking at his brother’s pant leg. And the smell like chicken on a barbeque. Then the screeching wailing that brought Mr. MacIsaac flying across the field and his mother sprinting toward the burning boy.

The bucket that Tommy sat in began to rock. Released from reverie, he grasped the bar holding him and Jacky in place. He heard Jacky’s shrill voice rising. Tommy stilled the emotions in his stomach while his twin’s protests grew blubbery. “Stop it, Jimmy Dog! Stop it! You’ll tip us. I’m scared.”

“Wheee,” cheered Jimmy Dog as the bucket swayed and jerked like a playground swing.

A man yelled from below. “Stop that up there! You idiots. You’ll tip it.” Jacky whimpered shamefully for Tommy to help.

“Okay, that’s enough, Jimmy Dog. You made your point. You got us scared to death. You happy?”

“Wheee.”

Sure, do it, thought Tommy. Make us fall. All three of us flipping over the edge like fish from a barrel, drowning in air, flipping, flopping, and just before we crash you will finally know, you idiot, what a mistake you made.

Sneering triumphantly, Jimmy Dog slowed the bucket and brayed,

"Told you I'd get you back for running off that day. And you too, Jacky, for not coming back like you were supposed to. I see you're still a crybaby."

Tommy did not feel the same righteous glow as when the purifying brook washed over him and consumed the remnant of sin, when he prayed that the cleansing power of our Eternal Father in Heaven, our Redeemer Jesus Christ, and the Holy Ghost would extend to his best friend whose memory was not as good as his, so that his immortal soul would not languish in Purgatory or be consumed in the everlasting fires of Hell. Then he knew he'd been heard. He knew forgiveness was granted though Jimmy Dog asked for it not.

A lot of water flowed down the Findrinny since then. As innocence grew into faith, perception improved. Sister Dot was right. Supplemental acts of penance could wipe away all trace of sin. But Jimmy Dog was right too. You could just as easily forget about it.

The twins wouldn't go on the Tilt-a-Whirl with Jimmy Dog. They wasted some money at the pin throw. The fun house wasn't fun—the surprises scared Jacky and he took to shaking.

"Look! The Crown and Anchor wheel," pointed Tommy. "Here's a quarter, you can go bet on something. The anchors remind me of the sailor suits we found in Aunt Didi's trunk. Remember them? And the bedroom story Mommy used to tell us when we were little kids?

"I remember. The one about the sandcastle war."

And here they imitated their mother's best Irish, their voices shaking with mock anger: "And you, Jacky, for shame to throw poor Tommy in the dirty sand. Wait till I catch you for that."

It was enough to steady a trembly chin and set a small smile creeping onto Jacky's face.

"Okay, anchors aweigh!" With one spin of the wheel they were three times richer, with another, they were three times more. A laugh burst from both their hearts. They thought no more about the Ferris wheel. And even when Jimmy Dog appeared, he was welcomed. Bygones be guy bonds. By mid-afternoon the three lads had spent all their coin and absorbed much of the dust and dirt the fair could kick up. Far from the madding crowd, they plopped to count their scant coupons.

Tommy peered up the midway, mesmerized by the sounds and movement of people flowing to and fro below strings of fluttering pennants green, red, yellow, and blue. He directed his face into a cooling breeze, closed his eyes, and breathed in the sounds of guns popping, wheels clicking, rides whirling, music from the carousel, the smell of cotton candy. Without his vision, these other messages were distinct, one from the other, not at all like the mayhem when his eyes got involved. Hear. Smell. Taste. Touch the grass. Until over them all came the barking of a carnie.

"Two hearts! Another lucky winner!"

He opened his eyes to peer afresh at the maze. Walkers faded into sunny motes and blurry shadow. Glints of light clashed with their like. Sunbeams danced from mirrored surfaces and swirled patterns in the dusty air. Out of one of these spangled rays emerged two damsels, drawing nearer, holding hands the way boys would never do, until they blocked the sun just feet from the lads' oasis. One looked like she had stepped from the pages of *Life* magazine: "The New China—From Inside." She wore a white dress brought puffily together at the waist by a shiny black belt. A neat black purse slung from her shoulder to her hip. She listened carefully to her companion, saying little and covering a tittering mouth. The talking girl was taller. Her honey hair, thick and full, was tugged into a ponytail that slung halfway down the back of her bumblebee t-shirt. Where had they come from? A different town? A different country? Shangri-La? And then they were gone, poof, swallowed up by the Findrinny Fair.

"Where are you going?"

He dodged through the crowd, keeping sight of his quarry. It was easy enough. Girls were dawdlers, smellers of roses, not at all like boys, beelining here and bumbling there. These two hovered and landed, sucking nectar along the way. He saw the way they laughed. To make her laugh like that would do, he knew. He saw them slip coupons to a head-in-a-cage. He did the same. He mounted close enough to reach and touch a flying ponytail. Music filled the air and around went the carousel pinto chasing the carousel dragon and the carousel bee round and round, up and down, merrily and fairyly, like kooky cuckoo clocks, and both so flirtsome and fluttersome he didn't know if he was on land or at sea or swooped through the blur like Airwinger's bride.

He pinched himself. It was true. Fair Hero and her lady-in-waiting had descended from the fairytale turret of Castle Fina. They had come to Findrinny Fair.

Katie Beaton laid scribblers, pencils, and books neatly on her desk, sat attentively, and when Mrs. MacDonald looked for volunteers she was the first to raise her hand. Sometimes she was allowed to pick co-workers, an easy task considering all the girls yearned for her friendship. She was awarded a star that first day. The backrows boys whispered, "Suck-up." "Brownnose."

Tommy knew that seat assignations were purely alphabetical, but he knew as well that God sometimes grants favours to his good and faithful servants. And so he was delighted and thankful for the miracle that placed him directly behind this voluble beauty. When she turned the most mesmerizing eyes upon him, he accepted them readily.

"Take them," she said. "Take them," shaking the stack of papers in her hand. "Take these and pass them along. Are you deaf or something?"

With his first words to her, in the third week of school, he asked if he could borrow her eraser. He had been looking for a way to let her know he could say her name exactly the way she pronounced it, which also happened to be the correct and only way. Mrs. MacDonald and everyone else had taken to calling her Kaydee. Entirely different. Just like his mother said: "My name is Bridget. Call me Biddy and I'll scratch your eyes out."

Katie's was a nearly new eraser, sloped on both ends and warm from her touch. Pink with blue lettering. Wiggletipped. It was nothing like the scuffed and rounded rubber hidden in the boy's pocket. He watched it move over pencil marks, lightly losing small greyed bits that he carefully blew toward the floor. When he returned it to her, unused tip forward, he overloudly declared, "Thanks for lending me your eraser, Kay-tee."

Her face said, Why overloud?

Jimmy Dog snickered, "Y-you're welcome, Tom-ass."

Tiny red lips moving in the loose folds of the teacher's cheeks spurted fact and fiction. They were doing a unit on local history. The arrival by ship of Colonel Dan Maroon and the Irish regimentals; the Jersey merchants Robin, Jones, and Cunningham whose names can still be seen on downtown stores; the immigration of the Scots and the Irish, and their encounters with the French and the Indians; and the legend of the Micmac scout, Sam Snake, who guided Dan Maroon on his famous trek into Indian country.

The teacher, Annie Big Archie MacDonald as she was styled, had girth that would make a cooper proud—a well-rounded belly and bosoms the size of butter churns. For badness, the boys called her Twin City Dairies.

"It's important to know the rivers of this county," she announced. "When Dan Maroon discovered and mapped this valley and the different rivers that flow into it, it opened up the interior of our county for settlement."

Tommy wanted to say that it didn't sound like Dan Maroon discovered anything. If Tommy knew Indians, and he did, he was pretty sure that Sam Snake knew every brook and river between Canso and Cheticamp. Maroon was just the first white man led there by the nose.

"Now I have a question for you," she continued. "Can any of you tell me what the name of the big river that flows past Findrinny means? Not this piddling little brook at the foot of the hill, but the big river that curves around the outskirts of town."

"The Ani G'nish," Katie said.

"That's right, Kaydee. But does anyone know how it came to be known as Ani G'nish?" A panoply of blank-eyed pupils stared back at her. "Surely one of your parents must have educated you on this by now. One of you. Anyone? Anyone? I'll give you a hint. You should think about the Micmacs who first lived here. Maybe that will bestir your memory." She scanned the sea for a spark of recognition. "Anyone?"

"It's Mi'kmaw."

"What?"

"I met an Indian in the woods up on Cape Clear. He told me you don't say Mick Mack, you should say Mig Maw. And he told me that the big river was named after a saint."

The teacher peered at Tommy suspiciously. When she realized the impossibility of his answer, her cheeks jerked and shivered.

"An Indian saint! There's no such animal. I'm quite sure I would know if there was an Indian saint."

"I didn't say the saint was an Indian. The man who *told* me this was an Indian. I can't remember what the saint's name was, Antioinkish or something like that. It has a T in it. He was a saint from ancient Greece."

"Is that so? Tommy, you can't believe what those people tell you. They'll make a fool out of you every time. They are tricksters, you know, all of them. There is no Saint Antigonish or whatever he said, I can assure you of that. That Indian was pulling your leg."

At this revelation, the class realized the extent of their classmate's gullibility. A howl from the back row spread forward to engulf him. The teacher's tiny lips drew together like a sphincter. She settled her class, turned her broad back, raised her chalk, and shook and shimmied as she drew four squiggly lines that joined as one.

"You see this river running from the northeast, and this one from the southwest, and this one that flows right through our town, and this one. You see how they snake through the valleys and all end up as one river, the Ani G'nish. But what does it mean? This is a question that still puzzles the historians. You see, Ani G'nish is in fact a Micmac word, but unfortunately no one knows with certainty what it actually means. Experts disagree. So if I were to ask you on an exam what Ani G'nish meant and you said, 'Snakelike rivers of fish,' you'd be right. But you'd also be right if you said, 'The place where black bears break branches while gathering beechnuts.'"

She grunted the words onto the board, underlining both interpretations, and returned to the class. "There is no agreement among the experts." And here her small lips stretched like a miniature elastic band. "But even though there is some confusion, historians do agree on something. They agree that our great river is not named after Saint Ani G'nish."

Her smirk gave the class permission to again express its derision.

"All right, all right now, class, that's enough. I'm sorry, Thomas, I couldn't resist."

Embarrassment blew hot and cold on his neck and face. Upon his yellowed wooden desk, he stared intensely at the carved words and doodlings of bygone seventh graders. To these hieroglyphics he added a word in lead etched deeply darkly carefully into the desk. He drew forth the memory of the drive to Cape Clear. The man who preached of Mi'kmaw things, salmon in the streams, sweetgrass, sweatlodges. With each new query the old Mi'kmaw closed his good eye and paused. Thomas wondered if the man had fallen asleep. When he did deign to speak, a sweet fragrance, fruit of the vine, filled the air and his one eye crinkled and winked. How many lies had he told?

He felt, not saw, Katie Beaton whisk toward the back of the classroom. His face had become hot. He dug with his pencil into the desk, his hand retracing the one word in hard black letters, snake, snake, snake, snake, snake, until the lead shattered and charcoal smudged and smeared a dark jagged line across the desk.

Katie was back and leaning into him. "Don't be embarrassed. It's okay. I have an idea." She spun her back to the teacher, held open before her a large red book, hard-covered, gold-embossed, and announced, as if orating to the legislature: "Be quiet, everyone. Listen! We shouldn't have laughed at Tommy's saint."

She held the book high like a priest saying mass. "See," she said. *The Lives of the Saints*.

"Saint Antiochus," she pronounced in a ringing voice. "Saint Antiochus was a Greek physician who was beheaded under the Roman governor Hadrian, he of the Wall. And when milk flowed forth in place of blood from the severed head of Antiochus, his executioner, See-ree... See-ree-ack... Cy-ri-ac-us was converted to Christ. And he himself also suffered martyrdom."

She shut the book with a smack of authority. The entire class was staring at her as she set aside her manuscript. Tommy expected her to say, "These words are coming true before you this very day." Half his classmates understood that Tommy had been right about something, and whatever upper hand Mrs. MacDonald had gained was now and forever vanquished. As for the other half, they were too disgusted with the image of white milk draining from a decapitated sainthead to even care.

On the boys' walk to school the next morning, Joe Dillon was intent on debating the meaning of their river's name. Which scholarly tradition should they follow? The Bears Breaking Branches academy or the Snakelike Rivers school of thought?

"Bears breaking branches and gathering beach nuts," Jimmy Dog sneered. "What the heck are beach nuts? Nuts you find on a beach? What kind of name is that? It's embarrassing that's what that is. I mean, we know the rivers meet here. It's gotta be about rivers meeting or something."

"Maybe it means bears scratching their nuts while playing with beach balls."

"And Micmacs breaking branches on their heads,"

To Tommy, it didn't matter that Mrs. MacDonald still insisted on her conflicting definitions. The vindication he felt was as sweet as a completed Hail Mary. Throughout the fall, his walk to school seemed sunny on a rainy day. At home, he read ahead in his books and completed his homework before supper. His cursive writing grew less sloppy, his sums more accurate, and Twin Cities more interesting. Tommy did not know what to call the feeling that gave wings to his school days. He was in virgin territory. His aunt asked him if he had a girlfriend at school. Cissy opined that her brother had a case of puppy love.

"Who is your sweetheart?" asked Cissy's friend Edy.

Tommy spurned all conjectures. To grant credence to others' misperceptions would only tarnish the magic. Still, he well suspected where the exhilaration originated. He knew it faded when Katie was absent for a day and returned in greater exaltation with her reappearance. He exulted in the ebullience as though it was a mysterious, newly discovered body part. A feeling that lay hidden and unbidden until kindled by Katie Beaton.

THE BISHOP'S BOWL

Mrs. Caffrey drained the dregs of her milky tea and pushed aside *The Crypt*. It had been years since she had time to read the entire paper. She listened. Saturday, so the boys were out the door at the crack of dawn. Cissy and the little ones were visiting Gramma and Grampa Dunphy's for the weekend, down in Port Hood. Portood, as they say. No laughter, crying, arguing, teasing, begging, banging about. How sad, she thought, to not hear a child.

The Crypt lay open before her. She had been pondering an article on the Pope in Rome. As she pictured it, one night under the light of a bright full moon the pontiff announced he would convene a council of all the bishops of the world, something that had not been done for hundreds of years. The cardinals thought he was off his rocker. They dismissed the notion as easily as a dream, if only because Pope John was such an old man, a mere caretaker.

The Crypt, it seemed to Mrs. Caffrey, had taken much the same viewpoint as the Curia. Even though this particular pontifical pronouncement had been uttered in December 1959, the paper did not until now, nearly two years later, deem it worthy of mention. One would think this could be a tad embarrassing for the editor-in-chief, Father Joseph McCarthy, who fancied himself a potent prognosticator of all things Vatican. McCarthy was a raging redbaiter in the mould of Pope Pius XII. For him, the Catholic Church in Europe was a besieged fortress. For fifteen years *The Crypt* screamed of terror in bold black headlines:

"Polish Clergy Suffering New Persecution for Their Faith."

"Church in Romania is Wiped Out."

"Reds Aim at America."

A different unholy threat to Catholicism came from within the Christian communion, not that McCarthy ever used the term. One rule *The Crypt* avidly promoted was Number 1258 of the 1917 Canon Law. This teaching set out that it is illicit for Catholics to assist at or participate in any way in non-Catholic religious functions. The editor felt this edict required faithful repetition, although as he generously allowed, "The Church in its lenience does permit the faithful to have a passive presence at non-Catholic funerals or weddings, if such is required out of courtesy or because of holding a civil office. However, these potent matters of perversion and scandal can only be tolerated with a bishop's approval."

One line in the article on Pope John particularly tickled Mrs. Caffrey. This was the expectation that Orthodox and even Protestant Church leaders would be invited as observers to the historic conclave. She would not have been surprised if McCarthy had screamed, "That should make them happy!"

"It's about time," she called at the slam of the screen door, the *scream* door, the twins called it. "Come here you two. Where were you? Get back here."

"We're hungry."

Like a border collie Mrs. Caffrey corralled the scamps. "No, you're not. You're coming outside. Didn't Daddy say he needed you to help him? Where were you? Hector, honey, you must have a job for these two. *Ìosa,* you're back and forth like a jouster. Hector! Hector! Just slow down and tell them what they can do."

"Should have been here half an hour ago. Where were ye?"

"Nowhere."

"Daddy," she sang with a warning look, well received. "Okay. Here. Boss, meet your crew. Crew, meet your boss. Do exactly as he says and you can eat when you're done."

The twins turned out to be useful enough ladder holders, wire pullers, carriers of coil and tool, hoisters of the almighty aluminum rod. Finally, with the aerial completely assembled and securely fastened to the chimney, Hector yelled, "Okay. watch out!" and tossed a brown coil of plasticized copper wire from the roof. "Now lead that into the front room. I'll be right down."

"All set for magic?" he asked.

"All set."

Hector clicked the power and clacked the dial slickly through its orbit, choosing the solitary number that served Findrinny Fair. Channel 9. Crackling voices and flickering faces told them he had found it. But barely so.

"I have to go back up on the roof. I have to adjust the aerial until the signals hit it just right. I saw them doing it at Tando's last weekend. You stay here and tell me if it gets any clearer. You kids will be the calling crew."

"What's that?"

"Like a bucket brigade, you know, for fires, except instead of passing buckets we'll be passing messages from Mommy down here to me up on the roof."

Willing as elves they were. Jacky stationing himself by the ladder and Tommy in the porch. Directions flowed from room to roof and back. "How is it now?" came down and up went, "That's good! No, no, turn it back. Lost her! Oh, do that again." With gathering precision, repeated along the line, satisfaction grew, until a clear unblinking black and white image glowed upon Mrs. Caffrey. She raced to the porch.

"It's perfect! Tell him to come down and see."

Hector stepped onto terra firma as his brother-in-law appeared in the yard.

"What's going on, Lucky?"

"You're lookin' at it."

"Comin' in? We just got the TV going."

Bridget barred the door. She would throttle him when she had him alone. "Hector. We talked about this, remember." She surveyed the neighbourhood. From where they stood she could see five verandahs, two of them occupied. A clutch of students, their jackets emblazoned with a large black X, passed by in the direction of the campus.

"Lucky, you can come in if you want, but you won't be getting a drink. There're some seminarians coming over to watch a ballgame in less than an hour. I don't want you being stupid and ruining our first TV social. You're already half sideways."

"What's the good of that? Watch the World Series and not even have a *dileag*."

"That's right," agreed Hector, "We don't want you drinking in the house. It's for your own good."

"For my own good. That's rich. As if someone besides me would know my own good. As if you two would." There was no mistaking the united front though. Lucky spun on his heel and marched away.

"Straight to the Legion, you can be sure." But she couldn't dwell on that. There were biscuits to bake and the front room to tidy and clothes to put away and those smelts that Danny dropped off and kids to feed. *Ìosa,* but the go-ahead. "Where's Archie? I haven't seen him since breakfast. You two go find your little brother. Bring him back here right away. He's probably begging for food all around the neighbourhood, the little *gommach*. People'll think we never feed you. Stay out of other people's kitchens, do you hear me? Hurry. Go find him."

"We're hungry."

"I know. So is he. Go get him and bring him back."

The guests landed on the tick of two. Her husband let them in, pumping their fists like champions, showing off his new teeth, and shoving them toward a yawning chesterfield. All scuffed velour and faded floral. She was thankful it was just their arses got a good look at it.

The baseball game, the whole reason for the visit, was of scant interest to Mrs. Caffrey. Upon her soul, she wouldn't know what to do with a baseball game. She could follow hockey, yes. You put the puck in the net. But baseball was as foreign as the Dead Sea Scrolls. The only woman huddled among seven males, she was determined to use the occasion for news gathering.

They were two Morrises and a Maroon. Gene and Gussy Morris were from down Port Hood way. Somehow related to her father's people. Fearful good stepdancers, both them and their sister. Imagine, two priests and a nun in one family. How proud the parents must be. Their friend was a tall, dark-eyed Maroon, somehow related to Hector's mother's people. They'd figure it out. For now, her husband was charming the Morrises to gales of laughter. She positioned herself next to the big Maroon, angling so he was forced to shift his rear end a half turn toward her and away from the TV. He seemed to be mesmerized by the box. It was a semi-fruitful maneuver. She got him talking, anyway. The Maroon could talk. But slow. *Dhia, Dhia,* he was slow. And then he would agree with what he had just said by means of great sucking inhalations, "Yuuuup." It was the Gaelic in him Mrs. Caffrey figured. Accent as thick as porridge. They were barely beyond boys now, but just think, in three or four years we will call them Father. They will forgive sins. They will transubstantiate.

"What kind of prayer do you do at the sem?" Hector asked the big Maroon.

"Mass every day, the Office," he started. "We have—"

"Do you pray the rosary?"

"Not so much, although I would like to. We always did at home, of course. Every Saturday and every night during Lent we were on the floor. At the seminary it's considered a kind of popular religiosity. Yuuup."

Hector was clearly disappointed but quiet in the face of higher doctrine.

"Well, I don't know what that means," said Mrs. Caffrey. "But we are great believers in the power of the rosary, aren't we, Hector? *Ìosa,* did that player just make the sign of the cross?"

"Yes," said Gussie Morris who was glued to the tube. "His name is Chacon, from Venezuela. He always blesses himself when he steps up to the plate. He must be a Catholic."

"Too bad for him God is a Yankee fan," said Hector.

The Morrises laughed then cheered and cheered louder still at some sudden action from the television. When the fuss died down, she made them relate the entire play.

"Okay," she interpreted. "So the little Venezuelan hit the ball and someone on the other team threw it into the place where the Yankee team sits."

"The dugout."

"Yes, the dugout. And so the other team couldn't get the ball and throw it after him, so he just kept going right to the next place."

"The next base. You got it. And now if somebody hits the ball he might come around to score."

"Around?"

"Around the rest of the bases and into home. That's called a run—like a goal."

"You're that excited and he didn't even score yet?"

Much had to be explained, this was clear. But what interested her more was the intensity of feeling among the men. How they rubbed their hands gleefully with each turn of the game, each ball and strike. Her husband stewed on each Yankee pitch to the plate and delighted when Whitey Ford threw strike three. The Morrises lost steam when a second Reds batter got put out. According to Hector, the Venezuelan looked to be stranded at second base. She felt the glee emanate from her husband.

"Look at him now," he said. "Dancing around, but he's not going anywhere."

"Big Frank is up," said Gussy Morris. "He'll knock him in."

Mrs. Caffrey made a spiritual connection with the God-fearing Chacon and an allegiance with the Yankee haters. "Okay. We need a hit. Come on Big Frank. Sit back there, Hector, you're making me nervous."

The Morrises took her encouragement personally. They cheered the batter like he could hear them. "C'mon, Frank! Bring him in."

And on the next pitch, with an audible smack she heard all the way from the Bronx, the ball sailed over Tony Kubek's head, over Tom Tresh's head, and nailed the outfield fence like it was shot from a cannon. The Morrises cheered. Little Chacon took an arm-wheeling cue from the third base coach and crossed home plate without a slide. The Morrises exploded.

"Yay, Frank!" Bridget yelled and she danced with Gene Morris. To be sure she knew what had just happened, she asked for an explanation.

"Just watch."

The just-occurred play was repeated on the screen. The ball again rebounded off the outfield fence. Chacon again crossed the plate and Frank Robinson, manfully clapping, again coasted into second base. Cincinnati 1, New York 0. Again.

Hector groaned for a second time.

"What's this?" she said. "Something new under the sun? How do they do that?"

"What?"

"Be able to show it all over again."

"Back off. Have ye never seen an instant replay before?" Maroon marvelled at his superior experience. After living in Toronto for two years, television was not a new revelation to the seminarians. "Well, Mrs. Caffrey, what you are witnessing is a miracle of modern technology."

From that point, Bridget began to take a lively interest in the game. Imagine showing again what just happened. She would have a second chance to catch on to things. The possibilities were limitless. There were other pauses, like the inordinate amount of time between pitches. The pitcher leaning forward on the mound trying to see what the catcher was signalling with his fingers ("You're kidding, right? That's how they talk to each other?"), shaking his head, shaking again, nodding, spitting, scratching, throwing dirt, pumping himself up.

Baseball was a spit and dirt game, a solitary game, a waiting game, a game of specialists. A pitcher staring hard and long before throwing his lightning. Between pitches, Bridget requested a snap analysis of what had just happened. In baseball, she learned, you could ask questions and a man whose team is leading is all too happy to oblige with colour commentary. The rules seemed impossible, but by the fifth inning she thought she was pretty sure of the difference between a run and a home run.

"Shhh, Mommy! You're asking too many questions."

It was during the seventh-inning stretch that the arse came out of the Caffrey's First Television Social. Ewen Maroon was in the middle of a snail-slow explanation of why the second baseman had to tag a runner, not just the bag, when a ruckus erupted out-of-doors, a rhubarb that signaled that an until-then highly successful affair was to go horribly sideways.

The twins raced to the front door and flung it open. Their mother called after to stay them. "Hold your horses, you two!"

"It's Uncalucky!" Tommy called, "He's on the ground."

Their father pushed them aside and groaned. Mrs. Caffrey squirmed into his side. What she saw was three men, two in clerics, one in bright plaid, standing grimly over a fourth, the fallen, flailing, familiar figure of her brother struggling like a hooked trout. Lucky, loudly and in obvious error, was attesting to his need for no further help. They should leave me be, he said, and all would be just "ine an nanny." The three men stepped away from the derelict. Left to his own devices, Lucky executed a few feeble failures to right himself, then dropped his bloody head until the fight left him. And there he sat. Ine an nanny.

Mrs. Caffrey saw the look on Hector. She knew it wasn't just her brother's condition that assailed him but the identity of his three handlers—his erstwhile rescuers or citizen arresters. First, Mr. Wilkie Cunningham, purveyor of all things tartan, who she knew would be enjoying the family embarrassment. What better way to wreak revenge on two thorn-in-the-side Samwell Hung lovers. Far worse, though, was the presence of two princes of the Church. The Most Reverend William Edward Power, bishop of the diocese of Findrinny, was the tall one in purple. The other was a dark-haired priest, calmly smoking a cigarette. She was sure she had seen him before but couldn't say where. The merchant did the talking.

"We were just finishing up a meeting about what to do about the Indians. Just leaving the meeting and who comes tumbling down the long stairs at the Celtic Hall but Mr. Lucky Dunphy himself. Me, His Reverence, and Father McCoy were all standing right there when poor Lucky came rolling by."

The two clerics nodded gravely, but when the bishop spoke to the man of the house the mood was softened by his mellifluous and reassuring baritone, "We wondered if we should take him to the hospital, but Mr. Cunningham said you would want your brother brought here."

"Yes, Your Grace. Yes, yes, yes, Your Grace," said Hector.

"There doesn't seem to be anything broken," said the priest.

The storekeeper continued with authority, "He's taken quite a blow on the mouth. Just look at him. Still spitting out blood."

"Oh, Lucky," said Mrs. Caffrey, "let's get you inside where I can get a look at you."

"Come here, Ewen," said Hector to the big Maroon. "Grab an arm and we'll get him to the sink. Lots of light there. Okay. Uuuuup. Can you move your feet?" he asked Lucky. They followed Mrs. Caffrey into the kitchen. "Don't worry, Your Excellency," he called, "Bridget will get him fixed up, you can be sure of that."

In the kitchen, she pushed back Lucky's lolling head, opened his mouth, and peered into the dark bloody hole, expecting to see missing teeth.

"That's ugly," she said.

"Sha's nothin."

Mrs. Caffrey dug out bandages, bottles of iodine, cotton batting, and towels, and sponged away crusted blood. "I don't know, Lucky. It looks pretty ugly."

"Ant we have a little..." requested Lucky.

"Not now. Not now."

On closer examination, Mrs. Caffrey saw that his lower teeth and gums were covered in clotted blood. A minute piece of the tongue seemed to have been bitten off, the source of the flow. Once she had determined a hospital visit was unnecessary, Mrs. Caffrey repaired the injured man as best she could and demanded he drink two tumblers of water. She laid him on the daybed, tucked two coats for a pillow under his head, and put a woolly blanket over his shoulders. He grunted appreciation.

"Ìosa, Lucky," she said. "You've really done it this time. Look at you. You're a veritable fountain of family embarrassment. I swear to God if you shame Hector one more time you can jump off Cape Clear before I'll talk to you." She wiped her hands clean, removed her apron, and rejoined the men, smiling as she approached the bishop. "We met at the CWL bazaar, your Grace."

William Power was a tall man with a creased face and kindly blue eyes. Recognizing her, he reared back and exclaimed, "You're the one who made the mermaid! Lovely to see you again!" He would certainly remember the woman who had shaped a voluptuous seawitch from angel food cake and just the right amount of chiffon frosting. It was the toast of the cake walk and a chance for the bishop to show off his sense of humour. For Will Power, the social perquisites of his position were as much a joy as his ecclesiastical duties. Though his territory encompassed the entire island of Cape Breton and a portion of the mainland, it had taken him little time to acquaint himself with the parishioners of the cathedral parish.

When he smiled his whole face smiled. He could charm the suit off a Sunday. "I understand you have a wonderful singing voice, Mrs. Caffrey. And I hear there's a move afoot to have you sing a solo at Midnight Mass."

"Well, Your Grace, you'll find that there's always a lot afoot in the Little Vatican. As for that particular rumour, yes, the choirmaster has asked me to try, but I have never performed solo in the cathedral. I feel I might be overcome with emotion before such a great congregation."

"Ah, but God will be with you."

She stuck out her hand to the priest.

"Father?"

"McCoy. How is your brother, Mrs. Caffrey?"

"He will likely have a sore head."

"For more reasons than one." Silence pungent as turpentine filled the room. It was Cunningham who spoke. There was no need to state the obvious, the plaid clad little potlicker. She could easily cut him down and have all the men smile at her triumph. Toss off a "zinger" as her sisters called them. But the presence of the clergy stalled her arrows.

"Yay!" yelled the twins.

Mother, father, bishop, priest, and seminarians all turned to the boys on the floor and to the box they were cheering. A pinstriped image was moving across a grey backdrop. It touched second, rounded third, winked. Fifty thousand fans were cheering in Yankee Stadium.

"He hit a home run. That Maris guy," said Jacky. "The guy you like, Daddy."

"It's the third game of the World Series, Your Grace," Hector explained seriously. "The series and the game are tied, but it looks like the Yankees may have taken the lead with that." He spoke as an obedient child to a parent.

Maroon said, "Watch this now. They will show an instant replay of the whole play." The room watched Roger Maris at the plate, swinging, slapping the ball into the right-field bleachers, rounding first, slowing into his home run trot, circling second, third, modestly keeping his eyes on the baselines, touching home, smiling and shaking hands with the excellent Mick.

"That could be the turning point in the series right there," Father McCoy said. "Great players find a way to make it happen. Maris is a fine player. He did well this year and not only because Mantle was behind him in the order. If I was a betting man, I would wager his record may never be broken."

The seminarians were glad to join in the patter, though in tones low and somber out of respect for the unfortunate calamity they were sharing. They seemed happy to agree that the Yankees had the superior team.

"Here's a further bet," said the priest, "and I'd put a hard nickel on this one. The record of the M&M boys together: a hundred and fourteen home runs by teammates. You watch and see if that'll ever be broken."

Hector let this sink in, a smile settling. "I like that, Father McCoy. Thanks for that."

All at once she remembered where she had seen the priest's face. It was in *The Crypt*. He was shaking hands with the president of the university over a caption that read: "Rev. Dr. Hugh J. Somers greets Father Steel McCoy, recently returned to the diocese after twelve years working in the cooperative movement in the Dominican Republic. Father McCoy will assume the directorship of the university's Extension Department." She hadn't read the accompanying article. She would now.

McCoy said, "Well, I do hope to hear you sing someday, Mrs. Caffrey. Now though, Bishop, I suppose we should let these good people get back to their ball game. It was nice to meet you all, though I'm sorry it couldn't be under more pleasant circumstances." He made a move for the door, but Power froze the priest in mid-step.

"Mr. Cunningham tells us," began the bishop, "that your brother is living apart from his wife?"

Mrs. Caffrey blushed. "Yes, so he is. It only just happened. I'm surprised Mr. Cunningham knew the gossip so quickly. I guess the air moves quickly in the Little Vatican."

On the hard cot Lucky Dunphy shifted his position, farted with authority, and fell again to snorting sour air through bloodstained bandages. By way of apology he belched, "Nothing but aaiirrr."

The bishop raised his eyebrows. "Was it sudden or had it been building for some time?"

"Yes, I would say it has been coming for some time."

"To me it sounded like that one had been building for some time," said Cunningham, "and now that it's out, it doesn't smell too good."

The bishop ignored the crudity. "Are there children from the union?"

"No. Yes. One. A boy, James. He's a... He's the same age as our twins."

Bishop Power pursed his lips in thought. He asked if he might venture a suggestion before taking his leave. Something for Mr. and Mrs. Caffrey to bring to the lost sheep. "There will be a retreat at the cathedral next month," he said, "for the men of the nearby parishes. Father McCoy here will be leading it. It might be a good opportunity for Mr. Dunphy to clean the pot, so to speak, to turn a new leaf. It would be good to see Mr. Dunphy, and you too, Hector. Come out for the retreat. They can be powerful experiences. You too, Mr. Cunningham."

After an uncomfortable silence, Hector explained. "Mr. Cunningham is of the other persuasion, Your Grace."

Bridget Caffrey said she would do her level best to get her brother to clean the pot. The bishop could be assured of that.

"Yes, Your Grace. Yes, yes, yes, Your Grace," agreed her husband.

Tommy had for two months felt a gnawing nocturnal warmth and discomforting hardness. But in all these wee hour imaginings he was unable to speak. His dumbness felt like a physical handicap, but in truth he just had nothing to say. Awake, too, he could not imagine what he could say to Katie when he had her alone. In the dream, he hoped she would fire the first salvo, but no, she would putter and preen, smiling or growing tired of smiling, waiting in vain for him to go first or, most often, walking away. From these dreams he woke feeling in every tooth the cowardly lion. He wished she would make a demand: "Can't you say anything?

Anything? Anything at all?"

As they passed under the stern painting of Bishop Fraser and out into an apple-crisp October afternoon, Tommy remembered Geronimo's mantra: *Be cunning and aggressive in the face of danger.* He needn't have worried. Once he spoke, she was off. She could carry conversation like Santa carries the mail. What will I do when I get home? Let's see, when I get home I'll call my friend Joyce. She'll come over and we'll listen to records and do our homework. We'll frug and bug. We'll twist and shout. We'll do the locomotion. Joyce is such a good singer. Joyce is such a free thinker. Joyce is so observant. Joyce has such a way with words.

She had already said good-bye when Tommy found his voice again.

"I wanted to thank you for the time you read the story of Saint Antiochus."

"Don't mention it. I just like showing off about what I know about saints. Plus, I didn't like Mrs. MacDonald making a joke at your expense."

"Thanks."

"But did you really think that the Ani G'nish was named for a saint?"

"Well, that's what the Indian told me. But I guess he was kidding me and I fell for it. I guess he was one of those tricksters Mrs. MacDonald talked about. Trickster Indians. Have you ever heard tell of them?"

"No."

"Tell me about another saint."

"That's a funny request."

"Sorry. You seem to know so much about them. I'm just interested."

"You don't talk much, do you?"

"I guess not." Again he turned a valentine shade. More than simple listening would be required of him. "Hey," he tried, "there's something I want to show you. Have you ever seen the Bishop's Bowl?"

"No. What's that? Some earthen vessel Bishop Power eats his porridge from?"

"No, it's really neat. You should see it. It's a big hill that we go tobogganing on in the winter. Come on, it's just up behind the high school."

"You better not be up to something weird, Tommy Caffrey."

"No, come on, I'll show you. It'll just take a couple of minutes."

They walked on in silence, passing a great white house that they knew to be the bishop's palace. It stood three storeys and had all the embellishments of the Second Empire—bracketed eaves, hooded windows, iron cresting. A foursquare white tower projected from its black mansard roof. She remembered his question.

"Okay, so you want to hear about a saint. Here's a story about my favourite, Santa Fina. Santa Fina lived in a beautiful walled town full of great towers. It was called San Gimignano. Inside its high walls the people felt safe from their enemies. So it was with their neighbours they competed. The men built higher and higher towers to show which of their families was the most powerful. Higher and higher the towers grew until San Gimignano became known as the Town of Fine Towers. Amid all these great marvels of human invention reaching high and mighty to the sky, there is a humble and narrow cobblestone alley. And down this narrow alley is a small stone house. You have to step down four steps from the alley to get into it. One, two, three, four. In this small stone house once lived a young girl named Fina. She lived there with her parents and her brothers and sisters, as happy and content as the rest of them. Then one day Fina committed a sin so great in her mind that she laid down upon a rough pallet and remained there so long the pallet and the girl became one. And each night, the rats would come to nibble her as she starved herself for forgiveness."

She told the story with great enthusiasm and in vivid detail, complete with death and miracles. By the time Katie had finished speaking of Santa Fina's short and bizarre existence, Tommy's heart raced with disgust.

"How weird is that."

"Weird and wonderful! But that's the life of the saints. Imagine the poverty of Santa Fina. Imagine the piety! Don't you find it romantic? I do." And her heart went out to the little *santa* and she prayed that she too would be so brave in what was asked of her. She sighed deeply and tossed her hair against worldly trappings. She snapped out of her reverie when they suddenly came upon the crest of a wide deep bowl, a green amphitheatre sloping majestically toward a lush and grassy bottom.

"So here it is!" Tommy swept an arm expansively. "The Bishop's Bowl."

Katie unstrapped her schoolbag and flopped to the grass staring. He dropped beside her. In silence they peered from belvedere to panorama, Tommy trying to picture the scene as Katie did, for the first time. They looked beyond the bowl and field, past a smattering of university buildings, and toward a forest on the field's far side. Like a Van Gogh it stood, alive in aspen red, maple orange, birch yellow, and evergreen, alive and swaying in the gently cooling autumn breeze.

"Whoa," said Katie, "I never knew this hill was even *here*."

"Me and Jacky and Jimmy Dog discovered it on a bike trip years ago. We just kept riding up here past the church, past the schools, past the bishop's palace, and then when we got up here the three of us just stopped and said, 'Wowwwww… Look at that!' You should have seen Jimmy Dog. As soon as he saw it he just raced his bike right to the bottom like it didn't have any brakes. I thought he was going to kill himself, but he didn't even wipe out. Me and Jacky were so scared we *walked* our bikes down."

"So Jimmy Dog rode his bike fast down there? And he didn't kill himself?"

"Yup, believe it or not. I can still see him speeding down the hill yelling, 'Geronimooooo!' all the way."

"He's kind of crazy, you know. He's like your best friend, right?"

"Yeah, I guess so."

"How long have you known him?"

"Forever. He's my cousin."

"He's actually kind of weird or didn't you notice. He's always picking his nose and wiping it on his clothes. And he's constantly making little grunting noises. It's very distracting. You know what? I don't even think he knows he's doing it."

"I didn't notice."

"Did you notice he hardly ever talks to anyone except you and your brother?"

Tommy hadn't.

"Well, maybe it's good that you chum with him. He doesn't have any other friends."

"Sure he does. He plays with Joe Dillon and some other guys too. Bart, Leo, other guys."

He looked her way as if expecting an answer to that insight. They were sitting close and she was talking again, though his heart made it hard to follow the thread of her monologue. She was talking outside herself now, free from all restraint. She was babbling about something nice her friend Joyce had said about Jimmy Dog being cute. Katie disagreed.

"His damned red hair spoils everything, I told her. What can you do with a redhead? Anyway, it's his behaviour that freaks people out. Why don't you say something to him if you're his friend?"

Tommy gathered himself to attention. "What am I going to say? He'll never listen to me. I used to try to get him not to do stuff, but he never listens."

"So you've given up. Doesn't that make you a coward?"

"No, that makes me a saint for being his best friend when nobody else will hang out with him." Having said this aloud, he immediately felt guilty. He wanted it back.

"Touché," she pounced. "But I think you might be overestimating your sanctity. I know a lot about saints, Tommy Caffrey, and you ain't no saint."

He felt disloyal to Jimmy Dog. He knew the Dog hated small talk about his psyche, good or bad. Insults and lies were the worst. Compliments were also discouraged. Jimmy Dog would decide what should be said about Jimmy Dog, nobody else. He wouldn't hit you if you said something nice about him, but he didn't have to like it. Tommy needed to change the subject. But as soon as Katie spoke, Tommy looked in her eyes and forgot the guilt. Two irises were upon him, glowing green perfection. His dumb face appeared in her pupils, horse-like, looking back at him. What wonder swam in such two small spots. But then her eyes and the equine image within looked shyly away and he realized he'd been staring. Embarrassment clung thick to the air. The silence that followed brought the first bugle of retreat. But he remembered Geronimo and another strategy emerged.

"Do you know what that building over there is? That's the Coady International Institute."

Katie's scarlet lessened and Tommy settled into the story he was saving for this moment. It was part of the plan.

"It was named after Monsignor Moses Coady. He was in the Ani G'nish Movement. They built a bunch of co-ops and credit unions to help the miners and the fishermen and the farmers. He died a couple of years ago. My dad played the pipes at his funeral. See that graveyard up on the hill? Moses Coady is buried up there." What could she say to that?

"So, Tommy," she asked, "is it true you have a photographic memory like Mrs. MacDonald says?"

Tommy shrugged. From Mrs. MacDonald the statement seemed like an accusation. From Katie it was part tease, part compliment. Cautious pride welled within him and he sank further under a spell of his own making.

"Do you?"

He wondered what answer would cast him in a favourable glow.

"I don't know."

"It sure seems that way," said Katie, "You are the only one in the class who knows all the provinces and all their capitals and all the states and all their capitals, and every element in the periodic table."

Tommy checked himself, not sure if he wanted to try again. "Sometimes I can't remember things. Other times I just look at something and I can't forget it. Like names on a map. I remember them all right away and they just kind of stay there."

"Well, I'm going to tell Mrs. MacDonald to stop helping you with your cursive writing even though you're still so sloppy. You shouldn't be acing everything. I won't be able to keep up. And we wouldn't want that." But she softened the threat with a flash of her fine teeth, then she cast her eyes about for new sights. She lifted a finger to point.

"Hey, there's the rink, isn't it? Down there."

Tommy had to touch her. Just his hand on hers. How would it feel? She was pointing to her right, past his nose. "See down that way, that's the college rink, over there. Look." He put his hand down where he knew hers had been.

"Yes."

"Neat," Katie said, "Funny to see it from above."

"Have you ever been inside it?"

Her hand came down on his. For an electric moment it lingered. The jolt entered Tommy's body at her touch and he felt his whole left side glow with heat, his heart quicken. He struggled to follow her words. His most bloodfull organs pulsated and palpitated.

"Oops, sorry," she said. "Have I ever been inside the rink? That's a laugh. Nearly every weekend in the winter, that's where you'll find me. Either in the stands for the games or on the ice for the skating parties. But I think it's so stupid that only boys are allowed to play hockey. I bet I can play just as good as you. My uncle floods the backyard every winter. I'd play out there every free minute I could, except when the ice won't freeze or it's too covered in snow and no one will help me shovel it away. My uncle says I skate better than him when he was twelve. Plus he says they are going to start a minor hockey program. I told him I wanted to be allowed to play. "

"What? You gotta be kidding. They won't let you play. You're a girl."

"Shhh. You want to broadcast that all over the Bishop's Bowl? *Breaking news: Girl playing hockey.* So what? I heard they allow it in some places in Cape Breton. Who knows, maybe they can do it here too. Anyway, I bet I can skate faster than you. Do you ever go to the skating parties? They're starting again you know. We could race there this Saturday. Or better yet, we'll have a race at the bantam tryouts. One-on-one. One end of the rink to the other."

Tommy felt no need to compete with Katie Beaton. Katie's manner was calming to him now. He expected her to go on and on when she talked. Like a lovely lozenge, it soothed his anxiety. The guys he hung with didn't talk at length, except little Leo Dillon the idler and he was a *gommach*. No, Katie was not that kind of talkative. She wasn't a pain in the arse. She was mesmerizing. Blindly he bought into her plot to crack the hockey gender barrier. The sun began to set, the horizon streaked in soft cloudy lines of pink and blue, blue and pink, pink and blue. Tommy saw rhapsodic images of skating Katie moving in figure eights. They played upon his mind. They pried open parts softly pasted shut.

"They should have a name for that colour," Katie said wistfully to the pink-streaked sky, and the shapes seemed to shimmer with greater delicacy and evanescence.

Tommy watched the dappled horizon in respectful silence. Their shared stillness thrilled him in its intimacy. He knew if he stared and thought hard enough the answer would come. "I know!" he cried. "We'll call it sky blue pink. It'll be our own pet name. Pink for girls, blue for boys."

"Perfect! Sky blue pink because anything boys can do, so can girls." And she laughed at the uncertain frown on his blushing face.

HEROES

The sergeant major spun on his one heel, clopped his peg leg, and boomed, "Attennn-TION!" Long columns of hard black shoes stamped loud upon rain-spattered asphalt. The pipe major turned to his band and called out the first tune. "Highland Laddie!"

At the head of the parade stood six foot six Big Ran'l MacDonald. His voice carried to both ends of Main Street. "BY THE CENTRE, QUICK MARCH!" The drummers began their rolls. Twelve Caledonia-kilted pipers blew great gulps of November air into their blowpipes, filling their tartan-covered sheepskins. With the second roll of the drums, twelve expanding sacs were tucked under twelve left elbows, sending through each set of three drones just enough air for the two tenors and the one tall bass to commence a harmonized hum. The split second the roll ended, the twelve pipers blew and pressed at the same time to deliver a sufficient quantity of air surging through the chanter reed and bang, as one, in came the chanters, "EEEEEEE," and the music began. And the parade was off. From Columba's Field up Main Street, past the Great Elm, the Five to a Dollar, the Brigadoon, the credit union. Behind the pipers, the swinging tenors and the rat-a-tat-tat of the side drummers and the boom boomity boom boom of the bass. And in front of them all, the sergeant major leading the veterans of the First and Second World War and the Korean Conflict, their jaws cocked at lofty angles, lurching toward the site of the annual memorial. Between Oak Manor and the red-bricked post office where the Red Ensign fluttered at half-mast, past the Celtic Hall, home to Scotia Branch 59 Royal Canadian Legion, the members of which would soon be cramming the place, parched warriors in soggy berets. Belly up to the bar, boys. The first drink's on the house.

When the war broke out, McCoy was a China missionary. When it ended, he was an army chaplain in Italy. Memories he thought he'd vomited away twenty years earlier came slinking back. Shanghai, criminal heads hanging from lampposts; baby bellies bloated with opium. Lishui, baptizing the dying while the bombs fell in the streets;

selling his own shit. Money for manure. And it was about to get worse, far worse. The Japs were coming. Their agents were already in the city. He tried to convince Curtin, the superior, to flee. The old man was as indecisive as Pharaoh's mother's mummy and nearly as deaf. When that failed, McCoy tried to convince the nuns. No, they wouldn't leave without the superior. What would the Japs do to them? Never mind. Steel McCoy wasn't going to fall into murderous hands. He took the next ferry across the river. From the far bank, he looked back with relief at the nuns and Old Curtin boarding a boat to escape. From there it was a forced exodus. Danger and dysentery dogged them every step of the way. Because he was the strongest, the others sent McCoy on even further. In Kunming he learned to play the black market so he could send supplies to the other missionaries. Not exactly why he spent five years studying in the seminary. Then it was over the hump to Bombay and on to the Holy Land and Rome. The occupying Americans adopted him as their chaplain. He learned to enjoy scotch. He celebrated VE Day in London. He was back in Cape Breton for two weeks when the Scarboro Foreign Missions sent him word he was assigned to the Dominican Republic.

It was Father McCoy's first time marching in the Remembrance Day parade. Wars on the other side of the world meant nothing to the *campesinos*. They had their own *dictador* to worry about. In the DR, November 11 passed without a mention.

The parade turned at the bend in Main Street. Father McCoy saw the Wheel and the turrets of the Fina and beyond them a brook, a bridge, and a sandstone column writ with the names of those who made the supreme sacrifice. Around the cenotaph, row on row, flocked the fine folk of Findrinny. The Caffrey clan was there of course. Bridget and her chickens, the littlest tucked into her ankle-length coat. Father McCoy nodded, doffed his cap, and spoke.

"Morning, Mrs. Caffrey."

"Morning, Father. Chilly day."

"Parade! Stand at ease!" ordered Sergeant Major MacDonald. "Parade! Stand easy!"

The program flowed like the brook babbling beneath the Wheeler's bridge. An opening prayer from Mother Vince. "Abide With Me" from Blaise Cameron, his bass baritone used to full vibrato. The bugler's last post. Two minutes of windblown silence. Pipe Major Hector Caffrey playing "The Flowers of the Forest." A bugled reveille, then the speeches, the laying-on of wreaths, the chaplain's closing prayer.

"Lord," intoned Father McCoy, "by your mercy and wisdom you have brought these men and women home from the peril and agony of war. Let us never forget the sacrifice made by those who did not return and the sacrifice made by these who did..."

"Your father and the other veterans are heroes," said Mrs. Caffrey, wiping a drop of evidence from her eye.

Tommy Caffrey pondered the garish green crosses and poppy-pinned wreaths lying about the cenotaph—an obelisk to remind you of the passion of Passchendaele, the disaster at Dieppe, the victory at Vimy, the streets of Ortona, the heights of Cassino, the taking of Coriano Ridge, the storming of Juno Beach, the liberation of Holland... Victims of bloodmuddy trenches, mustard gas, artillery shells, landmines, sunken ships, and friendly fire. The boys who won't be coming home.

What of the other side? The losers. The Jerries and the Japs. His mother told them once that their father had done everything he could not to kill a Jerry. He trained for the signal corps, he volunteered as a stretcher-bearer, he joined the pipe band. He hid the marksmanship that had once brought down two deer with a single shot. He was a conscientious objector. "After the war," she said, "Daddy vowed never again to fire a weapon."

If everyone fought like my father, Tommy thought, the Jerries would have won the war. We'd all be goose-stepping around yelling "Heil Hitler" like bloody idiots and lamenting our feeble philosophy of pacifism. His father's way was far from Geronimo's. When he was no older than Tommy, the Apache had already proved himself an intrepid raider. Told what it would cost him to have the girl he desired, he snuck into a Mexican army installation and stole the required dowry. Under cover of darkness he rustled twenty horses from a standing slumber and in the morning delivered them to the girl's father. *Be cunning and aggressive in the face of danger.* This was Geronimo's true way. His bravery was not mixed with hate until he discovered his beloved wife, their three children, and his own mother massacred by soldiers. It was only then that he cut off his hair and declared war on Mexico. To make war on a country, he called forth supernatural powers to defeat superior numbers. He could speak to bears and eagles. Bullets fired at him turned into water. He could control time. If he wanted, he could command the dawn to hold off for hours until his raiders had finished their work. The Apache flocked to his magic.

His parents had a picture of the Sacred Beaming and Bleeding Heart of Jesus above their queen bed. Above his, Tommy placed his Indian heroes. The scowling Geronimo, the noble Black Hawk on a sweater, and between them, a newspaper clipping of Diefenbaker and two other chiefs, all three in enormous ceremonial headdresses, Dief the Chief in the middle. Be proud, he seemed to say. Be loyal. Never give up. Never surrender.

Tommy would add another hero to his pantheon this November 11. He pulled the photo from *The Hockey News*, scissored it neat, and tacked it next to Geronimo. *The Hockey News* said that Pierre Pilote was small for a defenceman, certainly smaller than his perpetual partner on defence, the hulking Number Four, Elmer Vasko. Whenever Vasko carried the puck, the fans in Chicago Stadium would bellow in a low bull roar until the rafters vibrated. "Mooooooooooose!" they chanted. But Tommy knew. Number Four might be popular, but Number Three was the real leader of the Black Hawks. He flipped through his stack of cards, all ordered by team, and found Pilote's. He wore the home sweater, bold red with proud Indianhead, and on the left breast, the "C" for captain. Pierre Pilote's body was crouched in faceoff fashion, his stick on the ice, his chin cocked upward. Serious black eyes peered out from under a spiky black crewcut. Tommy wondered if his hero was tall or short for a defenceman.

Tommy asked, "How tall and heavy are you, Daddy? Five foot nine and a hundred and seventy-seven pounds! That's exactly how big Pierre Pilote is!" And so he knew Pilote wasn't small because his father was big as a bear.

In *The Hockey News*, the only pictures of Pierre Pilote showed him putting a hip into Boom Boom Geoffrion at the blue line or sending a Red Wing up and over his back while he carefully corralled the puck between his skates. Pilote was not as belligerent as Moose Vasko, not as nifty a playmaker as Stan Mikita, not as swift a skater as Bill Hay, and not as powerful a shooter as Bobby Hull. But he had all these gifts in good measure. He could score a few goals, not bad for a defenceman, and whether from crease to red line or from the blue line in, he was a pinpoint passer. If Bobby Hull was a lion, Pierre Pilote was a leopard. He relied on quickness rather than speed, surprise rather than strength. Sharp and intelligent play with lightning bursts from the ideal position. Not to say he wasn't strong, but that trait he employed only when needed most. For self-preservation. For standing a forward up at his blue line. For balance when the guy was rolling over his back. He liked to have one stretcher-case a game.

Jimmy Dog hated him. "What's one Stanley Cup? Rocket won five in a row."

"But too bad, Jimmy. Rocket retired and the Black Hawks took the Cup away from you. Too bad. So sad."

"He's just a friggin' defenceman who didn't learn to skate backward until he finished junior."

"A friggin' defenceman who led the playoffs in scoring."

"No individual trophies."

"Yet."

Never mind, Tommy thought. Never mind that Pierre Pilote was *just* a defenceman. Never mind that he couldn't shoot like the Rocket, skate like the Rocket, score like the Rocket, fight like the Rocket, strike fear like the Rocket. Never mind all the vitriol from the jealous and officious opposition. Pierre Pilote was doing one thing that Rocket Richard wasn't doing. The Rocket was gone and Captain Pilote was still playing hockey.

"Yeah, but he's still a fucking Indian."

The Celtic Hall, 294 Main Street, Findrinny Fair. As staid and square and white as its denizens. Up the main staircase is the dancehall, as busy as a beehive this Armistice Day. The ladies auxiliary is serving sugar doughnuts and hot chocolate to noisy queues of cubs and scouts. Downstairs a hundred or so members and guests of Scotia Branch 59 belly up to the bar and piano. Tinkling the ivories is Jolly Mabel Cunningham, as made-up as a corpse. It's as if she lived for this one day a year, the day when the men gathered up close to her backside, those who leered and those who sang.

There'll be bluebirds over
The white cliffs of Dover

Lucky Dunphy sneaks past a dozen brown arborite tables and parks himself far from bar and piano. He plunks his glass and proceeds to dig black dirt from his fingernails with his strongest and longest talons. Accumulating a sufficient quantity of jam, he squashes it into a small black speck and flicks it into his unwanted glass of ginger ale. He peeks out from under his cap. On the outside his comrades look like him. Pressed grey slacks, white shirt, striped tie, blue blazer pinned over the heart with red velvet poppy, blue beret adorned with legion crest and regimental badges and mottos: *Pro Patria, Je me Souviens, Semper Fidelis, Siol Na Fear Fearail*—The Breed of Manly Men. Upon their chests all wear rows of medals; in Dunphy's case, five: the Defence Medal, the Star of Italy, the France and Germany Star, the Atlantic Star, and the 39-45 Bar. France and Germany sicken him still.

"Hey, Lucky! Don't tell me you're not drinkin'. Jesus Christ, it's Armistice Day. I'll buy you one, man. Double Captain and Pepsi right?"

"No, I'm good."

Behind him the sound of a record being snatched and dropped, a scratchy rasp then the rich light baritone of Gentleman Jim Reeves:

If I see you tomorrow on some street in town
Pardon me if I don't say hello.

"Hey, Lucky, how about a snort?"

No, I'm good."

Just walk on by, wait on the corner
I love you but we're strangers when we meet

"Aw, turn that off. We can't hear the piano."

"Hey Lucky, get over here. Give us a song. Jesus those Dunphys can sing."

"When they're sober."

Lucky remains detached, spiritually, so to speak. That is to say everyone seems to be in better spirits than him. He sees the bartender fielding coupons, his comrades on their second and third, the conversation getting louder, the singers, arms locked in a sway to Jolly Mabel's jaunty piano, double hollering *inky dinky parlez-vous*. He envies them their camaraderie, and more so, their liquor.

"Mr. Dunphy."

"Padre."

"You may not remember me."

"Of course I remember. You're the priest that dragged me to my sister's place. I wish you hadn't done that."

"You were supposed to take in my retreat at the cathedral."

"I made a deal with them. I told them I'd go to the AAs instead and they were happy with that." Dunphy rises, grasping his glass like a talisman.

"I'd like to talk to you about something."

Lucky walks briskly away, shouldering through loud clutches of veterans sharing tales of fallen comrades. The sing-a-long is expanding, taking over the mood. Then whoa—it's as if a spotlight were thrown on her. Among those surrounding the piano is a sight seen only this once in Findrinny Fair, by Lucky Dunphy at least. A "blonde bombshell" was the going term out of Hollywood. Even in the navy blazer, she stands out among the females. No shapelier he supposes than Jolly Mabel, but Mabel's face could launch a thousand ships… the other way. And look at the hair onto her. Busty, blonde, and beautiful. It was not inconceivable that he had a shot at her. Once upon a time he'd had some success with the ladies. Usually liquor was involved. Or nylons. Or marriage. But months had gone by since his last piece of tail.

He is close enough to smell peroxide when his intent is dislodged by a pair of flapping lips belonging to Nosey Flynn. "What about you Lucky? D'ya get yer deer yet? I'll be in the woods above Bornish tomorrow at the crack. Bambis beware." The fiddler rubs his hands vigorously as if to massage away a dawn chill.

Lucky curses the roadblock. "What?"

It is as if Dunphy had not said, "What?" but instead had asked, "Flynn, was it you who plugged that twelve-point buck back in '56? Can you tell me that story?"

With a straight on, no escape engagement of the listener, Flynn is into it. "Damn right it was me. I was in my blind watching my pile of apples and up steps three doe and then one, two, three yearlings into the open field. One by one they dipped their heads to munch, the young ones first. I knew the buck was sending them to test the site for safety. Then sure enough, the big whitetail showed himself, majestic and powerful… POW!"

Throughout the rendition, Flynn is mere inches from his listener's face, enforcing interest with repeated elbows to the ribcage and exploding bilabial fricatives above, below, and square into Lucky's eyes. When the puff and spittle propels him to turn away, the perceived lack of attention brings yet another jab to the ribs, another jolt to the skeleton. Jab. Puff. Jab. Puff. Jab. Puff. Never has he noticed this quality to Flynn's Ps. Of course he has never until now been in such close proximity to the fiddler's lips.

"Puh-lugged him right between the eyes."

Lucky wipes his cheeks and chin, rubs his ribcage.

"You drinkin' pop? Please can I arsk you, what's the good o' that? One drink won't do you no harm, it'll just get you going. Jesus, you're as dour as the dead."

"No, I'm fine. Stayin' off 'er for the day."

"Then what about your free coupon. If you'll not be needin' it..."

Lucky turns away and moves again in the direction of the blonde. Behind his sober grey eyes, he harbours the same opinion as Nosey Flynn. Lubrication. That is liquor's true purpose, an opening of the senses and a lowering of the inhibitions. The trick is to get more out of it than it can get out of you. Most times it works out fine. He thinks of the slip in his wallet: *Angus (sponsor) 863-4040.*

Hector Caffrey interrupts the reverie. "How's it going Lucky? What's in the glass?"

"Ginger ale."

"Well, after that episode with the bishop, that's a good thing.

So you're on the wagon, eh? And did you go to the AAs?"

Lucky feels like asking, "What are *you* drinking?" But there is no doubt of that. The molecules fairly tickle his nose. Rye and ginger. Seagram's Five Star. It's not as if Hector has never gotten shitfaced. They all had it in them. Alcoholism that is.

"Doesn't one of those As stand for anonymous? I said I would, didn't I."

"Well, that's a good thing, then," says Hector. "How you makin' out with that?"

"All right."

"They teach you anything?"

"A lot in fact, if you want to hear about it. You see, they have this philosophy based on Christian perfectionism. Total Temperance, it's called. D'ya ever hear tell of it? 'Not one drink ever.' The idea is one drink's too many, twenty's not enough. One drink, they say, and bingo, back to square one. What are you drinking by the way?"

But Hector is backing away, waving, whistling, drawn into the larger chorus of puckerlipped smileycheeked twitterers. "Colonel Bogey's March!" Off he went, highstepping with all his good feeling comrades, raising pointy elbows, stamping their feet like it was 1945. Glowing in each other's free spirits, picking up the tune now, whistling like whippoorwills.

Hitler has only got one ball
Goering has two but they are small
Himmler has something sim'lar
And Mister Goebbels has no balls at all

Lucky pictures the propaganda minister naked, sans testicles, getting set to blow his xenophobic brains out. His wife and six children already spread dead about him. The Babelsberg Stud screeching out one last hateful screed against the Jews as the shotgun blast removes grey matter through the top of the hairless skull and splatters the bunker walls. Dunphy narrows his eyes to improve his memory. Something the racist bastard said that was true enough. He'd read it in *Time* magazine: "It is not propaganda's task to be intelligent, its task is to lead to success." Yes. That makes sense. That's the AAs all over.

"You walked away from me. Why?"

"Oh you again, Padre."

"How's that going?" the priest nods toward the full glass of ginger ale. He is a taller man. Handsome in a weatherbeaten way. Slowly hauling on a cigarette. Drinking scotch. Single Malt. Lucky sniffed. Glenfiddich. Too cool by half or half cut, one or the other.

"It's going."

"I've spoken to your wife, Mr. Dunphy."

"Ah Jesus, and what did the warden have to say?"

"She doesn't think you can do it on your own. She thinks you need to get out of town, away from this environment."

"I took the pledge. I'm going to the AAs. I have a sponsor. What more does she want?"

"I gave her the phone number of a new addiction recovery house in Frenchvale. A friend of mine, John Webb, started it a couple of years ago. It's called Talbot House. It helps men who are trying to stay on the wagon for good."

"Webb. He's a priest too, isn't he? Jesus. If the God-talk at one place isn't intense enough, they'll send you to another. 'Accept a higher power in your life. Ask those you've harmed for forgiveness. Make amends for your errors.' The day I accept a higher power is the day the war never happened."

"At least you know the steps, even if you don't accept them. What Talbot House does is give you a community. You won't feel isolated like you do here."

Lucky sees that the bird in the bullet bra has backed away from the lek, exiting when the whistling and wing beating began. No doubt out-of-control wings and hands had a way of finding her. She is sashaying toward the bar, cheeks aglow like ripe McIntoshes. Lucky wouldn't feel so isolated if he could rub up against Jayne Mansfield in a legion jacket.

"Okay, Padre," he relents, "let's talk if you want to. But tomorrow. You can buy me lunch at the Brigadoon."

The priest moves in on his prey until he is in breathing range. Scotch. "There's something else I want to talk to you about. The nuns up in the Tampakan tell me you used to be a manager for the mining co-op and then for Archer-Atlas."

"That was a long time ago."

"There is a story about the consent forms the B'laan signed. I want to get your version of it."

Lucky smells the breath of the priest. Rum there too. Sucks on the Scotch for show. One of those collar-warrants-respect types. Ah, what the hell. What difference does it make now? He won't be undoing what's done.

"What are you, a priest or a cop? Anyway, it was all on the up-and-up. Three hundred and some signed the consent form, more than fifty percent of the affected adult population. Check the records at the court house."

"Three hundred is not even ten percent of the people who live in that zone. Everyone knows that except the census takers. And I *have* seen the consent form in the court house. Are we to assume that any of those names knew the meaning of those English words typed neatly on the top?"

"Didn't matter. If they couldn't read, we read it to them. That's within the law."

"Couldn't read English? The nuns say that would account for a hundred percent of the signatories. Another thing. What if what you read to them was not the same as what was written? Is that within the law?"

"Listen Padre. There's nearly ten years of water under that bridge. What's done is done. You can't hold back progress."

"The nuns say..."

"Oh the nuns say, the nuns say. You take a lot of stock in what the nuns say, padre. Is my sister one of the nuns you're talking to? She's been up there nearly four years now. She knows the score. Sister Catherine-Under-God. You talk to her? Didn't think so. She'll be home for Christmas. Talk to her then. She knows what a dissembling lot those Indians can be and how gullible are her Little Sisters of Jesus. But let's save this talk for the Brigadoon. I wouldn't mind a free lunch. Got my appetite back since I took the pledge. Twelve noon sound good?"

With that Lucky tunes out the preacher's yabbering. Easy enough. Volume is peaking in the Legion Bar and Boardroom. Goddam busybodies those nuns are. Just leave good enough alone, why don't they? But even those bitches can't stop Big Ran'l when he gets something in his head. You can't stop progress. What is it he likes to say? 'If it isn't Archer-Atlas today, it'll be Falconbridge tomorrow.'"

Jayne Mansfield has moved to the bar and is looking in Lucky's direction. At his hair, he supposes. He approaches the quarry in a sidelong manner, keeping her blonde helmet in view as he zigs and zags. The platinum oddity opens a cigarette case. Findruine he guesses by the sparkle. He snaps a match aglow, holds it close, shakes his wrist and scuffs the matchhead into his pocket. "Not from around here, are you?"

She blows her answer toward the ceiling. Red lips, even white teeth. Her eyes, doe-soft and brown, are shaded in metallic blue, her lashes long and dark. The Italy Star emblazons her chest. Hard to miss. Her name? Mindy MacKay from Aspy Bay. He repeats it with her same lilt. No one ever forgets that name, he's betting. Lucky smiles and speaks his own. A good confident smile is all it takes for a man to dazzle. That and a scintilla of charm will get you to first base.

"What are you havin' doll?"

"I'm having a good laugh. It took you quite a while to get here, Lucky Dunphy. You've been checking me out for fifteen minutes. But on your way to see me you stop and talk to the fiddler, the whistler, the priest, and oh, look at that, I actually have to go in five minutes. See. You should have been quicker." She has a soft voice punctuated by squeals.

Lucky moves a step closer and sniffs. "Who's checkin' who out? Bobby! Rye and ginger for the lady."

He interrogates Mindy MacKay on her time in Italy. Maybe they crossed paths. She had been an angel of mercy in Andria, worked on the wounded in her sweet Alice blue gown, then on to Rome where she stayed for the remainder of the war. Lucky makes good use of this knowledge and soon they find common acquaintance among Highlanders and nurses.

Mindy MacKay points with her chin. "The big guy with the white hair and the one arm, who is he?"

"The one who's talking so much? That's Big Ran'l, Ronald Atlas

MacDonald, and you are the only one in here who doesn't know him."

"*Ìosa,* so that's Ronald Atlas. Of course I've heard tell of him. He's the big war hero."

Lucky could tell her the story of how Sergeant Major MacDonald lost his appendages. He'd had a front row seat, as did a half dozen other men in the room. Their platoon had been ordered to capture a German strongpoint along the Coriano Ridge. With his men pinned down by artillery, the sergeant major grabbed a pack of hand grenades and started doing the military crawl in the direction of the firespitters. Soon as he was near enough, he lobbed a grenade into the machine gun nest and finished the Jerries off with a spray of tommygun. With that one taken care of, Big Ran'l sprinted to the second position and splattered that nest of Nazis with a pair of pineapples and more tommygun. But when he went for the third position, the Jerries were ready for him. As he came sprinting through open ground, just five lengths from the nest, up pops a Jerry at point-blank range. This guy blasts a rifle-mounted grenade at Ran'l and finally he goes down. The blast covered him with shrapnel, shredded his left arm from the elbow and shattered his kneecap. Even this didn't stop him. Big Ran'l looked down at his barely attached forearm. It was still holding a hand grenade. He pried it out with his right hand, pulled the pin with his teeth and lobbed it sidearm right into *dummkopf's* face. How can you not be loyal to someone like that? But there was no need to draw any more attention to Big Ran'l. He had enough.

"Who are you here with?"

"Vera Palmer. You know her I think."

"Of course. You seem so sweet," he ventures. "And those eyes of yours. What colour are they? People must ask you all the time. I'm saying dark chocolate."

"Don't you get flirty with me, Lucky Dunphy. I see you have a ring on your finger."

"Not anymore." He dislodges the band and deposits it in his ginger ale.

Mindy MacKay from Aspy Bay interprets this action incorrectly. All Lucky is trying to prove is that he's available. She thinks he's revealing something entirely different. A word he's never heard tell of.

"What does that mean?"

"It means you dislike women and what they stand for."

"That's harsh."

The wedding ring bubbles like a set of false teeth freshly dunked. The smell of peroxide wafts in and out of his nose. It mixes with every smoke, spillage, and spirit in a ten foot radius. He won't bother to look the word up. He looks away, sucking his teeth. His heart measures eight pulses.

Mindy MacKay turns to the crowd frowning. Plenty of fish. No need to settle on a cold cod who can't converse. "Well, see you." She sails through the closeness of the crowd, a battleship in a fleet of corvettes. Promises, promises. Lucky examines his non-alcoholic drink, fingers the coupon in his pocket. Dry tongue slides over lying lips. *The sacred pint alone can unbind the tongue of Dedalus.*

Big Ran'l MacDonald observes Lucky critically and orders one of his minions: "Carl, go get this man a double rum and coke."

"No, I'm not..." starts Lucky but Carl doesn't break stride.

"You know that padre you were talking to? McCoy. What did he have to say that was so important?"

"Oh, him," says Lucky. "He thinks he's Dick Tracy. Dickless Tracy more like it. He was asking me about the consent forms. I set him straight."

"Is that it? I heard he's been snooping around. Talking to the Indian nuns. *Dhia!* Get rid of that piss in your hands. What the hell's swimming in there. Jesus is that your wedding ring, Lucky?

Big Ran'l draws a few more veterans into his circle and nods toward the priest. "Did you hear the story about him, how he got the name Stainless Steel? It was a story that happened in the sem. McCoy was in his first year, young, just two years out of university, but he was doing well, making friends with good guys. Three in particular. Then all of a sudden he just decided to cut them off. All three of them. He would scarcely say hello to them outside of class. But what was the reason? What turned things sour? That's what you won't believe. It seems one evening the rector gave a forceful lecture on what they called in the sem, 'particular friendships.' It was as stern a warning as the lads had even witnessed. The rector said, 'These types of relationships are highly inappropriate. Dangerous even. None of you should ever form an exclusive bond with another seminarian.' Obedient as the scabbard, McCoy responded by cutting ties with anyone who had been diverting his attention. The three good fellows were the first to get the cold shoulder. He wouldn't want them to get the wrong idea, you see. McCoy's three seminarian pals couldn't figure out what the big deal was. Jesus, they were no more interested in particular friendships than they were in getting their hands dirty."

"How do you know?" Lucky says. "Maybe they were."

"Jesus, are you talking about homos?" says Carl, handing Lucky his rum and coke.

"Yes, of course we're talking about homos," says Big Ran'l. "They fly to the seminary like moths to the flame. And poor McCoy flew the other way so fast he gave up all chance for friendship, even with the non-homos. He's the same way now. Look at him. Standing there like a tombstone in the back forty. Here stands theese Pair McCoy. Outstanding in his field."

The tale causes general amusement among some of the veterans but in others, a sense of respect for the youthful seminarian. All glance his way whether in curiosity, superiority, or humility. As they watch his inscrutable mien, they see him joined by a very blonde and very busty woman. She accepts a light from the Sky Pilot.

MacDonald snorts to regain the crowd. "But that's just half the story. There's a better one. Jesus, Lucky, will you drink your drink? You're making me nervous. Listen to this. A few years before McCoy entered the sem, he went to Toronto with the boys from the Bay. The lads picked up some skank on Yonge Street and brought her back to where they were staying. It turned into a gang-bang. Everyone had a go at her. But McCoy would have none of it. When it came his turn, he locked himself in the bathroom until she left. Even after she'd cleared out, McCoy stayed put. The boys had to get a crowbar and pry the door open. And here's the best part. When we finally got the door open, what did we find? Stainless Steel McCoy, sitting on the toilet, head down, crying like a baby. Crying like a goddam baby."

The trees were bare now and autumn leaves lay thick and still. Tommy Caffrey shuffled lazily through, his crisp crunch and kick mingling with the distant rush of the rain-swollen brook. He accepted where his feet were taking him though he was in no hurry to arrive. It was for this mission he carried his tomahawk again. Where would it take him today?

The spot he'd selected for that long-ago ambush looked bare and exposed now. The bush he hid behind, the tree where he tied his tripline. The scene was as dull and unthreatening as the sunless sky. Across the stream, where once a savage creature lurched and lunged, there was but a scattering of cars and a few listless shapes entering and exiting the Five to a Dollar. He waited. The water moved slowly and steadily past him, higher than it was that summer day. Had it been as high, he thought, its waters would have protected him. The walker would have been swept away like a broken tree. There would have been no need to defend himself, no need to maim or kill or be killed. No need for a dread secret. Not even to Jacky had he spoken of it, nor would he ever.

Why does such guilt reside in the midst of bravery? Bravery, he surmised, is more evident when someone is saved besides yourself. Katie for instance. If Katie had been in danger and his tomahawk had saved *her* life, that would be a different story. Oh, to be in her eyes as she was in his. Oh, to be in her. No guilt would live.

"Come on. You'll be late."

Tommy's heart jumped into his throat. He turned. A boy stood there, coal-black hair, skin the colour of earth. He wore an open vest that crawled with flat black snakes. When the boy spoke, his face pulled sharply into high, proud cheekbones.

"You'll be late for the water ceremony. The sun is already high. Aren't you coming? You can come with me."

Over his shoulders, the newcomer drew a blanket of wool and leather, trimmed with brown buckskin. On it, too, wriggled and writhed the black beasts with their strange flat heads and devilish dark eyes. Tommy looked up. There was no sun in that sky, just one patch of cloud brighter than all the others.

"W-Where?"

"You don't know? It's that way, south, where this stream meets the Big River."

Tommy eased a breath into his lungs and stood to follow.

"What is your name?"

The Indian narrowed his eyes in surprise. "My name is 'Who you see before you.' That's my name. What is yours?"

"Tommyhawk."

"I see. Don't you know it is not polite to ask a brave his name before you have come to know him? Perhaps you are not a brave. The warclub in your hand, how did you come to possess it?"

"I found the stone in these woods. It was in a hole in the trunk of a tree."

"What tree?"

"A giant elm tree in a grove near Columba's Field." The Indian looked at the sky. "You speak of the Treaty Tree. A Mi'kmaw made that stone. He hid it there so you would find it. You and only you. Did you know that? You did, didn't you. Yes. He put it there because he wants you to do something. Something that will restore the relationship that the whites and the Indians once held.

"Since you are so bold as to ask my name, Tommyhawk, and because you have been chosen for special things, I will tell you the name my people call me. My name is Sambath. Sambath of the Clan Kat from the tribe of Mi'kmaw. I have walked two days to be present with you at the water ceremony." He held out a hand in friendship and swiftly they flew along the boy-browned leafy trails toward the mouth of the Findrinny Brook.

Presently, the sojourners two came upon a gaggle of pilgrims. Tommy's guide identified them as members of the B'laan tribe. They had quit their homes on the Tampakan Ridge and had trekked the distance of the brook, moving slowly with small children and elders, camping along the way. The braves carried machetes and spears and were ever on the alert for rabbits, squirrels, coons, snakes, or other edibles. The elders carried the blankets and trinkets and cookpots. The younger women, bent forward as if shielding their faces from the wind, seemed to shoulder the greatest burden. If one did not have a child pouched on her back, she carried a basket of wild rice or Indian corn or potato. The women wore sandals, dusty and dirty from their journey. The men's feet were bare and gnarled, tough as tree roots and wide as plates. Their toes were flexible grasping mechanisms built for the climb.

Where the rivers met, Tommy and Sambath of the Clan Kat stood upon a knoll, bare but for one tall branch-deprived tree. "We can see better from up here and the wind will blow their voices for us to hear." Tommy surveyed the scene, taking in the meeting of the waters, his little babblebrook being swallowed by the Big River, the Ani G'nish, revered by Indians and Findrinnians alike for its salmon, trout, transport, and beauty—the liquid backbone of the entire district. Across the river on the apple tree island he looked upon a tight concentration of Indians who were doing the chanting and drumming he had heard for the last mile.

Around this group, spinning and shuffling in a slow-moving circle, were the Mi'kmaw dancers, their moccasins mesmerizing in their rhythmic movement.

A great many more watched and listened, the blankets on their backs glistening with black and red and blue and yellow animal designs. Wolves, bear, moose, lynx, beaver, eagle, and black snakes like those which adorned the blanket of Sambath of the Clan Kat. The kye-aye continued on and on as dancers whirled and circled the drummers.

Wey u we he haiya, Weu we he haiya.
Wey u we he haiya, Weu we he haiya.

The rise and fall of the voices was hypnotic and the thunder of their drums joyous and frightening amid the chirps and shouts of the dancers, until the chanting ceased and the drums fell silent.

Next appeared a group of brightly clad young women, heralded by a heaven-sent tinkling of a thousand bells, dancing in sways and circles, moving slowly forward as they swirled. Their hair as glossy black as the crows and piled high on their heads. From these creations gaudy wooden combs stuck out like eagle feathers. Their unsmiling lips were painted a startling vermilion and from their ears hung dark coloured beaded necklaces that shook and shimmered as they moved. Each wore a dress that fell the length of their slim bodies and ended at a pair of one-strapped yellow sandals, all that protected their dainty feet from the dirt. Each dress was striped in the batik style of the B'laan—black, red, black, gold dotted with blue; black, gold, red, gold, black, blue spotted with gold; black, gold, red, black, up and up. And over their chests and bellies they wore capes of blue and black and brown and gold, dotted with blue batik. As they danced they flipped this cape alluringly to and fro to reveal an azure underside so it seemed like their swirling was like the lifting of the great blue wings of a wonderfully painted heron. Each dancer wore a wide belt with brassy tassels that reached to her thighs. From the tassels hung these thousand bells made of a metal less tarnishy than silver, more malleable than gold. The sweet, rich sound that announced and remained with the dancers throughout their performance came from this tinkling chorus of finest findruine.

The face of each girl was different from the one next to her, a fact that unnerved young Tommy though he knew not why. This one was catlike. Her flat wide nose and her laconic look suggesting feline security. Her eyes were narrower than the next girl who looked downcast and tearful. Hers was a yellower face and round as a melon. They were all different though all the same as they sashayed toward the gathering at the forks.

Three men separated from the crowd and stood with their backs to the Big River. These men wore the same colours as the dancers. The middle man, the *datu,* wore a flat white leather cap. From it, white bristles descended like the brittle hair of a grizzled old man. The cap was decorated with dozens of clumped-close dingleballs, small and soft as cotton. These dangled in long braids from the back and in short tickling bunches like cherries over his determined, piercing eyes. He held wide his arms, well-muscled and tattooed. Some of the crowd cawed to silence the muttering masses. Immediately the datu's voice carried to the boys on the wind.

"Do you know what he's saying?"

"He's speaking the language of the B'laan. Different from Mikmawisimk. He says there is a Mi'kmaw woman here, a *sachem,* who has come from Unama'ki to bless these waters and the great gulf where the fish go to mature. He says that our sisters and brothers, the salmon, no longer return to their spawning grounds on this brook, though they return to all the other streams along the Bong Mal."

"Bong Mal?" Tommy asked.

"The B'laan do not call this river Ani G'nish. They call it Bong Mal. It means big river. For six seasons now, when the salmon have returned to the big river from the gulf, they have avoided this brook. The sachem has come to bless the waters so that they may welcome again the salmon who bring life upstream.

"The datu speaks of the relationship between the B'laan and the Mi'kmaw, of the two sons of the cougar who went to the west of Unama'ki, and the third son who stayed in the Tampakan under the protection of the Three Sisters. He tells of the findruine that the Clan Kat were taught to make by Dan Maroon. He tells of the miners, the many young men who worked with their sweat running down to produce the ingredients of peaceful cooperation, so that we might all profit, for we are all treaty people. Our findruine has helped to maintain peace with the white man despite the many Mi'kmaw who have died from sickness, starvation, and the bounty of Cornwallis. It has kept your greed in check, until now. He thanks the Mi'kmaw for coming to this place, Nartigonneich, the place where the rivers meet, to assemble with their brothers and sisters, the B'laan, and to speak with one voice to Kisu'lk, to Melu, to the Great Spirit."

The sachem then appeared, speaking some words of B'laan before reverting to her mother tongue. She slowly semicircled the bank while waving an eagle feather in blessing of the land she stood on, and gently, as if in conversation, explained her movements and their symbolism. She turned and raised her arms to the Big River and called on Kisu'lk to cleanse this brook so that the salmon may again wish to swim in its waters.

When they were six, their father took the twins to the hatchery for Stocking Day. He told them of catching salmon by the dozen in the Findrinny Brook, baskets full of them, before the law made it a more sporting game. People from all over North America come to fish the Ani G'nish. He spoke of the spawners dropping their roe way upstream and the little parr that try to survive for two years in their brooks before they sense the call of the sea. But only one in a thousand make it that far. Tommy had often seen their glassy shapes hiding in the weeds, schools of them darting in the big pools, resisting the pull of the current. Then the smolts flush to the ocean and somehow change their lungs to breathe in the salt water. They travel all the way to Greenland, and two or three years later, thirty, forty pounds heavier and strong, find their way back to the Ani G'nish, back to his babblebrook and all the other brooks all the way to Mount Kitanglad.

Tommy watched the brookwaters mingle and disappear into the swift currents of the Big River and together rush toward the harbour and the gulf and the ocean. But no salmon or trout or gaspereaux made their way back up his babblebrook now. Not since the Archer-Atlas Smelter and the polio slime appeared. Now only dumb grey ugly longjaw mudsuckers like evil trolls skulked and teemed in the shade of Findrinny's bridges.

The sachem pointed to the poplar tree that stood near the boys. The tree had scant branches, except near the crown. It was not a climber, but she called for a boy to plant the flags of two nations, B'laan and Mi'kmaw, in the top branches.

"You can do it," Tommy said.

A young sachem's assistant swayed toward the willing boy, findruine bells ringing, and passed to Sambath of the Clan Kat the flags of two nations. Roughly he stuffed the cloths in his belt, strode to the tree, and without hesitation grasped it between his feet and hands. As he shimmied, the sachem praised those salmon who sacrificed their lives to feed Glooscap, the Creator of the Mi'kmaw. She thanked the salmon for continuing to offer their lives to feed the Mi'kmaw and the B'laan and the pale people. She prayed for his babblebrook that it may be made worthy of the promises of Kisu'lk. And to the sound of bells and *kuglungs* and drums and rattles, Sambath of the Clan Kat hoisted high the flags of two nations.

Wey u we he haiya, Weu we he haiya
Wey u we he haiya, Weu we he haiya
Wey u we he haiya,
Wey u we he haiya, Weu we he haiya
Ta Ho!

GRACE

Aggie Dunphy had the privileged blue eyes and fleshy milkmaid face of her mother. From her father's side she gained intelligence, facial warts, and a helmet of brown impenetrability. She entered the convent the year she graduated from Port Hood Academy. No one was surprised. She spent her novitiate at the motherhouse, studied to be a nurse, and upon reaching the status of fully professed, Aggie Dunphy paid five dollars for a block ad in *The Crypt*. It read, "The person formerly known as Agnes Margaret Dunphy of Port Hood, Inverness County, Nova Scotia, has legally changed her name to Sister Catherine-Under-God, nothing more, nothing less." It was a profligate act and vain, but it did the trick. No one could call Aggie Aggie now but the chosen few.

When she left Port Hood for her first two-year stint in the Tampakan, she was unperturbed. Only twenty-four months. The Scarboro missionaries did it all the time. Off to China or Japan or the Philippines or some Godforsaken place on the other side of the world, never getting home even if your mother dies. If *they* can do it, *I* can do it. But that was wishful thinking. It was the isolation in the midst of many that brought her chest-to-knees on the floor one rainy afternoon. Indian shock, her brother called it. Among the B'laan her sharp tongue was limp as a dishrag. Her ear was just as much a clunker. Twelve months learning the language and still, entire rat-a-tat conversations could register zero on the comprehension scale. She knew the pain of being left out. She knew the paranoia of gelotophobia. She suspected her assistant, Erita, a young woman with birdlike accusing eyes, of theft, influence peddling, and spying. The little sneak had the gall to enter Sister's cell unannounced only to find the big nun curled up in a tight fetal ball and hiding in the darkest corner she could find. Sister Catherine-Under-the-Bed.

"Oh, Bridget, if I could only speak," she wrote, "then perhaps I could relate to them."

It was the hikes into the forest that saved her. The days when she closed the clinic in Kiblawan Town, took the jeep far up the Tampakan, left it at a trailhead, and hiked the highlands with Erita and one or two of the houseboys. For the farther-flung trips, they hired a guide who chewed *mami* and smoked weeds found on the forest floor. They tread the paths of the virgin forest and at each cluster of isolated houses, held precariously above the ground by skinny stilts, the houseboy would call up, *"Maayo! Maayo! A dunay bay masakit?"* Is there anyone sick here? And they would set to work, questioning, probing, diagnosing, remedying. Sister Catherine's hospital experience and Erita's bush medicine were on a different footing in this forest. There was much, she came to acknowledge, that a nursing sister could learn from the ways of the B'laan. She learned to identify medicinal plants and to name them by their English, B'laan, and Latin names. She learned to harvest their parts in the right season, to take only where they were in abundance, to leave some to propagate and for others who may need them, to make infusions and decoctions and tinctures and poultices. Still she was a novice compared to Erita. The girl's knowledge seemed innate. She grew on Sister Catherine like a willful child who is right more often than not. Still, she was a proud girl and one that needed taming.

Was Erita embarrassed, wondered Sister, by her sallow and long-eared aunt whose smile produced crooked rows of orange teeth and whose spit hit the planet like asteroids? Or the old uncle, wonderstruck when he heard Sister would be going to Findrinny for Christmas. Not that he ever heard tell of Christmas. It was the destination that left him in awe. Sister saw how he pointed to the sky and said something incomprehensible. Erita, usually so swift to translate and spin, said nothing. It was the houseboy who later interpreted. "He says you go very far. Farther than the moon. It is because he thinks the moon is closer than Findrinny is. He has never been to Findrinny, but every night he sees the moon."

This impossible distance between the Tampakan and Findrinny was easily traversed by letters. Dear Sister, they began, or Dear Mama, Dear Mary, Dearest Bridget, Dearest Aggie. Questions, advice, jokes, commentary, and gossip followed. Aggie's carried schemes galore. These usually involved Hector building or buying something and putting it on a bus to the *bukid,* as Aggie called her new home. Or some cockamamie scheme to make money to publish a book on herbal medicine. Or some human rights abuse she thought they should stir things up about.

For her part Bridget stuffed her offerings to Aggie with snippets from

The Crypt, family snapshots, and school photos until…

Dearest Aggie,

You will be home soon and I feel I must warn you. Lucky is not good. He has been on a bender since Armistice Day. Sometimes I wonder how he can keep it up. He's messing up big time. Mary is at her wit's end. She put him out of the house again.

There is another thing. I am leaving Tuesday for Sydney. I have to get some tests done. The doctors at St. Martha's think it's best. They have all the modern labs up in Sydney. I don't think they will find anything. I wouldn't even worry you about it except I won't be here when you get in. I may only be getting out a day or two before Christmas, later if they have to do a procedure.

Hector will pick you up as usual and you will stay with us if you can handle the kids. Pack of wolves, I should say. Hector took a job working for the mining company. He'll be working in the boiler room keeping the smelter all fired up…

Sister Catherine-Under-God would always remember the moment, the day two worlds collided, she would always say. She was looking at the hanging calendar, thinking, When do I leave? When do I get in? How many days before I see Bridget? Should I go to Sydney? She heard the houseboys running up the steps, stepping lightly through the hallway and standing erect waiting for her signal. She adjusted her coif and veil and with a deep inhale composed herself. The older of the two spoke. Shot to death, three road crew workers in the employ of Archer-Atlas Mining Company. The houseboys' cousins witnessed it. The three huge earthmovers were still running when the constabulary arrived. They are blaming a former mine employee of leading the attack, a certain Diggy Capion.

Sister Catherine knew him. He was a kind of modern-day Geronimo and brother of Erita. "Our peace has been shattered!" she wailed.

Erita remained impassive.

"You'll have to find out where he's hiding," said the nun finally, "and tell the authorities. If he's guilty, he'll have to pay the consequences. If he's innocent, the truth will win out."

"You are really that simple."

Aggie was impressed. Erita could insult her with sarcasm. She measured the lopsided brown face and saronged body. The girl was fifty pounds her junior. A mere flyweight. Her brown animal eyes no match for icy blue.

"It was cold-blooded murder, Erita. Even the B'laan who witnessed it have said so. It was an attack from the jungle with no provocation shown and no warning sent."

"No!" Erita said. "It was not cold-blooded murder. It was not that. You are wrong, Sister Catherine-Under-the-Bed. We B'laan do not know cold-blooded murder. We know hot-blooded murder. That is what you see here, Sister. Revenge killing with hot blood. You believe that the truth will win out. But you do not say the whole truth. You do not know the whole truth. You ask me to tell the constabulary where my brother is. But when do you say to Iron Claw, who is your family's friend, is he not? When do you say to him, 'Why do you claw such terrible holes in the Three Sisters?' When do you say to your brother, Mister Lucky Dunphy, 'Why do you live among the B'laan for ten years and trick them like a Trojan Horse?'"

"These are questions you, Erita Sagada, have no business asking," said her shocked employer. A lesson had to be learned from the outrageous exhibition. The young woman was dismissed. When last seen, she was marching toward the forest with not a glance in the direction of the nun.

At a desk lit by kerosene lamp, Sister Catherine read again her sister Bridget's latest missive. And read it again. Hector left his job and went to work for Ronald Atlas. He's going to be keeping the smelter running. Lucky had been on a bender for five weeks and was causing trouble for everybody. Bridget was going for tests. This was what stopped her each time. How Sister Catherine hated the word. Tests. Each time she saw it, she felt time itself close in on her. In a week, she would be making her first home visit in two years. She had hoped it would be a joyous occasion, but it was sounding more like she was jumping from the Tampakan frying pan to the Findrinny fire.

But it is time I did take a break from the *bukid,* she thought. I have aged fifty years in four and am now a dumpy old crone no longer able to lift myself from where I squat at my desk. Do you have a piano tied to your arse, dear?

But rise again she did and lowered her lamp and knelt and prayed over the day's events. She blessed herself and stood to prepare for bed. She removed her black and whites, her white coif, her black veil, her woolen belt, her rosary, her cross, her holy habit, her sleeves, her ring, her shoes, her socks, her underskirts, her underwear, and her scapular.

She snorted at Erita's sackable insolence. Hot blooded murder indeed. What sense can you make of that kind of delirium? And the questions! Sister Catherine peeked at the small mirror she kept for vanity's sake. With her other hand she brushed the hair on her thirty-year-old head. She had told Erita she had no business asking those questions, but the truth was that they were questions Sister Catherine had long ignored. Questions that would only embarrass the family. Questions about quislings. She thought of Ronald Atlas MacDonald, the pompous accumulator, the biggest man in Cape Breton they say. Untouchable they say. And Lucky, the family disgrace. I wouldn't put it past him. He was malleable enough. And poor Bridget being tested in the hospital, worrying about that fool when she should be thinking about herself. She raised high over her naked self a soft white flannel nightgown and let it fall over head and bare shoulders and plump breasts and belly and dimpled strong rump and bushy brown bush and legs and feet. Sister Catherine-Under-God knew she could not fix everything. But she vowed she'd do what she could. "When I get home," she said to the small mirror, "I am going to put the fear of God into Mister Lucky Dunphy."

One afternoon, when flakes as big as silver dollars and light as angel's breath swept and swooned from the sky in sweeping swirling minuets, the overhead lights in Mrs. MacDonald's classroom flickered once and then flickered again. Children and teacher waited for the third darkness. It came and stayed.

"No school!" cheered Jacky. "What are we going to do, Tommy?'

"I don't know. How about you, Katie? What are you gonna do?"

"Go tobogganing of course. Wanna come?"

"Sure. Hey, remember the Bishop's Bowl? It's the best tobogganing hill in all of Findrinny."

Katie and her friend in their furryhooded snowsuits scratching vinyl against vinyl pulled their sleds past the Royal George Hotel and the post office and dashed across the town's busiest intersection. They met the four boys at St. Columba Street.

"Hi, snowmen," Katie said. "This is Joyce Hung, my best friend. Maybe you remember her from an earlier grade. She's a Buddhist. Isn't that neat?"

Katie yammered as they strolled along, making up stories about Joyce to test the boys' gullibility. "Joyce is from Hong Kong and this is her first time tobogganing. It never snows in Hong Kong. Can you believe it? I'd die. Before she came to Canada she thought snow came down from the sky all in one clump and landed on the ground like a blanket. She never dreamed there could be something like snowflakes."

"Katarina Anna Maria Beaton, you are real funny. You know I've tobogganed a million times. Don't believe her, you guys. Have you guys ever been to Stewart's Hill? Katie and I go there all the time." But then they reached the crest and the wide, snowy treeless hill came into view, and Joyce stopped in her tracks and exclaimed, "There must be a hundred kids here."

Compared to Stewart's Hill, the Bishop's Bowl was a mountain, an amphitheatre, a volcanic cone crawling with children throwing snowballs, tossing toques, catching snowflakes on their tongues and eyelashes, building ramps, chewing mittens. They trudged uphill and scampered out of the path of onrushers. They cried and catcalled. They yelled, "Wait for me!" "Look out below!" "Get out of the way!" "Geronimoooooo, here I come!" and "Move, Angus, or I'll cream you!" They sped downhill on shiny aluminum toboggans, round-nosed wooden toboggans, sleek wooden sleds with red metal rosebud runners, flying plastic saucers, patched-up inner tubes, bellies, backs, bottoms, and pieces of floppy cardboard salvaged from garages and garbage bins. At the base of the hill they jumped from their crafts and crowed, "Look at how far we went!" and "New world's record!" and "You're gonna die for that, Harry!" Hearts thumping, the new arrivals ran to the crest of the Bishop's Bowl. Snow was everywhere. There wasn't an adult in sight.

Afterward they drank warm milky cocoa at Katie's house and she said, "This is my new kitten, Beebee. See how she points at you with the tip of her tiger tail, Tommy? I think she likes you." The cat coiled and purred. "Meeemeee," said she, and Katie laughed.

They stayed and played in the Beaton backyard. They stayed and shaped angels upon the snow that hid her hockey rink. They stayed and played after Mrs. Beaton turned on the porch light and said, "Aren't you kids hungry yet? Your mothers will be looking for you." They stayed and played after a voice from over the fence called Joyce home. They stayed and played until Tommy ran into something unseen and lay on his back rubbing his throat, his head wet and warm in the cold snow. She came to him then like a guardian angel. Her face was close to his in the stillness. He could see the warmth of her breath come toward him. He could smell honeyscented hair under her hood. Her eyes above him were wide, round, and concerned. She said, "You fell like you were shot, Tommy. So sorry about that. The clothesline should be higher. Are you okay?"

Tommy rubbed his throat and heard himself croak, "I'll be all right."

She grinned into his face. He answered artlessly. She moved her face lower until all was darkness within their hoods. They were closer than two people had ever been. Their noses touched and then their lips. A warm wave of comfort spread from him and conquered his entire body. It soaked him to overflowing. His heart hammered.

Jacky ran up from behind and said, "Is he okay?"

Using Tommy's chest as a springboard for her hands, Katie leapt to her feet. "He's okay. Tag, you're it!" said she and ran away. And only after many minutes did his happy hammer subside. They stayed and played until Katie's mother said she wasn't going to call her anymore. Katie waved goodbye from the doorstep and Tommy knelt in the snow staring at the porch light until Jimmy Dog said, "What are you waiting for? Christmas? Let's go!"

In bed that night, Tommy remembered the snow day, the tobogganing, the cocoa, the cat, the snow angel, and the darkness inside the hoods. For many nights, he replayed that one golden mythologically embellished moment so that its memory and meaning would never fade. Remembering it, he would run his damp tongue over his lips and whisper softly to the image floating above him, "I'll be all right." Then he would close his eyes. So many other memories meant less for him then.

Cissy Caffrey punched her pillow. She didn't mind doing the lioness's share of the work, but there had to be fringe benefits. Now he's asking her to assemble the twins and Archie. A sort of meeting of the elders. Then and only then would he tell her what news he was withholding. That was baloney. She should have been the first to hear. The boys arrived redfaced and wet from chasing a football around the Protestant schoolyard. She suspected what the news would be and was already preparing her argument.

"Your mother is going to be in the hospital for a little while. She's staying in Sydney for at least another week."

"What's the matter?"

"She's having more tests. She'll have some decisions to make. *We'll* have some decisions to make. I'm going back up the day after tomorrow. She needs me to take some things to her."

"I want to go with you. I want to see Mommy."

"I'm sorry, honey. You have to help with the kids."

"That's what you said last time. What's wrong with Auntie Mary? Or Aunt Aggie—I mean Sister Catherine? She'll be home soon."

"Aunt Mary will help out, but Sister Catherine might come to Sydney with me. Somebody has to be here all the time. Everybody has to pitch in, including you. We'll just be gone for two nights."

"When will Mommy be home? Will she be home for Christmas? She's supposed to sing at church."

"We're not sure. It all depends."

The twins tried to mine an intelligible vein in the conversation. The rapid-fire Q&A between sister and father was not doing it for them. Cissy was like a well-informed detective simply filling in the missing pieces to a puzzle, pressing an agenda. A regular Nancy Drew. Such was her facility for deduction, she seemed rarely surprised by an answer or dissuaded by evasion, able to make bold assertions about individual rights. But then Cissy said something she shouldn't have said. Their father was momentarily dumbstruck. All went quiet. He swore in Gaelic, cursed her worse in English, shoved a hand into the small of her back and frogmarched her to the stairway.

"Suas ahh!" yelled Hector Caffrey. "Get up there!" Any attempt at defence was cut off severely. "Shut up," her father said. "Imagine saying such an unholy thing. You'll skip supper, young lady, and be in your room for the night."

"I didn't make it up."

"Suas e!"

Such was Chief Cook and Bottle Washer Cissy Caffrey's inglorious and hasty dispatch from the family confabulation. The conference was disbanded on account of the outburst. Later in her room she blubbered her pain into her pillow. She knew what he had called her. She knew the Gaelic was bad and You Antichrist of Hell was worse. Whatever it was she said, she didn't deserve that. He should apologize for making her cry.

A soft knock padded on the door. Cissy sat up and smoothed her dress.

"Just a minute."

She wouldn't let on she had been weeping. She would show dignity. She would apologize for her part. That would soften him. She would say, "But you shouldn't have swore at me and you shouldn't have pushed me, Daddy. That hurt."

"Come in."

It was the twins.

"Get out of here. You're not allowed in my room. Get out!" A pink slipper slapped the slamming door behind them.

The twins knew they would get nothing from Cissy. Those jaws were clamped like a vice. But perhaps between the two of them they had heard enough to piece the puzzle together. Frank and Joe Hardy at your service. They set out to restore the order of the words, hoping order might make sense of things. It was like the old days, hoping twinstincts took over. The two as one.

"Cissy was saying she wanted to go to the hospital with Mommy, then she was talking about her singing at church, then there was that next thing," said Tommy.

"Yeah, that was the Unholy Thing."

"Yeah, that's right. Cissy said she heard someone talking about Mommy going to have an abortion. Going to Halifax to have an abortion. Right? That was the word, right?"

"She said she heard Aunt Mary say it."

"Yeah, but Daddy said it's not true. It's an Unholy Thing. People should mind their own business."

"But he also says they have a big decision to make."

With mechanical instinct their eyes found one another. They were mirror images, eyes, chins, freckles. They stared into the gold-green iris of the other. Still made no sense. It was agreed. They would have to consult *The American Peoples Encyclopedia*.

The church was three-quarters full when the Beaton family arrived for Midnight Mass. The congregation was as restless as they were excited, cheery as they were solemn. They prayed, probed missalettes, hacked, shushed, tittered, waited upon the first carol to lift them to their feet.

Katie had insisted she be allowed to come. She had a friend in the ceremony. She had bought a yellow beret special. The mirror told her she looked as prim as My Fair Lady. She sparkled like Tinkerbell. To be safe, she needed only to stay close to her mother.

A purple pop-eyed man approached the Beaton bunch. A high starched collar cut his goblin neck to overflowing. He wheezed. "Still room halfway up this side, Mrs. Beaton, argh ar ar."

Katie drew back from him in alarm. "We'll be going up front," her mother said.

Five minutes before mass, the Caffrey crew landed. Hector was breathless. With him were Cissy, Archie, and Molly, with Daisy in his arms. The twins and Bridget had come earlier. Hector, his long face saddened by a less than Christmas mood, looked dejectedly at the filled pews.

A purple head popped into view and a voice stringent as vinegar wheezed at them. "Full house tonight, Hector, but still a wee bit o' room toward the front on the right. Argh ar ar argh. See there, where Angus is indicatin'. Maybe you need to fit in two pews. Filled up early tonight."

Trailing the family was Hector's brother-in-law, Lucky Dunphy. Many in the congregation knew the former mine manager had been on a spree that started in September, was waylaid by a hopelessly short three-week hiatus, then gathered enough new steam on Remembrance Day to take him through to 1962. What none of them knew was that the binge had hit a serious speed bump seven days before Christmas. A speed bump named Sister Catherine-Under-God. He spent the last week of Advent in his old man's house locked up in a bedroom and drying out to a steady diet of righteous indignation from his mother, father, brothers, sisters, and wife. When he tried once to escape, Sister Catherine-Under-God lassoed him like a heifer. Lucky Lucky not so Lucky. After that little piece of rodeo, he had to make a few concessions before he again saw the light of day.

The penitent removed his fedora and picked his way between the children to Hector. "I'll just sit down back. I'll squeeze in somewhere. Yes, yes, you go." When Hector led his troop away, Lucky remained, eyeing the big centre doors as they opened and closed. His sister may not have put the fear of God into him, but she sure as hell put the fear of Catherine-Under-God into him. Attending Midnight Mass was just one of the conditions of his release.

The bishop and a small band of clerics, whitegarbed under stoles splashed in gold and green embroidery, emerged from the vestry to sweep all-powerfully down the side aisle. Their appearance was a multiple sign. To the undertaker who moonlighted on the organ, it was the signal to step upon the pedals and strike the first key. To the Marian Boys Choir it was a signal to tense. To the Adult Choir it was a moment to regard the choirboys, their preparedness, their confidence.

To the Knights of the Altar assembled at the narthex, the bishop and priests' appearance was a signal that their procession was to begin.

Two dozen shuffling servers, clad in red soutane and white surplice, gripped tightly their brass candlesticks, their holy bibles, their rattling censers and their long-handled crucifixes. Earlier, coming down the side aisle, Tommy listened as his soutane swung with the swishswishswish of fifteen others. It was his first time wearing the scarlet. He drew in the stiff aroma of lacy surplice that covered him to the waist, smelling of starch and December air and ironing board. Smelling white.

On the weeks when he and Jacky served mass, for they were always paired, they had oft peeked beyond the tall door in a corner of the servers' vestry, not to wear the long red gowns that hung inside but to longingly touch them. Until this night, they were only allowed to slip the black over their heads. Off-limits was the red, except twice a year, Easter and Christmas. Each time they clasped the tiny fasteners of the black soutane, from black-slippered toe to buttoned-down neck, they imagined that someday they might wear the scarlet vestments that hung in the end closet. How humbled and thrilled and reverent he felt now that the day had finally come. Someone pinched Tommy's arm, wrinkling his surplice and pressing the red soutane into his flesh. Tommy noted his interrupter's eyeballs. They were the colour of his vestments, only in reverse. Red on white, and bulbous. Looking pretty bulbous tonight, Uncalucky. A twinge of sadness fluttered in Tommy's chest. Unlucky in life was Uncalucky.

A voice cackled, "Looking pretty special tonight, Chief." Lucky tussled the boy's hair and with a few wide strides he scampered toward a full back pew. He dropped a knee that failed to touch the floor, mumbled gratitude to his pewmates, knelt, and blessed himself like he was waving away mosquitoes. His head dropped as if he had been shot. Chin to chest, eyes groping the red marble floor. From above, great golden lamps gleamed upon his Brylcreem-slicked pompadour.

Tommy looked along the pillared nave he would be treading shortly. Now he raised his eyes to the pillartops and the galleria. Miraculous events, each portrayed in ten-foot diameter tondos, lined the middle of the vaulted ceiling. The Nativity. The Resurrection. The Ascension Into Heaven. As if reflecting on these life-of-Christ moments, two rows of saints posed above the pillars on either side of the centre aisle—Saint Cecilia, St. John the Baptist, and all the apostles, exalted in robes and halos, carrying their symbols. Now he examined his sculpted candlestick. Now he set his gaze on the acolyte who would give the signal. Resolute, he waited. Holding a candle was the most important job, his mother told him. Fire signified the Holy Ghost.

On your mark, get set, and two columns of cotton and lace launched forward slow-oh-so-slowly through the nave. In the balcony above, an organ droned and the boys' choir sang.

O Come, O Come, Emmanuel
And ransom captive Israel
That mourns in lonely exile here
Until the Son of Gaw-aw-awd appear

His mother was in the loft, he knew, and his father, sisters, and Archie were somewhere in the throng. And another who would wear yellow on her brow.

Rejoice, rejoice, Emmanuel
Shall come to thee, Oh Israel

Bishop Power welcomed the congregation to the celebration of the birth of the Christ child. His deep baritone created a mood of joy and wonder commingled with solemnity, filling the flock with holy anticipation. The bishop and his retinue approached the high altar and the sacrifice of the Eucharist began.

Tommy looked out upon the congregation, surreptitiously, for his was a role that demanded grave engagement. No, now was not the time to scan for the yellow beret. The bishop was reminding the people by means of the *Orate fratres* that the Eucharist being offered was not his alone but theirs as well. Tommy and his fellow massboys exhorted the Lord God to accept their sacrifice for the praise and glory of His name: *Suscipiat Dominus sacrificium de manibus tuis, ad laudem et gloriam nominis sui, ad utilitatem quoque nostram, totiusque Ecclesiae suae sanctae.*

During the offertory, Bridget Caffrey moved to the front of the choir to pose in profile beside the organ. Her face turned to where she would project her voice, to the ornate altar that dominated the sanctuary. Beside her, the choirmaster placed his mortician fingers to his organ, squeezed off a few short blasts, and again rested those bony hands upon his lap. He nodded to the soloist.

From where he sat in the distant dark pews that ringed the sanctuary, Tommy looked out into the mass of faces in hopes of spotting the yellow beret. Everything was still, except for his mother's lone voice surging like a current through the hushed congregation.

O holy night! The stars are brightly shining
It is the night of our dear Saviour's birth
Long lay the world in sin and error pining
'Til He appeared and the soul felt its worth

Tommy's eyes roved like snipers through the centre seats. She said she'd wear something yellow so she would be easier to see. It was her favourite colour. But wait! There! A yellow beret and a black coat. He widened his eyes upon her. At the moment she was looking over her shoulder and up toward the singer, his mother. It wasn't allowed. He would get yanked frontward for such an indiscretion.

Without warning, they were looking at one another. Katie lit like a highbeam. Tommy raised a finger. She smiled and flapped a hand without moving her arm. Like a hummingbird wing it fluttered and disappeared. She widened her green eyes and pointed at him, at his soutane. Tommy nodded, raised his brows and whispered, "The red one," though of course she couldn't hear.

So, thought Tommy, she had come just as she promised. She said she wouldn't miss the chance to see him in a long red dress. He liked when she teased him like that, as long as no one else heard. Just for them it was. She meant something to him, that much was sure. Not what Mommy teased about puppy love. Not a crush either. Not like what Edy Boardman said either. Not a girlfriend. Something deeper and more abiding. Something that no one else had ever felt. Something that did not demand reciprocity.

Katie had turned toward him and her head wiggled jauntily on its neck. Her yellow beret dipped side to side. Tommy knew she was teasing because he had been staring and it wasn't polite to do that. He looked down at the two hands folded upon his clean white surplice, down his scarlet soutane to his slippery black slippers. He slid them softly upon the gleaming red marble and smiled because he suspected then that he knew what Katie was to him. What she meant to him. And once the suspicion took hold, a current of nervous warmth grew within and the Answer descended upon him like a litany.

She was his
Honeybee, she was his
Bumblebee, she was his
Buttercup, she was his
Fleur de lys, she was his
Mystical rose, she was his
Evening star, she was his
Epiphany, she was his
Easter, she was his
Pentecost, she was his
Princess, she was his
Queen of hearts, she was his
Sweetheart, she was his
Sacre coeur, she was his
Silent night, she was his
Silver bell, she was his
Spectrum and his prism, she was his
Rainbow, she was his
Angel from above, she was his
Ave Maria, she was his
Amazing Grace, she was his
Bonny wee lassie, she was his
Cris mo cridh, she was his
Dreamcometrue, she was his
Cinderella, she was his
Snow White, she was his
Rapunzel, she was his
Rose Red, she was his
Juliet, She was his
Katarina, she was his
Hero, She was His.

Fall on your knees! O hear the angel voices!
O night divine, O night when Christ was born
O night divine
O night, O night divine

In rapt silence, the congregation listened, afraid to disturb the awe. No coughing, no shuffling, no glancing at watches, no thinking beyond the moment, no undue movement from the multitudes. Adults did their best not to look back. Those who did, both the confident and the non-compliant, pivoted stiffly and smiled toward the voice. Tommy felt his chest fill and tighten over and over. And a man with a gleaming pompadour and bulbous bloodshot eyes, his tears streaming silently down windburned cheeks and falling upon an unfeeling floor, opened his eyes to suffering sweltering desire for a higher power in his life.

He knows our need, to our weakness is no stranger
Behold your King! Before him lowly bend!
Behold your King! Before him lowly bend!

For some hymns there is only one way to do the angels justice. That way, in the case of "O Holy Night," is contralto *a cappella* from the loft of a grand cathedral, naturally on Christmas Eve. The ancient melody floods a great church in operatic grandeur as the faithful in sin and error pining make worthy their souls and listen to the simple words reverberate with a thrill of voice, clear as a silver bell, in great expectations of a new and glorious morn.

The mass had ended and the people were sent in peace to love and serve the Lord. Clouds had blown in swiftly from the north to shelter the town and separate it from the distant, still shining stars so far, far above. The peaceful filed down the aisles, shaking hands, greeting with felicity the season of joy. They praised the bishop's powerful sermon and remarked on the choir.

"Did you hear that lady sing 'O Holy Night'?"

"That was Bridget Dunphy from Port Hood married to Hector Caffrey."

"The hair was just standing up on the back of my neck."

"Wasn't she just heavenly."

"Wasn't she just."

"She should sing at the rink."

Outside, snow was falling. Flakes as big as communion wafers swirled, sparkled, and shimmered in shadowy light. A soft, white benediction carpeted car tops, the parking lot, the little needles on the pine tree sentinels, the slate roof of St. Columba, and the tiny white crosses set atop *Tigh Dhe,* the House of God. And down Cathedral Hill, on the lane that sloped toward St. Columba Street, an unblemished ribbon of snowy white pointed the way home, a pure holiness that bathed the town in twinkling glory.

An assemblage of sensible shoes, high heels, children's sneakers, winter boots, and rubber galoshes passed out the side and centre doors and down the whitened stairways. The thin white diaphanous layer broke into a slop of black footprints. The massgoers parted merrily, cheerily, dreamily. Some sought vehicles that started with happy roars and the slow slap of windshield wipers. Others descended gingerly the hill to wind their way home. Before them lay their weary world, hushed, snowfrosted, sugarplum-dreaming.

And slumped behind the Main Street Texaco, fedora between his feet, black hair covered in snow, the town drunk wept, his body and soul shot through with the mercy of God. Christmas had come.

PART TWO

TO THE BACK OF BEYOND

EXILES

Louis Riel lived in exile. Bonnie Prince Charlie. Napoleon too. But there was one major difference between them and Jimmy Dog. Jimmy Dog didn't give a damn about going home. Not unless he was carrying weapons. All he desired was to evade the cops and truant officers until he made the hockey team. Then they couldn't send him to reform school. He'd be too important.

Other than the tryouts at the rink, Jimmy Dog was seen as a fleeting figure and only in the moonshine, often shouldering a sack, hobo-style. A silhouette and boottracks keeping to the dark corners of Findrinny Fair, stepping off Church Street by the Greening Mansion, trodding the woodspath between brook and intervale, disappearing into a dark, tangled but somehow penetrable ten-foot brambly hedge. Through a hole he cut in this wall, Jimmy Dog slunk. Beyond, amid a high grove of spreading elms, their far-reaching branches bare and black against the running clouds, the boy with the orange hair made camp—a humble lean-to of spruce, a stone firepit strewn with blackened tin cans and piles of assorted empties camouflaged by branches. On one of these, the exile spilled his sack. He had rifled the brookbank and invaded the drinking spots. He'd swiped from backyards and garages. He'd scored in bushes and hollow tree trunks, along Liquor Lane back of Hillcrest, and in bins behind the West End Market. The bins were the worst. Maggots, millions of them, swarming over choke-me-til-I-die stinking carci. He got to know them by their smell…at twenty paces.

Calculate. Eighty bottles will get me a dollar sixty at Beets Backup. Plus the longnecks. Another fifty cents. That's two-ten this week. Twenty weeks, forty-some bucks. At that rate it'll be May before I can go to the Canadian Tire. There's got to be a better way to make money in this world.

"So why are you collecting empties? What are you, some kind of Junior Hammy Hammerhead?"

Jimmy Dog had been discovered. He leapt to his feet not knowing how to greet his finder.

"I saw you crossing Church Street and ran to follow you. Don't you know they're looking for you on the radio? They have a missing person's bulletin out on you. Redheaded rooster last seen at the rink."

"That's bullshit. Nobody gives a shit about me. If anyone wanted to find me, they can just go to the rink. Obviously no one gives a shit."

"Jeeze. It's frigging cold out these days. Do you really want to be sleeping outside if a snowstorm comes? Why don't you come to our place? My parents will let you. You can sleep on my top bunk."

"Nah, I'll just go find a barn," Jimmy Dog mellowed.

"Why are you collecting bottles?"

"Why do you think, dope? I'm going to line them up and have target practice."

"That's neat. Let's get some rocks."

"Right."

"Then why?"

"You figure it out."

"You need money. What do you need money for?"

"Right, Sherlock. I need money. Now unless you're going to help me, you can make like the birds and flock off."

"I'll help. Okay, this is what we need to do. First we need to get a big wheelbarrow like Hammy Hammerhead, baggy green pants, and extract some of our teeth. Then we get hats like Hammerhead and walk around hollering at everyone who laughs at us."

Jimmy Dog laughed in spite of himself. "Screw you. You and Hammy Hammerhead too."

"I have a wagon," Tommy offered. "How about we get some more sacks, you fill them all up, get them over to Church Street, and I'll wheel them over to Beets from there. No one would have to see you, and you could still sell your bottles. Two or three trips and we're rolling in dough."

"*I'm* rolling in dough. *I'm* doing all the work."

"Okay, but listen. It sucks that you got kicked out of your house, but just come stay with us."

"I didn't get kicked out. I ran away. I wouldn't go back there if they paid me."

"Well, come stay with us." Tommy stuck out his hand. "Deal?"

Jimmy Dog eyed the coats, blankets, and pillow littering his bed of fir, more sleek and less prickly than spruce but harder to find; the cold firepit that bragged only three stolen burnt black beancans; the measly two bucks worth of bottles. In his heart the boy wished for the good things in life. But then you are called retarded by your so-called parents. And then you are called Basket Boy by arseholes like the Zealot. And then you don't get what you need for Christmas even though you beg and beg and beg and don't give up, and still she says, "We're too poor." Then maybe you do need a helping hand. Maybe you do need a friend.

"Deal."

Excitement was in the Findrinny air. All through the district a great recruitment was occurring. The word went out by school and church, by paper and poster, by radio and phone line. A minor hockey school was beginning. Big Ran'l was throwing some money at it, the oldtimers would run it, and the young studs would coach it. There'd be competition for all ages. It was a grand undertaking, everyone said. Sydney has minor hockey. Why not Findrinny? The thirteen- and fourteen-year-olds were called bantams. The only bantams these boys knew were boxers and roosters. They saw themselves as a cross between the two, tough and cocky. From all through the district they came, townies from the Protestant school, Bishop Fraser, Braemore, and Findrinny High—some who lived at the rink—and country bumpkins from coastal villages and inland farms who had never seen the inside of one, all on a journey to the human cull known as tryouts.

Dan Alec MacEachren stood behind the player's bench sucking on a stogie. The lesser coaches took notes in the stands or ran drills on the ice, whistling for stops and starts, slamming sticks and echoing, Go, Go, Go, Go.

From the stands boomed the voice of the Venerable Bede: "Wheel,

wheel, wheel, wheel!" "Corners are good!" "Chisholm, move your Jesus arse!"

Bede MacLean was born in a goaltenders crouch. When his playing days were on the wane, he took up coaching. He just knew the game better than anyone. Knew what the forwards needed to do to score on him. Screen. Use their teammates. Shoot high, blocker side. Open the five-hole. He knew, too, what the defencemen needed to do to stop them. When he hit fifty, the town hired him as recreation director. In this guise he built a playground, baseball diamond, and a cinder track made of a secret recipe of sand, ash, and waste oil. He recruited a crew of cronies to organize minor hockey at the college rink. The Venerable One would remain in the background, a sort of Hindenburg whose word carried weight even in retirement. He told Coach MacEachren he'd take charge of shooting drills—Jimmy Dog Dunphy's favourite activity and the goalie's most dangerous.

Jimmy Dog was built like a wrassler. He knew how to get leverage, but taking slapshots against the barn wall was not like standing and swinging on shaky skates. As often as not, he fanned on the shot and looked like an idiot doing so.

"Dunphy! The hundred dollar wind-up and the five cent slapshot. Get off the ice!"

By the second practice, the Dog was making the adjustment from backyard shooting to shooting on ice. By the third session he was dinging pucks off goalposts for a challenge. But it wasn't his shooting that grabbed the coaches' attention.

"Back, back, back! For Christ sake, Dunphy! Get the hell off the ice if you're not gonna backcheck."

The consensus of the parents was that the Dunphy kid would be a decent little hockey player if he skated harder. But he didn't. Plus he had a chip on his shoulder. In the first red and white game he went toe-to-toe with Simon MacDonald who was six inches taller and dumb as dogshit. The Zealot took the on-ice bout, but the Dog beat him in the second round. That one occurred in the odiferous refrigerator they called a dressing room. Without removing his gloves, the Dog smoked the Zealot four or five good ones upside the temples before Coach MacEachren broke it up. Dan Alec abhorred violence unless it came from his own mouth. He fired the fighters a volley of profanity so blue with bastards that the scrappers settled on the spot. Jimmy Dog had gotten revenge with zero chance of rebuttal. This suited Jimmy Dog just fine. Oh yeah, he was good with that.

The biggest surprise in the tryouts was the presence of the fairer sex. Just one, but could she skate. She liked to fly up the left wing, then cut into the middle for a pass from her defence mate, raring to dart through the opposition. Whether the puck came with her was another story. A few of those bumbles and her partner looked elsewhere to pass. First synopsis? All flash and no finish. She had hands of stone.

Coach MacEachren made his second set of cuts and taped the names of the remaining twenty to the cement wall. Just fifteen would be chosen—three lines, five defencemen, one goalie. The last attempt to impress the coaches came on January 6. Jimmy Dog had the date circled in red on the Caffrey calendar.

The lads who piled into the dressing room afterward were less boisterous than they'd been since their first practice. A coach poked his head into the hall and said, "Tell Katie to come in."

The Zealot snorted to his buddy the Goon. "Maybe the girl will beat one of you guys out."

That Katie was still hanging around made no difference to Jimmy Dog. She had a cat's chance in a burlap sack. For her to make the team they'd have to break their own rules. Girls weren't allowed to play hockey in Cape Breton. This was a good thing. But if you listened to Tommy, you'd almost think she had a shot. She was improving, he said. She always had the legs for it, now she was working on carrying the puck, slowing her feet to match her hands, her touch a little softer, keeping her head up, not seeing but feeling the puck on her blade, doing what the boys could do. Stickhandling.

Jimmy Dog loosened his laces and removed a cold, bare, blistered foot from a too-tight skate. He groaned the other foot out of its soggy boot, ripping open a blister. He felt a burning pain and warm water draining down his heel.

"Sheesh, that's ugly." said Tommy.

Jimmy Dog massaged his feet, avoiding the open sores. His thumb slipped over blisters, fat or runny, always painful. "You said she's not allowed playing, right, Zealot? It's just a boys' team, right?"

The Zealot had already learned his fortune. But unlike the other boys who got the brand new Black Hawk sweaters and left for home, he had stayed to watch the odds narrow on Tommy and Jimmy Dog. He wore his new issue to gloat. He had counted thirteen sweaters leaving the room. Two spots left.

"Yeah," he said. "But you can always break the rules."

"Piss off, Zealot. Anyway she didn't score one goal the whole tryout. She won't make it."

"Well, she is a defenceman, scoring goals is not a big thing for us." said Tommy.

The three boys saw the coaches' door open. Katie Beaton, still in the full uniform from skates to Habs sweater to stocking cap, smiled back into the room and slipped into the corridor. They looked to see if she was carrying the other sweater. If she was, it was bundled beyond recognition, but the Zealot claimed he could tell.

"Looks like it's between you two. Too bad one of youze is gonna get beat out by a girl who can't even stickhandle."

"Jimmy! Your turn!"

The coaches' room reeked of sweat and steam and smoke. Jimmy Dog glanced at the horsey face of Dan Alec MacEachren who was staring back at the beefy enigma in front of him.

"Heck of a slapshot, Dunphy," said the coach. "Must practice it a lot."

"Yeah. I g-got a net painted on my barn."

MacEachren studied the downturned face. "Not many kids your age can one-time it like you. You trying to be Bobby Hull out there? Is he your favourite player?" He gave Jimmy Dog a lopsided grin meant to indicate friendliness. Jimmy Dog's eyes flickered toward the man across the desk and back to his lap. The intensity of a moment's contact with another's eyes was as much as he could take sometimes. These moments revealed much. The eyes he saw in that instant were gentle and alert. The smile was kind. The coach was listening.

"No, I like the Rocket better."

"Great player, the Rocket. But he wasn't one for slapshots. Wrist shots were more his style."

One of the underling coaches, his head in a hockey bag, his arse upturned and facing Jimmy Dog, piped up. "For your favourite, you should pick a player that's still playing."

Probably a Leafs fan, thought Jimmy Dog. Probably thought Frank Mahovlich was the second coming. "I'll pick whoever I want."

The head coach smirked at his notes. The boy had a mouth. Not a bad thing in a leader. "One of the coaches said he saw you play last year. Said your skating seems a lot slower this year. I'm surprised that you're not working harder out there."

Jimmy Dog waited for a direct question. When it came, he shrugged and flicked his eyes toward his inquisitor. "It's only practice. I'll skate harder in the real games."

MacEachren leaned back on his chair and rubbed his chin. He had the reputation as a fine judge of hockey horseflesh. What he saw in Jimmy Dog Dunphy was natural ability, toughness, and a wicked slapshot. But he placed a premium on skating and hustle.

"That's not a good answer. The coaches are trying to evaluate all the players based on what we're seeing out on the ice. How are we supposed to make a proper assessment if kids aren't trying equally hard? What do you have to say to that?"

"I try hard."

"You just said you didn't try hard."

"No, I didn't say that. I said I'd skate harder in the real games."

"Jimmy, can you look up, please? Look at me while we're talking. I don't mean like that, for a split second then look down at your lap. You know, there are not many first year bantams who are going to make this team. Five or six is all. It's mostly the second years who'll be picked, the ones who turned thirteen before the new year. Says here your birthday is this month. So you'll still be a bantam next year and a big one at that. You made it past two cuts, so that means we liked what we saw. But you need to work on some things. Get that skating figured out and you'll have a real good shot at making next year's team. You work on your skating, strengthen those legs, skate hard at tryouts next year, and you'll have a good chance. Real good."

Katie Beaton had lately been surprised by the changes in her body. Big changes, from bumpy to bloody to hairy. Trouble was, there had been little or no warning. Nobody had told her how disgusting it would be. Her mother maintained that she had indeed given Katie enough information to eliminate the element of surprise. If there was more she needed to know there was no time like the present. She showed her again the picture of vagina, uterus, and ovaries. To Katie, it looked like a cooked lobster splayed out on a dinner plate. Her mother said what was happening was a beautiful thing.

She spoke to Joyce about it. Down deep? Emotionally? Yes, she admitted, there was pride. A virtual swelling in the chest to match the real ones. After months of examination, there had been a definite breakthrough on the bosom front. She could feel them taking shape. Her nipples had grown darker, larger, definitely larger, and small bumps had begun to encircle them. She slapped her hips. Almost overnight she had developed a bubble butt. Suddenly she had curves. There was contentment. Yes, the universe was unfolding as it should. But there was also a quiet calm like the viola to the right of the orchestra. Her body was a well-strung instrument ruled by a level-headed girl.

She was growing stronger too. She could feel muscle being defined from her buttocks to her thighs to her calves. She was strong on her blades, her bubble butt powering a skating style that few of the boys had mastered. One day her coach told her, "I notice you never get tired, do you, Katie? You could skate all day and not get tired. Is it true?" To the girl, this was not a revelation except that it told her that other kids might not have the same gift.

"You have strong legs and a stronger heart," said her coach. "You should take up track and field in the spring."

From Confusion Square, Katie kept her eye on the rink door. The sign above it said Memorial Arena. No one called it that. It was just "the college rink," a cold barn made of steel, ice, boards, and chicken wire. She watched hockey games there, and skated on Saturdays round and round to circus music. Now she would be the first girl in the history of Findrinny Fair to play hockey there.

The Goon and the Zealot came out laughing. They'd made the team too. Jimmy Dog exited alone. She didn't ask. When Tommy emerged, she knew as well. How could she not? He couldn't suppress the smile.

She said, "Since we're going to be playing on the same team, how about we do our homework together." They dumped his hockey bag and continued on to Caledonia Road, taking turns carrying hers and gabbing. The talk went from school to hockey and back. Katie's cello calm, it should be said, did not quiet her tongue. This force of nature spewed forth its commentary with openhearted charm.

"Oh my God," she said, "but I loathe roll call. I hate them calling my name first. Like I have some choice in it. Roll call is just a pointless malingering vestige of childhood. Hopefully next year our Grade Eight teachers will come up with some wiser way to record attendance, or somebody named Anderson, or Armstrong, or Barry will move to town. I know what that stupid Zealot and his friends say. They call me the teacher's pet."

"Don't worry about those dummies," said Tommy. "I'll take care of them."

"You? You mean we. We're going to be teammates with those morons."

She allowed him into her inner sanctum. Twin beds, high and soft, laden with puffy pillows and stuffy bears from the Findrinny Fair, prettily spread with padded quilts made from snipped patches of clothing and curtains or purchased from the Five to a Dollar. Above her bed, a picture of Paul Anka, a starburst in his eyes. On high shelves, a curious congregation of handmade saints. Around the walls, posters and slogans from three different Findrinny Fairs: It's a Findrinny Affair, Pony on up to the Fair, It'll be a Fair Day in Findrinny.

"And that is my sister's record player." Katie pointed to a portable phonograph sitting atop a squat chest of drawers. She drew up its baby blue lid to show off the insides, the playing mechanism, the tonearm with its diamond stylus, the turntable, the loudspeaker. "She lets me play my records if I'm careful with the needle. She won't let me play hers because I scratched one once. I bought her a new one but she still is being a sook about it. So I started my own collection. Since I started getting an allowance I have been going to the music store every Saturday morning. See, this is my stack. I've bought almost twenty. Look at this one. Ben E. King. It's the best. I must have played it twenty times in a row when I brought it home. Tracy was yelling at me to take it off. Do you want to hear it before we start working?"

A soft sporadic scratchiness filled the room. Vinyl vibrations. Katie reacting to their invitation, holding a small fist inches from her mouth and swaying to the sweetness of sound.

When the night has come
And the land is dark
And the moon is the only light we'll see

By the swooning of her *O*s, the extension of her *E*s, by the hope in her *A*s, by the longing in her *U*s, by the electricity in her eyes, she told Tommy what she wanted from him.

No I won't be afraid
Oh, I won't be afraid
Just as long as you stand, stand by me

She flounced upon the bed and with a pat to the crazy quilt beckoned him. Come. She clasped a book upon her right palm showing four rounded fingernails painted pink like no hockey player ever before, and thumbflipped to the homework pages. She patted the quilt again.

If the sky that we look upon
Should tumble and fall
Or the mountain should crumble to the sea
I won't cry, I won't cry
No, I won't shed a tear
Just as long as you stand, stand by me

And darlin', darlin'

Tommy Caffrey tracked his cousin's trail to the elm grove. The lean-to had blown down. The fir bed and the firepit were covered in snow. Four miserable longnecks and two pop bottles sat where once there were a hundred. The boottracks led to the forks, to the same rocky hillock where Tommy had watched the water ceremony with Sambath of the Clan Kat, to the same tree the brave had shimmied up to hang two flags, Mi'kmaw and B'laan.

The flags were long gone.

"There's a bad storm coming," Tommy said. "Better come home. Supper's going to be ready soon. Apple pie for dessert."

"Leave me alone." Jimmy Dog descended the hill. Tommy fell into step at his side, asking what was wrong.

"It's my goddam skates. They've been too small for me since last year. My toes curl up in them and my feet are numb every time I wear them. I have blisters on my blisters. I wanted new ones and my stupid so-called mother wouldn't buy them. And then she said she would buy me new ones for Christmas and lied about that and lied again and again. How could I make the team on those useless fucking skates?"

Tommy thought he observed a twitch in Jimmy Dog's lips. A shiver in his chin.

"I can't believe she wouldn't get you new skates if yours are so small. You need them. Why wouldn't she get them?"

"Because she's a bitch and a liar. First she says the old man is not giving her any money. Then she tells me that she always gives into me, which is bullshit, and I have to start doing stuff to earn what I get. She made up a goddam list. And you know where she got that idea from? From talking to YOUR stupid mother."

"My mother?"

"Yeah, your friggin' know-it-all mother! She told my mother—and that's the last time I'm going to call her that—that she shouldn't be giving in to me all the time. That she was spoiling me. That I should have to do something in exchange for getting new skates like cleaning the fucking house or doing the fucking dishes or taking in the fucking wood. I said I'd do it once I got my new Tacks. But no, that wasn't good enough."

Tommy considered the information. "You could just get a pair of used skates. That's what my mom did. Get your mom to call Phone Fun Time on the radio and say she wants to buy a pair. "

Jimmy Dog hissed like a snake, "She's not my mother anymore. Got that? And there's no f-frigging way I'm going to use Phone Fun Time skates. I've seen your skates, the ones that say GARRETT on the inside heel in big black sloppy letters. You're just retarded if you think secondhanders are cool. If my old man and that stupid bitch won't get me a pair of new skates, I'm going to buy them myself. I've already saved two dollars and sixty cents. And by the way, if I had new skates I would definitely have made that team before you. You can be sure of that. You saw my feet. I couldn't skate with the blisters. No way should you ever have beaten me out for that team. Come here. I'm going to show you something."

They arrived at the brook, just upstream from its confluence with the Big River. A thin layer of ice covered its surface, glassy, reflecting the full moon. The water could be heard below, burbling.

"See those two holes over there? Those two holes in the ice? Those are my skates." Jimmy Dog threw a rock to indicate two ragged gaps in the ice.

"You threw your skates away?"

"I told you. I'm not playing hockey again until I get new Tacks. I need forty bucks so I can buy a new pair. Ones that f-frigging well fit. That's why I'm collecting empties. That's why I need money."

"Come home with me."

"No! Get out of here!"

"What will you do for food?"

"What do you care what I'm doing for f-food. Here's the thing. I need forty bucks for new Tacks. If you want to help me, help me do that. Otherwise leave me alone. I still have a long way to go to reach that much and I'm having to look farther and farther to f-find bottles. And now there's snow everywhere."

An alcoholic uncle had once lavished a five-dollar bill on Tommy, but his mother had snatched it away. Other than that fleeting visitation, Tommy had never been a wealthy person. The monetary sums they were discussing now made his brain spin like a roulette wheel. He glanced loyally at his friend for having the capacity for such grandiose schemes.

Jimmy Dog dug doggedly at a rock the size of a Christmas turkey. Stick after stick broke. Anger and humiliation shone on his face. "Help me."

On this rock I will build our friendship. As he joined Jimmy Dog's struggle with the buried boulder, Tommy felt a tightening in his chest. It was always thus between the two of them. He who pulled me from the Brobdingnagian Pit. We who held hands till we were six. I who made excuses. I who didn't tell. I who stuck up for him no matter what. But what is friendship if it always depends on doing what the other person expects you to do?

"Last time I was at the bottle exchange," Jimmy Dog grunted as his excavations grew more intense, "I saw someone bring in a big pile of copper wire. He got more than twelve dollars for it. Meanwhile I never see anything more than a two dollar bill. Look at all those bottles there. I'll get two sixty-six for all those damn bottles. Copper, that's where the frigging money is. If I could only find some copper I wouldn't have to go digging through stinking ditches and thorny bushes and maggoty fucking trash bins looking for bottles."

A twitch curdled Tommy's stomach and a tremor moved into his chest and upper arms. They weakened him. He knew. He knew of a coppery coil wound tight round a wooden reel. Its reddy brightness twinkled like Mars the one and only time he saw it, that night after Cape Clear when it sat bold as brass in his father's garage. But even as he watched his friend's shame turn to torment, a bond stronger than friendship prevented him from telling Jimmy Dog about it. In that instant, in the moment of formulating this selfish secret, he was shocked by a crashing noise and a tall plume of water that soaked him into a standing, dripping wet, ready-to-run-home position.

Jimmy Dog had freed the boulder from its ancient resting place and with a great heave sent it smashing down upon the thin ice. In the blameless brook a gap appeared, agush with water bubbling and spewing from submarine depths. Like blood flowing from an exposed artery, the troubled water rose and spilled like a killing plague over the skin of his babblebrook.

Malice aforethought is a key factor in distinguishing a premeditated crime from the passionate variety. Several considerations can aid in determining this important legal differentiation. One item of interest to an investigator would be when the accused acquired the weapon used in the crime. The time that lapses between a motive-defining injury and the perpetrator's violent reprisal will also be factored into the judgment. The greater the time lag, the less passion might be assumed. As contrary as it might seem, if there has been a struggle, as so often happens, the defence will enter this as evidence that suggests the accused had been surprised in the act of carrying out a much tamer plan. The defence would like a jury to believe that the accused was, in fact, provoked by the victim or victims. On a societal level, such a defence is mounted as an argument for war. It might even exonerate the killing of innocent non-combatants. Surprise, you see, can lead to passion. In the heat of the moment, even mature grown men can do despicable things for which they needn't be blamed, depending on the motive and other extenuating circumstances.

Jimmy Dog came running from his mother's house, tomahawk in hand. The police sirens wailing up Church Street were coming for him. Another car screamed up Kirk Street, blocking his primary escape route. He ran into the overgrown orchard with its craggy apple trees and thick hide of hawthorn.

"We've got him surrounded." He could hear them now, shouting his name, darting their shafts of light through the branches. Did they really think he would answer? Fat fucking chance. They would not find him in the Unseen Hole. He knew the pit from Tommy times past. He quietly covered his body and his overlarge head with leaves, slippery elm and maple and birch that blew up against the gnarly apple to be drawn down into the Unseen. When his burial was complete he felt for the tomahawk so that he might clutch it close to his pounding chest. Still. Free. Still. Free. Still. Free.

His mother could bleed to death on the floor for all he cared. Stupid bitch. If it wasn't for her stupid decisions it wouldn't be Jimmy Dog in a cold wet hole, it would be Jimmy Dog on a hockey team.

The cops had come so close he could smell their cigarettes. Other steps crunched close above.

"It looks like she'll be all right," a voice said. "He mainly just busted up the walls. She said he had some kind of hatchet. You should see the place. Holes in every wall. Christmas tree chopped up. Ornaments strewn everywhere, busted, broken. Mrs. Dunphy is all right though. She said he pushed her and she hit her head on the stove when she fell. Let's go. We'll catch the little shit tomorrow. We'll catch you tomorrow, you little shit!"

Still. Free. Still. Free. Still. Free. But with the subsiding of the flashlights, Jimmy Dog Dunphy felt no relief. No relief at all. He tried to let the tomahawk go but couldn't.

The presence was warm at first, a swirl of wind and a rustling of leaves. Something was in the Unseen Hole with him. It spoke a word and the word was "Come." Jimmy felt millipedes under his clothes. Crawly. Stinging. Movement without mass seeping into his stomach, writhing like pinworms, only to be stilled by the rustling and the return of the voice, "Come." A warm wind that spoke of summer. "Come. Let go. Let's go." Then pinworms again. Maggots. Ugly, stinking vermin like the ones he saw in the bin, writhing on and under dead flesh, falling in great maggoty clumps off the wooden lid. Now he saw a-swirling from his mind a small and tall shack. In it a naked man lay on his back, his belly swollen hard as a watermelon. People had gathered around his carcass and were moaning and mourning his loss. They cleared their throats, spit and muttered. Beriberi. Beriberi. Beriberi. Beriberi.

When the first tapeworm evacuated through the man's mouth, the people pointed and clucked their tongues. As more crawled from lips and nose, the mourners retreated, retching, screaming. They climbed down from the shack, leaving the fetid corpse alone with his parasitic companions crawling along his bloated carcass seeking the dark or falling through the floorboards to the hardswept earth below. Jimmy Dog gripped the tomahawk harder, a grip that could not be relaxed. Again the leaves rustled and the voice spoke.

"Come. Come with me. Come to the home of the B'laan, to the village of Datal-Alyong in the district of Bong Mal."

He had only to let go and they flew, Jimmy Dog Dunphy and his Unseen companion, over the path cut by the Findrinny Brook, upstream from the town, past the Archer-Atlas copper smelter, over the snow-covered farms and higher and faster, swooping over the Dream Valley of the Indians.

The Unseen spoke to him now as a teacher. The B'laan, he said, once inhabited the entire coast from the Strait of Canso to the Dream Valley to the Tampakan and beyond. Always retreating from the settlers, they survived by going north, always north, higher when they could, but always north where they live on just one ridge now, one last ridge and valley where still the Three Sisters safekeep them as they sleep. Their Creator is Melu who abides in a great expanse above the clouds. Melu's teeth are made of gold. He is so prodigiously clean, he has rubbed himself ivory white. It is Melu who sculpted both the Earth and the B'laan's first ancestors from great mounds of his own rubbed-off dead skin.

The B'laan were created to feast on the bounty of forest and stream and have done so for their entire existence. They are hunters and gatherers. They were nomads in times past but can no more roam at will. To earn paper money they mine the rich seams of copper that crisscross the Tampakan. They mine another mineral said to be more precious than copper, but the metallurgists of the Clan Kat permit no one to hint at the existence of this other. Stories from faraway lands have told the Indians how some white men, driven mad with greed, are willing to kill and enslave to fill their pockets and sacks and crates and boats and boots with the yellow metal.

You see their houses now. They are clustered in forest clearings and stand on stilts to protect them from the creatures and spirits that wriggle on the earth. See how they use the skinny trunks they slash and the bark they strip and the boards they whittle. The thirty houses we see make up the village of Datal-Alyong in the district of Bong Mal on the backside of the Tampakan Ridge. That one is the home of Juvy Capion. There she lies on a thin homewoven mat, hugging her son John Mark, the one she calls Jun Jun. Splayed on a second mat is her daughter Vicky, four years old, and her other son, Pop. He is the same age as you, James. It is his job to prepare the *pamahaw.*

Jimmy Dog watches Pop descend the hand-hewn ladder to the swept patch of red earth that surrounds their *balay.* Pop relieves himself by a nearby tree and with both hands primes an iron pump that stands nearly as tall as him, splashes water on his face and arms, and catches a quart to fill his kettle. Soon the kindling is alight, steam is rising from the kettle and smoke obscures the big pot that contains the leftovers from the evening meal. Pop pours his coffee and listens to a scattering of cocks crowing their reveille. The sun appears wide over the ridge to the east. He gazes at the red sky in the morning.

He squints as though he sees something shiny, something that should not be there. A glint. A warning. Jimmy Dog sees them too. Men dressed in camo, carrying Armalite assault rifles, quickening their pace. They have been told that rebels are hiding here. The soldiers are hunting them. They semi-circle and point their guns at the boy named Pop.

Jimmy Dog feels but cannot see the tapeworms and pinworms and maggots and centipedes. They invade him as quickly as they leave the body of Beriberi. They consume the soft parts first. He grips harder still the tomahawk, but it is too late for that. Imagine some foul and putrid corpse that has lain rotting and decomposing in the grave, a jelly-like mass of liquid corruption. Imagine such a corpse a prey to flames, devoured by the fire of burning brimstone, and giving off dense choking fumes of nauseous loathsome decomposition. And then imagine this sickening stench, multiplied by a millionfold and a millionfold again, from the millions upon millions of fetid carcasses, massed together in the reeking darkness, a huge and rotting human fungus. Imagine all this and you will have some idea of the horror of the stench of hell. You will have lived what Jimmy Dog lived.

Indoors, little Vicky has risen. She walks in small tidy circles on her heels, thumb in her mouth, naked but for a Mickey Mouse t-shirt. Her baby fat belly bulges beneath Mickey's shoes. *"Asa na Pop?"* and she moves on her heels toward the door. She stands in the doorway and smiles for she has found Pop. Now her six-year-old brother smells the coffee. Stretching like a cat, Jun Jun shakes the sleep from his head and the jet-black hair from his face, arches his smooth brown back, and reaches to the ceiling, sharply breathing in like it was his last morning on earth, his eyes still shut. The lad has learned to make the sound of cocks.

"Hmmm," murmurs Juvy Capion, blinking at her rooster son. *"Ang adlaw maabut."* The sun is up.

Pop turns to face his sister. He raises his hands to halt her descent into danger.

Fourteen Armalites open up. Their flames are seen first, short bright bursts easily visible in the weak light of morning. Their terrifying roar follows in but twenty-five beats of a hummingbird's wings. The gunfire awakens the entire village of Datal-Alyong in the district of Bong Mal on the back of the Tampakan Range.

We are creatures of the forest. We are men and women and girls
and boys like you, says the Unseen. We are B'laan. We are Mi'kmaw.
We are Apache. We are Cree. Still free. Still free.

COUNTERPARTS

The antiseptic smell assaulted him. It emanated from the cold corridors, pungent as horse piss. The smell would always remind him of reading the test results with Bridget. Every word like a snort of Javex. They had read them aloud to be sure.

Parents and doctor may have a difficult decision to make at the expense of the baby.

The phrase struck Hector as inhuman. He went straight to the university ethicist. The priest was unequivocal. In the context of eternity we are put on this Earth for a blink of the eye. Through the power of conception we increase humanity, through the power of the sacraments we bring their eternal souls to God. The soul must be saved.

The stench he smells is bleach. The hospital uses it to denature and destroy the microorganisms that spread disease. On every surface, it reacts with the protein of millions upon millions of microbes. Like bubbling water changes an egg to a boiled egg, so does bleach turn bacterial protein into clumpy masses that never regain their original form. They die a silent death. The nurses assure him that the smell is a sign that the hospital is a clean place, a safe place.

Hector Caffrey quickened his step. Once he saw Bridget again, he knew the stench would be quenched.

She had her finger to her lips. She pointed to the next bed where a white-gowned chaplain held a gleaming chrism.

"Good Sunday morning, Mrs. MacGregor," the priest repeated. "It's Father McKenna, dear."

"Hello Father," she said, looking from face to chrism and chrism to face.

"I've come to offer you Extreme Unction."

"What did you say?"

"I've come to offer you Extreme Unction, dear."

"What did you say?" The woman's tongue slid awkwardly over her pale lips. Intent on improving her advantage, she reached for her glasses but came up empty. She felt the right side of her head for a long lost electroacoustic device. Gone as well.

“Come closer!”

As the crone straightened, the priest stood with dignity, unsmiling except with a shift of the eyes toward Hector, unmoving except to secure the chrism with a second delicate hand.

“I’ve come to offer you the Unction of the Sick.”

“The what?”

“THE LAST RITES, DEAR. I’VE COME TO GIVE YOU THE LAST RITES.”

“That would be goooood.”

Hector was caught flat-footed. His wife had covered her face with *The Crypt*. He knew she was suppressing laughter behind there. She made it all the harder for him. The priest came to her side. “Come out from behind there, Bridget.” And when she wouldn’t, he teased, “Good Sunday morning, dear, it’s Father McKenna. I’ve come to…”

“Father Neil!” Helpless from laughter, she lowered her cover, wiped small tears from her cheeks, and ordered him to stop.

“If not for the love of God,” said the chaplain to the couple. “Oh, and did you hear? You’ll be moved upstairs today, Bridget. I spoke to the staff and they agreed. It’s crazy for you to be down here. Crazy. I mean, what were they thinking? You should be up in maternity. Of course you should.”

Hector bore three gifts. *The Agony and the Ecstasy*—she was a voracious reader and lately preferred the novel of the day. Flowers were always appreciated as long as there was space. He brought chocolates too, though she never ate them. “Thank you. For the kids,” she said.

“Still no sign of Jimmy Dog?”

“No,” he said glumly. “We’re organizing a search party, but it’s hard in the middle of winter.”

“Just now you’re organizing a search party? Two weeks after he was last seen?”

‘Well, turns out Jimmy Dog is the boy who cried wolf. He’s run away so many times in the past that no one was too concerned, not even Mary. The twins say he's probably holed up in a barn out in the country, drinking milk right from the cow, stealing eggs and eating them raw."

"Oh my God, that's terrible. Poor Jimmy Dog. No one deserves that." She reached out her hand and he hugged her. "Well, it can't be. The boys are right. If there's anyone persistent and willful enough to spend two weeks on the lam, it's Jimmy Dog." She laughed with her crying. "He can be such a sweet kid when things are going well. So funny in his stuttery way. So full of beans. Oh, poor Jimmy Dog. Tell the boys to come here with you tonight. We need to talk to them about it. And how about Lucky? Were you talking to Aggie?"

"Yeah. She saw him before she had to head back to the Tampakan. He's still over in Frenchvale at that Talbot House. Sister Catherine told him our worries about Jimmy Dog being lost. Looks like he's just going to stay put there. I don't know what's wrong with that man. If it was my kid..."

"It's not that. Lucky is finally doing something about his drinking. Getting away from all the triggers is what Father Neil calls it. He says Lucky needs to find the truth of his inborn goodness."

"That will take some time."

Her optimism and even-handedness often puzzled Hector. To her peril, she never gave up on a person. He had seen Lucky Dunphy in action and not just overseas. The Wild Man of Borneo pretty well summed him up. Truth of his inborn goodness? Certainly his wife was allowed to have all kinds of opinions and he encouraged this trait in her, but there were certain things you had to take on faith, like Lucky being an alcoholic. And she should take the teaching of the Church at faith too, but she did not. Not in its entirety. The test results were all the example you'd need to see that. Never had they needed the guidance of the Church so desperately as when they received that letter. But it wasn't to the Church she went but to her own conscience. He marvelled at how she could approach a question so differently from him. More confounding still was that she would argue even after they came to the same conclusion. It was as if she *wanted* him to debate.

He had some gossip for her, via Cissy, via Jacky. It seemed that their

Tommy had his first kiss at the lips of one Katie Beaton. It happened a month prior, but so detached had Hector been, it escaped notice till now.

"Oh, isn't that sweet? Pinned him down and smacked him in a snowsuit. Like two snow angels coming to life. Do you remember our first kiss?"

Such moments were alarming for Hector. The unexpected segue. *You have a rectal exam in five minutes Mister Caffrey. Can you change out of your barn clothes and put on this johnnyshirt?*

"Of course I remember." He hugged her. Not sufficient. "Okay. Let's see. It was in a barn. In Glencoe, almost to Bornish. John Angus Rankin's. Way the hell out there. There were horses. There were fiddlers playing in the house..."

"Am I part of the story too?"

They say you never forget a lover's first kiss. Sex might be forgettable, but a first kiss is not. Bridget remembered everything about it. A long warm night. June 1940. She wore a sporty blouse and skirt combination like they were wearing in Boston. The bob of her chocolate-brown hair was inspired by Vivien Leigh, pasted, centre-parted, and poofed on the sides. Her lips were coloured bright red.

The guest of honour was announced by a horn-blowing commotion, cheering, clapping, and backslapping. She studied his entrance and his modesty and how he joined his brothers under the Rankin's great horsey tapestry, eight duns with faces white from the sun, running and splashing toward the Caffrey brothers, with evergreen forests and the Rocky Mountains in the background. He looked so delicate, so shy, and yet so peaceful in the midst of the stampede. She would forever believe in love at first sight.

Hector's brother Jim was home from the States with his new wife, Mary, the terror from away. With venom in her spit, she denounced Hitler, Mussolini, and their Fascist collaborators—the puppet governments of half of Europe. She championed America's isolationist policies, loud, long, and drunkenly declaring her undying support for

FDR. Then she turned on her position, insisting that Roosevelt ought to declare war that very night. “He’s dying to anyway, don’t you know, the old cripple.”

The trenchers groaned with oatcakes, johnnycake, biscuits, blood sausages, and *maragans* galore, a big pot of beef stew, a steaming dripping leg of lamb, lobsters from Port Hood, oysters from Mabou, quarts and quarts of bully beer, and some good hard homemade cheese.

On the fiddle was Angus Chisholm backed by Nosey Flynn and Jessie Belle Moran, with Maybelle on the keyboards. After a liltingly slow air, a solo from Chisholm, barely touching bow to strings, the foursome kicked into a few appetizing strathspeys and finally snapped full bore into a set of reels. Old Peter the Bridge and Duncan Gillis leapt to their feet, both of them dancing in tight, tidy steps. Toe to heel and kicking out briskly those hard black shoes. Tamerack’er down on the hardwood floor. *Suas e!* Now you’re talking. Glencoe on the floor and we won’t give ’er up.

A full moon had risen enormous in the western sky. As the red orb crested the barn, guests came out from the house to ooh and ahh. Bridget boldly intercepted him: “So you’re the man of the hour. How are you enjoying the attention?” The smell of horse sweat, hay, and manure wafted past. Moonlight streamed into the yard and onto the trucks and carriages parked haphazardly throughout. Horses could be seen between their wagons and buggies and shays, and in the stables, munching patiently, their muzzles dipped in feed bags and broken bales. She pointed to one, stroked his twitching flank, pressed firmly into its dark muscular energy.

He knelt and pretended to inspect a hoof. She looked at his back. Not the back of a soldier. Too lean. Too gracefully young. “So you’re off to join the army. Everyone thought you were planning to be a priest.”

“Maybe someday. I need to be sure. I’m waiting… I’m just not sure yet.”

“It’s the only reason the girls have left you alone, you know.”

“What?”

Bridget had already made up her mind not to be coquettish. She would move straight ahead toward her goal. She might never see him again. “I’m going to college next year,” she said. “The nuns think I’d make a good teacher. I like to read. I like kids. And…" She showed him two fists and a disfiguring frown, "I can be tough and in control when I need to be." Releasing her ornery pretense, she laughed and stared at him, her head cocked. She considered him calmly until he again began to study his gumshoes. "I don't know much about horses really," she said. "But my sisters, Marie and Aggie, are wild for them. Not me. When they're out romping with the horses and running through the fields, I'm inside talking to Mama, helping her in the kitchen, singing songs. My favourite is *"Hò Rò Mo Nighean Donn Bhòidheach."* Do you know it?"

"Yeah. I know it. "

Bridget slowly moved around the stallion and stroked its other flank. The moonlight rested on her face now. "About all I know about horses is that they smell bad and feel good. When do you leave?"

"Day after tomorrow. I'll spend tomorrow with Mama and Papa."

"Are you afraid at all?"

"I'm sometimes afraid when I think that I might have to kill someone," he offered honestly. "I'm not afraid for myself. God will take care of me. When you look at all that is happening over there and you know that other people, other Canadians, are putting their lives on the line, it makes you feel... Brave is not the right word. I don't feel brave, but I don't feel fear either. The young men that I see in the newsreels don't look afraid. They look like they're doing a job that needs to be done. They belong to a brotherhood that I want to be part of. I'm sure there are times when fear must rise and dominate every other thought and emotion you have, but I don't feel it now."

Party sounds carried through the stilly night, the fiddles mixing with cheering voices. A warm breeze awakened the barnboards. She waited again, but he was finished. He had looked into her eyes the whole time he spoke. She liked that he found the words and trusted her enough to say them aloud.

"It's my birthday today. I'm sixteen."

"Oh, happy birthday!"

"I want you to give me a birthday present."

"Me? What could I give you?"

She looked down as she moved closer, watching her black shoes step, step, step. When she stood directly in front of him she tilted her chin upward, grasped his suspenders, and said firmly.

"I'll tell you what you can give me, Private. You can give me a kiss. My first kiss."

"Are you old enough to be kissed?"

"What is the age limit to share a kiss? Have you never kissed a girl before, Hector Caffrey?" Her eyes grew teasingly wide.

"I should have said, how do you want to be kissed?"

"I've thought about it," she said confidently. "Does that surprise you? I don't stay awake at night thinking about it, but I'm glad you asked. I just get so far and I don't know what happens next. To start, let me move a little closer and you put your arms around here. Good. Now the only other thing is for you to put your cheek next to mine and hold it there for a while. What happens next you decide."

He bowed and felt his head fit nicely into the crook of her neck. He closed his eyes and breathed in the apricot scent of her flesh. His lips touched the fair skin that covered the long muscle along her shoulder. He kissed her neck, tentatively. His heart beat heavily, sped on by the feel of her body pressing lightly against his own, cheek to cheek, her languid breathing near his ear. He pressed carefully into her then rested his lips on the bone, lightly, pressing, releasing, then pressing again more confidently. Every moment, every movement seemed infinitely important. She moved gently toward him and their lips were together. Breasts pressed softly through flimsy fabric against his beating chest. She tasted the moistness of his upper lip and pressed softly, firmly, softly into him. They breathed together for a few moments then she stepped away and showed her pleasure.

"Thanks," she said. "That was nice. Well, I better go now. My mother will be looking for me."

She backed away slowly, snapping his suspenders against his shirt, smiling at the sound. She was flushed. But he was worse off. Weak-kneed, palpitating, not knowing if he could move if he had to. She saluted and with gathering purpose, strode toward the house.

Weekly the winter weather worsened. The landscape of the District of Findrinny became alternately a still white desert and a roar of wild snowstorms. Winds wailed in from the northeast, shoving and packing the drift ice that had pitched camp in the Gulf of St. Lawrence. Temperatures plummeted. In banks as high as henhouses, boys created bright blue underworlds where they scampered on all fours, driven by a constant niggling fear in the hippocampus. Death by smotheration.

Hung's Brigadoon Restaurant was a beacon on these snowy nights. The last to turn off its lights. The last to serve a sleepy town. The cooks' helper slapped the orders together. The eldest Hung girl, Joyce, packed and ferried the takeouts to the front desk where Violet or Rose handled the customers. Over the course of an evening, Joyce Hung could skim off enough chicken balls, rice, and ribs to make a hobo fat. And so she did.

She'd seen him enter the barn twice. She recognized him from the day at the Bishop's Bowl. She asked around. Turned out no one had seen Jimmy Dog Dunphy for weeks. Kicked out of his house. Hadn't been to school. The cops were looking for him. Someone said they saw him floating belly up in the river, but he was going too fast and vanished before they could pull him out. Probably ended up in the harbour. Katie said he'd likely come back to haunt us smelling like seaweed. On the third night she watched him ascend into the mow and disappear behind a wall of bales. She spoke to him from outside his fortress. "I'm leaving the food here for you. It's all made today. I put a fortune cookie there too." When she came back the next morning there wasn't a trace left. He was like Old Yeller. Best left in the dark or he'll bite your arm off. She called softly to the fortress, "I'll be back with more tonight."

When he did say thank you it was like a voice from a hollow tree. The voice of fear. He would not come out until he told her his nightmare. You can be the judge, he said. Joyce was allowed close to the fort so she could hear his low voice. It had cracked since she had first met him on the hill by the Bishop's Bowl. She thought he was funny then. Not very cute, but funny. And full of life. Now he was dull, coughing between sentences, wrung out, and thinking the lunacy he dreamed was real. It made no sense, she convinced him. Guns, blood, death in Findrinny Fair? "James," she said, "things like that do not happen in our world."

She cured him with common sense and sweet and sour chicken balls, pork fried rice, honey garlic spareribs, beef and broccoli, egg foo yung, and lots of fortune cookies. They were leaning against bales of hay in the mow when she sprung it on him. "I think it's time for you to go back to school."

Jimmy Dog stuttered out the arguments for remaining at large.

"The temperature is going to drop to below zero the next two nights," she said. "Cold cold cold, then it's going to shoot up forty degrees by Friday. Gonna rain all weekend like a winter hurricane. They say it'll melt a lot of snow. You'll either freeze or you'll drown in here.

"N-No way. I am not going back home, that's one thing for sure. H-Hell no. I never want to see the inside of that house again."

"Listen to you coughing. That's from living in a barn. What would you do if I wasn't bringing you food? You'd be stealing it."

"I'd do what I have to."

MacLellan's horses snorted thick puffs of vapour. A mare stamped her hooves and shook and shivered the gathering chill from her chestnut coat. Even with pilfered coats and blankets and a blockade of bales, Jimmy Dog would not sleep well tonight.

"Well, you know what?" continued Joyce, "I steal. I steal food from the Brigadoon every night and bring it here to you. I'm not threatening to stop. I'm just saying that I'm already a thief because of you. And you know this food I've been bringing you for two weeks? I'd value it at forty dollars. Forty dollars my parents are short. If you even just had that much money, you could buy your precious skates with money left over."

"What's your point?"

"My point is, there's money to be made on the outside. You already work hard, you just need to be more creative."

She packed the take-out bag with the garbage to be dropped in the Brigadoon bins. She looked at him, his eyes downcast, his fingers laced as if in prayer. She regarded his lips, the top thick and shaped to cover his buckies and the bottom drooped into a Presley pout.

"You know what I think," she said, *sotto voce,* "I think you have beautiful lips, James Dunphy. Big, thick, beautiful lips. I could kiss them, I could. Katie did it to Tommy that time. Why can't I do it to you?"

She did it quickly, audibly, hands on his cheeks. He drew back in shock. She raised her eyebrows in "Well, what did I just do?" suspension and flashed her famous dimples. She held her eyes on him. Angrily he began, "If you do that once more..." His eyes were on her too.

It was perhaps the symmetry that stopped him short. Two divots to melt the heart of a harpy. Two more to melt Jimmy Dog's. Two eyes to hold him accountable for his actions. Two lips to kiss him better.

"You'll what?"

"If you do that once more I promise I'll start school on Monday." It was a good answer. If he was going to bargain away his freedom, he may as well get some more smack. And so, on a Friday morning after a bitterly cold night and with the warmth of first kisses still on his lips and in his heart, Jimmy Dog strolled into the cop shop and turned himself in. Before the week was up he would be a recognized hero.

February 1962 was nearly in the books when a wild gale blew in from the North Atlantic. Cold hard sleet, then hard, cold, unrelenting rain fell for two days. On the third day the wind shifted, the weather warmed, and a soft rainy mist enveloped the Little Vatican so that you couldn't see the cathedral from the street. High in the hills, the thaw began. Black water seeped from imperturbable highland tarns, pestilential fens, shrub swamps, and fissure springs, and by means of a hundred insignificant rills, storm-dug ditches, and secret trails, passed unseen through bedrock, gathering strength and velocity as it rushed through the boreal. The mist turned into rain that grew heavier by the hour. From the north, the headwaters of Tommy's obsequious babblebrook hurried downhill, collecting tons of melting snow and fresh fallen rain. The brook spilled into the Dream Valley as an angry roiling redbrown torrent, moving swiftly and purposefully through the vale, narrowing into wild cascades as it compressed through the Split, sweeping aside beaver dams, sending thick tree branches careening and digging into its gravelly bed and banks, ripping asunder two bridges, bursting the slag ponds of the Archer-Atlas smelter, and tearing through the town, flooding parking lots, streets, cellars, and Columba's field.

Tommy and Jacky were certain school would be cancelled. Their mother told them otherwise. She was home from the hospital again and again ruling the roost. She had agreed to take Jimmy Dog into her care despite Hector's objections that the boy be sent to reform school. "We'll see how it goes for a week," she said. "Just one week and we'll start looking for someone else to take him in."

When the boys entered their classroom on Monday, the teacher yelped a welcoming cry. With a hand on Jimmy Dog's shoulder, she led the former vagrant to his familiar seat, leaned close to his ear, and spoke quietly, intently, as if they were co-conspirators. She finished with a motherly hug, staunchly resisted. Annie Big Archie MacDonald was the mistress of the second chance. Findrinnian born and bred, she knew the fathers and the mothers of all her charges, the good apples and the bad eggs. Every day she saw the impact of negligent parenting. They were the derelicts, not the children.

For Annie MacDonald, morning roll call was not just a recitation, it was a communal news bulletin. "Kaydee Beaton," she started.

"Here, Miss."

"Class, you know, I am sure, that the bantam Black Hawks won a big tournament in Sydney this weekend and Kaydee scored the winning goal. Kaydee is the first girl to ever score a goal in minor hockey in Nova Scotia. Isn't that right, Kaydee?"

"Yes, Miss." She glowered quietly in her front row seat. She knew what the word on the playground would be.

"And I think that deserves a round of applause."

Bishop Fraser school was a square redbrick affair. The north side facing the cathedral was the girl's playground. The boys were let out into the south side facing Findrinny High into which this year's Grade Sevens would enter next September. The fast-moving grey clouds still held one last drizzle of rain, a last contribution to the great flood of '62.

At recess, a clutch of four boys made haste to a corner that kept the rain at bay. A fifth followed them in a roundabout route, out of sight and tucked into a near corner to listen. Simon the Zealot recited her crimes. There was the incontrovertible fact that she sat in the front row, the better to be seen. She was right up the teacher's arse, always talking to her when she didn't have to. Now she's getting compliments for doing something all of us have done—just because she's a girl.

"And," added Philip the Goon MacKenzie, "she's always the first one called at roll call."

Tommy could zip his lips no longer. "Are you serious? I know you're not the swiftest fox in the field, Goon, but even for you that's rich. Haven't you figured out that she's called first because her name starts with a B?"

"Andy Fraser's name starts with an A. Why isn't he first?"

"You're kidding, right?"

But Katie Beaton was safe from their wrath. Safe on the other side of the school. Had Tommy not blown his cover and been chased off by the Zealots, he would have known what danger she was in.

By the end of the school day, the sun had made landfall. Separate cumulus clouds sailed like ships over patches of blue. Girls deprived of a weekend of skipping got out their ropes.

Daisy, daisy, who shall it be?
Who shall it be who will marry me?
Rich man, poor man, beggar man, thief
Doctor, lawyer, Indian Chief

The Zealots gathered on the girls' side of the school to watch. How rare for them to stay beyond the bell. And why would they station themselves there? Why but to eye one particular skipper clapping and singing her insipid ditties.

How many children shall we have?
One, two, three, four, five, six, seven...

Simon said, "We'll wait till she separates from the herd."

As Katie skipped and the Zealots leered, Tommy and Jimmy Dog became waylaid from their homeward journey. The objects of intrigue were an open manhole and six flickering fiery smudgepots to warn of danger. Two yellowhats worked the hole, one up and one down. Their task seemed to be the production of an oozing stinking mound of mud and slime to mark the entrance to Hillcrest Street. The workers took advantage of the spontaneity of the boys' visit to pursue some public relations. As they deftly turned tobacco onto paper, they did what came second nature to the adult denizens of the Little Vatican. The short brownskinned workman with the glistening gold tooth asked first Tommy: "What's your father's name? Caffrey. Hector Caffrey? Yes, of course. How is your mother? Don't you look like her."

It was Jimmy Dog's turn.

"Elvis Presley."

"Very funny."

The taller of the two men drove his shovel deep into the muck. He cupped a cigarette in red bony hands and snapped it alight. He remained erect as he smoked, leaning one elbow on his long-handled spade like two thirds of an American Gothic. He looked like the hands of a clock, straight up and down. Tommy imagined the man's backbone was similarly made from a long-handled shovel.

"That's right," said Jimmy Dog," My father's name is Elvis Presley. Haven't you ever heard of him? He's doing a show tonight at the Parish Centre. You should go and catch him."

"Whatdyathink, Ron. Little smart alec look anything like Elvis Presley to you?"

Six O'Clock answered. "Not too much, Norm. Elvis has black hair. Hard to believe he could have a kid with a big orange mop like that."

"His father's name is Lucky Dunphy," Tommy said to a snarl from Jimmy Dog.

"Told you to shut up about my name, arsehole."

Six O'Clock said, "Yes, yes. You know Lucky, Norm. He used to have a big job up in the copper mines."

"Oh, Lucky, of course," said Goldtooth and examined the urchin before him for resemblance. "I know who you are. You're that runaway."

Jimmy Dog turned on his heels. "Why did you tell them who I was,

Tommy, you friggin' Judas. Just keep your mouth shut, would you? Why don't you just dry up and die."

At the base of the hill skipped Katie Beaton, still singing her rhyme.

And now you're married you must obey
You must be true in every way
You must be kind, you must be good
And make your husband chop the wood

Down the hill the Zealots flew. It was an ambush. Four against one. "Come on, let's get her. Geronimoooo!"

Katie saw the vigilantes charging down the hill. She sprinted across St. Columba and turned down College toward home and safety. The open flap of her backpack clapped crazily. The books in the bag slowed her flight. With each stride, the Zealots, propelled by the steepness of the hill, closed ground. She was on the bridge when they caught her. "Grab her! Grab her!" yelled the Goon. When all four had laid hands on her, one of them yelled, "Let's hold her over the river!" The boys hoisted her to the railing and, without thinking, over. Tommy couldn't see Katie's face. The Goon and the Zealot, Andy Fraser and Bartright who couldn't fart right shielded her from view.

"Help!" she yelled.

Katie dangled upside down with four pairs of hands clutching her leotards at the ankles and calves. Her hair and skirt reached toward the Findrinny Brook. Her leotards were pulled toward her knees by the boys' clumsy hands. Her panties, pink and patterned, were revealed. Tommy saw the contents of his friend's schoolbag fall into the raging river far below. Books, scribblers, pencils, pink rubber eraser sloped on both ends, all disappearing into the rushing current, all pulled by invisible gravity, that most powerful force, so powerful as to heat the interiors of stars and planets to extreme temperatures, to direct the tides, to hold planets in orbit around their sun, to coalesce all dispersed matter and therefore account for the very existence of the Earth.

"Help!" she wailed. "Help, please. Don't let me go!"

Tommy stood frozen to the planks of the bridge. What were they doing? If they dropped her she would surely drown. Fear and disbelief overwhelmed him. It was impossible to think straight. Maybe they were trying to pull her back up and couldn't. They weren't strong enough. He looked at the Zealot's grimacing reddening face, a head above the others. Should he rush to help? Should he yell, "Don't let her fall!"

"Help," she yelled a third time. "Pull me up. Pull me up. Please, pull me up!"

The scene was a blur of boys, arms, hands, leotards, plaid woolen skirt falling down the wrong way, pink for girls blue for boys, hair streaming down, arms flailing, Katie pleading. Tommy immobilized. Jimmy Dog, crowing like a cock, scampered up with the two workmen. The three reached over the gang and pulled Katie up, up, up and over. Katie slumped sobbing on the sidewalk as her tormentors backed away. Goldtooth put his coat over her. Six O'Clock was transformed. The cords in his red neck tightened like springs. On his heels he spun, sweeping a long skinny arm at the vigilantes.

"Get home, you little devils! Clear the hell out of here!"

Jimmy Dog tackled the Zealot, whom he hated grievously, and threw him to the pavement. He pounded his head into the sidewalk. Blood issued from the Zealot's ear. Goldtooth pried them apart. Jimmy Dog knelt beside Katie and asked if she was okay. The question turned her sobbing into great gulps for air.

Tommy hung uncertainly on the sidelines, hearing Six O'Clock's curses ring in his ears: "Clear the hell out of here!" Tommy ran. At the driveway of 79 St. Columba Street he slowed and stopped. Minutes crept by. Goldtooth and Six O'Clock were re-employed with their spades, a safe distance away. His cousin who would have news of Katie was not coming home. Tommy slunk off, taking the back way to the scene of the crime. The fury of the risen brook rushed past. Above him a raven croaked from a bare elm. *Gorach*. A dog ran by, a rag of wolf's tongue redpanting from his jaws. People passed over the bridge unaware of the drama that had unfolded there. The workmen knocked off. Jimmy Dog did not appear. Tommy slid like a dottery otter down a slippery bank into a tangle of alders, maples, and birch. Deadly ice-chunks and tumbling branches hurtled past a body length away. He pulled himself free from the clutch of branches. Fog chilled the air. Sun set and streetlights lit.

Tommy walked slowly along the edge of the swollen brook.

He replayed Katie's terror until he bumped into the tilted shell of a wringer washing machine and fell to the ground, rubbing his knee. He leaned against the derelict appliance and peered over the sound of the brook to the dim beacons of Main Street. If he stared hard enough he could see through the darkness and fog and straight through stores and banks and restaurants and rows of houses. He could see through them all, all the way to Katie's house. Mrs. Beaton had turned on the back porch light. Tommy should cross the river and go to her. He should. To make sure she was safe in her bedroom. Sleeping. Not remembering. He heard a voice call his name. If found, he would not see Katie tonight. Approaching footsteps raised a panic within him. If he was going to jump, now was the time.

"Tommy! Tommy, where are you?"

He looked again through the rows of buildings to the porch light in Katie's backyard, beckoning. He had to get to her. He flushed like a partridge from his hideaway and leapt into the rushing river, hearing one last time Daddy's windblown call.

The strokes he flung into the brown water were as futile as fairywings. He thrashed his arms wildly in the direction of the light. To no avail. He felt himself sailing helplessly on the swirling unrelenting current, the cold water pulling him toward the iron track of the Church street bridge. Sickeningly he slammed into a low branch of a slippery elm. The furious sound of the water rushing past was replaced by submarine silence then swelled again in his ears as he popped, gulping to the surface. Now he was hooked to an overhanging branch. He held his head above the water and with numbed hands grabbed for a hold. Grab a hold! But his feet slipped and his legs were back in the river, weighing him down. His jacket clutched and choked his throat. The zippertop cut into flesh. Out of breath now he reached once more, felt an arm, and clutched its strength. Suddenly he was being pulled up and out of the water. He heard but could not see his father panting, thanking God, swearing desperately, tucking the shivering body of his son in his burly arms, running like a fullback for home. "Holy old savanagan God! What were you trying to do? Kill yourself?"

Blood was trickling through the mud. Both the boy's boots were missing, presumed drowned. Father looked into son's wide-eyed, frightened face and blurted a desperate screed. "How many times have I told you to stay away from that God-forsaken river? How many times? How many times?" Then calming, he said, "Thank God you're safe. Your mother is just sick with worry. The whole neighbourhood is looking for you."

Bridget ran a bath then stripped the boy, cleaned his wounds, and had Hector lay his quaking fetal form into the steaming water. She cooed over him like a dove. Having earlier invoked Jesus, Mary, and Joseph, she thanked all three. Hector informed the rest of the searchers and paced the kitchen as if it were a waiting room. Drawing fingers through his black and silver hair, he looked in on the bath to ask, "Is he okay?"

Later Hector would lower Tommy's pajamas and give him two sharp slaps on the bare bum. He looked at him and repeated what he had already said, "You are never to go near that river during a flood. Do you understand? You know I've never spanked you before, Tommy, but this is a very serious thing. You could have drowned. You made your mother sick with worry."

Tommy ran upstairs, put his face to his pillow, and swore he would never make his mother sick again and never again give his father cause to spank him. He recalled his father's sadness and the serious speech he gave until every word was emblazoned in his mind. His solemn oath was pledged with eyes tightly closed in his pillow, knowing in the deepest recesses of his heart that a promise is forever. He would not go near the river. He would not make his father angry. He would not make his mother sick with worry.

"I promise, I promise, I promise."

The next morning, Tommy trailed Cissy and Jacky to school. He stared straight ahead in silence trying not to remember, trying not to see the fenced-in manhole or the black and fiery-eyed smudge pots nefariously glowing. Along the base of the Mount St. Joseph hill they strode until they turned toward Bishop Fraser School. They blessed themselves at the sight of the huge brownstone cathedral. *Tigh Dhe*. House of God. St. Columba's. In the name of the Father and of the Son and of the Holy Ghost. I confess to Almighty God and to you my brothers and sisters.

Mrs. MacDonald started her roll call.

"Not present Miss."

The teacher peered over her Dame Ednas.

"Kaydee couldn't come to school today, Mrs. MacDonald," announced Fiona Finnegan. "She had a bad accident yesterday. I mean she had a bad incident yesterday. Her mother wanted me to give you this letter." The self-important one dismounted and strode to the front of the class to deposit an envelope in the teacher's beefy hand.

As she read the enclosure, the teacher's belly jutted toward the class. From time to time she shook her head as if trying to loosen water from her ear. She lifted her head six times and six times she looked for a different boy. When she finally set the note on her desk, her wrinkled cheeks were flushed under a determined head of steam. She wiped mist from her glasses and said that a very serious thing had happened.

"First," she said, "I want to praise a boy in this class for being a hero yesterday. James Dunphy helped save the life of one of your classmates and we should all give him a round of applause. James, I personally want to thank you for helping Kaydee Beaton yesterday. And her mother also wants to thank you."

Then she opened the bottom drawer of her oakenwood desk. From it she drew a length of limp black leather. Treachery was whispered around the classroom. "She told on them."

"Simon MacDonald, Andrew Fraser, Bartholomew Cartright, Philip MacKenzie, and Thomas Caffrey. Come here, you five, and stand at the front of the class."

They knew the drill. Left arm extended, palm up and flat. Right hand out if you are left-handed. You will not complain of being unable to hold your pencils to do your work. Beginning with Simon, each received two thwacks. The Goon pulled his hand away so that the teacher strapped herself. He received extra in anger for insolence.

Whack whack.

Whack whack.

Whack whack.

Whack whack whack whack.

Tommy kept his eyes on the floor, not caring whether the others cried. The crime was cowardice and the punishment was humiliation. Mrs. MacDonald took his left hand in hers.

Whack whack.

Blood shot down his straightened arm and turned his hand to flame. Pain shot through him and settled in his eyes, ears, and brain. In his throat he caught the pain and buried it deep within him forevermore.

"You may go back to your seats now," ordered the teacher as she concealed her weapon. Head down, Tommy stared hard at his desktop, at the blue ink circles, snakes, and spirals etched there. "You five will stay in for recess and lunch."

Walking home after school, Jacky caught up to Tommy. "Whoa! That was pretty crazy. I never saw five guys get the strap all at once. It was like historic. That was your first time, wasn't it?"

Tommy was resolute in his silence.

"Look Tommy. You didn't deserve it. Not like the others. Jimmy Dog said you were just standing there. You weren't helping, but you weren't really part of it either. The main thing is you didn't cry. You took it like a man."

The comment made little sense to Tommy. He had just stood there. Like a lily-livered yellabelly little limp-dick chickenshit coward, he had just stood there. He did not take anything like a man. He deserved what he got and should have cried like a baby. He decided never to reply, never to speak again, ever, ever, ever again to speak of the part he had or hadn't played in the torture of his fallen Hero. In humiliation he would turn away from her. That's what a man would do.

THE DEAD

There was word of an encounter in the Tampakan. The constabulary had killed three B'laan. In the week that followed, dozens of families abandoned their homes and fled on foot to the School of the Nativity, run by Sister Mary Immaculata and Sister Marie Joseph of the Little Sisters of Jesus. The sisters were struck by the ragged appearance of the refugees. They remembered a time that poverty was unknown among the B'laan. Their needs were simple and easily met from forest, stream, and estuary. It was the same among the Mi'kmaw who also relied on the Earth's bounty and acknowledged these sources of abundance in their clan avatars, the Moose, the Salmon, and the Eel. *T'iam, Plamu, and Kat.*

To both the B'laan and Mi'kmaw, the production of findruine was always a sideline. A cooperative coming together of Indians and settlers for the purpose of friendship and enterprise. The B'laan found the rich seams of copper, digging it out by pick and shovel and later with the aid of water turbines, mining deep into and under the solid rock, then removing and refining the ore. It was back-breaking work shared equally among the young men. Four times a year the secretive metallurgists of the Clan Kat arrived to perform their magic. For the B'laan, these were times of wonder and celebration. Never would they forget the heat emanating from the melting copper mounds, as the men of Clan Kat poured into this molten lava the other ingredients that turned the copper into ingots, sheets, and coils of white or red findruine.

These once proud people arrived at the school in desperate need of the basics: food, shelter, medicine. In the schoolyard, the men squatted on their skinny haunches, smoking gravely, looks of shock on their weathered faces. Inside, the women and children, terror-stricken, drew clutching-close. They peered mistrustfully at the black-and-white clad creatures who moved like great exotic birds that might yet turn them over to the authorities. The first group of twenty men, women, and children had fled to the forest as soon as they heard the shooting. Only when the constabulary's jeeps had left Numnum and returned to their base did they brave the roads to the mission. Over the next few days a terrifying picture of the encounter began to emerge.

"You have come to our school seeking sanctuary," Sister Mary Immaculata announced on the second evening of the crisis. "You can stay here as long as you like. If you have family in the forests, if you can get word to them, they can come here as well."

It was only on the fourth day that the constabulary issued their first report. Armed Indian rebels under the command of Diggy Capion had infiltrated a village in the back of the Tampakan Ridge in the district of Bong Mal. A unit of the constabulary, under the command of Lieutenant Alex MacKillup, was hastily dispatched. An exchange of gunfire took place. No soldiers or insurgents were among the casualties. Three civilians died in the crossfire. One was wounded.

That evening, two new refugees arrived. A slim, intense girl called Sabina and her chubby companion and protector, Ling. Ling said barely a word but carried a machete and a *kuglung*. Sabina asked the houseboy if they could see Sister Catherine-Under-God. When they were told that Sister Catherine was at her clinic five miles away and would they like to speak to the other nuns, they conferred and Sabina spoke.

"Tell them we have been sent by Erita."

Sabina and Ling were brought to the one room in the school that had a lock on the door. Inside they were asked to sit amid the clutter of filing cabinets, desks, small machinery, and a large iron strongbox. On top of the strongbox sat a reel to reel recorder. Opening a wire-bound notebook, Sister Mary wrote the date and under it in clear and horrifying script: *Interview with Sabina and Ling, two girls from Datal-Alyong, sent by Erita Sagada to report on the massacre of Juvy Capion and two of her children.*

Sister Marie moved the recorder to the desk, affixed two reels, one full, one empty, and holding a microphone, spoke in the B'laan dialect to the frightened girls. "Do not be afraid. This machine will record your voices so we can listen to your words at another time and if you agree, others can hear them as well."

Sabina spoke clearly and in great detail. Ling shivered and wiped away tears during the worst of the exposition. Afterward, the tapes and notebooks were placed in the safe under combination lock. Sister Mary sent word to the bishop that they required assistance. They would not publicly release the collected testimonies until their investigations were complete and the witnesses assured of protection. But, and this is where they needed his immediate help, they could not complete their investigations without a visit to Datal-Alyong and this could only happen when they had been cleared for entry. Did the bishop know a judge that would make this visit possible?

Bishop Power spoke to Judge Hughie about securing the sisters' clearance. As his emissary to the Tampakan he sent Father Steel McCoy, a middle-aged priest of the Scarboro Foreign Mission Society. McCoy had served in China before and during the war years, narrowly escaping the Japanese advance by making his own long march to freedom, one that would rival that of Chairman Mao. His post-war mission stints were in the Dominican Republic and Panama. A great promoter of the cooperative movement, a thorn in the side of dictators, he was just the man the university wanted to direct its Extension Department, a job once held by the esteemed Moses Coady. McCoy posed just one question to the university chancellor and the president when he signed on as director: "Bishop Power, Father Somers, when do we start walking with the *nativos?*"

McCoy arrived at the School of the Nativity on a Tuesday, a week after the massacre. The sisters had pieced together a very complete picture. The movement of the constabulary was easy enough to track. Various tribespeople saw their jeeps head up and over the Tampakan. They drove through the village of Numnum as the cocks began to crow. They left their jeeps on the outskirts. From there it was a mile hike to Datal-Alyong.

The soldiers claimed that their mission was the apprehension of Diggy Capion, the leader of an armed group that opposed the activities of Archer-Atlas Mines. Capion was wanted for the murder of three workers employed by Archer-Atlas. Informers had reported seeing this man in Datal-Alyong, presumably in the company of his wife, Juvy.

Fourteen soldiers crept into the village. They carried closed-bolt Armalite assault rifles. Widowmakers they are called in Northern Ireland. The soldiers, hushed, came from the east and with short swift sprints stole into the clearing between woods and village, whispering and signalling one to another in practiced commands, separating one house from the other thirty. They had planned to enter the village under cover of darkness, but they were late. In the yard, firelight crackled with life and smoke rose like incense. Faintly, the sounds of waking children could be heard within. The soldiers quickened their pace, rifles at the ready, safeties unlocked, coming closer and closer, until at the village perimeter they formed a semi-circle, crouched over their short-sighted weapons, elbows bent, fourteen scopes set on one stilted shanty. They saw a man, a boy really, grasping something in his hand, turning toward them.

What happened next is the only contested part of the story. The villagers all agree the Armalites opened up first. The constabulary claims there were shots fired from inside the Capion house. Both sides agree on the casualties: Juvy Capion, age twenty-seven, and two of her children, killed; a third child wounded. The husband of Juvy Capion, Diggy Capion, leader of a tribal armed group opposing a project of Archer-Atlas Mining Incorporated, escaped capture.

Sister Marie said, "The constabulary are treating it as the site of an encounter and using this claim to deny access to reporters and human rights workers. Even family are being kept at bay. They allowed the mine people in though, the one the people call Iron Claw, and the site manager, Slate. They blew in on a helicopter with Colonel Bravo, stayed for half an hour then got back in the helicopter, heading south toward Findrinny. Colonel Bravo says his men must ascertain the number of rebels who camped in the village that night. What they are really doing is covering their tracks."

"Your last statement is speculative, Sister. For now let's stick to the verifiable evidence. How do you know all of this? Are your witnesses reliable?"

"There is a woman we know who lives in that village, a midwife named Erita. She is also a trained human rights worker," said Sister Mary. "You see those two young women singing outside, Sabina and Ling? They are from the back of beyond, Father. They don't speak English, only their native language. Erita sent them to tell us in detail about the massacre."

McCoy looked at the girls. They were no more than seventeen years of age. Skin the colour of caramel. Their eyebrows were plucked to narrow lines and their cheeks were painted with a reddish hue. Their clothing was of the western style, but shabby. The slim one wore a t-shirt and red skirt. The other wore a white flowery, flouncy dress that puffed at the shoulders and hung to her knees. They wore no shoes, just flip flop sandals. Their only accessories were strings of cheap beads and an ornamental comb.

The husky girl plucked her homemade guitar while the other in a clear voice sang a song the two had composed to commemorate the deaths—a mournful song in unsparing detail. The elders squatted, chewed their *mami,* and grunted agreement. The mothers listened quietly, sadly, rocking, cooing, and stopping the ears of their children. The young men paced and snorted like wild pigs caught in a trap.

McCoy spoke Latin, Mandarin, Spanish, some French, some Gaelic, some Italian, but he could not speak to Erita's two emissaries. He asked Sister Mary what they were saying.

"They are singing now about the day after the massacre. The constabulary returned and made a show of finding bullet casings near the Capion house. They are saying that the soldiers planted these casings themselves and will use them as proof that the rebels were in the village and had fired first."

"Speculation again. Anything else?"

"Yes, Father," said Sister Mary Immaculate, "Sabina tells us that she herself heard Juvy Capion shouting at the soldiers to stop shooting. She shouted, *"Tama na ayaw namo sige ug pabuto kai naigo nako."* It means, "Please stop firing your guns for I am already wounded." Sabina saw two soldiers go into the house. There was one more shot and the soldiers emerged laughing. Then she heard the Lieutenant, MacKillup, say, "Finish off the boy. It's better that there are no witnesses."

Father McCoy nodded to the girls. "Ask them what happened to the bodies." He followed the nuns outside, Sister Mary Immaculata, sixty-something, and Sister Marie Joseph, nearly as long in the tooth, bundled up in their habits, their faces like sugar cookies peeping out from veil and crown.

Sister Marie spoke to the slim girl and then to McCoy. "Sabina says the soldiers ordered the villagers to carry the bodies into the square and lay them out for all the people to see. Like a kind of warning. They laid the three children and the mother side by side on the bare ground. The soldiers left laughing. Erita crept from one body to the next, quickly examining them for signs of life. The wounds were terrible. I won't describe them. It was then that Erita saw the eyelid of the little girl, Vicky, flicker. Just a twitch. She was breathing. When the soldiers had left the village, Erita took the little girl into her *balay* and cleaned and bandaged her wounds. The girl was still alive when they left to come here. Erita would have come herself except she had to care for the child."

"Did they bury the bodies?"

"They buried them as they always do," said Sister Marie. The old nun's wrinkled cheeks, squished against their stays, turned a shade and looked askance from the priest. "They wrapped them in tree bark and hung them from the highest branches of a tall tree in the forest."

Father McCoy was aware that the nuns were often chided for their tolerance of heathen practices. This factor alone nearly led to an early end to their mission. Even so, it struck him as odd that Sister Marie would shy away from including this element of the story. So much of the rest of it was beyond human comprehension and care.

"Do they have any hard evidence? Shells, photographs?"

"Yes, Father," said Sister Mary. "All the human rights trainees have cameras. After the killings, Erita took pictures. She sent the camera here with the girls. It is in our safe. You must take it to the bishop when you return to Findrinny. They also collected a sampling of shells. They were all the same. All constabulary issue."

"What will you do now?"

"First thing tomorrow we will go to Colonel Bravo and present the letters you brought from Bishop Power and Judge Hughie. With those, we expect you and Sister Catherine-Under-God will be able to visit the village."

"Where is she?"

"Should be here any minute."

"And yourselves? Are you not making the trip?"

"We must stay here for the sake of the refugees, especially these two girls. They are not safe in the village. They were seen collecting shells. There may be those who will tell the constabulary. Some of the men in the compound will go with you and Sister Catherine. She can speak the language well enough and Erita can speak English."

Sister Marie added, "What we sent the bishop is our summarized report. We will add more detail from the testimony of these girls and from what you and Sister Catherine learn on your site visit."

Site visit. To Father McCoy it had the ring of an engineer inspecting a dam or a building. He looked from the report signed by Colonel Bravo and Lieutenant MacKillup to that signed by Sisters Mary and Marie. Conspicuous by their absence from the one, and heartbreaking in their brevity in the other, were the names of the victims. As a summary of young lives cut short they were so very inadequate: *Juvy Capion, age 27; her son Jordan, known as Pop, age 13; and her son John Mark, age 6, were killed in the massacre. A girl Vicky, age 4, was wounded.* The report of the sisters also noted that Juvy Capion was three months pregnant at the time of her murder.

"And the soldiers, what did they do when they left the village?"

She faltered now, the slim, bright-eyed girl who had always been so direct in her answers. She opened her mouth but no words gushed forth. The nuns hung their heads and reached out to touch her on either wrist. With a choke she aborted a second attempt. Languid Ling stopped playing her *kuglung*.

The girls remained silent. Father McCoy realized he had not bathed or shaved since leaving Findrinny a day ago. Pale-skinned, long-nosed, eyes shielded behind thick-rimmed glasses, he must seem quite a sight and smell to the girls, who seemed sensitive to every nuance of the moment. He reached for his cigarettes, then stopped. Time had stood still and a presence stronger than his ego, not felt since his days in Domingo, filled the room. These are the excluded, the stillness whispered. These are the innocent of which I spoke: "But whoso shall cause one of these little ones that believe in me to stumble, it is profitable for him that a great millstone should be hanged about his neck, and that he should be sunk in the depth of the sea." And, Father McCoy thought, these are moments for which songs are sung and books are written. In moments such as these, vocations are understood.

A husky female voice broke the stillness. It was Ling speaking, the hate in her voice distinct in every word. Cookie-faced, squeaky Sister Marie translated for the benefit of the priest. "Ling says the soldiers just walked into Numnum, set up a roadblock, and had a big breakfast. Sausages, eggs, rice, beer. Then they got in their jeeps and drove away."

Ronald Atlas MacDonald started his lumber career with a handicap, two in fact—the left forearm and the half a leg he left in Italy. His coming home present was his father's lumberyard and the land the old codger had gained in tax sales. Big Ran'l spent his disability money on new saws and the best prosthetics money could buy. He plodded his way through life in short steps and short sentences. When homes were needed for returning veterans, he sold the town a parcel of floodplain previously used only for pasture. With the hard cash, he bought a fleet of new trucks and logging equipment. When he asked Yolanda to marry him he told her he'd put rings on her every finger. By their tenth anniversary, MacDonald had put enough short sentences together to be a millionaire and Yolanda had a fistful of diamonds.

MacDonald hired tree scouts to scour Crown land and paid lobbyists to work the halls of Parliament. He contributed bigtime to the Tory party even when they were on the downswing. He kept abreast of the latest developments in resource extraction and government largesse. He saw development on Indian land happening all over Canada. When an opportunity arose to secure a government permit to take timber off the Tampakan, Atlas Lumber was there. A few short sentences later and MacDonald had acquired substrata rights.

Archer-Atlas Mining Inc. was the latest manifestation of a shell game's worth of companies that, at the bidding of MacDonald, had made camp in the Tampakan. From each company—by whatever name it took, Archer-Atlas, Glencore, X-Strata, Indophil—Atlas gained a finder's fee, secured all surface rights, and retained a stake in the mine. This last payout was directly dependent on the progress of extraction, a fact not lost on Big Ran'l. After seeing the games the companies played, he insisted that Archer-Atlas take a more active interest in his venture's success and that he be installed as vice-president in charge of all Cape Breton operations. In two months the company had a fully constructed office in Findrinny Fair. On the lower floor was a warren built for bean counters and secretaries. On the upper floor, Vice-President MacDonald, Aussie the geologist, and Slate the site manager had their offices. The most substantial upper room was the long, plain, rectangular boardroom that looked out upon the belching stacks of the Archer-Atlas Copper Smelter. MacDonald pointed through the window, through the billowing smoke, and out toward the ocean.

"Storm clouds brewing in the south," he said. "Have a seat." Five chairs scraped across genuine Atlas Lumber flooring, high-grade oak sold at a premium price, stained lightly to hide a multitude of sins.

The boardroom's only adornment was a large map of northwestern Cape Breton. The towns of Cheticamp and Findrinny were indicated, as were a few smaller villages with French or Celtic names. North and east of these settlements appeared to be fully forested wilderness. Within this terra incognito, bold black lines enclosed a large grey area called Tampakan Mine Site Project. The site was riddled with blocks, lines, and captions indicating the locations of access roads, power stations, transmission lines, drill sites, an explosives magazine, a concentrate pipeline, and a tailings pond the size of Lake Ainslie.

"Well, well, Clemmie, I'm just tickled pink you can be here with us today. You must be fearful weighed down with work in Ottawa. A shame you couldn't make it to the grand opening."

The Honorable Clementine O'Leary was the first female elected to represent any Cape Breton riding. O'Leary had made her way on serious-minded intelligence and frugality earned at the elbow of her farming parents. She remembered the depression before it was given that distinction. "Cape Breton never had a depression," she barked at a parliamentarian from Upper Canada. "Nothing changed in 1929, nothing at all. We didn't have two dimes to rub together before or after. We just kept on the same way as we always had."

MacDonald put up with her platitudes. He knew she grew up down the coast, far from well-to-do Findrinny. Poverty was something of a badge for her ilk. Big Ran'l looked at it rather as the worst kind of weakness and one that was easy to exploit.

"Ah, it was a grand opening indeed," Big Ran'l continued. "Lots of food. You would have liked it. Now we five here, Mr. Aussie, Mr. Slate, Mr. Cash, Mr. Law, and myself, are very concerned, I'm sure you understand, about the talk coming out of your high office about an investigation."

"I'm sorry, sir, but what I told the press is simply that it is up to the courts to determine culpability."

"Well, you see, Clemmie, this is not necessarily the case. Mr. Law?"

"This is correct. The courts are not required to determine anything in military matters. In nearly all cases, military matters are decided by military courts."

"But it seems, Clemmie, that you are pushing things in another direction. Or am I mistaken?"

"Three non-combatants are dead. A mother and two children. It doesn't look good, sir. You got that priest making a racket. You got the guerrillas creating panic. Maybe the best thing is to let the courts decide. Get it over with. If it's true, as the constabulary claims, that they were surprised and provoked to retaliate while carrying out their lawful duties, then they have nothing to fear."

Slate the Site Manager cut in. "There *will* be an investigation. This is certain. I was served the notification two days ago."

"Two days ago. I'm surprised you wouldn't know that, Clemmie," MacDonald, wide-eyed, mocked. "You being a valued member of the government. Now you see, an investigation is not just something that you merely and foolishly promoted. It is a certainty. Now we want another certainty. The certainty that the constabulary will be exonerated. Because you know what, Clemmie, if the constabulary is found guilty, the goddam savages would have some martyrs on their hands. Archer-Atlas will be dragged into it. The mine and the military are hand in glove. There's no need denying it around this table. If one goes down they both go down."

Mr. Aussie reassured them. He'd seen it before in the Philippines, in Honduras, in the Congo. There would be a clamour, it was to be expected, but the evidence was amply clear. Despite the unfortunate outcome, the tension and volatility of the situation necessitated the soldiers' response.

"Certainty," boomed MacDonald with a fist to the table. "Certainty means getting the right judge appointed to the case. Or at least don't get the wrong one. Don't get that goddam MacPherson who gave the sisters the okay to go snooping around the site of the encounter. You must be able to do that for us at least, Clemmie. Jesus, can you do that for us? It's the Minister of Justice who appoints judges to this case, is it not."

"You know me, sir. I'm like a bull's dick. I go where I'm pushed."

"Well, that's good, that's very good, Clemmie. See if you can get old Archie Carter from the mainland. He's a fair man, I know him well. Let's see that you do that. And now Mr. Cash, I believe you have some information from the world of high finance."

Mr. Cash spoke at a brisk clip. "The foreign investors are willing to go ahead despite these unfortunate encounters. Yet, they are getting nervous. They want to see some action. Here we have a state-of-the-art smelter operating at twenty percent capacity. We will finish digging what the permits allow by the end of the year. Whatever the hold-up with your government is, you have to right that ship."

"The hold-up with the government is sitting right here at this table," said MacDonald looking at the woman he called Widesides O'Leary behind her ample back.

"Clemmie, dear," he said, "the deputy minister, Mr. Roy, paid us a visit in October. We took him to Cape Clear, you'll remember. You know about that. You helped make it happen and we thank you for that. But do you know who met Mr. Roy at the airport? You might think it would be me, or Mr. Slate, or Mr. Law, or perhaps even my good wife, Yolanda. But no, the first person to meet the deputy minister was the bishop's man, McCoy. First mistake. A mistake that set us back two months."

"That was Mr. Roy's initiative. He knew Bishop Power in Montreal."

"Mr. Who? Mr. Wah?" puzzled Big Ran'l.

"Yes, Mr. Roy. He knew—"

"The only thing I asked was that you get Indian Affairs in our corner. You should have sewed up Mr. Wah like a spider sews the fly. You didn't push hard enough. You let things fester until the Indians went all Geronimo on us. You know why people are getting killed in the Tampakan? It's because of these goddam government hold-ups. We know that. The investors know that. If we get the permits to move on up the Ridge, if we get the permits to start digging gold, you're going to see rivers of money flowing around here. A lot of jobs. A lot of spending. All this opposition you see now, it will disappear like ice cream in the sun. You see, Clemmie? What we need is a stronger advocate in Ottawa, someone who won't rest until all the forms are signed, sealed, and delivered. Speaking of forms. Now another wrinkle has appeared and Clemmie, my dear, you're caught up in it like a willnot. It's the old canard of the phony consent forms."

"The consent forms? That's old news. Nobody believed what those Indians said back then. Why should they believe it now?"

"They shouldn't. It's just that goddam McCoy. He's trying to get the diocese to contest the forms, saying they're not legit because the Indians were tricked into signing them. If Judge Hughie, the good Catholic he is, gets pressure put on him by Bishop Power, it's only a matter of time before you get hauled in to confirm their validity."

"All I can say is, as far as I knew, the Indians were fully aware of what they were signing. That's what I believed at the time. Your good friend Lucky Dunphy was the one talking them into signing. Talking B'laan like he was, how would I know if he was duping them?"

"And do you still believe that now?"

"I've heard things."

"Yes, well, when you use words like 'duping' and 'as far as I knew,' it makes me wonder what you believe, *and* what you would say under oath. If it comes to that, it would not just be a scandal for you, it would be a scandal for the government. All I care about is it could put the kibosh on our project. But if all goes well, you won't have to worry, you'll be a former Member of Parliament by then and the fallout will be minimal. You may not even be called to testify."

"Former MP? What's... What's going on here?"

"Oh, you won't be left out in the cold, Clemmie. The Chief has taken a liking to you. You do for the party, the party does for you. There's board appointments, ambassadorships, even Senate seats. Patronage is the lifeblood of the party. A good word from the right people and I'm sure the loyalty of Cape Breton's first lady MP would be handsomely rewarded. And a woman who grew up in such dire poverty should never look a gift horse in the grinning teeth."

"I don't know where you get off. I am not going to give up my seat over a maybe, or an if that might lead to a maybe."

"A maybe is maybe I won't fund your campaign this year. Or maybe I'll put money behind MacInnis's campaign. Or maybe the Chief hears about a potential Munsinger in his caucus and doesn't appreciate being misled just before an election."

MacDonald rose heavily and caned his way to the window. He peered at the nimbus scene and breathed deeply as if to ingest the smell from belching chimneys. "Snow's starting again. What a winter, eh? Rains for a few days, all the snow goes, then boom, another big snow. Maybe you'll be stuck in Cape Breton for a few days, Clemmie. Take a little furlough." He turned to look her in the eye. "Look. Clemmie. You don't have the stomach for hardball. We're not asking you to resign. We're telling you to."

"And this 'stronger advocate.' Just who do you have in mind for this role?"

He stood up and led her to the door. "Who do you think? Mr. Cash, these foreign investors whose money we need so badly, what are their names again?"

"Mr. Sy, Mr. Danding—"

"Yes, them fellers. What kind of money are we talking about them investing in the Tampakan project?"

"It's complicated. They have a forty percent stake in a company that's got about forty million dollars invested in Archer-Atlas specifically for the Tampakan project. You figure it out."

"Well, I want you to get on the horn with them today. I want you to give them tycoons some good news straight from the Little Vatican. I want you to let them know that they will have Ronald Atlas MacDonald going to bat for them in Ottawa. Tell them they will have a full-time paid lobbyist working the halls of Parliament." All the men laughed long and loud at his gall.

Fishy Friday found the two friends in their favourite window booth. Katie let the story of her near-death experience pour out over fish and chips, weeping. There was anger. There was fear. There was humiliation at having been out-run and overwhelmed, at being turned upside down for all the world to see her underwear.

"When I got home, you know what I did? I was so mad, I took those panties off and threw them right in the garbage can. Joyce, it was the most harrowing thing in the world. Looking down at that water, seeing my books disappear into it, thinking I was next. I was completely helpless. But when I think of it now, I realize those boys who held me over the bridge had to be strong enough not to let me drop. At the time, all I could think about was that awful river and pray they wouldn't let go of me. Now, I get the shivers whenever I think, What if they couldn't hold me?

"Mommy was so angry that she marched right over to Philip MacKenzie's house and spoke to his father. I heard he tanned Philip's hide but good. When Mommy came back home, she told me to let it go. Don't let my anger get the better of me. Then she took me to Cleopatra's to have my hair done and after that, she bought me a new dress."

Joyce said, "She's trying to make you feel better. To restore your dignity."

"I need more."

"What is it? Do you want to get back at the boys yourself?"

"Something like that."

"But in a dignified way?"

She sighed. Humiliation and dignity were concepts Katie never had to contemplate. "How do I do that?" she asked.

Joyce took a sip of green tea. "My mother says that a gem is not polished without rubbing. She says that a lot. Whenever someone in my family is having a *kao yan* she says that. She says polishing the gem that you are is not about making you more prideful. Pride and humiliation can improve you or they can destroy you. Pride is good if it helps your self-confidence, but if you are truly self-confident, there is no need for pride."

"And what about humiliation, how can that be good?"

"Humiliation is bad when it leads you into shame and guilt or makes you do vengeful things. It's good when it is a guard against false pride. Humiliation is one of the ways we become humble. Think about our Santa Fina. Think of her humiliation. Every night visited by rats. Now, that's humiliation. Seriously."

"Yeah. Then I think you're supposed to say, 'And yet...'"

"Let me put it this way. It's all about courage. The Mahatma says fearlessness is the first requisite of spirituality because cowards can never be moral. If you deal courageously with this humiliation, you can increase your dignity. If you can deal with it bravely, straight on, keeping your pride in check, you can achieve humility."

Katie wasn't sure what this meant, but she knew Joyce, like Gandhi, had paid for what she peddled. Oh, the indignities of growing up Chinese in a white man's world.

"Remember the day we were sitting here and Rose made the joke to those old biddies about the McHung tartan?"

"Yeah," Katie never forgot a good giggle. "They were apoplectic."

"Well, the man down the street who sells the tartans heard about that and got very upset with my dad. He wanted him to take the tartans down. When my dad said no, he tried to have his club get people to boycott the Brigadoon."

"You mean the guy with the big black-rimmed glasses and the squinty eyes that blink and blink and blink?"

"Yes, him. Tartansocks."

"But your tartans are still up."

"You know what's funny? Dad had planned on taking the tartans down at the end of the summer, but after the tartan guy came to visit, he decided to leave them up. He said it would be cowardly to take them down."

"Good for him."

"Is it? That's what's not so easy about being dignified. Tartansocks was talking about us like we're some kind of terrorists. My sister said they could try to hurt us, but my mom said, 'No, it's in how we react that will either increase our humiliation or increase our dignity.' You can give in, or you can go for revenge, or you can do what my father did and let it be a judgment on your detractors."

"So what happened with Tartansocks?"

"That's the best part. We heard all about it from some guy named Lucky who came to visit my dad. Tartansocks took his grievance to his club, but they called it a stupid complaint from a cultural buffoon. Instead of chastising my poor dad, they made him an honorary member of their club."

Katie inhaled from her cup then placed it upon its saucer. "Something like Santa Fina becoming beatified, I guess."

"Something like that. Humiliation doesn't have to lead to shame. It can lead to recognition. It can and should make you stronger."

Katie thought about Santa Fina of San Gimignano, the city of fine towers. Daughtered into a declining noble family. Extraordinarily kind. Devoted to the Virgin. Desirous that her soul might separate from her body in order to meet Jesus Christ. In sickness and in humility, refusing a bed and choosing instead to die on a wooden pallet, though the rats and worms came to feast.

Think of the miracles accomplished in her name! The woman cured of her paralyzed hand, the falling man saved, the bells of San Gimignano spontaneously ringing at the hour of her death, Amen. Think of the mess in the morning. Think of her mother. Think of the family—her humility was both their humiliation and their immortality. Living with a saint is more grueling than being one.

"Then that's what I will do," said Katie Beaton. "I will be who I always was, but I will be stronger. I will be faster. Those boys will never outrun me again."

Hector Caffrey looked at his watch and at the locomotive that impeded their progress up the hospital hill. He would be late for his visitation with Bridget.

"The train should have passed by now. Why is it sitting there still? Does it make sense to have a train crossing right at a hospital entrance? What if there is an emergency? Cissy, can you think of a game to play while we wait?"

"Let's sing railroad songs," Cissy suggested helpfully and in moments the car reverberated with strains of "I've Been Working on the Railroad," and "Little Red Caboose."

The train lurched forward to accommodate freight handlers at the depot.

Chuggin' down the track track track track
Smoke stack on the back back back back
Little red caboose behind the train, train—

"Shhh!" Jacky yelled. "Look, it's snowing."

"Sure enough. They said it was going to snow," Hector noted grimly. "You can't trust March. It can be warm and sunny one day and a blizzard the next."

Cissy broke into *Snowflake, my pretty little snowflake,* but all grew quiet as they watched reverently the wet fluffy flakes building on the car windshield, slowly obliterating the rusted boxcars. Hector let them grow magically thick before clicking the wipers into slow-paced action.

Tommy slouched, mute and reading, during the railroad trilogy, "Trivia game people. I know you know the Nile is the longest river in the world, but do you know the next longest?"

"Next? I think it must be the Amazon in South America," his father answered.

"Yeah. And what's the longest in North America?"

"I'm not sure. The Mississippi maybe? It runs the whole length of the United States. But the St. Lawrence and the MacKenzie are very long too."

"You don't even know for sure the longest river in North America." Tommy sneered.

"Do you know?"

"Yeah, it's the Mississippi of course. In fact if you count the Missouri, which runs into the Mississippi, the two together are thirty-seven hundred miles long—the third longest river system in the world. Hell, the MacKenzie is only twenty-six hundred and fifty miles long."

"Don't say that word," Cissy ordered.

"Is that right? Kids! Be quiet, okay? Don't get into it or I'll turn around and go straight home. Cissy, can you start another song?"

Tommy looked disdainfully at the man behind the wheel. His father's temper was shorter these days and other weaknesses were being uncovered. For one, he had no idea how to cook. The best he could do was open a can of Campbell's soup. He didn't care a hoot for the children's hygiene except to say, "Tommy, your teeth are after turning right yallow." He couldn't teach Tommy as the great books of knowledge could. He did not possess the encyclopedia's certitude, the cool comfort of irrefutable facts. The tallest waterfall: Angel Falls. The biggest country: the Soviet Union. The largest lake: the Caspian Sea. The longest river: the Nile. His father's only interest seemed to lie in visiting their mother in the hospital.

The children weren't joining Cissy's latest interlude and she fell silent. "Shut up!" Jacky shrieked at Archie. Molly fidgeted and Daisy cried. And he knew it was all on his father to fix. This realization bit him as only guilt can, with a niggling in the stomach and a gnawing in the gut. In anger and pride he had wounded his father.

Those with true obsessions never see them as such. Tommy was no different. What mattered most to him was the pledge he had made to himself and his mother: to name the child that grew in her belly. The saved child. And that obsession was fed by the books stacked like city towers alongside his bed. For better or worse, Tommy was firmly in the grip of the river gods. His self-confidence buckled but recovered with their inspiration.

Tommy asked, "Daddy, what's your favourite river?"

"Okay, Tommy, I'll answer you if you sit between Jacky and Archie and keep them from killing one another until we get to the hospital."

He crawled over Jacky and squeezed between them, holding squirming Archie's arm firmly in place at his side. "Dad?"

Hector began, "Okay, my favourite river. Just wait. Cissy, can you put Molly on your lap, she's leaning into me so hard I won't be able to drive. I don't know if I have a favourite river, Tommy. Why do you want to know?"

"I don't know. If you don't have a favourite, is there any river you always wished you could see?"

The children grew hushed as they watched through the curved openings on the windshield the softly falling snow and the long locomotive beginning to crawl forward, bringing its train slowly into squealing, hiccupping motion. Rust-brown boxcars filled with coal, bullet-like tankers and crude logging flats creaked past slowly, gathering momentum, flashing by, overcoming their cars' tranquil interior with a furious clicketyclack of steel wheels on steel rails.

"During the war I had a furlough," Hector began. "I knew people from Ireland, so I went to visit them. They lived in Limerick. The river that flows through Limerick is called the Shannon. I didn't like it. It seemed to breed cold and damp like viruses breed disease. After the war, when I asked Mommy where she'd like to go on our honeymoon, she said she wanted to go to Ireland. Imagine, Ireland. We had no money to go to Ireland. She wanted to kiss the Blarney Stone, to walk through the monastic hills of Glendalough, to see Dublin's fair city where the girls are so pretty, to see the forty shades of green, to take a boat ride up the Shannon. She wanted to see Brian Boru's fort and the shrine to her namesake, St. Bridget's Abbey, where a perpetual fire burns. To hear her talk about it, the Shannon was the most beautiful river in the world and Ireland was the nearest thing to heaven, even though she'd never even been there. I didn't have the heart to tell her that what I saw of the Shannon was not very pretty at all. It was downright depressing."

He stopped there, thinking he had said too much for childish comprehension.

"So did you go?" asked Cissy Caffrey.

"Well, no, we didn't. We couldn't afford it. And now, well there's all you kids to take care of, and Mommy's sick and…"

Cissy waited. They all waited and watched unflinchingly the speeding train whip past their field of vision so furiously fast it blurred and stung and moistened their eyes and urged them to squeeze closer for warmth and protection. They waited as a wailing whistle cut the morning in two.

"No." Hector recovered. "We had a lovely honeymoon though. We got married in Port Hood and spent our wedding night in Lawrence's

Cabins, above the Harbourview beach. The next day we motored up the coast, spent three days on the Cabot Trail, and ended up back in Port Hood. Your mother loves the beaches there. Where else would you rather be in the summer, she always says."

The clacking of the train rendered inaudible his trailing voice. He stared with longing through the rumbling cars, the intermittent wipers, the falling flakes, silver and dark, dark and silver, as the shrill far-off lonely whistle penetrated the thick snowy air, penetrated and transfixed six children and their pondering parent.

Tommy remembered the last words of a book he had read. It was the Shannon that brought them to mind, but the book was about the Liffey. Whenever someone crossed a Liffey bridge, an epiphany was to occur. Each person surprised by his or her fate. The acolyte, the Indian, the bazaar boy, the dreamy stay-at-home, the gambler, the con man, the unfortunate bob, the failed writer, the sad counterparts, the longsnout, the painful case, the patriots, the mother, the drunkard, the dead Michael Furey. They were the last words and they were the correct words and they were the words that would stay with him. Yes.

Yes, the newspapers were right: snow was general all over Ireland. It was falling on every part of the dark central plain, on the treeless hills, falling softly upon the Bog of Allen and, farther westward, softly falling into the dark mutinous Shannon waves. It was falling, too, upon every part of the lonely churchyard on the hill where Michael Furey lay buried. It lay thickly drifted on the crooked crosses and headstones, on the spears of the little gate, on the barren thorns. His soul swooned slowly as he heard the snow falling faintly through the universe and faintly falling, like the descent of their last end, upon all the living and the dead.

RIVERRUN

"And this stillness of life did not in the least resemble a peace. It was the stillness of an implacable force brooding over an inscrutable intention. It looked at you with a vengeful aspect. I got used to it afterwards. I did not see it anymore."

Joseph Conrad, *The Heart of Darkness*

Inside the hospital the Caffrey family stalked corridors as cold as charity. The same sickening antiseptic smell assaulted them.

"Hello, darlin'," Hector said and they kissed.

"Oh," she exclaimed, taking a bouquet from her eldest. "Thank you, Cissy, they're beauty-full." She reached for a vase. "Here. Can you dump these old mums? There's a garbage can in the bathroom."

"You've all got snow on you," Bridget observed. "What kind of morning is it out there? I can't see from here. Is it bad?"

"Wicked scandalous altogether," said Hector.

Bridget coldly touched a cheek and smiled at Tommy. She was a shade paler by the day. "How are you, sweetheart? Have you thought of a name for the baby yet?"

"I'm making a list like you said and crossing off the ones I don't want."

"What ones are left?"

"I can't say. Lots. There's only going to be one left when I'm finished and that's the only one that will count."

"Oh." She looked at her husband, shrugging. She thought of another angle.

"What ones are crossed off?"

"Well, St. Lawrence."

"St. Lawrence? You mean like the river or the saint?"

"The river. I crossed it off because it has a big mouth. I don't want the baby to have a big mouth." Lawrence, patron saint of comedians, roasters, and butchers. Martyred on a gridiron by Valerian. Crying out, *"Assum est, inquit, versa et manduc!"* This side's done, turn me over and have a bite!

"Well, it's good you crossed that name off. Any others?"

"Amazon."

"Amazon?"

"It has a big mouth too. And it means something I didn't like. And I crossed off Fraser because it is too wild and dangerous. It's a good river though. It—"

"Are all the names river names?" Bridget interrupted.

His father had an ah-hah moment. "I think I know what's going on. The book list you made for him and all the questions he's been asking me. All those books that are piling up in his room. Now we know why. It's all about picking a name for the baby."

"But Tommy," his mother said, "you can't just pick a name of just any river. You can't, for example, give a baby a name like Mississippi."

"Why not? Haven't you read *Huckleberry Finn?* The Mississippi is a very old, proud, and helpful river. It protected Huck and delivered poor old Jim from slavery."

"But not every river name is appropriate for a baby, Tommy. You can't call a little baby Mississippi, or Zambezi or Ani G'nish."

"Why not?"

"Why not? Why would you?" his father asked. "Why would you saddle a kid with a wacky name?"

They would not dissuade him. Tommy had seized this task like Arthur had seized Excalibur. Just like Daisy was the right name for his little sister, the name he chose for this new life growing inside his mother would be the right one too. It would be a name that would also give meaning to his friendless and dismal life. It would extinguish the hurts of the past. It would make sense of loss and imbue a clouded future with silver linings. What name could possibly salve such desperate needs. It had to be a river. A river was the cause of his torment and a river would be the resolution.

It had to be the right river. The name was less important than what the river was like—how fast it flowed, what history took place there, how the people lived on its banks. The mighty, the deep, the meandering, the drudging all had their place on his list. To eliminate a river just because his parents thought the name sounded funny? That did not compute.

By the end of April, Tommy had read all the fiction his mother had unwittingly recommended. *Dubliners, The Adventures of Huckleberry Finn, Heart of Darkness, The Bridge on the River Kwai, Death on the Nile*. He reread a geography book with stories of Abdul of the Nile, Sumai of the Yangtze, Simba of the Congo, and Roshik and Moti who lived in the great delta formed by Mother Ganges and the Brahmaputra. He moved all twenty volumes of *The American Peoples Encyclopedia* into the bedroom where they were stacked six and eight high.

He pulled one from the top: Volume 14, "Mormons to Optimism." As was his custom, he first studied the picture on the inside flap. It was a dramatic illustration of the French masses storming the Bastille in their fight for freedom, July 14, 1789. The peasants wore angry faces and tricorn hats or frilly bonnets. They wielded savage sickles, two-pronged pikes, cutlasses, and longrifles fixed with bayonets. A man in striped trousers waved a double-bladed axe from atop the besieged prison. Tommy, laying belly-down on his bed, flipped through pages to find the article he was looking for.

The Murray River is Australia's longest river (1,609 mi), rising in the Muniong Range of the Australian Alps, for much of its course (1,200 mi.) separating New South Wales from Victoria, and draining an area of about 270,000 square miles. It debouches into Lake Alexandrina, and after leaving, it flows into Encounter Bay, where a bar prevents the entry of deep-draft ships. For lighter draft craft the Murray is navigable in the wet season to Albury, about 800 miles. The chief tributaries are the united Murrambidgee and Lachlan, and the Darling on the right bank, and the Gouldbourn and the Loddon on the left bank.

Tommy reviewed the article quickly and closed his eyes for a brief time to commit it to memory. Then, as was his custom, he studied the picture on the back inside cover. It was of the inventor Eli Whitney of New Haven, Connecticut, circa 1800, showing a companion the first gun made of interchangeable parts, the rifle which inaugurated mass production. A uniformed officer stood between them, surmising the possibilities and potential of the terrible weapon.

Tommy looked at his river list, then guided another volume from the stacks. He studied the inside flap and turned to an article on the Volga, the longest river in Europe. Baby Daisy began to stir. She called and Tommy lay aside his reading, slipped into the girl's room and peered over the top of the white wooden crib cooing. Shhhhhhhhhhhh. He reached into the crib, pulled a knit blanket about his sister's shoulders and cooed some more. Baby plopped two fingers into her mouth, sucking energetically, then less and less so, until she dozed off.

Daisy. Named by Cissy. Well-named, Cissy. A happy flower, long willowy green stem, sunflower yellow centre, dainty petals that spring loose with the tiniest tug. She loves me, she loves me not, she loves me, she loves me not, she loves me. When Daisy is awake and her belly not hungry and her bottom not wet, she gazes at Tommy as long as he will gaze at her. They laugh aloud and she giggles helplessly till he tickletortures her not. But when she's bottomwet or bellyhungry, Tommy carries her downstairs where someone will take care of the crybaby, crybaby, don't cry, baby Daisy, don't cry, little girl.

Except for these activities and for meals, church, and school, Tommy remained secluded in his bedroom during the lessening winter and emerging springtime. Thomas Leander Caffrey reading *The American Peoples Encyclopedia,* Volume 19, "Trent to Weld," in the boys' bedroom, 79 St. Columba Street, Findrinny Fair, Cape Breton, Nova Scotia, Canada, North America, the World, the Solar System, the Milky Way, the Universe, circa April 1962. Daisy Patricia Caffrey sleeping, giggling, crying, babbling, gazing, sucking on fingers in her crib, same time, same place.

Jimmy Dog called on him most days, bearing money-making ventures aplenty. Sometimes he ignored the knocking or pleaded sickness so as not to interrupt his study. Now, though, the door opened and Jimmy Dog appeared in his sanctuary. It was unheard of. The new housekeeper must have let him in. For months now, housekeepers had been appearing to take the place of their mother. Most of them fought constantly with Archie over food. "Itt yer porridge. Itt your porridge or you shan't get any meat." And Archie would act as if boiled oatmeal was found under P for pig slop in the Canada Food Guide. He told his father that the housekeeper had threatened to shove *maragans* down his throat. A new one appeared, a kinder one, but one who failed to understand the regulation about not letting Jimmy Dog Dunphy, known tomahawk thief, upstairs.

Jimmy frowned at the mounds of books. “I’m going jiggin’ mookies off the King Iron bridge. D’ya wanna come?”

“Nah, I don’t think so. I’m just kind of reading.”

“Yeah, sure looks like it. Don’t you want a break from all these books?”

“No. Besides isn’t it too early for mookies?”

“No, they were under the bridge yesterday. Andy Fraser saw them. They’re early this year. Come on. Andy says we can get fifteen cents a mookie from Missy Ming this early in the season.”

“Nah, don’t think so.”

“C’mon! Let’s go. I bet we can catch twenty in one hour. Kids just throw them back and then we can get those easier cause they’re half dead and stupider than ever. I watched them yesterday and made me a jigging rod today. It’s easy. Nothing can go wrong-o. Twenty mookies is three bucks. An hour’s work and three bucks. And I’ll catch more the next day and the next day.”

“I don’t want to jig mookies. I’m reading.”

“What is that? Since when did you start reading encyclopedias. Since when does anyone just read encyclopedias. Let’s go. I can make a rod for you if you want or you can just help me. I have a bucket to carry them in. Let’s go. Let’s go.”

When there was no response, he pulled Tommy by the leg. “I need someone to help me with the bucket at least.”

What Tommy intended to utter was, “I said no,” but what he emitted was more like steam being released from a boiler. He slammed his book shut and shook his head, “I said no! You’re always after me to go scrounge for bottles or look for stuff to steal. I want to read.”

“Let’s fucking go, man.” Belligerent as a battleship. The quiet persuasion was over. “Come on!” Jimmy Dog yelled and his eyes held hate and his mouth frothed like a mad dog. He was adamant now and would no more likely change than a demon would shed its horns. There would be a blow up.

To resist, Tommy thought. What would it take to resist? An iron will to stay my anger, an uncaring attitude to calm my revenge, perseverance equal to my adversary. And why bother? Surrender meant peace in our times; though it wouldn't matter, this surrendering of his time, for in the next instance of insistence, the slate would be wiped clean. Past capitulation would count for nothing toward future compromise. Jimmy Dog would forget the victory like the wolf forgets its last victim.

"Resistance is fertile."

"I wish," said Tommy. "Okay, okay. Go make a rod for me and I'll be over in half an hour."

"It'll only take me ten minutes to make a rod. We can make it on the way. Come on. Now! NOW!"

Off the King Iron Bridge they dropped their hooks, scraping the murky, muddy bottom and jigging, ripping upwards into the throats of shadeseeking mookies. Through the intervening air, flashing squirming heavy ugly torpedo fish propelled upwards still sucking uselessly through bloodpink gills and airswallowing bottom feeding maw.

Badboys swarmed the bridge. The air was punctuated with cheers, chants, curses, and insults. The usual bad words the boys had heard in the Bishop Fraser school playground seemed impotent next to the unfamiliar and overused oaths of the older boys, and the same word being used as an all-purpose part of speech—intimidating adjective, nasty noun, and venal verb. Fuck you. All fucked up. Fuck a duck. I'd fuck her. Fuck me gently. Fuckin' rights. Motherfucker. Go fuck yourself. I'll give fuck a good goddam.

Most jiggers unhooked and flung their catch back over the bridge to be caught again. The most injured throwbacks, suspended three feet from the bottom, were set upon by the ravenous unmaimed who tore clumsily at cream coloured innards oozing from widening wounds. Only when the unfortunate floated beyond the shadow of the bridge, did the cannibals abandon their gruesome meal and leave it to flipflop listlessly downstream on bloodugly currents, unpursued and soon forgotten, its skyward facing belly showing dumb, useless, senseless death, a fleshy feast for something above or below its place in the food chain.

The most sadistic of the jiggers tortured their catches. Goon MacKenzie lit a cigar, coughed a high, raw, smoky exorcism, and propped the wine tip into a mookie's grey lips. Grey killing smoke poured from its gills. Wayne the Gimp threw one onto the bridge applauding like a maniac the bonecrushing gutsplattering power of a passing milktruck. Mudsuckers, heaved onto nearby railway tracks, had their very existence obliterated into crushed and spewing fragments of flesh, bone, and vitals.

Upstream, along the railway track, were the ramshackle homes of the coloured people. Unpainted walls, bare windows, dusty yards, small kids dancing round a shriveled grandmother who sat rocking and smoking, rocking and smoking.

"Nigger, nigger," someone yelled into the shocked May day. "Lazy nigger smoking a homemade pipe."

"Hey, Mumbo Jumbo! Put you on some voodoo there."

Jimmy Dog paid no heed. Of all the jiggers, only he was intent on catching and *saving* as many fish as possible. Tommy gave him what he could catch, grimacing dramatically as Jimmy cut fish free of hook. Jig, pull, extricate, flop, thud into a pail for Missy Ming.

All of it—the killing, the swearing, the racism—made Tommy sick and afraid, and the terror he felt pounded out in a booming rhythm along the Congo riverbanks as a dugout canoe crept warily through the crocodiles and a chant went up, and chant and drum and flame bespoke of death.

BOOM, steal the pygmies,
BOOM, kill the Arabs,
BOOM, kill the white men.
Hoo, Hoo, Hoo.
Listen to the yell of Leopold's ghost
Burning in Hell for his hand-maimed host.
Hear how the demons chuckle and yell
Cutting his hands off, down in Hell.

Bright spring sun spattered the wrinkled face of the proprietor of Ming's Variety. In her flat, broad sun hat and knee-length silk pants she squatted barefoot in a dung laden garden. In one jade-encrusted hand, she held a spade. All around her, skinny stakes hoisted a crisscross of wire leads.

"Hi, Missy Ming. Mommy sent me for a Surprise Bag."

She squinted, pivoted toward the voice, and showed two uneven rows of long yellow teeth. "You Kay-tee, no? Kay-tee Beaton?"

"Yes. And I want a Crispy Crunch bar too."

"You go inside. I meet you there." Creaky, crinkly, smiley Missy Ming rose from the good earth.

Bells, buzzers, balls bouncing off flippers greeted Katie inside Ming's Variety. A boy was at the buttons. He flippered, batted, and rattled pinballs to and fro, tensely jerking his apparatus just enough, shaking it but not tilting.

Bent over like a question mark, Missy Ming entered from a back door wiping her feet on a wiry mat. "How your mother? Good?"

"She's going to a funeral today. My cousin Fiona's grandfather died. He was sixty-nine. My sister and I went to the wake this morning."

"You big girl now."

"It was my first time ever seeing a dead person. But instead of going to Mr. Finnegan's parlour, we went into the wrong room, only we didn't know it. Mommy said we were suppose'ta kneel and say a Hail Mary, but there was no kneeling place. So we just stood there and said our Hail Mary out loud to show extra, extra, extra respect. Then we shook hands with the relatives and went home. Mommy said it was an honest mistake. She said it was a Mr. MacLeod in the other parlour we went to and he was a Protestant. That's why they didn't have any kneelers, because Protestants don't kneel when they pray. She said we were not supposed to say the Hail Mary because Protestants don't say that prayer. She told our aunt what we had done and they giggled so much that my sister got mad. How were we suppose'ta know who was in the coffin? My sister closed her eyes when we got close and I could only peek. Anyway, it was an interesting thing to do, but I sure don't like to see dead people."

The storekeeper climbed a four-step ladder and from the topmost shelf lifted a stapled paper bag. Eleven similar bags lined the length of the shelf.

"And a Crispy Crunch," Katie reminded her.

In one hand Missy Ming held out a chocolate bar and a Surprise Bag and dropped coins into the girl's hand from the other. "No tax-ee, no tax-ee."

"What's in the Surprise Bag, anyway?"

"Your mother not tell you, I not tell you."

Katie skipped out onto the sidewalk. Sunlight streamed through the bare elms and gave the houses and pavement a tigerstripe look. Ahead, she looked into the slanting light to see two boys turning onto her street. They walked abreast, hands attached to a shared cargo.

Swinging their bucket forward to gain momentum, the two fishmongers swayed toward Ming's Variety. At the wholesalers they had dumped their fishing poles and were now walking sideways, facing one another. They made no eye contact, such was Tommy's hatred for the task at hand. They carried and rested at twenty-second intervals. Sweat bristled on their brows and beads bubbled above their lips. Inside the bucket, perishing, puckering, gasping mookies slid dismally, helplessly, hopelessly among their dead brethren. Tommy looked at the giant elms and budding maples casting skeleton shadows over Morar Street. There was no joy in the brilliance of sunshine. His cousin's singleminded pursuit had poisoned his slim interest in the gory enterprise. "I need a rest," he said, lowering the cargo. "How much money do you think you'll get."

"Twelve mookies. That's a dollar seventy."

"Are you sure she'll give you the money?"

"She better. Fifteen cents each. That's what the Goon said."

"What if he's tricking us."

"Well, I didn't do all this work just to be shystered. If she doesn't give me what she should, I'll figure out some way to get it from her. Okay, let's go," and they heaved the bucket up between them. Dead sloshbreath foulsmellingly puked from the lurching pail.

Tommy did not spy her until they were almost upon her. A girl holding up a bag to the sun as if to see inside. As neutral as Switzerland she greeted them. His past came back instantly, as it does for any guilty man who in an unguarded moment remembers that he hasn't forgotten. His partner dropped the weight of their longjaw mudsuckers so that Tommy's hands jerked downward in concert.

Jimmy Dog yanked a handkerchief from his back pocket and made a show of wiping his brow. He groaned like a victim of torture.

Katie rolled her eyes skeptically. "Wow, you must be so strawwng, Jimmy Dog. Lifting that heavy bucket. Look at you, your face is red as a cherry bomb. Where are you going?"

"We're on our way to Missy Ming's. Can you get us a drink of water, please?"

"Sure. What's in the bucket?"

Jimmy Dog flashed back at her. "What's in the bag, nosey?"

"I don't know what's in the bag. It's a surprise for Mommy and me."

"Well, what's in our bucket is a surprise for you too." Jimmy Dog leaned over, both hands on his hips, squinting into the pail. "What is that anyway, Tommy? What would you call that anyway?"

Tommy went along with him. "I don't know. Sure is ugly."

"Let me see," said Katie.

She shrieked at the sight. Her body convulsed and she fought off tremors with flailing arms. "Oh gross. Gross. Gross. Gross. Gross. You guys! Uyyuck! What are they? Dead fish? Are some alive? I saw one move. On my God, they're still moving their mouths. Oh, how horrible. You're disgusting." She recrossed the street, excoriating as though gizzard and stomach and spleen had become one combined revolting organ.

Jimmy stomped his feet and burst into a loud bray.

Katie narrowed her eyes and set her jaw. "You laugh like a donkey or a goat. You are so stunned. He is so stunned." For allegiance she looked to Tommy and folded her arms. "Tommy, make him stop."

She said it in an exasperated way, as if she thought it was something he should know to do himself. But boys don't help with things like that. Let her swish her ponytail all she wants.

"I wish you'd stop him."

He saw her still shivering and trembling. He saw his cousin's antics cross from merriment to mockery. "Shut up, you arsehole," challenged Tommy to no effect, so he more forcefully repeated his command. "Shut up, you fucking retard!"

They both stared at him now in stunned silence. Their looks distinct. Katie all lips and wide green eyes, her breath held. Jimmy Dog sneering with disgusted incredulity, his head shaking, his nose snorting one last time. "I was only having fun."

Tommy drew menacingly close. "Well, it doesn't look like it to Katie and me. So you'd better shut up."

"What are you doing getting in my face? Are you trying to protect Katie now? It's too late for that, you coward."

They flew at each other. Tommy's knobby wee punches and Jimmy's wild jabs cutting the April air like aimless switchblades, four fast-moving fists deforming friendship. Jimmy Dog got him in a headlock and grated one into his rival's scalp. Tommy threw all his weight against him and they tumbled onto the street. An orange head ricocheted off the curb like a basketball and blood seeped into the shaggy mane. They fought until their energy was spent and Jimmy Dog, weak and in pain, cried uncle.

Tommy fully expected the last word counterattack. It had never been otherwise. Instead, Jimmy Dog angrily brushed himself off and rubbed vigorously the budding wet welt on the side of his head. Huffing, he snatched the fishbucket with both hands, carried it awkwardly a few paces, set it down, again picked it up, dropped it and began dragging it along St. Mary Street. Tommy watched the slow, strained, scraping, unrelenting progress. From behind he heard, "You'd better go follow your friend."

Her slim counsel given, Katie opened the front door, glancing back for a second before she and her surprise bag of tampons vanished from sight. Jimmy Dog, too, disappeared around the corner. Tommy stood alone in purgatory, letting the stillness of his solitude wash over him, wash over but not cleanse him of the shameful pricks that chilled and consumed him body and soul.

Missy Ming teetered through the gate and bent her torso perpendicular to the sidewalk, her face dropped close to the mouth of the fishbucket. "You not from here," she said warily to Jimmy Dog. "Where you from?"

"Highland Drive," Jimmy Dog lied. "I caught these f-fish off the King Iron bridge. Someone told me you buy them for fifteen cents each." His eyes met hers only furtively when his pitch had ended.

"Fifteen cents. Hah! Who say I pay that? Ten cents what I pay." The woman pronounced cents like "sin" and so Jimmy Dog did not understand her at first. When he did comprehend, he gaped mookielike at her, then at the fish.

"Too many," continued Missy Ming. "Maybe I buy four, five, but this too many. I buy five. For five I give fifty cents."

"Can't you buy them all? I was counting on this money. I have to buy new skates."

"Where you skate now? No ice now."

"No, no. I'm saving for next winter. Can't you buy more? And aren't you supposed to give fifteen cents each?"

Missy Ming was not given to impracticality. Running a store whose currency was nickels, dimes, and quarters, did not allow for flights of fanciful charity. She squinted at Jimmy Dog as if solving a riddle. She spoke incomprehensibly as she climbed into her establishment.

The boy, redfaced and pacing, saw his cousin lurking across the street. "Get lost," he yelled. His plan was in shambles. He did not want Tommy gloating over the wreckage.

Missy Ming's gap-toothed smile reappeared in her doorway. "Okay, I give five cents each for other. Good for fertilize garden. Bring in here."

Jimmy Dog knew he was in no position to bargain further. He feigned thankfulness and heaved his cargo off the sidewalk and up the cement stairway one step at a time. He trailed his benefactor into the confectionery, swished the bucket past the clanging pinball machine, alongside the counter, then down a stairway lined with bottles of aftershave and cases of vanilla extract. A rusted deepfreeze snored fitfully against a dark wall. Missy Ming put five of the suckers in a deep and stained sink and, one by one, tossed the remainder into a dilapidated wooden barrel in the backyard, counting them as she did. Jimmy Dog watched silently, a queer clammy feeling settling over him.

Back at the counter Missy Ming hovered near the register while a radio blared fiddle music. She dipped sallow fingers into the till. She smiled at her vendor so that her black eyes disappeared into a yellow sea of wrinkles.

"You play hockey?"

Jimmy Dog grimly accepted a handful of dimes and nickels. When he returned to the street, he saw that Tommy was already gone. As he thrust the coins into his pocket he thought of payback. He thought of the bottles on Missy Ming's cellar steps. He thought of vanilla for sale and after-shave for the hardcore drunks. There were better ways to make money and for a lot less effort.

How incongruous of Mrs. MacGillivray to leave me this copy of *Ladies Home Journal*. What can I possibly gain from it? Well, there's this—I did not know it's taboo for the press to raise with Natalie Wood the topic of her relationship with Warren Beatty. Is she too impulsively intense? Is he too fancifully aloof? And I did not know that nowadays eyes without make-up look as undressed as lips without lipstick. Neither did I know that black and white is sweeping the nation. Anyone can wear it and it looks terrific with a tan. And oh, here's my Marilyn. She turns thirty-six in June, same as me. *Ìosa,* it's almost as if we live parallel lives. The *Journal* is big on ailments as well, plenty of maladies, chronic and acute, mild and severe—pain, swelling, stiffness of joints, burns, breakage, inflammation, rashes, dryness, wetness, foot rot, heartburn, unforced flatulence, diarrhea, constipation, and laundry woes. Thankfully a cornucopia of remedies abound in the form of Bayer aspirin, Lycra girdles, stinging nettle, Solarcaine lotion, fibreglass splints, Vitamin D, Johnson's baby powder, soothing emollients, feminine napkins, Dr. Scholl's Zino-pads, Tums for the tummy, yoghurt, Pepto-Bismol, Ex-Lax, and Javex, to name but a few. No cure for cancer, though, and time is short.

"Hello, Bridget."

"Hello, Henrietta! I didn't expect to see you again so soon. Come over here and give me a hug. Who's with you?"

Henrietta had visited before, twice in March and once already this month. "I had a knot in my womb too, Bridget," she confided on the first visit. "I had blood spottin' my underwear. I got in the bathtub and slid a finger up there and I found what I knew I was going to find. It was like someone lodged a marble up there, near the neck of my womb. I told Day, "You better take me to the doctor. I'm bleeding and it ain't my time."

Henrietta's fuller story came out in the second visitation. Her tumour had grown at a terrifying rate, she said. The doctors ordered radiation. "I remember being wheeled into the operating room and being surrounded by huge glaring lights and all them doctors and nurses in white hats, masks, gowns, and gloves, all so white, so very white. They gave me something and then I don't remember a thing until the next mornin'. I found out later that what they did was they sewed a plaque filled with radium to the outer surface of my cervix and packed another one against it. Then they slid rolls of gauze inside of me to help keep the radium in place. Then they threaded a catheter into me so I could pee. That took care of the tumor. After that, they just gave me X-ray shots, putting lead inside me to protect my colon and such. For three weeks I got that radiation shooting steady into my womb. When I showed my cousin Sadie what they did to me, when I showed her from here to here, from my breasts to my pelvis, Sadie whispered, 'Oh, Hennie, they burnt you black as tar.' And I said, 'Lord, it feels just like that blackness be spreadin' all inside me.'"

Bridget looked with acute interest at Henrietta's companion. It felt uncannily like looking in a mirror. The woman appeared to be about Bridget's age. The face was more angular, the nose sharper with a Neapolitan hook, the skin a more olive tone. But the eyes and mouth were identical and her hair was as dark and curly and uncombable as her own.

"This is Gianna," said Henrietta. "She joined the sodality just a couple of days ago. She asked if she could come and visit."

"How are you, Bridget?"

It was the simplest of questions, yet Bridget felt an invitation to unburden to this woman who exuded joy like an aura. "Pleased to meet you, Gianna. How am I? Do you have an hour?"

"I understand you have made a difficult choice."

"Yes, very difficult. Very difficult indeed."

"As did I. Tell me about yours, will you, *per favore*."

Bridget caressed her swollen belly with an open palm. "It was a choice only I could make. I could not allow my husband to make such a terrible decision."

"Why?"

"Why? Because he is not a realist. He believes too much in miracles. And because I did not want to have him live with the decision, should it go badly, I mean."

"But he will have to live with the decision."

"That's true. But he won't have to live with the guilt of making the decision, one way or the other. This is why I say it was my choice and mine alone."

Henrietta sighed. "At least they gave you a choice, Bridget. With me they just started in on the radiation and by the time they told me their treatments would stop me from having more babies, it was too late. I don't believe I'd have gone through with the treatments had I known."

Bridget took Henrietta's hand in her own. Just like piano keys, she thought, ebony and ivory. "Oh, Hennie, darlin', I know. It is a terrible thing to give up the gift of bringing life into the world."

"You know what I believe?" said Gianna. "I believe one's life is like a river. Our lives are rivers and like all rivers, we have a name. In this river is a boat. It may be smooth sailing for that boat, but it won't always be. There will be shallows and rapids. The boat can go through this channel or that channel, it can sail straight into a strainer that tips it upside down. Or with adept paddling or safe portaging, it can avoid the danger that leads to ruin. Sometimes what is required is heroic action. But even the little choices we are presented with have the power to prepare us for heroic action. At those times in the river of life, if we surrender ourselves to God and his will for us, we become better prepared for even more difficult choices downstream. Our boat is less damaged and better able to navigate the length of our river. This is what you have done, you have lived a life of genuine holiness and wise choices and God has entrusted you with a personal vocation."

"Is that it?" asked Bridget. "What if one's life is like Henrietta's. We don't all get to make our choices. Even the doctors here practice what I call benevolent deception. They were ready to withhold even the most fundamental information from me on the pretext that they didn't want to confuse or upset me. I had to fight to find out my diagnosis. Is that part of God entrusting me with a personal vocation?"

Henrietta said, "Do you know what Gianna told me today? She says because of me, thousands of lives have been saved and the terrible scourge of polio has been wiped out. My doctors never told me anything."

Gianna seemed to be examining her conscience. "We doctors must learn to be more forthcoming, yes, but if we are not, women like you must shake us out of our reverie. As for your persistence, Bridget, this is who you have become, a person who asks questions, who wants answers, who makes informed choices. It is part of your make-up. It influenced the vocation that God has given you."

"Lord, Lord, I'm tired," said Henrietta, "I think I'll sit down while you two talk. Why don't you give me that magazine on your lap, Bridget. Do they still have that column in it about saving marriages? I would always read that one in the waiting room."

Bridget talked as she flipped through the magazine, "Yes, I know the one you mean, Henrietta. You like that column? I never read it, not since I saw the kind of advice they give to wives. No matter what the couple's problems are, the counsellor always finds a way to blame the woman. Like the one where the counsellor tells the wife that to refuse to have sex with her husband after he hit her would just touch off another inevitable explosion. Can you imagine claiming that the wise and loving wife is one who accepts this twisted treatment as a form of ardour? That was it for me. I'd rather read the phone book. Oh, here it is, 'Can This Marriage Be Saved?' I think it would be better called '*Should* This Marriage be Saved?'"

Holding out the magazine, Bridget looked up into the eyes of the duty nurse. Her visitors had faded away as swiftly as they had appeared. The nurse looked wary as she held out the pills. "Have you had any visitors this evening, Mrs. Caffrey?" she asked. "It can get awful lonely up here without someone to talk to, can't it?"

BONANZA

From *The Crypt,* May 1, 1961, under the headline:

Capion Murder Complaints Dismissed

In a resolution dated 26 April 1961, prosecutor Archibald Carter ruled that pieces of evidence submitted by the complainant, the Diocese of Findrinny, are insufficient to establish probable cause to find Lt. Alexander MacKillup and 13 other members of the constabulary guilty of murder. In his resolution, the prosecutor gave weight to the testimonies of MacKillup and other soldiers who claimed that a legitimate encounter took place at the Capion house that resulted in the death of Juvy and her sons. Carter based his ruling on the physical evidence that the spent M-14 and M-1 Garand casings reportedly found at the site of the encounter could only have come from the rebels. Father Steel McCoy, representing the Diocese of Findrinny, said, "The killing of the Capion family bared the true face of the constabulary and how they are being used to protect the interests of investors. The fact that they can evade court proceedings against them shows the impunity enjoyed by Archer-Atlas Mines and the company it keeps. The Diocese of Findrinny intends to continue to pursue justice for Juvy Capion and her children."

Tommy awoke before the sun rose, tiptoeing, stealing through darkness, pulling a wagon laden with coppery cargo. Squeaking, straining past wooden wimpled heads of the sisters of our lady, a monsignor's stony granite gaze, the one-fingered cenotaph pointing to Orion—an obelisk to remind you of the soldiers for pride and glory dead in Flanders Fields where poppies grow between the crosses row on row, and across the Wheeler Bridge to where looms Castle Fina. And who, Castle Fina, do you keep hidden high high in holy solitude. Who is in your keep? Cinderella? Sleeping Beauty? Rapunzel? Rapunzel let down your honey hair. A beauty spinning golden honey thread from honey golden hair. Climb, I will climb to you and kiss and spin about your castle keep, dance and spin and kick and kiss and kiss and kiss and kiss and kiss. I am Sir Thomas, knight-errant of the table round. With my chariot red and coppery treasure, rolled on reel, to purchase thy freedom and mine. Spin for me a silvery spidery web of finest maidenhair and I will spin for you a terrible tale of tyrants, dragons, ogres slain in thy name.

No time for dawndreams. Work to do. Heigh ho, heigh ho. Here I hide my coppery cargo. Here. I hear but do not see the brook babbling by. Silvery sounds and sparkles in the starlight. Hear the brook flowing, glowing by, my little babblebrook. Haul thy treasure now and heave it here in hideaway hidden. We will see my coppery confession by sunlight later when we three walk past. The past. Too much the past. Too much the past. Turn the page. Turn the page. Toss it away for a rainy day. Wonderful, it would feel wonderful to be free of it. But you protect, you see, you protect the past by treasuring it. Tommy, can you see me. It is the future arrayed before you, the frightful future. No, it's the present. I am Tommy in the present with Jimmy Dog. I am sacrificing my soul for Jimmy Dog Dunphy.

Need a bottle too. Bottle will be his bait, later, when by water we come again to Castle Fina to find our buried treasure. But hark. Hear? And look. See? A faint light on the horizon. See! From the gloom a turret appears, rising, pointing, beckoning for me to come. From such height did sweet Juliet to Romeo call. But soft. From such height did the guillotine fall. But hard on the neck of the guilty Antoinette. Lost her head poor thing. From such height did lovely Hero wait and mark the way night after night for her lovely Leander to swim across and lay his head on her bare breast and kiss its curve and its nipple pink and lick with lingering longing upon the pink the sky blue pink nipple where Daisy sucks her loving rich sweet thick milk and I remember too my mouth on her nipple sucking for all I was worth on her belly crawling like an insect toward my lifeblood and feeling it burst into me willing myself to live.

Need a pole too. A good hard one. Something that can stretch and not break. There, near the castle, perhaps a pole. Amid the debris, the not-make-believe refuse of a not-long-for-this-world putrid-smelling filling station. But yes, by yon fender lies a shaft of broken Sherbrooke, a busted but strong shinny stick. Remember how free the ice under his skates, the cheering children, the puck skipping,

skipping across the Salt Ponds to the net. Shit, it's stuck. Dig it out from greasy grass, a dirty bladebroken stick lying in a stench of rubber, gas, catspray, piss, puke, oil pooling in footprints, spiralling in puddles, purple polluting paisleys of petroleum. Smells to make you sick. Dipping his finger in an oilpool, he touches forehead, chest, and shoulders. An oily pretend blessing. It's oily make believe.

See the first streaks of rose red dawn creep upon the door. Door ajar. Everything's bilingual these days. Push. Push again. Creak open into interior darkness. What if? Yes, a stairway spiraling, ascending to the keep. Should I finally see what so oft I dreamt? And still I wonder. Yes. Feel my way with feet and hands slowly, step up, step up, step up, rounding, spiraling, dizzy if too fast. Ascending round slow steps, sounding soft but loud as cannons because only me. Loud as the charge of the light brigade with cannons to the left of me cannons to the right of me into the valley of what awaits only me. Fina Castle in your castlekeep what do you hide? Pirate treasure, pirate sword, sleeping beauty, sleeping whoo-er. At the top, another door awaits. Yes yes yes. Push. Push the door and see inside the keep where so oft I entered in my dreams. See Aurora's rose red rays creep. Rose is the colour of my true love's room in the morning when I rise. In the morning when I rise. See? Yes a princess on a calendar. 1957. No, not a princess. Pretty but no princess. And no pirate treasure or fearsome dragon or magic mirror or table round. No Launcelot. No Guinevere. No honey haired princess. Sad, paling Aurora shines only on curled and bloated girlie magazines, corrosion oozing batteries, busted brown beer bottles, cigarette butts beneath and around a rusted busted bedspring.

Close my eyes and stand still. If long enough, the scene will correct. Tightly close my eyes against sight, my nose against smell, my ears against sound, my mind against the end of innocence. Hark! She speaks. A princess lying on rose red rusted spring. Tonguing her dry lips she beckons me to her side.

Brave Knight, why have you ascended high to my mean estate?

I have come to rescue the lady of the turret. If you be that lady, you are the one I have come for.

Who are you?

I am Sir Thomas. Who are you? And why do you lie in misery?

I am Fina. I do penance for my sins.

What terrible crime did one so young?

Many.

The worst, tell me. Confess and I will absolve.

On a day meant for dalliance I read the rhyme
Of Launcelot and allowed love to master me, then
With another of my tender age was guilty of a crime
I gave this boy an orange sweet wet ripe and red
But when my conscience spoke guilt was my reward
And now I lie on cruel springs and will 'til I am dead

For this you suffer fair Fina?

I do by my own decision, I do but for the Lord
In the company of mice who squeaking come
To nibble scraps and crumbs that fall upon my floor.

Holy Santa Fina fair and true
Over this you suffer and die? An orange!
May miracles be accomplished in your name
God be with you. You are released of your bondage to sin.

Sir, are you such a mouse?

You are released from your bondage, I say.

Why are you here?

I smote the dragon and am here for thou.

Why do you call me Santa?

You are the promise of innocence and the depth of suffering
Lying alone with only rodents
To remind you that life exists outside this keep.

Yes, they are my friends in the dawning
Chased by the rays of the sun
To appear again in the gloaming.

With that, Fina faded and his eyes beheld the sad same scene, brighter now and void of rose red hue. Seeing, accepting till sadness consumed, he crumpled to the dead floor staring with burning eyes at the littered remains of his daydreams, feeling the sadness of lingering loss. And now they would take Daisy away. So Cissy said. She who knows all. They were finding a home for Daisy and the new baby. Katie, his mother, now Daisy. Within the female was the acceptance he longed for. But why do they leave? Different reasons, the same result. Loneliness. Learning. Starting again. Losing again. Learning nothing. Starting again.

A raven appeared in the branches beyond the shattered glass. With a maw that opened and closed like a clockwork closet, it mocked his foolishness.

Gorach.

If he could go to Katie and say to her, remember we were friends once. Remember the time in your backyard, snow angels, hot cocoa, your honeyscented breath in my face. Do bees follow you around, Katie? Do bees sense your sweetness and want to drink of your nectar?

Gorach.

Don't stay away forever, Daisy. Grow and laugh and learn but don't stay away forever. I'll give you a daisy a day, dear. I'll give you a daisy a day. I'll love you until the rivers run still and the four winds we know blow away.

Gorach.

I will decide, Mommy. Won't keep you waiting, wondering, worrying, waiting for me beyond where the rivers meet. I will give you a name.

Dawn had fully broken when the boy escaped the tower's must. Homeward he pulled his barren squeaking wagon, not seeing on his right the sympathetic gaze of the bishop, saints, and sisters who mutely whispered advice. Not hearing on his left the silvery stream's sage counsel. Be free like me. Homeward bound he trudged morosely bitten by a banished dream, assuaging bitter pain with faint hope, rubbing into open wounds the stringent balm of reality.

Ach, you're as *gorach* as the crows.

My thirty-sixth birthday. Just me and this little life growing inside. If I could only see. *Ìosa,* why do they put the window so out of the way; you'd think I was going to leap to my death.

Is the sky grey with the coming of rain? With little girls' faces pressed to a pane and hopes of a picnic dashed to the earth? A day with no hope of laughter or mirth, when dreams of an outing seem to pass with the splish splash splatter of water on grass. But my sister Marie said it won't matter, dry the tears from your eyes, we'll make up a platter and head to the barn. We'll have us our picnic just you and I. I can still smell the smell of the last of the hay, the horse in his stall, the new lambs at play. With our dolls we sat on my fifth birthday on the wide threshing floor as daintily we sipped at our hot sweet tea and rocked up and down on a wagon with wheels taller than me, high wooden wheels much taller than we, we rocked and we talked of what summer would bring. We'd be free as the breeze that rustled the leaves. Over the flume she would run to Papa making hay, or climb in the mow and jump up and down, and swing on a rope and do all of the stunts Mama warned us about. I'd sing of Loch Lomond and the Rose of Tralee; she'd dive from the wharf and swim in the sea. We'll sit on the beach and tan in the sun. O think Marie of all of the fun. We'll sit round a fire and listen to fiddles and soar through the air like the down of a thistle.

Is the sky clear with but wisps of white? Is it as it was on the day I turned twelve with ribbons in my hair and new leather shoes, when Papa said round the islands we'd cruise. And we all laughed my brothers and sisters and I, and my mother bore a basket of biscuits with butter, and I bumped my head on my first boat ride. The salt in the air and the wind in my hair and they said I looked the fair bonnie lass on the prow with a squint in me eye and a dimple in me cheek. The mackerel they caught on invisible lines, all blue and grey with flashes of green like emeralds from the sea in which they had swum. They seemed to know their time had come but not with sad eyes just the smallest of frowns, with flashes of life like the kick of a colt, slippery, sliding, slapping their tails like all fish do, from the smelts to the blackfish, the silver darling herring, the trout and the hake, the glistening gaspereaux they catch with a rake. For my birthday round the islands we toured on a boat with a sail that flapped like a flag, and swung past our heads when they tacked with the gales. Look out below! A frightening commotion when the men would arise and dash to and fro, with clamorous calls, and laugh they would laugh when all was okay. And we'd sail with the breeze to'rd the island of hay and she'd open her basket and tell us to dig, and we'd dig at the biscuits and brownies and squares, there's lots here for all, so we'd fill to the gills and off again we'd go with the wind in our sails.

I remember another one blossoming May, just Hector and I in the last light of day. Sweet sixteen, so young and yes handsome, or so I'd been told, young and so handsome, clever and bold. Though love would be distant, a wartime away, and other boys kissed me at the end of the day, it was his tender touch that stayed with me, my darlin' dear, and lingers still now in my memory clear.

Is the air hot and dusty, sultry, shimmering, gay, as on that day when I boasted hurray and showed them my pay, my very first pay. And Papa brayed, "We'll be out of hock and eat chicken tonight!" The pay wasn't great but the benefits were, for there's not a child that I taught who's ever forgot Miss Dunphy the Stern who made them laugh and still made them learn. Those earnest wee girls and serious boys tracing line after line in search of the divine with fingers rough from pulling and chopping and digging in stuff. I wonder now did they know what Blake meant? What dread hand indeed, what immortal eye? Or did by rote they learn my own blind faith, untested by tragedy, temptation or hate, nor loss of direction or life's evil jeer or kismet, fate, destiny's leer.

Whose cruel jest does test this faith so well?

Hector says that all we need to do is believe and pray to the Virgin Mary. He gave me a novena that he is praying. "The Virgin Mary is a demanding mistress, sir," said I to him as Mrs. Bread said to Newman. She'd seen it herself. All the prayers and petitions, down on their knees beating their breasts, fasting and flagellation. Mary demanding and merciful. Pure, holy, and unattainable, mother yet virgin, human yet immaculate, sadistic yet mild. O mystical rose. O tower of ivory. O mother of pearl. O Mary most chaste by the men. If you're over the age of twenty-three, don't you think you should be marrying? Either that or join the convent. Is it true, I wonder, that story of the girl munching coal dust to repent for her sins? Thinking, she was, that the Virgin Mary told her to do it. That's what Anne Marie MacDonald said. But it's only the few take it too far.

Anyway, Hector does enough praying for the two of us. He expects a miracle. That note he sent me when I was last in Halifax. I cried when I read it, and I cried too for reasons that I could not speak about.

I keep it in the drawer here next to me but I don't need to read it. It's been committed to memory.

God made such a wonderful decision when he brought us together. No two people could have loved one another more. You are the perfect wife and a model mother. I know God will leave us together for many years to enjoy our dear little family.

It makes my heart ache. I had a choice and I made it. But I had a choice. I had a choice. It was mine to make and no one else could make it for me. Not the Church, not the doctors, not Hector. It was my Gethsemane. My agony in the garden. The sorrow in my heart is so great that it almost crushes me. He left his disciples then and went to pray and I prayed with him. He threw himself face down on the ground and I threw myself down with him. My Father, is it not possible to take this cup of suffering from me. He went to his disciples then and found all three had fallen asleep. Keep watch he said, and pray that you do not fall into temptation. How do mere mortals make such a decision? Only in faith. Only in faith can we be strong enough. It is the greatest gift. In my darkest hours, I pray for faith.

I know God will leave us together. There is so much to live for. So much that is beautiful. In a garden, a place of beauty he prayed, amid the flowers and the trees and the pools and the vines and dates and figs and olives and grapes, and the moon shining from above. So much to live for. The sound of bells, the smell of roses, the sight of sunset, the taste of strawberries, and oh my lover's touch. The spirit is willing they say, but the flesh is weak. But oh the joy of flesh. Caress me with your fingertips so that I might feel again the pleasure of love. Gaze into my eyes so that I might lose myself in you and you in me and hold these precious fleeting moments for as long as we both shall live. Grow big in me and never let me go.

I know God will leave us. Will I too cry, *"Eloi Eloi lema sabacthani?"* I will be dead and dead I will lie on a flowery bier, in a casket of wood, on a pillow of satin, cold and still, and the children will come to kiss their cold dead mother and I will not be there. Where will I be? Will I be? Will I be far away from Findrinny Fair, stretching ghostly arms across a gulf so great that my consolation cannot pour out into them. A still decaying body. The flesh is weak. We all will die and dying our flesh will fall away as my flesh diminishes even now.

I know God. And I pray to God. I pray that ministering angels be at my side in my hour of need, that guardian angels stand always by my little ones. I pray for this little one growing inside me, that she or he will know a mother's love. I pray that they will all know how much I love them and that this sacrifice will be for all of them a sign of my love, and they will know the good shepherd will leave her flock to assist the one who may be lost, be it the first or the last.

I pray for Hector that he will be strong and gentle. For the world, that hearts will be full of love and free of hate, that prejudice and bigotry and misery be banished, that the high and mighty will be brought low and know the lowly, that the rich will know the sting of hunger before it's too late, that those who say they are not rich may see how wealthy they really are, for all should be fed and nourished and nurtured.

I pray to whomever might hear me, let me know that you are with us when we pray to you, and yes, maybe its sign enough what Molly Bloom said... "God of heaven theres nothing like nature the wild mountains then the sea and the waves rushing then the beautiful country with the fields of oats and wheat and all kinds of things and all the fine cattle going about that would do your heart good to see rivers and lakes and flowers all sorts of shapes and smells and colours springing up even out of the ditches primroses and violets nature it is as for them saying theres no God I wouldnt give a snap of my two fingers for all their learning why dont they go and create something..."

This far upstream they had never ventured. Explorers three on a rambling path through tumultuous tangles of new green they flew. And oh the buzzing of the bees and the lemony trees and the ripe catkins like caterpillars hanging from willows by the brook and birdsong filling birch and bush. A dirt path worn smooth by sneakers and bicycles and oh, there's a grackle, flying close over the brook. Look how green blue black his head. Look how iridescent.

"Guys, hey, taste this. It smells lemony, but it's sweet."

"No, I won't taste some sticky, stinky bud fallen from a tree. See, even you squirrel up your mouth. I can tell it's awful. Hahaha, Jacky ate some bud and now he's nearly throwing up over there. Look,

Tommy. Your other half a brain is barfing up a lung. And the brook is so low. Remember how deep in February? Deep and scary."

"Let's play cowboys and Indians. I'm Geronimo."

"I don't want to play that. That's for kids. Let's go this way."

"No, let's stay near the brook."

"A squirrel! Drift a rock at him!"

"Don't do that, Jimmy. He's not hurting us."

"Just a friggin' squirrel. Andy Fraser took me huntin' last week. He picked off a squirrel and a chipmunk."

"He shouldn't be doing that."

"What's a frigging squirrel? They're good target practice, that's all. I'd shoot one some quick when I get my pellet gun."

"You shouldn't have a gun if you're going to be killing innocent animals."

"Innocent? Innocent? Are you retarded? They're only friggin' squirrels. It's not like they're on trial or something."

"Let's skip stones! Let's slit the devil's throat!"

Quicksilver splashes sprang and vanished zzzp zzzp zzzp and his mind went into the river with them, to the contraband hidden a half-mile downstream. When all were in bed and the lights turned off, he had gone looking for it in Daddy's superorganized electrician's shop. They had it out the day they went to Cape Clear, the day Big Ran'l's buttermilk-breath and chewing tobacco voice droned on and on about all that mining crap. It wasn't with the bigger spools of thick black wire or the smaller tinny reels. The coppery roll was tucked behind a false wall, as if hidden from sight.

Tommy said, "Do you think it's a sin to hook something if you do it to help someone who needed it more?"

"Maybe not," said Jacky.

Tommy said, "Every morning before daylight, Huck or Jim would slip ashore and hook a watermelon, or a mushmelon, or a punkin, or some new corn, or things of that kind. Sometimes Huck would snatch a chicken if he could find one. They'd cook the food on their raft and go to sleep with full bellies. Huck's father used to call it borrowing, so Huck thought that it was okay. What do you think of that?"

"Sure, why not." answered Jimmy Dog, "As long as they're not borrowing *my* frigging chickens."

"Huck said his pa taught him it was fine to steal stuff if you were meaning to give it back sometime. But Huck's father was no good, and the Widow Douglas reckoned it was stealing. Jim figured they were both half right, so he and Huck decided not to take *all* of the stuff."

Jimmy Dog offered a thoughtful reply. "Sounds like stealing to me. But if they needed something bad enough, it's alright that they took it. Too bad when you're in trouble you can't just ask and someone would help you out. There's lots who need things and lots who have more than they need."

"What bridge is that?" Jacky said, pointing ahead. "There's no bank to walk on. Hey, I know where we are. Let's go up that path. It takes us up to the Wheel."

Tommy didn't want to leave the brook. The hidden reel was just beyond the shadow of the bridge at the edge of the fairgrounds.

"But the water's so shallow. What are you afraid of? Just take off your sneakers if you don't want them to get wet. My feet are hot and sweaty anyway. The water will do them good."

"Shit, are you kidding?" Jimmy said. "Look at that polio slime. And there might be broken glass under there. No frigging way. Meet you on the other side.

Under the bridge, shadowy cool calm replaced the light of day. Sneakers slung, trousers rolled to the knees, Tommy walked alone. The splashing of his feet made an echo, so he tried his voice. "Findrinny," the bridge repeated with a hollow tone, but he had to watch out for the unseen slippery bottom with its glass and rubbers and shrapnel, and the lurid green algae clinging to its stones. Worse was the smelter waste drifting microscopically into the river, joining with the cleaner waters downstream, and flowing out to an accepting harbour, filthy and purifying like the Ganges to the Hindu. Tommy knew something about the Ganges. He knew that tens of millions of Indians who live in the Gangeatic Plains defecate daily in the great river and that all that shit flowed in freely as well from its many tributaries. This shit will not kill the river.

He also knew that hydroelectric dams were being built along Hindu's most sacred waterway. They will obstruct the Ganges and choke it. Neither will this shit kill the river. The Ganges will defeat the dams. It will send tens of millions of quartzite granules to penetrate the stainless steel turbines. The dams will clog and die. And the Ganges will remain as incorruptible as a mother's love.

Sunlight.

Tommy called, "Hey, Dog, come down here. I think I see a beer bottle. Two more pennies toward a new pair of skates." But the bottle was mere bait. The treasure lay beyond.

"There's something else here!" cried Jimmy Dog from the bank. "Lookee here. Look! Look! Holy shit! Look, Jacky! Jesus, come look at this! It's a bunch of copper wire all rolled up nice and neat. Man. This is worth big friggin' bucks. I can't believe it."

"Jeeze, I wish I'd went for that stupid bottle," Tommy lamented. "Then I would have found the copper. Looks like it's all yours, Dog."

"You're friggin' right it's all mine. Finders keepers, losers weepers."

"Reckon must be worth nine, ten bucks."

"Whoa! D'ya think?"

"Sure looks it. Hey we can take it to Beets now. It's right there. And look, there's a hockey stick. We can carry it with that... Cool, a Sherbrooke, my fave, man."

Beets Backup was an unholy trinity of store, yard, and bottlebarn. The Store part was a dingy walled-in verandah attached to the Horthon Street side of Beets Fraser's house, functional-minimalist in style. A high counter ran the length of the dark room. A heavy cash register squatted at the far end. Behind it rose dark shelves stocked with nuts and bolts, fishhooks, hockey cards, chocolate bars, bubble gum, cans of Libby's beans in molasses sauce, tins of tuna, pickles, rat poison, flyswatters, No-Pest Strips, matches, pouched tobacco, rolling papers, lost and found golfballs, baseballs and pucks, pine tree air fresheners, chainsaw oil, Brylcreem,

.22 calibre bullets, bottle openers, vanilla extract, and aftershave. Through an open doorway into the house proper, the boys could see blood. On the chesterfield, flopped over like he'd been shot, lay a member of the family. Above him hung a brace of rabbits dripping blood on a splattered circle of newsprint.

"Hey, Mister," Jimmy Dog yelled at the corpse. "Wake up. Wake the fuck up, you old drunk."

A low rectangular box sat in a corner. Along its front was written Nesbitt's ORANGE. Jimmy Dog snapped open the lid and lifted it high. Five rows of identifying caps faced the boys. Batlike their bottles hung from metal runners, necks grasped loosely in the slots, orange, green, pink, black bubbly bodies hanging into the cold vacuum.

"Anybody got any money?"

Tommy said. "I got a dime. I'll get a pop and we can all split it. We're rich, right?" He laughed and clapped an unsmiling Jimmy Dog across the back. "Kiddiiiing! Dog's rich now. But he'll pay me back. Right, buddy?"

"Let's go out," said Jimmy Dog, and the three of them stepped from darkness to bright sunlight. This was The Yard, undulating, hard trampled, where half-tons and Chevys as long as lobster boats unloaded trunkloads of bottles and departed ten minutes later pocketing a greasy wad of mad money.

The third member of the Beets Backup complex was The Bottlebarn, the money-maker in the triumvirate. All around its earthen floor, swept hard and clear of debris and pockmarked with trampled bottle caps, stood cardboard boxes and wooden crates of empties, stacked six feet high and just as deep—three full walls of Moosehead, Oland, Alpine, Keith's, Schooner, Ten-Penny, Red Cap, Molson Ex, Molson Canadian, Labatt 50, and whatever other malted oddities Findrinnians might drink.

A gaunt man in loose fitting clothing shifted boxes from one stack to another. Fucking the dog, Beets would call it. His black hair was piled into a greasy, compulsively-combed bouffant. A bloated red growth like a giant June bug reared from his neck. From the back pocket of his baggy-arsed trousers jutted a long leather billfold umbilicalled to his belt loop by an even longer iron chain. The stacker kept up his charade until he was sure no adults were with the party. Still ignoring the boys, he raked a comb through his thick slick hair, then pinched tobacco from pouch to paper, rolled a makings, and snapped a match.

"Is Beets here?"

"Gone to a ball game. I'm in charge. Ya got something?"

"Copper," answered Jimmy Dog manfully. He stepped aside to show off his bonanza.

"Where'd ya steal that?"

'We didn't steal it," Jimmy Dog said. "We found it by the river. If you don't believe me, ask them."

Jacky couldn't tear his eyes away from the purulent neck inflammation even when the man stared and asked him something.

"It's true. He found it." Tommy pointed to Jimmy Dog. "We were walking down the river and there it was under some bushes.

Carbuncle removed his twisted wire of a cigarette and curled his upper lip. He eyed them suspiciously. "By the river, eh? Looks pretty goddam new. Couldn't have been there very long. Why would all this *copper* be just sitting beside the river? Tell me that. We sure as hell ain't going to buy any stolen copper here."

"I don't know. Maybe somebody hid it there and forgot about it." Jimmy Dog felt his jackpot slipping away. "Anyway, finders keepers, right? What will you give me for it?"

"Give you for it? I'll give you for it. In fact I just might ask you little shits to leave this copper here till we hear if anyone lost a roll. The town cops might be interested in seeing it too."

A long Ford crept into The Yard and emitted an adult customer, a tiny-lipped woman wearing a shin-length flower-bedecked dress and Dame Edna glasses. The man grabbed the reel and made for the office, yelping foolishly over his shoulder like a dog riding its tail. The boys hustled to catch him.

"You can't come in here," Carbuncle slammed the door, but it caught Jacky's foot and rebounded into the room. "Little Christers. Get in here and get this over with quick. I got customers."

He pointed to the weigh-scale. "Hoist 'er up there." He tapped on the counterweight until the numbered bar leveled, pulled a pencil stub from his shirt pocket, wrote a few figures, and showed the paper to Jimmy Dog.

"Thirty-four pounds. Ten dollars and twenty-five cents!" the boy yelled. "Can you believe it, guys? That roll was worth ten dollars and twenty-five cents. I'm rich! I told you the money was in copper."

"Okay, you little shits. Now shut up about it. Once you get your money, you're not going to say another goddam word about copper and selling it here. You got that? Not a goddam word. If you did steal it, and I think you did, I'm not getting in trouble for buying it. Let's go into the store and get your money. Move it."

The shadow of Annie Big Archie MacDonald darkened the doorway. Amazing how the teacher's attitude toward them had flipped since Katie was hung from the bridge, when Tommy became the coward and Jimmy Dog the hero. She put her hand on Jimmy Dog's Herculean head and asked him a question. The old Jimmy Dog, the one who had no use for teachers, would just have lied and went about his business. He would have said we brought in a bag of bottles and are just getting our money. Automatic. But something about this teacher who was nice to him would not allow him to do it. The Dog just stood there, his mouth opening and closing like a mookie.

"James? Jacky? Thomas? Have you all gone deaf or dumb?"

Jimmy Dog put it to her straight. "We found this roll of copper by the river. Thirty-four pounds. He thought we stole it, but we didn't. No big deal."

Carbuncle moved in front of the reel. "We sure as hell ain't going to buy any stolen copper here at Beets Backup."

Mrs. MacDonald looked like she just smelled a jar of earthworms that had been too long in the sun. "I can vouch for this boy, sir. He's one of my pupils. He's honest and trustworthy."

"Well," said Carbuncle, giving the heave-ho gesture. "That's good enough for me. Let's go get your money guys."

The teacher looked dubiously behind Carbuncle's back at the newly found reel. Her gaze continued around the office taking in the broken-armed typewriter, the overflowing trash can, the pin-ups, the rifle propped in the corner. She looked back to the reel and gave the stacker a withering look.

Annie had grown up on a farm in Bornish. Nothing fancy. No fine clothes, no make-up, no accessories, never even heard the word. She got her first piece of jewellery when she turned sixteen, a locket with a small diamond set in red findruine. Her mother hung it close round her neck where the diamond dazzled and the findruine gave colour and mystery to her plain round face. "Annie dear, you have a good mind and you will go places. But you are no beauty, so use what you can."

"I'll take a closer look at that reel, if you don't mind, Mister… What is your name by the way?"

Carbuncle gave her a name and stepped aside.

"Well, Mr. Dort," she said, "it looks like the boys have something a lot more valuable than copper here. But perhaps you already have an inkling of that. The boys do not seem to know it themselves. If you haven't concluded the deal, perhaps you can tell the boys what thirty-four pounds of red findruine is worth. Something more than ten dollars I should think. I bet you could give these boys oh, six or seven hundred dollars and Beets will still make a tidy profit when he sells it to the merchants. Is he in? Oh, too bad. I'll mention it to him next time I see him."

Jacky and Jimmy Dog were leaping like they had just won the Stanley Cup. Jimmy Dog jumped and pounded his fists in the air, hollering victory and lunacy and the names of all the things he would buy. Jacky right there with him, the jerk.

Tommy stared wide-eyed after them. "A new… rifle?" he said aloud, forcing the last word into the open. "What about the new skates? Wasn't skates what this was all about?"

"I'll get skates too. I'll get the best hockey sticks. I'll get an air rifle. Shit, I'll get a .22. Why not. I can buy whatever I want. I'm rich."

Tommy followed them from The Bottlebarn and watched as they ran ahead of Carbuncle into The Store. He thought of a red squirrel sitting bushy-tailed on a low branch, its dark eyes rung by a ring of white, an acorn spinning expertly between teeth and claws. Pow! Off with its head and all that's left of that life is a redspewing decapitated carcass twitching on the forest floor.

"Thomas, Tommy?" he heard Mrs. MacDonald's voice speaking from an authority that seemed alien among the pungent smell of stale beer, musty earth, and damp cardboard. The sound of her clipped voice registered like a radio droning in the background.

"You know I think it's time you let go of the past. It is not right to hold a grudge, you know. It was a very mean and dangerous thing to hold Kaydee over the bridge. You did something wrong and you were punished for it. But it seems you have a hate on for me ever since. I had hoped you would learn something important from it, but instead it seems you have lost that opportunity. Other boys were punished many more times than you during the year and their... their trespasses, were often less serious."

She waited for Tommy to turn around and agree with her. It wasn't as though she didn't like the boy, but his behaviour, which was outwardly mannerly, suffered from a scornful introspection. She recognized her own disdain. Once trust is broken, she liked to say, one is always on one's guard.

The boy kneeled in the dirt, picked up a bent rusty nail, and began to dig at an embedded bottle cap. He flipped it loose, threw it against a stone to knock the dirt from inside, and shoved it in his pocket. He began to write on the ground with his nail.

"Am I right, Tommy? You may have doubted that I meant well for you, but I did. Everything I did was for your good. I hope you can see that."

He stood to face his accuser. Sunlight slanting in the front door engulfed her from her black flat-heeled shoes to her shimmering hair. The stream of dusty light ended in an even black shadow upon Tommy's sneakers.

"I didn't do it."

"What didn't you do?"

"I didn't try to hold her over the bridge. The other guys did. I just stood there like a coward. Maybe some of them were actually trying to hold her up. Did you ever think of that? They didn't let her go. That's what I was afraid of. That they would drop her. I know I shouldn't have just stood there. And they should not have treated her so roughly and scared her so much. Poor Katie."

"You didn't hold her over?" The teacher scoured a three-month-old memory. "Well, why did her mother say that you were one of them when she wrote her note to me?"

"Yeah, I was there, but I didn't grab Katie. Jimmy and I came running up afterward, but he brought the workmen with him. I didn't help at all. Just stood there like some stupid coward."

He looked from his shoes up into the teacher's dark and silent silhouette. His meek attitude and a face that displayed a pathetic need for answers softened the teacher's certainty. When she did answer, her voice was unsteady. "Mrs. Beaton's note said what boys were there and that James helped Kaydee. She said James helped Kaydee get home. I assumed the rest… When I asked Kaydee later who was there, she said she didn't remember." Mrs. MacDonald stopped speaking and asked Tommy to approach her. As he obeyed, he emerged fully from the shadows.

"Is that true? You didn't hold her over the bridge?" she muttered.

As his eyes adjusted, Tommy felt he could see this was significant information for her and detected also a willingness in her to believe him.

"Yes. It's true."

There was a momentary slackening of Mrs. MacDonald's piercing gaze. Then she shifted it to the earthen floor, her jaw set tensely with the anticipation of admission. "I'm sorry, Tommy. If what you say is true, you really shouldn't have been punished just for standing there. You weren't a coward; you were probably just scared. I am really very sorry." She adjusted her large frame to shadow the rays from his squinting eyes.

Tommy frowned. Shouldn't have been punished? Shouldn't have been humiliated? Shouldn't have lost my Hero? Does she have to stare at me like that with her glassy eyes and her fat, ugly face and her little painted-on lips? Probably just scared? That's what a coward is, scared stiff. A coward cowers when others are being brave. A coward is so guilty that others cannot even put words to his cowardice. Only he knows the depth of his shame. Shouldn't have been punished? Didn't they know he would admonish himself enough, that the juices in his stomach would conspire against it, burning ulcers into its hidden folds and crannies? His chastisement with a leather strap just made public his own internal humiliation.

Like two gunfighters they stood in the sunlight and shadow, waiting. Why did she stare so? Was it forgiveness she sought from him? Only a priest could absolve someone of sin. She should go to confession, kneel in a dark place, and say an act of contrition. It was not his job to absolve her, and besides, to do so might steal from him that which had grown like a cancer, a malignant tumour, invading locally and expanding by metastasis. Not a cervical kind of cancer like his mother had, but guilt, guilt, unrelenting guilt compounded by humiliation, guilt nursed in silence, guilt fermented by time, guilt as familiar as the face in the mirror. Guilt that not even the grace of God could relieve.

The other two had returned, Jacky carrying cold bottles of lime rickey, cream soda, and orange crush; Jimmy Dog fingering a bill. "He gave me a twenty dollar bill and some change for the pop machine. We'll get the rest when the bank opens on Monday. Thanks again for speaking up for me, Miss."

"Yeah, thanks," repeated Tommy, "thanks a lot." With a backward glance he followed the woman moving to the open trunk of her car. Spangles of light glinted from her spectacles and reproached her for her interference, her age, her ugliness, and her stupidity. Tommy shook his head and snorted away any pity he may have felt. "Old bat," he whispered, "too bad *you* don't get cancer and die."

"Right now," said Jimmy Dog, "Right now! Let's go to the Canadian Tire. I'm gonna buy me a .22."

"That's not your money," said Tommy.

"Not my money? Like hell it's not. Finders keepers you said."

"We were with you when you found it and all you're gonna get us is a bottle of pop?"

"Okay, I'll buy you guys each a Daisy Red Ryder. C'mon, let's go look at them."

"What's a Red Rider?" Jacky asked.

"It's an air rifle. It shoots BBs. They can shoot the eyes out of frogs and chipmunks, anything like that. Then I can blast them to smithereens with my .22. The frogs in Bullfrog Swamp won't stand a chance against us."

Jacky waved his arms and squawked like a blue jay, "Dad! Dad! Dad! Alright, he's stopping. C'mon guys, we'll get him to drive us to the Canadian Tire."

"You said you were going to buy skates, not get a rifle to kill animals. That's why I wanted to help you."

"I just told you now, didn't I? I can buy a rifle *and* skates, and Daisy rifles for you two if you want them. C'mon."

Tommy wasn't going to talk Jimmy Dog out of it. Even if he admitted to placing the contraband, he would not be believed. Jimmy Dog did what he wanted to do and molded his viewpoint to suit his desires. It had always been so.

"It was probably you who told Katie's mother that I was on the bridge."

"What are you talking about?"

"It was probably you that told Katie's mother that I was on the bridge that day. You were the only one who could tell her."

"You're more retarded than I thought you were."

They locked on each other's eyes as if looking away would constitute a retraction. Jimmy Dog folded his arms and intensified his glare. Still staring, Tommy held high his bottle of pink pop and tipped it menacingly. The liquid moved up the bottle and fell gushing from its height, splashing onto the trousers of the two boys.

"Jerk!" steamed Jimmy Dog, jumping back. "Look what you did." His fists tightened, but a blast from Hector's horn pulled him away.

"C'mon Jacky, let's go spend some money. Leave that arsehole here."

The Strato-Chief pulled away. Tommy could see immediately Jacky's mouth motoring into the story of the red findruine find. One essential way the twins differed was in the power of discretion. This just might be, Tommy realized, the fatal flaw in the entire Copper Caper. If Tommy was discrete, Jimmy Dog was like Fort Knox. Jacky, not so much. Unless they swore him to secrecy, and they hadn't, he would blab it all over town. Already he would be in breathless braggery to their father. Jimmy Dog's primordial secrecy would be no match for this orgy of truth-telling, no defence for how quickly Jacky's impulses would jeopardize his fortune. Hector Caffrey was no fool. Thirty-four pounds of reeled red findruine—now where do you suppose that came from? Thirty-four pounds of findruine worth more than his father would see in a month, two months maybe. Not two minutes after it left, the Strato-Chief reappeared, a look of deep puzzlement plain to see in its driver's eyes. Tommy got the hell out of there.

Diefenbaker had dropped the writ. These were the words that Ronald Atlas MacDonald had been waiting for. He told one of his senior legal staff, "You're on my team, Bill. In fact, you are my campaign manager. Here's what I want you to do. We'll seize the momentum and keep 'er moving through the election and right on through to the opening of the Archer-Atlas Gold Mine. First thing is the nomination meeting. Make it quick and make it big. Get ads on radio and TV and in *The Crypt*. Invite every registered Tory. Get Clemmie to move my nomination to show there's no breakage in the ranks. I'll go after bigger fish. Get Mr. Diefenbaker on the phone.

"John, I want employment to be the main plank of my campaign. And the Tampakan Ridge Project will be the sheen on that plank. Mining has always been the backbone of Cape Breton and with the development of Tampakan Ridge, mining will be more lucrative than ever. It just fits, you know. It's like Yolanda says, 'All the stars are aligned.' Just think of the jobs. Now if the party can help by sending Mrs. Fairclough here for my nomination, well, that would be just the cherry on top, wouldn't it. You'll do that for me. Thank you so much John. If she could come here and see for herself the preparation we've done, and how close we are to creating more jobs, more wealth for the people of Cape Breton Highlands, I have no doubt that she will authorize the next stage in our plan. We'll double our copper production by year end and within a year we can start taking out the gold. And how about yourself? Do you remember that promise you and Olive made? Within the year, you'll visit Findrinny Fair. Well, how does a whistlestop tour of Cape Breton sound, with a Saturday evening rally in our fair Findrinny?"

His nomination was staged at the parish centre. Bagpipes led the dignitaries to the stage, ten sets of them exploding into the echoing hall. Media from the Halifax *Herald,* the Sydney *Post,* the Findrinny *Crypt,* and every radio station on the island brandished microphones and scribbled in pads. The Minister of Indian Affairs was treated like visiting royalty. Her speech touched on the history of mining in the area, hinting just enough that the best was yet to come. Lame duck O'Leary moved his nomination. She was seconded by a man from the Acadian Shore. "Covering all the bases," was how the campaign manager put it.

MacDonald had shrewdly considered the content of his acceptance speech. There was no one opposing him, of course, so the nomination wasn't a concern. He could make a target of the Liberals, but they had been trounced so badly last time, they were of little concern. They would serve only as the butt of his jokes. In deciding on his theme, the nominee was entirely preoccupied with the opinion of the Minister of Indian Affairs. If Mrs. Fairclough remained in her job post-election, it was her say-so that would open the Tampakan for massive development. If the minister saw the overall worthiness of the project, the wheels could start turning immediately. The sound of five hundred Tories chanting her name, "El-len, El-len, El-len," was like grease in those wheels. The fact that Mrs. Fairclough had come to Findrinny at all was mythical. That she came to crown a shoo-in nominee soon to be a shoo-in Member of Parliament meant one thing to Ronald Atlas MacDonald: mountains of gold and copper and whatever else the Tampakan had to surrender.

After a few potshots at the Grits, MacDonald went into his old woodcutter act, using his clanging left arm for effect, pounding out the step by step way that a hard-working man can get ahead in this world. He extolled the party faithful to trust implicitly in their own potential for greatness.

Greatness was jobs. Greatness was regional revitalization. And behind them all, the riches of the Tampakan, which would be in the grips of communist guerrillas if not for our brave constabulary. Resource development. Jobs. Jobs. Jobs. A chicken in every pot.

"These are our rights," he said. "And here we have a choice. Do we want to go up or down? Do we want to go up to reach man's age-old dream, the ultimate in individual freedom and prosperity, consistent with law and order, or do we want to go down onto the ant heap of totalitarianism. We choose to go up! This is the essence of the new Conservatism that Mrs. Fairclough and I espouse."

The Tories would be back in power in Ottawa, that was a given. Diefenbaker had won the biggest majority in Canadian history just four years previous and O'Leary had won the local riding by an unheard-of nine hundred and fifty votes over some Liberal upstart from the university. It was the power of the Chief, most said. Not just that, said MacDonald. He was there. It was organization.

According to MacDonald, elections in Cape Breton Highlands were won and lost not by campaign platforms but on two jobs. One was the party's capacity to get out their vote. It was easy enough to know how people would vote, but some needed a boot in the arse. Complacency would not be tolerated with party loyalists. The other job was to sway the less than ten percent of Cape Bretoners who were open to influence. Both parties considered this remnant electorate as a bitch considers the runt of the litter. Weak. Willing to suck the hind tit. Incredibly, though, it was this rump that sometimes carried an election. What influenced them was no great mystery, he said. Name recognition was important to some, but a bottle of rum was equally important to just as many. That the undecided could be swayed by platforms and policies was a curiosity that MacDonald dismissed like a spit of tobacco juice.

The national strategist said, "Perhaps we should start with name recognition then."

The rest of the team laughed till manager Bill raised his hand for silence. "If someone in Cape Breton Highlands hasn't heard of Ronald Atlas MacDonald, they must be deaf in both ears and dumb in between. He's the most famous man on the Island. He's a successful businessman, an employer, a community volunteer. He's a war hero, for Jesus sake."

In the orchard behind the Caffrey house stood an apple tree unlike all the others, as squat and gangly as the forty others that surrounded it but far more tempting. The lowest branch was a simple mount, always was. It lead to another uncomplicated step and another, until magically you were at the crown and the way back down looked as complicated as chess.

From the tree's highest perch, Tommy surveyed his neighbourhood. The entire orchard was a bouquet of pink and white blossoms; behind him the Protestant school and CJFF; to the front, his house, the woods, and his babblebrook hidden behind spring foliage; and far below him, beyond tangle and branch, the cold, damp earth and the Brobdingnagian Pit.

Tommy doubted. The day before, he had trundled down the cathedral hill, his confession done, his penance said. What good did it do him? The priest's forgiveness salved just the surface of the soul. This doubt filled a gulf between his earliest memories and this complex present. The doubt he felt gaped like the distance from his treetop perch to the hole in the ground below. The great hole he avoided out of desperate fear of never emerging. The pit filled with memories of fingernails coated with clawed dirt and the sound of his own voice calling, Mommy, Mommy, help. The pit, despite the branches obscuring its blackness, was ever-present. It recalled ancient fear, desperation, and sweet salvation. He was five years old then, new to the neighbourhood when he had been swallowed. He could see the sky above. He could hear the chickadeedeedees out there somewhere, maybe in the apple tree. Whooo are you-oo-oo? they whistled. How he had wailed. How he had languished before help arrived. He pleaded with his cousin. Don't go, don't go, don't leave, and prayed that he would come back with the rope like he promised. And Jimmy Dog did return, tied his cord to the apple tree, and helped Tommy pull up up and out, turning the pit from tomb to womb and its inhabitant out into sunlight reborn.

Through all the intervening years they'd been best friends. Comrades in adventure from the Salt Ponds to the woods, from the Bishop's Bowl to the college rink. Sure they argued about the Canadiens and the Black Hawks and fought on different sides in the Indian wars, but Jimmy Dog was always true. Their small differences, once just expressions of themselves, were now etched in history and defined by reputation. Jimmy Dog the Hero and Tommy the Coward. Whatever had been their relationship, it had fallen like last year's apples and lay rotting in the dead black leaves deep in the womb tomb pit below.

Now the boy descended the apple tree, noticing how everything had grown smaller, the distance between steps, the last jump to the ground. The Pit was so deep then. Now it seems I can stand in it and it would scarce swallow me.

Once in, knees tucked to chest, butt wet, the smell of damp soil and fermenting apples about him, he closed his eyes. I am not big, I am small. I am ten, I am seven, I am five. His breath came unevenly. He kept his lids shut because to open them would extinguish the fear. And with it the memory. The trick, he remembered, was to *breathe* away the fear so that the memory would return in crystal controllable clarity. "Mommy!" he wanted to cry out. "Help!" But his mommy was in the hospital amid the smell of ammonia and roses. He breathed away the need to call out. Jimmy Dog would appear, they would be joined by a cord, and Tommy would ascend into light. That was then. He did not need Jimmy Dog anymore. He did not owe him; he had paid for his life with a reel of red findruine. He opened his eyes.

A beam of sunlight shone in the hole. Tommy looked away, blinded temporarily, and sought relief in a dark corner. Leaves and apples had piled deep in that spot. Black except where it was lit by a lone shaft of Sol. Funny that the beam shines only there, thought Tommy. How long had yon compost waited for its corner to be warmed. A soft, sizzling smell escaped the pile as if being cured of frost. The beam moved over it like light through a magnifying glass. Something was there.

He pulled at the earthy, leafy, woody appley pile. It was darker and wetter in its belly. No warmth was there in the absence of sunshine. No way to wake the fetid gut from its wintersleep. There *was* something. He was certain now. There was a protuberance below. Hard stone and slick wood. It was miraculous. There in the belly of the fearful pit was his long lost tomahawk.

It was a sight. Stuck with mud and leaf like tar and feather, worm-eaten rawhide, decorations ruined, shellac tarnished. Disgraced and abandoned. But what of the life of its creator? How his fortune had fluctuated in its absence. Not since it disappeared did the woodsboys play war. There was the fiasco of his fall for a girl, a foolish ride that began in Hero worship and ended in cowardice, humiliation, and loss. There was the evergrowing rift with Jimmy Dog. Tommy hugged the talisman to his chest. There was so much to tell. There was Daisy being taken. There was his mother withering away. And to add insult to injury, there was the Black Hawks' humiliating loss to the Toronto Maple Leafs in the first round of the playoffs. The Toronto Maple Leafs had won the Stanley Cup for God's sake.

The tomahawk, wiped clean of mud and leaves, restored to its past magnificence, would be handled differently now. Its worth would climb to apotropaic echelons. Never would the amulet fall again into the wrong hands. In his cousin's possession, it had been used for destruction and evil. Treated with respect, the tomahawk would bring good fortune, he was sure. Only he, Tommyhawk, could give it the measure of awe and purpose it deserved. He would keep it hidden from prying eyes. He would touch it twice during a day, at first light and when darkness fell.

When it was too much to bear, he let his excitement slide out of him in waves of joy. Like the tide, the excitement returned again and again. Generously released, generously received. Tommy Caffrey couldn't believe his luck. His fortunes were rising like a Bobby Hull slapshot. He clutched the tomahawk tighter. He couldn't wait to be alone in the woods with it. Only, he didn't have to wait for the woods. This pit would do.

The presence was warm, a swirl of wind and a rustling of leaves. Something was in the Pit with him. Something Unseen. It spoke a word and the word was "Come." The boy felt worms under his clothes, crawling and creeping into armpits and underwear. Under the earth, dirsh and gungy sluggish snails dripping trails of silvery semen, hinching closeward, forward march to stink of flesh. Unfresh earthworms winding, shining, brown termites squirming, swarming maggots wakening, slithering around the rotting pine box. "Come."

The worms left him then and he was off flying over Findrinny Fair for many a lightning mile following his babblebrook through the farms and fields, through the Split, and over the verdant valley of the Indians, high into the Tampakan and beyond, over the forests of yore, with trees like skyscrapers. Here were the crystal clear rivers and brooks of his dreams rising and settling with the rains. Here were the pristine savannah and boy-browned trails, crossed by armies of ants. Here was a dusty village of thirty stilted homes. Here in the back of beyond the B'laan lived like savages, early to bed, early to rise. Except, when under the spell of Yullgai, they would gather to watch the moonbeams play on Bong Mal and brighten their view of the Three Sisters.

Tommy hears explosions, fourteen stuttering, echoing bursts and it is over. A blood-drenched stillness descends upon the village, but only for a moment. A woman cries out. Loud voices grow in escalating and commanding fury: "Stay in your houses! We will search you one at a time!"

Another shot. Calculations are made. Another shot. The search lasts a half an hour, while four bodies lie bleeding. The lieutenant calls his troops together. The constables, nodding through pinched lips, listen to his instructions. Gesturing angrily, the lieutenant barks at the people, "Lay them in the square so everyone will see them. Leave them out till the moon comes up, then do whatever it is you pagans do with them."

The soldiers go laughing to Numnum. When they turn their backs, a woman rushes forward. She is a water ceremony dancer, a midwife, and a healer. She goes to the mother first and holds her wrist, raises her eyelid. The boys are dead too. She feels the baby girl, Vicky, here, there, here, there, and hustles her away.

The soldiers will not be back until the next afternoon when they come to plant shells that they themselves will find.

"Do you see their faces, Tommy? Do you see what is left of them? Do as I tell you. The horrors you have seen here are not a dream. They are happening at this very moment in time. Speak to your friend James. He too has seen these terrible things but does not believe. Find him and tell him to come to the chapel tonight. There you will meet my messenger. She will confirm what you have seen this day. Then you will seek out the wisdom of an elder of your tribe, someone you trust, and tell all that you have seen. Choose someone who will know what to do. I insist on this. It is what you must do. You will not hear from me or see me again until you return the stone of this tomahawk to where it was given to you a year ago. Do you not remember what I told you then? You will have this gift for a year. You are to care for it and believe in it. You do remember. Yes, I see you do. When you do as I demand, you will be born again with the strength of the tomahawk upon you. Go now from this pit to do your duty before it is too late."

The Sunday after he became his party's candidate for the June 18 general election, Ronald Atlas MacDonald began a kind of see and be seen campaign. The tour began with 8:00 a.m. mass in Port Hood, followed by the ten in Mabou and the twelve in Shean. He arrived late for each and made such a clang-bangthankyoumaam that entire congregations went forth and shared news of his Convivial Presence. It was great fun. After the noon mass at St. Mary's, the candidate had opportunity to talk politics to a group of party stalwarts. To the right of the church they met, the scent of sure victory fueling their self-importance. Near the end of their cigarettes, Big Ran'l edged closer so they could smell the buttermilk on his breath. He spit and lowered his voice, surprising, since there wasn't a Liberal within fifty yards.

"Did you hear about old Cameron up in the highlands?" he said. "The old *bodach* was having a wolf problem, see. The wolves were eating his sheep and other farmers' sheep, all through the Margarees. So didn't they send a woman up from Halifax to talk to the whole lot of them. Well, here she comes and she's going on and on about how the wolves are such and such and such and such and the best thing is not to kill them but to capture them live, then castrate them. She didn't say castrate, mind you, that would have seemed too violent. She said, 'You neuter them, you see.'"

And here Ran'l made a pinched face and a snipping motion, like an old woman slicing a blade through rawhide. "'You neuter them, you see,' she says, but old Cameron's there at the back scratching his head, looking at the other men like this woman is definitely not from around here, and finally he stands up and says, 'Lady, you're not understanding the problem here. You've got it all wrong. The wolves aren't fucking the sheep, they're eating them!"

The tale won a guffaw from the men, even those who had heard it before. He told it so well and with such certainty that it actually happened. Pretense trumped all for his believers.

On the Fourth Sunday before the Election, the candidate travelled an inland route to John the Baptist in Whycocomagh, then on to St. Joseph's in Glencoe Mills, and to a second St. Joe's up the Southwest. On the Third Sunday before the Election, he attempted a five mass marathon. By noon, he had been to morning masses in Pleasant Bay, Cheticamp, and St. Joseph du Moine, spoke at a late luncheon put on by his Acadian supporters, and made it back to Findrinny in time for a Presbyterian tea. At the stroke of seven, he was clanging his way up the cathedral's centre aisle, just ahead of the opening procession, all eyes upon him. In the one day, Ronald Atlas would be seen by two thousand worshippers.

The preacher at the cathedral was a certain Father Willie Gillies. He was competent enough, though enfeebled by a droning toneless delivery that had them nodding in the pews. On this evening, though, and despite having given the same homily at earlier masses, Father Willie felt imbued with a sudden conviction in the fine words he was spouting. It came out in his voice. All took notice, the rector included. "My God," he said, "you gave the same sermon this morning, Willie, and I was unmoved. Was it all in the delivery?"

Father Willie wondered himself. "All I know is that it felt as if my voice was given supernatural vent. It felt like it wasn't me talking but someone through me."

"Perhaps there was someone," said the rector, "speaking through you, I mean. That kind of oratory can only come from the Holy Ghost. Appropriate, I suppose."

"What do you mean?"

"Appropriate. It being the season of Pentecost."

From where he was looking at his watch, the candidate for Cape Breton Highlands had enough of the preacher's overflowing sermon. Not so much because of the tone and content as these were uplifting to be sure, inspiring even. If he could just wind it up. That was the problem. Big Ran'l still had the 8:00 p.m. mass at the college chapel to catch. They were a different sort down at the university, snobs and fairies, reverend doctor this and reverend doctor that. A priest in every residence. As nosey as grandmothers. And like grandmothers, they would forgive a hard-slaving student for being late, but not an old codger like me who has nothing better to do than hang around until Sunday to go to mass. Maybe I should have had my driver wait for me instead of telling him to pick me up after the chapel mass.

Had his thoughts not drifted to such banal meanderings but remained attentive to the message from the pulpit, Big Ran'l MacDonald might well have avoided what was to befall him. He might well have avoided the chapel altogether.

MacDonald always had trouble negotiating the one and only stairway to the lower campus. It was a two stage cement and brick invention with a sturdy black iron rail for support and vine-covered side wall for beauty. In the winter, forget it, the snow and ice broke an old priest's leg or a professor's arm every second year. But by now spring had taken hold, darkness came late, and he was man enough to cover the distance in five minutes and arrive just ahead of the opening procession. He took the first step down, the second. The next five steps were easy enough. But just then a young woman came blasting up from the lower campus, running like a madman, three steps at a time.

"Oh," she said with her hand on her chest, "I didn't see you there. You scared me."

Strangely, it wasn't his significant handicaps that did him in this Sunday evening, it was an awkward pivot into a too-fast turn so as to get a view of the runner's young ass. The *cromach* that faithfully held his left flank in good walking order slipped and went flying from his grip. His lower left appendage, taken by surprise, was not up to the sudden jolt. The leg crumpled. He sought balance instinctively with his good right arm. MacDonald had taken the precaution, as he always did, of having his strong flank positioned near the black iron railing. So strong was his right that he was certain it could take his two hundred and sixty pound girth and fling him over the rail like a pole vaulter. But the ivy creep, even in May, had begun and the green unfurling leaf buds confused and tangled his fingers. Safety hazard he thought in a flash, as the vine snagged his good arm and his useless left arm swung round behind him like a backward haymaker and with a dull iron clank struck the rail. Boom. He was crumpled on the first landing before he knew what hit him.

Within three long laborious breaths, two young women were panting over him like puppies. One was the runner with the unassessed ass. The other was an Indian. Her coal-black eyes bored a hole in him. She was removing his tie, opening his white shirt, with the practiced hand of a healer.

"Are you all right, Mister?" said the runner. "We can't get you up, you're too heavy."

"You go get help," the Indian said.

"Okay. You stay here with him, Erita, I'll get some campus cops. Big ones. We only have a few minutes to get to mass."

The Indian scuttled around him like a beetle. Lifting his head onto her lap, she pulled a lacy veil from her purse and dabbed at his brow. "Get some water too. I'll need it to clean this cut on his forehead."

"Ow, Jesus! Easy with that rag. Leave me alone. I can manage on my own."

MacDonald's pinstriped suit was a patchwork of scuffs, his fashionable fedora as flat as a Legion beret. He slapped it against his good leg and moved onward stiff, sore, and staunch, the Indian trailing in case he dropped again. He did the chapel steps gingerly, but the sight of the congregation seemed to revive him so that he threw off his helpers like Samson crashing the pillars. He lurched into the back pews, jostled a startlefaced student, and moaned like a wounded cow about his bruised arse. Young faces turned to the disorder of sanctity. He ignored them. What did they matter? They would be voting in other ridings. Jesus, they would be voting in other ridings. It dawned on him now how foolish he'd been, putting on the Pharisee for a congregation that was half come-from-aways. But he couldn't leave. He could barely stand up when the time came. Or kneel. How the Jesus was he going to accomplish that trick? He stood up, he sat down, he zoned out. Young voices purred, "Praise to you, Lord Jesus Christ." Missed the gospel, he thought. What does it matter, I've heard it four times already today.

The homilist moved into position in the pulpit.

I have much more to tell you, but you cannot bear it now.
But when he comes, the Spirit of truth,
he will guide you to all truth.

With slow and burning recognition, Ronald Atlas took in the voice of the preacher. Jesus, it was that potlicking McCoy who was up there. MacDonald perked up as if he were catching the priest in an unguarded moment, spying on him so to speak. What in the name of God does he have to say about truth?

"When the apostles spoke to the crowds at Pentecost," McCoy continued with a flourish, "they were able to preach to all these visitors to Jerusalem, people who spoke a dozen different languages but could not understand one other. The apostles were able to preach and have everyone understand them because they had been imbued with the Spirit of Truth. No matter what language those people thought they understood or didn't think they understood, they understood the men from Galilee. This must be one of the Spirit's greatest gifts. To have people hear you despite their limitations and despite your own limitations. It can only be done with the help of the Spirit.

"We have with us here today, a young woman who will speak to you about the truth of her life. What I ask is for you to hear even though you do not think you can understand. I say this because we are in conflict in our community and it is time for us to take sides. You cannot remain neutral, for to take no side is to side with the oppressor. What is happening is too important to ignore. I have invited someone to speak to you this evening. She will complete my homily."

The last comment drew a reactionary swell that lasted for two heartbeats then subsided. MacDonald, for his part, tried to prolong the murmur. "Goddam woman sayin' the sermon. That can't be right."

The Indian he'd met outside appeared like a wisp from the side aisle, chin held higher than demure. On her head, out of respect for the customs of the church, she wore a small square, a paper napkin perhaps. It made her look foolish, MacDonald thought, as she ascended the winding iron staircase. Twenty-five years old, he guessed, never could tell with those people. He elbowed the startlefaced youth, "Why couldn't she wear a proper bloody veil."

"And thank you to all of you for having me. You know when Father McCoy invited me to come and speak to you, I said I would be afraid. He said, 'Don't be afraid. This is your chance to speak truth to power.' So thank you, Father. It is a rare privilege. You know, my people have a name for your Father McCoy, We call him Padre Steel, so I will call him as my people do. We call him this because he has proven to us to be strong and incorruptible and we want him to remain that way." She smiled at the priest and took a deep breath.

"I am Erita Sagada. My people are the B'laan. We live far from here on the Tampakan Ridge. We live under the guardianship of The Three Sisters and show respect to our benign creator Melu who lives beyond the clouds. We are real people. Padre Steel tells me I have some truth to tell you. I do. It is this.

"I will speak to you of my brother, the *plamu,* the salmon. Each year, when the leaves turn orange and red and yellow, the salmon come. Each year the Indians come from all their villages, from Cape Clear to the Three Sisters, from the back of the Tampakan, to the villages at the foot of Kitanglad. From all over Unama'ki we come. Mi'kmaw and B'laan, we come to the rivers with our spears and our baskets. We come with our children so that we might teach them. The salmon we greet joyously for they have come so that we may have life. They leave their eggs so that more of their kind will be born. We thank them as we spear them.

"The river that you walk over every day on bridges so that you do not have to touch her, the small river you call Findrinny Brook, for us is called Miabut Plamu. It means She Who Brings Us Salmon. But now she does not bring salmon. All the other rivers bring salmon. But not Miabut Plamu.

"O people of Findrinny, have you not felt the departure of the salmon and the trout and the gaspereaux who once filled your stream? As you suffer downstream eating mudsuckers, we presume, we suffer upstream with no fish for us. It is only the beginning. A great rain is coming that will poison the waters, but that is not a positive message either, is it Padre Steel? I am sorry.

"My positive message is you can do something about it. You can stop the source of the problem. You can stop the Archer-Atlas Copper Smelter. The owner of the company is here in this church right now. I met him on the way here. Good evening, Mr. MacDonald."

The congregation turned toward him because that is what you do when someone points. Even if you never poke your nose into gossip, you will automatically react to a fingerpoint. Look over there. Where?

There. Jesus, it's Ronald Atlas. You're right. Big Ran'l himself. Look at the look of him. Is he loaded? Who is that young lad he's up against? And those who chummed with him and those who were employed by him and those who did business with him and those who listened to his sermons, looked at him askance for the briefest of moments. And still she ranted like a true Newfoundlander.

"Mr. MacDonald is running for election. He will be interested, I am sure, in what you have to say about the salmon and why they no longer swim in the Findrinny Brook. Do you not know why we Indians no longer produce findruine, that beautiful gift that made rich the people of Findrinny and made peaceful the relations between our people? Do you not know that it is because of the poisoning of Miabut Plamu? Do you not know that when our river is clean and our salmon return, we will again mine and create and bring to you the gift of findruine? Mr. MacDonald knows this, but he does not want it to happen. He has no interest in findruine because he cannot control it. Why do you think he works so hard to get mining rights and timber rights?

"One last thing I have to say before I step down from this high pulpit, perhaps my only chance to speak to you, and I see some of you are leaving. Good-bye, Mr. MacDonald. This is a prayer for my sister-in-law, Juvy, who died with her children in what the soldiers call an encounter. Please pray with me. Let us pray that the souls of Juvy, Jordan, and John will find peace and rest. Let us pray that justice will make their deaths not in vain. Let us pray that the salmon may again swim in the Findrinny Brook. Amen and thank you."

The two cousins were assaulted by antiseptics and disinfectants. The iodoform pierced Tommy's lungs like a heart attack and the ammonia cleared his sinuses like catpiss. So sick, so sick, he wanted to throw up. Why would someone inflict such a malady on another, as though bleach was the most normal inhalant in the world. He followed the smells to his mother's sickroom. We have got to get you out of here, now! Mommy, this is awful for you. It is frigging poison in here, Mommy. I swear to God you'll die in here if you have to keep smelling that. Out of the way, let me puke. But he held them in, the words and the vomit both.

Icy fingertips touched and lingered on his cheek. From her wrist, a watch swung loosely.

"How are you, sweetheart? Have you thought of a name for the baby yet?"

"I'm still making my list and crossing off."

"I know. It's an important decision. Stick with it, sweetheart. You'll do it."

Jimmy Dog said, "Get on with it."

"On with what?" she asked.

When Tommy had gone to Jimmy Dog about their mutual nightmare, the horrifying deaths they had witnessed, Jimmy Dog claimed he had no clue what Tommy was talking about. He would not go to the chapel mass to prove anything. The next day, too, he remained in denial.

"You have to remember! My spirit guide said you would know the names of these people who were killed."

"Your spirit guide. Hah! What are you now, some junior Geronimo?"

On the third day, Tommy brought a clipping from a yellowing edition of *The Crypt*. Big black letters: **"Three Killed in Tampakan Encounter."** Names were named. Jimmy Dog laid aside the paper and turned his back to Tommy and lowered his big orange head. "Was his name Jordan?" he asked.

"Yes," said Tommy. "Like the river."

"I thought it was Pop. Maybe Pop was his nickname. Pop Capion. I liked the name as soon as I heard it. I would like to say to him, 'Hey Pop, how ya doin' buddy.' But I can't do that. He's gone. He was the same age as me and you. Now he's dead. So what are we supposed to do about it?"

"We're supposed to go to the hospital and speak with my mother. She'll know what to do."

"Visions," said Bridget Caffrey, putting aside the clippings Tommy handed her. "Visions are very hard to trust, aren't they. You can never know if what you have seen is true or imaginary. You boys are very lucky to have each other. You have a kind of confirmation. But what a terrible thing to confirm." She reached out to her brutish nephew who flashed his eyes as briefly as ever. Some things never change. She let go of his hand. "You know, when Indian boys are about the age of you two, many of them are sent on a vision quest. They go to a secret place and pray that they may have a vision, one that will help them find their purpose in life, their role in the tribe, how they may best serve their people. Maybe that is what happened with the two of you. You went to this secret place, this hole in the ground you both knew about. Maybe you felt afraid, maybe you felt that something important was going to happen, but whatever spurred it on, you had a terrible vision. A vision that no boy should ever have to see. Do you hear me? It is beyond the call of duty even for an adult. Perhaps this vision does not have a short-term answer. Sit with it for a while, then come back and tell me what you think, what else you have observed, and we will talk some more. You know what I think? I think in time this vision will help you find your role in the community, just like visions do for Indian boys."

Tommy, clearly not getting it, said, "People are dead, Mommy. I don't want to think more and more about it. My spirit guide said you would know what to *do*."

"Me? Look at me," she laughed. "I'm eight months pregnant. I can barely get out of this bed to use the bathroom let alone lead a charge against the constabulary. *Ìosa,* I'm practically chained to the bedposts. Maybe one time I could have raised a ruckus, but not now. I'm afraid there is not much I can do, Tommy."

"He said you would know. Everything else he said came true. These killings, what Jimmy Dog saw, the woman who spoke at church, everything. Now you are supposed to know what to do about it. You have to." She wasn't even trying to have an idea, thought Tommy. In six months she had gone from strong to invalid. It was this room. It had addled her brain. It was the goddam Javex. It had turned her brain to jelly and her body to mush. Just waiting for the baby to be born, as if that was her sole purpose in life. As if that was her role in the tribe. She has six other children. What about us?

A nurse in black-banded cap wheeled a metal cart into the room. "Your meds, Mrs. Caffrey," she began brightly. Then, seeing the boys, she said, "What are you two scamps doing in here? Visiting hours aren't for another five minutes."

"It's okay, Josie, I think it was by design. They wanted to catch me alone." Mrs. Caffrey took two pills and chased them with water in a paper cup. Her eyes told the nurse she could leave now. She opened her drawer and latched onto a box of chocolates. She handed the box to Jimmy Dog. The boy opened the Pot of Gold. Inside were six half-eaten confections, soft whites, pinks, and coffees nibbled and left in their spots. Jimmy Dog grimaced and handed the selection to Tommy. This was all she had to offer them.

"Let's go," said Jimmy Dog.

"We can't go until we know that she is going to do something. The woman who spoke at church said there is an election coming up. She said maybe we could speak to our candidates. Big Ran'l was there in the church. She said we should talk to him about salmon in the Findrinny Brook. Maybe she meant you could speak to him."

"Hah," she laughed sarcastically, "Yes, I am sure I can convince Ronald Atlas MacDonald to do anything."

She took their hands again in hers. "I don't know how this tomahawk you are telling me about could have the power to make you see things in another time and place. But you tell me you didn't see these clippings until after you had your visions. I have to believe you. But I can't see how two thirteen-year-old boys can be expected to get involved in something so foreign to them, so far away. I'm sorry."

"If you can't do anything maybe you can think of someone who can."

His father entered the room and looked at his watch. "When did you two get here?"

Tommy deflated. Their time alone with his mother had been a waste. Her uselessness rocked his trust in the vision. He watched his father bend to kiss her on the cheek. It would be just the two of them now.

"A letter arrived for you, darlin'," his father said, handing it to her. "From Sister Catherine."

"Let's go," said Jimmy Dog.

The boys made their way down the stinking corridor, Jimmy Dog in the lead, Tommy trailing him like a zombie. What was the point of it all? What was the point of any of his tomahawk encounters? The drunk he nearly killed in the brook, the trickster in the forest, Sambath of the

Clan Kat, and a cowardly rampage that killed three innocents. Jimmy Dog would have been better off believing it was just a nightmare and nothing more. I should have left him to it.

They were already outside when Hector caught up with them. "Tommy! Wait! Your mother wants the two of you to come back to the room. She says she thinks she knows somebody who can help you."

She was still holding Sister Catherine's letter when the boys returned.

"You asked me to do something. Well, I don't want to disappoint you. This is what I've come up with. Hector, I want you to drive to Frenchvale tomorrow and bring Jimmy's father back home. There is something that Uncalucky has to do for us. Something the spirit guide has asked him to do."

"Lucky?" Hector's eyes grew incredulous. He paced in tight circles and pumped his arms in protest. "How are you going to pry Lucky out of that place? He hasn't left it in five months. You boys go stand over there. Shoosh. Listen, Bridget, I'd do anything for you. But darlin', darlin', to bring Lucky out of that place is a bad bad idea. He hasn't had a drink since Christmas. That's a good thing, believe me. What could be so important that you'd want to break that streak? And besides, he won't come home anyway. He wouldn't come when his own son was missing. What does that tell ya?"

"It tells me that Lucky knew Jimmy wasn't lost, he was hiding. Lucky will come if I ask him to come. And while you're at it, tell Sister Catherine I want to see her too. It's time to rally the troops. Good news, boys!" She waved to them yoohoo. "Good news. My darling husband is leaving tomorrow morning to fetch a soldier to carry out your mission. Private First Class Lauchlan Dunphy. Jimmy, your father is coming home."

BLOOMSDAY

On a day in June, trees blossom pink and white and lady-slipper red. In long-forgotten orchards, applebuds burst to life. In fragrant meadows, flowers abound in carpets of dandelion, waving daisies, buttercups, and tufted vetch clinging to green stems light as bluebird feathers. Timothy, alfalfa, clover purple and white all burgeon into hay, the cattle's delight. From roadside canopies, lupines leap pink, white, blue, and merrily.

It was on a day such as this, so abloom with life, that two chiefs journeyed to Findrinny town, the one chief long dead but still filled with maniacal fortitude. This leader of men travelled in a metal box in the trunk of a Chevrolet that had left New Glasgow that morning and would arrive at the Capitol Theatre by noon.

The second chief was the Prime Minister of Canada. Ahem. John G. Diefenbaker is on the train. Hail to the Chief. He was a striking sight, Diefenbaker. Six feet tall. Kinky ridges of tightly combed, well-oiled grey hair radiated back from a brow that projected a lawyer's intellectual ardour. Unavoidable eyes, quick, friendly, dominant. What betrayed the Chief, though, was the loose jowls and slack skin round about his throat, quaking wattles that exposed him as a flappable paranoid. In the face of disloyalty, his shaky pouches bristled blood red and the Chief drew daggers with his icy eyes. Disloyalty, he said, is the first step toward outright betrayal.

The prime minister made his way toward the back of the Special Edition Judique Flyer, thanking all by name. When he reached two men in a four-seater, he tugged a folded paper from his inside jacket pocket and passed it to the premier of Nova Scotia. "It is a memorandum," he explained. "It was prepared by the US State Department for the Kennedy visit a year ago. I want you to read it and tell me what you think."

Robert Stanfield unfolded the note and read the letterhead. "How did you come to be in possession of a personal memo prepared for the president?"

"Because he apparently tossed it into the waste paper basket right after our meeting. Regulations require that the baskets be checked at the end of every day to ensure that no secret documents find their way there. Well, this bit of confidence did land there. Go ahead, read it."

The memo was stamped "SECRET" in square red letters and entitled, "What We Want From Our Ottawa Trip." It was written on State Department letterhead under the name of Walter Rostow, Policy Planning Director.

A Harvard lawyer, Stanfield was a cautious and disciplined man. He read the words lugubriously, moving his jaw as if chewing a cud. When he finished, he rubbed his bald pate in discernment and handed the note to his seatmate, the Tory candidate for Cape Breton Highlands. The premier peered at the Chief from under shaggy brows. "They use the word 'push' a lot, don't they? And they certainly have definite ideas about how Canada can support their foreign policy."

Diefenbaker hummed agreement and waited, wanting to hear if either man, the premier or the candidate, had an opinion before proffering his own.

The premier had of course heard of the controversial memo. "So you saw this some time after the meeting? It must have made you look back on the gathering with a different perspective."

"Exactly." The Chief lowered his voice. "For one thing, I asked myself whether Kennedy had gotten his way on any of these points, and I was satisfied that he had not. We did not change our positions on the first three points. As for the fourth, we had already decided to increase diplomatic force on the North Vietnamese. The Americans feel that if the North Vietnamese continue their aggression, the United States will have to send in combat troops for the whole of southeast Asia. If you can believe it, he even thinks New Zealand and Australia will fall to the Communists. I think it's preposterous, but my personal point-of-view isn't relevant. We have already said we are prepared to do all we can to make the International Control Commission work. So they were one for four and that was a foregone conclusion."

He growled softly to himself as might a leopard coming back for the afterkill. He removed the memo from the candidate's grasp, folded it, and slipped it into his inside breast pocket.

Ronald Atlas MacDonald, the candidate for Cape Breton Highlands, and a good friend of the prime minister, mentioned a related controversy, one that brought the religious majority in his riding to righteous alert. Catholics were understandably shaken by the anti-papist sentiment expressed in some quarters of the American midwest. Their loyalties fell instantaneously behind Kennedy, and beware the politician or protestant who slighted the president. Diefenbaker had warily dodged a Liberal attack in this vein. The Liberals claimed, and there was none who denied it, that the American president scribbled something on the State Department memo. In a clear reference to his Canadian host, he wrote, "This is one son of a bitch." There was something cloyingly photogenic about Kennedy's miscue. The Liberals were onto it like hounds on a fox, the press served the fresh kill on a platter and hoped the public would eat it up.

"Well, I appreciate that you didn't get into a backstabbing match with JFK," said the candidate. "We love him in the Little Vatican."

Diefenbaker growled with the resilience of a man who lost three elections before he starting winning. "No problem. It did the Liberals little good. They made some quick press points, but they should have known that an affair of this sort would not endear them to the Americans. The Yanks would have preferred the story never hit the newspapers."

Stanfield slowly withdrew the pipe from his lips and held its smoldering bowl. "I daresay, the Liberals have since been fine-tuning their tactics on getting in bed with Kennedy. "

"Yes," said the candidate. "They'd better get used to sleeping with a hippopotamus."

The three rich Tories laughed in a satisfied way, as if they knew they were making history, and when they had settled, the premier asked, "How will you approach the Americans and President Kennedy now?"

"I think it's obvious," answered Diefenbaker. "I'll approach them with one hell of a lot of caution."

The morning of whistlestopping from Port Hastings to Judique to Port Hood to Mabou and Shean and now on to Findrinny had been a medicinal tonic for the prime minister. The weather had been phenomenal, the crowds wildly supportive, the hecklers easily put in their place. He told his handlers he wouldn't mind campaigning in Nova Scotia the whole of the spring. They believed him.

The election campaign of 1962 had been marked by many setbacks. For one, midway through the campaign his Finance Minister decided to de-peg the dollar. The result was disastrous. Letting the buck float on the open market sent it into a near ten percent freefall. The Liberals printed stacks of ninety-cent Diefendollars and distributed them at street corners. A great time was had by all at the Chief's expense. But that was just mockery. There was violence too. On May 30, Dief stepped onto a Vancouver stage and was greeted by organized anarchy. Ten thousand British Columbians gathering to hear the prime minister were prevented from doing so. Only a human barricade stopped the rabble from gaining the stage. Then, just last Saturday in Chelmsford, Ontario, the Chief gave a speech accompanied by the sound of rocks hitting the walls and windows all about him. He was struck on the head by a placard. Good old Olive doubled over the signwielder with an elbow to the solar plexus. "That to me was the turning point in the campaign," Diefenbaker joked. "Olive stiffin' a hooligan."

Tommy followed his father into his room. Shiny black brogues lay at the foot of the queen bed. On the bed itself, as if laid out from toe to head, were his father's thick green woolen hose, his polished white spats, his Caledonia kilt, his horsehair sporran, his chromebuckled belt, his uniform doublet, his wraparound pladdie, and his jaunty feathered glengarry. His father stripped to his underwear and strapped on the kilt.

From the kitchen, Gramma Caffrey ranted and roared. "Well, I never thought I'd see one of my own turn Tory."

"I didn't say I would vote for him, Momma. I said we should think about it. I am employed by him after all." He hid his sniggering and insisted that Tommy follow suit. He had her going.

"I wouldn't vote for that Ran'l MacDonald supposin' he had silver balls."

"Oh, don't worry, Momma, I'm just playing the pipes for him. The whole band played for the Liberal candidate. It wouldn't look too good for me not to play for the Tories."

"It's good the whole band played for MacInnis. He deserved it. Let the Tories play for Diefenbaker. It's bad enough he's letting the dollar go to hell, but after that row he got into with poor President Kennedy. It was Diefenbaker started that. I was embarrassed to be a Canadian living in the States."

"Why does Gramma hate the Chief so much?"

His father diverted him from a concept that was too strong for one so young to understand. "She doesn't *hate* him, Tommy. She has a hard time with any Tory. But Diefenbaker took something important away from her. We used to have a post office in our old house. Gramma was the postmistress. It was a good job and she was able to earn enough money to live there after Grampa died. As soon as Diefenbaker got elected, they gave her job to a Tory. Gramma ended up having to move to Boston to get work."

Tommy thought about this for a moment.

"Why'd he do that?"

"Diefenbaker?"

"Yeah, why'd Dief the Chief take her post office away?"

"That's what happens in politics. One side wins and they hire their own people wherever they can. But you know something, these things happen for a reason. Gramma was very happy in Boston."

To be with her son's family in time o' need. This was the blunt message Margaret Caffrey gave when she quit her job in Boston. Things are not good with the wife. The monsignor protested. He offered to hire her back when she was able to return. No, she said. There was no sense looking that far in the future. She may be in Cape Breton for months, if not years. The young priests cried like it was their own Irish mother abandoning them. As she boarded the train that would bring her home to Cape Breton, who showed up but the youngest priest in the rectory, her darling Father Fraher, George he insisted she call him, running toward her along the crowded platform, holding high his hat. He kissed her and passed her an envelope. With this last vestige in hand, she watched the city and suburbs of Boston flash by, the industrial parts, not the beautiful Melrose neighbourhood where she had lived, with the grocery stores and sidewalks and the electric heat and running water to make her more comfortable than she'd ever been in her entire life.

And her daughter, living a few blocks away with the three darlings. Things were easy. No lugging water from the brook. No splitting kindling, milking cows, and draining blood from pigs' throats for black pudding. No trips through the snow to the shithouse.

From her purse Margaret withdrew her new letter-opener, a gift from the monsignor to use on all the mail they would send to her. Inside the envelope was the most beautiful card she'd ever received—ivory, embossed with a rose bouquet and adorned with lacy fringe and pink ribbon. Over his signature Father George Fraher had written, "I will miss you so much, Mrs. Caffrey. I wouldn't trade you for the Virgin Mary if she walked in the door tomorrow."

At first the children were overjoyed. Housekeepers were a thing of the past. Now they had Gramma Caffrey. Cissy was cleared out and the guest room was given over lock, stock, and bureau to Gramma. She unloaded a suitcaseful of old-lady dresses and got set for the long haul. Her routine for the children would have worked well in a logging camp. Uptimes, mealtimes, bath times, bed times. Managing a household was of little concern to this mother of five, midwife of 75. What did have her worked up, though, was the nightmare of contemporary politics. A Tory with the largest majority in Canadian history acting as prime minister. A Tory acting as premier of Nova Scotia. Tories representing Findrinny federally and provincially. A big Tory living right next to her son. Now to top it all off, she had this pompous protestant prime minister laughing off good John Kennedy's criticisms.

"No two ways about it. If John Kennedy called Diefenbaker a son-of-a-bitch, he must be one or worse."

Hector and Tommy escaped the kitchen. Past the wooden houses and trim front gardens of St. Columba and Church Streets, they drove toward the hospital. Tommy, his elbow resting on the open window, sniffed profusions of purple lilacs. All of Findrinny was aflutter for the Two Chiefs. Cars were being washed, hedges trimmed, and dandelion-dotted lawns mowed in a communal storm of beautification.

At his father's touch, the radio filled the car with melancholy.

As I walked out in the streets of Laredo
As I walked out in Laredo one day
I spied a young cowboy all wrapped in white linen
All wrapped in white linen as cold as the clay

"I'm getting out here," said Tommy.

Columba's Field stretched out lush and green, ringed by grand white elms all the way to the river. On this June morn, it was sprung to life with practitioners of all things track and field. Athletes from twelve to twenty-five threw the discus, heaved the shot, arced the javelin, tossed the caber, shucked the sheaf, vaulted bar and hurdles, and dashed in short sprints along the freshly oiled oval. In the middle of it all, the Venerable Bede cast a sharp eye from one sport to another, barking his commands, stirring the recalcitrant, laying down the law.

Katie Beaton and a dozen other girls, their long hair falling toward their sneakers, pulled tight on the straps of their ankleweights. Snug so they didn't jiggle. Up the bleacher steps they highstepped, then sidestepped down and up and down and up and down again and again, feeling the muscles from foot to thigh strive hard against the resistance of the weights.

Two boys approached a pristine part of the track, its four lanes clearly painted, pulling a baseball backstop, an ugly makeshift affair of green fish netting stretched between three two-by-six planks. The coach, bounding and scowling, turned on them like a storm trooper. "MacNeil! Chisholm! What do you think you're doing? Highland Games in a month and you're dragging a goddam backstop over my track!"

The boys immediately ceased their activity and drew away from the offensive apparatus.

"Don't just leave it there!"

The entire squad of balltossers dropped their mitts and raced to the backstop. Counting manfully, they hoisted the awkward structure and in a wave of cheers, swept it into position behind home plate, all carefully avoiding the sacred tracklines. With shouts of joy one team took the field. The rest sang out the batting order.

"MacNeil! Chisholm!" the coach hollered again, waving his right fist. "Get some rakes! Snap to it! I want that track smooth as a baby's arse. The way I had it. And repaint those goddam lines while you're at it."

The coach gave the okay for the girls to unstrap their weights. On legs bursting with energy they stretched muscles and cantered the track. Soon five of them were toeing the line. On your mark, get set, go. Katie Beaton had a slower start than the others, but with the burden of the anklets taken away, it seemed like her feet barely touched the track. Her hair, like a thoroughbred's tail, flew straight behind her as she passed one runner and another, but the finish line came too soon.

Coach lumbered over and laid a hand on her shoulder. He had learned to expect questions after each race. For a man known more for critique than compliment, the coach was positively eupeptic when it came to this one. Some of his athletes had talent but no desire. Some had desire and little ability. Some were full of ability but did not attend to the technique of their sport. This was especially true of the sprinters, who expected running to come naturally to them. Sprinting, well, they did that all the time. With the other disciplines, it was clear they had to be learned from scratch. Not so for Katie Beaton. She ate up technique like she ate up hagiography. There was something more the Venerable Bede saw in Katie Beaton, though. An intangible rarity for one so young. In twenty years he had never seen anyone with more enthusiasm to go faster.

"Goddammit," he liked to say, "it's like she's being chased by the hounds."

"I came third." Katie was not a happy sprinter.

"Don't get discouraged, girlie," said the coach. "You're the youngest kid on the track team. Look at yourself as learning for next year when you will be racing against kids your same age, not against girls older than you."

Katie said, "I'm not discouraged. I just wish I could go faster. And I know I can. Tell me what I have to do."

"Well, you have good technique already, but good can always be better. Let's talk about your start-up. You need to focus and use your impulse to build momentum quickly. Come here, I'll show you. Other than that, considering most of the girls are taller than you, you are doing well. What they have in leg length you can make up in strength. Maybe not this season, but you keep working on it and next year you will win some races."

"I want to win this year. I want to win the Highland Games. Would it help if I cut off my ponytail? It feels like it's weighing me down."

"I don't know about that. You've heard about Samson in the Bible, haven't you? He got weak after his hair was cut."

"I've heard of Samson, yes," Katie replied. "The Philistines stuck swords in his eyes. But have you ever heard of Saint Rose of Lima or Saint Joan of Arc? They cut their hair to make them stronger and it worked. Maybe I will before the Games. Maybe then I'll win."

"I think it's more important if you learn how to get a good start out of the blocks. Here's how."

Many of the girls were afraid of the coach. Katie knew their fear detracted from what they absorbed of his advice. She would have none of that. Fear was a vestige of the past, associated with false pride. The point of being on the track team was to know her body better and what it could do. Katie listened intently to the coach. She pictured herself at the start line, her body crouched, her right palm flat, fingers pointed forward, her left hand lower and pointed back. She imagined her crouch deepening and the power in her right leg pushing off from a precise angle.

But now the coach was veering off from his instructional message. Nothing escaped the critical eye of the Venerable Bede. "Jesus Christ," he said, seeing what was occurring behind the equipment shed. "Are they doing what I think they're doing?" Then he was trundling in the direction of the shed, bellowing, waving his arms.

"Dunphy! Caffrey! What the hell are you two doing there? Put that out. First it's the smoking, then it's the drinking, then it's the goddam women."

Katie ignored the gesturing and the griping. She gave not a second thought to the evils of cigarettes, liquor, or laddies. She put her mind to her angles. She set into the starting blocks and pictured how she could increase the power transfer from leg to foot to blocks. The track beneath her feet was soft and familiar. The girls limbering up were her new friends, older girls who could teach her a thing or two. Soon they would be travelling together for road trips. Amherst next weekend, then New Glasgow, Halifax. And then all the track teams in the Maritimes would gather for the final and biggest meet of the season when the whole of Cape Breton would see her take on all comers at the Findrinny Highland Games.

Tommy Caffrey, hands in his pockets, feet crossed at the ankles, leaned against his father's two-tone green Strato-Chief. A Pontiac, like the Indian. He spit out the taste of his first cigarette and watched a team of volunteers pull a banner across the train station's brick façade. Others stretched red, white, and blue bunting along the front of a hastily constructed stage. Nearby, drummers paradiddled and pipers screwed drones up and down. A chanter, sprung unfettered into the air, squealed in dreadful discordance. The pipe major cocked his head to the tone of his pipe, removed his chanter, fiddled with the reed, blasted the eight note scale up and down, then returned the chanter to its stock. "All right!" he called loudly. "Pipers!" and in short order ten kilties had assembled and were playing the slow air his father first taught him, "Hector the Hero."

With the first notes, Tommy moved toward the long steel rails. Daddy had given him a practice chanter for Christmas. He called it MacCrimmon, as did the man who used to own it, Private First Class Gordie MacDonald. The two of them played in the Cape Breton Highlanders band. Daddy said Gordie was the first CBH killed in the war. Tommy could still remember the story his father had told him: "Gordie was a very good friend of mine," he said. "We shared the same trench and pup tent at Ortona. He had a girlfriend in the Hebrides, a Gaelic speaker like himself. They were going to marry when the war was over. On the day he died, I went to the cookhouse with him and gave him some rations. They were still in his greatcoat pocket when his body was found. One night in our Ortona trench, while we were practicing tunes on our chanters, Gordie and I agreed that if one of us didn't survive the war, the other would keep his practice chanter as a remembrance."

His father taught him the scale and three tunes, but when Mommy got real sick Daddy lost interest in teaching him. Nobody seemed to notice that Tommy played MacCrimmon no more.

In the distance, car horns could be heard, coming nearer, growing louder. A wedding? Must be a big one. The motorcade turned toward the train station. Shouts, whistles, and hoots poured from open windows. Placards bobbed and waved from farm trucks and convertibles. "John Diefenbaker: A Great Canadian." "Youth Back Diefenbaker." "Vote for Jobs, Vote for Ronald Atlas." By the time the blasting petered out and the entire cavalcade had parked, four thousand people swarmed the station grounds, all anxious to hail the Chief.

A man shouldering a bag of ice cream treats approached Tommy. "Better move back from that track, boy," he said. "Train'll be here in a couple minutes. Here, have a tub. It's on Big Ran'l. Here take a wooden spoon."

"Is that on him too?" He didn't understand the entire chain of connection, but in Tommy's mind, Big Ran'l was directly responsible for murder. He was a criminal. Tommy couldn't wait to hear what a real chief would have to say about the murderer's poison plans. The hammer would finally come down on Iron Claw MacDonald.

A long urgent train whistle split the air. The crowd erupted. The pipers skirled into action. "Scotland the Brave." Like an eel, Tommy slid through the masses until he touched the apron. Seconds later, in a cloud of dust and smoke, a great locomotive drew up like a snorting dragon. It pulled a train of four club cars and a bright orange caboose—the Special Edition Judique Flyer on a whistle tour from Hastings to Findrinny, and there was no better place to be on the Island that day. A door in the caboose opened. A man in plaid jacket, pencil thin moustache, and huge grinning teeth emerged to wild cheering. Hughie Grant. Following Hughie came the most well-dressed people in Cape Breton, the men wearing two piece suits, Tory blue ties, and shiny shoes, and the women in riotous pastel chiffon hats and dresses to match. Two by two they stepped onto the platform, waving.

The last pairing emerged, stood, and smiled. The woman wore a filmy blue dress and a hat like a feathered lampshade. The man clasped his hands above his head in a victory salute. He stood tall and gleaming, dressed nattily in glossy grey pants and suit jacket, white shirt and the thinnest blue line of a tie. Kinky ridges of grey hair ran even as cornrows back to the crown of his head. He clasped his wife's hand and raised it in another gesture of victory. He had the mien of a

British Bulldog. The man wore no feather headdress, but Tommy recognized him even before the chant rose from the crowd, "Dief! Dief! Dief the Chief! Dief! Dief! Dief the Chief!"

From his pocket, Tommy pulled out the Brownie Automatic his mother had given him. The boy had no sooner clicked his camera when he heard a familiar pleading voice. She was with her Chinese friend with the enormous dimples. "Oh! Tommy, can you take a picture of us?"

"Oh, hi." Tommy replied. "I can't. I'm saving my shots for the ceremony."

"Oh please, please, please."

"Alright, I guess."

"Okay, here we are. Cheese! Can you take two? One for me, one for Joyce. You remember Joyce, don't you, Tommy?"

"Yes, from tobogganing." He turned away. They were hard to look at with all the polka dots on them.

"So you're here to see the prime minister too?"

Tommy didn't answer. He was transfixed by what was happening on the stage. His father's friend, the polluter and racketeer, Ronald Atlas MacDonald, was lurching slowly and purposefully toward the microphone. Oh my God, what would that elephant do with a microphone? Sure enough, a bellow and a terrible screech from the sound system made ladies and gentlemen grab for their ears. It didn't stop Big Ran'l for a second. Tommy could hear him already, blustering like he did on the radio or bragging like he did on television in ad after ad, interview after interview, rally after rally, boasting on how he was going to make Cape Breton great again.

"Listen to me, folks. We are through with losing here in Cape Breton. We are about to become winners. I've been a winner all my life and I'm telling you folks, you get on my coattails and get ready for the ride of your life. We will all be winners. We will be an island of winners."

What a blowhard.

But instead of rattling on like his advertisements, the candidate swung around on his good foot like a ballerina and gestured to two rows of chairs filled with esteemed members of the Tory travelling show, local party stalwarts, and anyone else Big Ran'l deemed worthy of sitting on his stage.

"Ladies and gentlemen, la-dies and gentlemen, boys and girls, distinguished guests. This afternoon I have the greatest honour I have ever been given on a public stage. I am here to introduce a man who has given the country five years of powerful leadership, a man who has been a good friend to all Maritimers and a great friend to all Cape Bretoners. This is his seventh stop today and I can tell you the prime minister is just chomping at the bit to talk. To talk to YOU! Ladies and gentlemen, I give you the Prime Minister of Canada, Mr. John George Diefenbaker!"

The Chief advanced to the microphone. Tommy snapped his Brownie.

"I want to thank Mr. Grant for organizing this rally, and my good friend, Ronald MacDonald, for that wonderful introduction. I want to thank you, ladies and gentlemen and children, for coming out on this glorious Saturday. It is awe-inspiring to stand here on this platform and look out at these vast forests sweeping back over the hills. I pondered these forests from the train window on our approach and I thought of the farms that were cut from such inhospitable terrain. One glance would tell anyone that not one of your ancestors and none of you is a stranger to hard work. What farmer isn't? And I say this. I say this. It will be my undeviating purpose to do what I can to assure prosperity for the farmer. Without agriculture the Canadian economy cannot be maintained. Agriculture must remain dynamic and not static. My purpose, ladies and gentlemen, so long as I am prime minister, will be to continue to press to assure that those steps be taken that ultimately will bring about a comprehensive policy for agriculture and give to the farmer of Canada that hope which has often been lost to him."

His next words were lost to the crowd's applause. When he couldn't hear himself speak, Diefenbaker smiled and waved, his jowls flapping, his wattles bristling magnanimously. He stood back from the microphone to look toward his wife, Olive. A proud acknowledgment passed between them. A catcall beckoned.

"What do you know about farming!"

Diefenbaker pounced on the remark. "Excuse me, excuse me,"

he said, waving and silencing the crowd. "Could you repeat that, sir?"

When satisfied that the entire audience had heard, Diefenbaker smiled and thanked the plant for the question. His tone mellowed to a wise, comic tenor that preceded the telling of a tale designed to strike mute an opponent and bring cheer to supporters.

"I was once asked that question, sir, by the chairman of a farm delegation from Saskatchewan. A Mr. Wesson. He assumed that I, as a lawyer, now ensconced as a politician in Ottawa, could not appreciate the problems of the farming family. In reply, I reminded Mr. Wesson that many years previous, he himself had stopped at our homestead shack for breakfast en route to his new home in Maidstone. My mother gave generously of our larder and sent him on his way with a blessing. Mr. Wesson had forgotten that visit. I had not. No sir. And you, sir," he said with a wobble of his great head toward his inquisitor, "you needn't worry that becoming a lawyer or a politician will ever dim my memory of farming life and farming issues. It will always be in the forefront so long as I am in office."

The heckler smiled and clapped with the congregation. Tommy joined in the cheering. The Chief, smiling, patiently waving, soaked in the adulation. He drew back and waggled his finger to the distant green hills and the farms carved into them. Tommy snapped.

Diefenbaker growled, "In the twenty years before my government was elected, the number of independent farmers in Canada decreased by thirty-four percent and the total farm labour force had fallen by forty-five percent. We wanted to put a stop to that trend. Our program for farm rehabilitation involves better farm use, consolidation of small farms into more productive economic units, facilitating off-farm employment, better agricultural training, and extension of Unemployment Insurance Benefits to some farm workers. We are putting fifteen million dollars a year into this program. And in the next government, we'll increase that amount."

The audience cheered wildly. Tommy tried to decipher what meaning the speech had for him and his problems. It did not look good that the Chief was sharing the same stage with the very man who poisoned Findrinny Brook. Could he yell out a question like the heckler did?

"Are you going to the show today?" Katie interrupted his thoughts.

"I remember how much you like Indians."

Tommy looked at her and snorted softly. "Yes, of course I'm going. Wouldn't miss it."

Joyce said, "I already called James about coming with us, but you can come too."

"James?" said Tommy.

"Yeah, James. Jimmy Dog."

"You called him?"

"Yes. That's right. I asked if he wanted to go to the show with me. He said you never go to the show with him anymore. Always reading, he said. Aren't you guys friends anymore?"

"One Canada, I say to you. One Canada!" Diefenbaker shouted, a prim white fist held high. "The responsibility of the Canadian government is to consider Canadian interests first. But this should not be misinterpreted as being anti-American."

"So why are you here?" It was Katie.

"Shouldn't we be listening to the speech?" said Tommy.

"You like Diefenbaker?"

"Yeah, I like Diefenbaker. It's not every day you get to see a real live Indian chief." Tommy looked back toward the stage. "Only I wish I could hear what he's saying."

Katie followed Tommy's gaze back to the stage where the prime minister was shouting into the microphone. She looked at a placard. Dief the Chief.

"Did you say you think the prime minister is an Indian?" Katie asked.

"I know he's an Indian."

Joyce pressed. "Do you mean he's an Indian from India or a North American Indian?"

"No, not an Indian Indian, an Indian from Canada," said Tommy, stopping short of calling her an idiot. "From the prairies. Saskatchewan. He's probably a Plains Indian, Blackfoot or Cree or Creek. Maybe even a Lakota Sioux like Sitting Bull."

Katie shook her head doubtfully. "He sure doesn't look like one to me. Does he to you, Joyce?"

Joyce waggled her chin. "That's one pale Indian."

"He doesn't look like an Indian because he doesn't have his feather headdress on like in the picture on the wall in my bedroom. Now be quiet, please, so I can hear what he's saying."

A man next to Tommy yelled abruptly through his hands. "Hey, Dief! What's this spat between you and President Kennedy, then?"

"There's our hockey coach," said Katie. "Maybe he'll know."

"About what?" asked Tommy. "About the spat with President Kennedy?" How was it, he wondered, that that squabble was known to everyone. Did they all have the same opinion as his grandmother?

"No, silly, about Diefenbaker being an Indian..." but her voice was lost as she turned and the man on the stage silenced the crowd.

"Who? Who said that?" the prime minister hooted at the interruption. "You, sir? I want you to repeat that question for everyone." The Chief held his hands outstretched for quiet. His pale blue eyes pulsated until the heckler had been heard by all.

"You want to know about Kennedy and me? I'll tell you about my relationship with the American president since it's in the news so much these days."

The crowd tensed as its Catholic and Conservative loyalties collided. Tommy noticed the shift in mood but knew the Chief would set things aright.

"You know," the prime minister said confidentially, "I visited President Kennedy shortly after he moved into the White House. A goodwill gesture on my part. And when I walked into the Oval Office I noticed that since Eisenhower's departure many changes had been made. Gone were the old pictures of infantry battles and generals. Now there are steel engravings of American naval engagements adorning the walls. You know Kennedy is a navy man. I was air force, but I don't hold it against him." He paused to affect a smattering of polite laughter from the audience.

Tommy looked around and saw that Coach MacEachren was trying to shush Katie so he could listen to the Chief's yarn.

Diefenbaker continued his storytelling. “I noted that some of those beautiful engravings were from the war of 1812. So I asked the president, ‘Where are the British victories?’ President Kennedy rejoined that his reading of history did not indicate there had been any.” This brought from the crowd bleatings of patriotic indignation. Diefenbaker calmly shook his great head and signaled peace.

“So I informed President Kennedy about the encounter of the HMS Shannon with the USS Chesapeake. I pointed out that the American ship was routed in a mere fifteen minutes and the Union Jack was hoisted to where their star-spangled banner had waved. Then the Shannon hauled the disgraced American frigate all the way here to Nova Scotia and deposited it in Halifax Harbour. I'll give the president credit, though. When he heard the tale, he was quick to remark. ‘If I had a picture of the Shannon and the Chesapeake I would put it right there on that wall. I'd create a place of honour for it.’ I am now trying to secure a steel engraving of the battle and intend to send it to him as soon as it's done. History will be served.”

Diefenbaker waved and clucked as the crowd understood his meaning. We'll be cordial but bold, cooperative, never cowering.

Katie was poking Coach MacEachren again. Like a dog with a bone.

“Hey, Tommy,” she said, “Sorry to break this to you.”

“What?”

“Coach says don't be crazy, Diefenbaker's not an Indian. There hasn't even been one Indian elected yet, let alone getting to be leader of the country. They're only just starting to vote.”

“Sorry to break it to you. I've seen a picture of him in feathers with a bunch of other Indians. Indian chiefs!”

“I saw that too, Tommy,” Dan Alec MacEachren butted in, hoping to put the matter at peace and retune his ear to the Chief. “That was when Dief gave the Indians the vote. About two, three years ago. That's when you saw the picture, right? The chiefs were just honouring him. Letting him know how much they respected him and appreciated what he did for them. But Dief's not an Indian. As a matter of fact, his father was a German and his mother was right from Scotland, a Grant.”

Like a burning Ponderosa map, the photograph was emblazoned on Tommy's brain. Two dark Indians with Diefenbaker in the middle. That was one palefaced Indian.

Katie shrugged and said to Joyce, "I didn't think the prime minister would be an Indian."

Someone yelled, "What about jobs?"

Throughout the exposition Tommy had mustered a veneer of defiance, but when they stopped paying attention to him, he was filled with doubt. Maybe the Chief wasn't an Indian. Maybe it was right that Katie set the record straight. She had a knack for doing that. Maybe she wasn't being a friend when she corrected Mrs. MacDonald about that milk-for-blood saint, Antiochus or whatever. Maybe she was just setting the record straight. Maybe she just couldn't stand someone being wrong. Maybe she was a brownnosing snotbag.

"What about jobs!"

Diefenbaker called for the candidate to join him at the microphone. The moral cripple ambled forward, the sharp lines on his brand new suit cracking the sunlight. Except for a stiff limp and a stiffer *cromach,* there was no sign of the mechanics that held him upright.

"When you think of wage-earning jobs in Cape Breton you think of mining, and when you think of mining you think of Ronald Atlas MacDonald. This man has done more for employment in your riding than any other private operator you can name. And I know, even before he stood for election, he was working hard to bring the Tampakan Mining Project into reality. And he is the right man to do it."

Tommy turned away from the stage and pushed his way through the cheering Tories.

"I'm outta here."

"Where you going?" Katie called, "To the show?"

Cheeks burning with embarrassment, Tommy huffed past the pipe band standing at ease, escaped the gravitational pull of the station, and broke into a run at Dot Falt's mill, hearing the last words of a dislodged hero ringing in the air.

"One Canada," Diefenbaker shouted to the throng. "That's what I say. One Canada! To those who would say special privileges for Quebec,

I say One Canada! To those who say let those Eastern so-and-so's freeze in the dark, I say One Canada! To those who say we're going to become the fifty-first state, I say One Canada!"

"One Canada!" he shouted to their cheers as the entourage boarded the caboose and the pipe band began a farewell. "One Canada! One Canada!"

Over the bridge Tommy raced, between Keltic Motors and the War Memorial Arch, past Elm Gardens, the courthouse, and Miss North Grant's flowery pink-trimmed cottage; past the barber poles and Veronica's Confectionery; past the rubbydubdub Elmwood Lodge; past MacDonald Brothers Grocery, credit to all and sundry through bad times and good; past Wilkie's Celtic Court, your findruine and plaid emporium in the Tartan Heart of Nova Scotia. At the white church he wheeled left, legs tiring but with the will of one possessed by an Apache spirit.

"Slow down there, mister," his grandmother said. "What's the big hurry."

"The show," he panted. "Need a quarter. Can I have one, Gramma, please? I really need to go."

"You need to go? The bathroom is right there, fool. Go!"

"Not the bathroom, the show. I need a quarter for the show. The movie. Please. Daddy's still at the train station. He always gives me one."

She dug in her purse and out the door he flew, racing toward the theatre, straining now and feeling a pain in his appendix. When he saw the guys on the College Street Bridge, he pulled up and stared. "How come you're not at the show already?"

"Doesn't start for ten minutes," answered Jimmy Dog. "What's your rush?"

"What if we don't get in."

"Don't get in? Are you kidding? Everybody's at the train station. There will hardly be a line-up."

Archie said, "Hey, look Tommy, we're catching spinners. Watch. I'll get one!"

Tommy stood on the bridge catching his breath, staring hard at a spot downstream where the brook turned left and disappeared from sight like suicide. Maple keys twirled past his face, breezeblown propellers landing softly on the asphalt beside him, fluttering into the open air above his babblebrook, eluding the grabbing hands of the woodsboys. They twirled as the spinners did, spinning free on the span, eyeing upward while they spun. Traffic seemed to have disappeared and his brothers and cousin seemed the only ones in town. Far, far away a whistle wailed for a wasted wish.

"I got one!" Jacky shouted and held high a two-point maple key. "I got one! I caught one in midair!"

Archie cried with joy. "Yay, I got one too!" He held it aloft, then moving to the rail, let it drop. The four watched its spiralling descent until it was swallowed whole by the gentle brook. Spin, drift, and drown. Gone forever. Tommy shivered and shouted, "Let's go or we'll be late for the show! Race ya!"

In a flash they were off and darting past the bowling alleys, galloping down College Street.

"Hey, wait! Wait for me!"

But they didn't wait. Tommy wheeled abruptly across the street and into the sunless pathway between the tavern and the Knights of Columbus building. He lost his footing on the gravel and Jacky was at his heels crossly bumping against unseen walls as he tried in vain to pass. Tommy brought down his breathing in the narrow blackness between the two buildings. Through his nostrils, he drew steady draughts of cool dank air. His feet flew along the path to the tune of "Apache." He exhaled from his mouth in hard puffs.

Jimmy Dog, off to a late start, entered the alley yelling, "I'm on your ass, Archie, get out of the way so I can catch them."

Into the brilliant sunlight burst the lead pair. Past Sobeys' great wooden garbage bin of rotting lettuce and cardboard boxes they scampered. Neck and neck now. Legs reaching. Chests straining for the finish line that was the Capitol queue. Cowboy versus Indian. Pumping like madmen all the way. Their screeching halt carried them out onto the pavement of Main Street. A car horn sounded. They argued about who won the race or was it a tie.

"What's this show about, anyway?" asked red-faced Archie when he joined the others with a shoulder check to each brother.

Tommy pointed to the marquee and the posters standing to the side of the theatre. "See. *Geronimo,* starring Chuck Connors."

"Geronimo. He's that Indian, right?"

"He's an Apache who would never surrender. He's the most described person in America."

"Described? Does that mean he was a good guy or a bad guy?"

"Depends," Jimmy Dog butted in, "if you like a tomahawk sticking out of your head." Jimmy Dog had given up the chase when he knew he couldn't win. He acted like there hadn't been a race.

The line-up inched forward. "Do you have your quarter, Archie?" Jacky asked. The youngest of the lot held out a cariboubback for proof. "Okay," Jacky rehearsed. "It's twenty cents to get in. We each give the woman our quarter and she'll give us a ticket and a nickel back. Then we buy some popcorn or candy. Can you remember all that?"

"I know all that, idiot. I've been here before."

An oncoming blast of horns demanded their attention. The Tories were coming, hurrah hurrah. The lead car, a longfinned, chrome glistening Mercury convertible, white in colour, with royal blue interior, eased its way into view. Three young men stood on its back seat. Across their chest, stretched a slick banner written in perfect blue letters: "Vote for Ronald Atlas. Vote for Jobs." The Merc was followed by twenty more carloads all waving arms, showing off placards, and calling slogans.

"Vote Tory!" they yelled. "Vote Tory!"

"Vote Liberal!" a queuemate answered and shook hands with another man.

The banner wearers rebutted this slight show of opposition. "The Chief will take parliament by storm just like last time," they promised.

"Geez," Tommy called back, "my grandmother says the only parliament Diefenbaker should be in is a parliament of owls because he looks like one."

"Watch what you say, kid."

"Leave him alone," Jimmy Dog threatened. "Hey, that was narsty, Tommy. Parliament of owls. Good one."

A car stopped in front of the theatre. Two girls in rock and roll fancy polka dot dresses stepped out.

"Hey, Joyce, I saved you a place." Jimmy Dog elbowed the boys aside and stuffed hands into his pockets. He produced a pile of bottle cap liners. "Check this out, Joyce. We don't need to pay to get in. See, I found a bunch of Nesbitt's orange caps. Seven liners gets one person in the show for free. Here, take seven. You'll get in for nothing. You can save twenty cents."

Joyce looked doubtfully at the rubbery discs. She held one in her hand. "Seven?" she asked. She fingered the liners in Jimmy Dog's hand to find those less dirty than the others and snapped them into her purse. "Thanks James, that was very sweet of you."

"Were you guys at the train station?"

"Yup."

"How'd you like that?" asked Jimmy Dog.

Katie answered, "Kind of fun. We got free ice cream. The prime minister wasn't wearing any feathers though. That was a disappointment." She turned her green eyes on Tommy. They showed no malice, just the same magnificent magnetism. He looked away. If malice wasn't her intent in teasing, what was? What did she have to say to an ignoramus. Even she knew that Diefenbaker was a pretend chief. And there was what would never go away—cowardice, the sin that slithered unbidden out of weakness.

"So you must all be looking forward to this movie; especially you, Tommy, loving Indians so much. I just hope there's not too much killing in it. But what can you expect in an Indian movie, I guess."

Then Tommy said something he should not have said. Something that was a confidence between the two of them. The mood turned sour and Katie turned away, red with anger or embarrassment.

The convoy passed, horns and shouts fading, and Tommy prayed he had heard the last of Dief the Chief whose visit to Findrinny only boosted the fortunes of Big Ran'l. He should have known. What a fool he was to put his faith in a phony. One final salute came from the exhaust pipe of a backfiring Chevy as it turned the corner and disappeared into history. Fart to the Chief. Big ear-splitting obnoxious stink-up-the-bedsheets rumbling fart to the Chief.

The enticing aroma of buttery popcorn filled their nostrils. Jacky, Archie, and the two girls went straight for it. Five cents a bag. Jimmy Dog spent his quarter on crackerjacks, pop, and two Crispy Crunches, one for him, one for his date. The sweetness turned Tommy's stomach. He dropped his unspent nickel into his pocket and lagged behind the rest of the revellers. He was not here to make friends. He was here for what Geronimo could teach him.

Little Archie led the way, bold as a buck bunny at breeding time, passing his coupon to the ticket-taker and choosing seats halfway to the screen just as the lights came down. He erred just once when the plush curtain parted and the projector began to roll.

"This doesn't seem much like an Indian movie to me," he whispered.

Jacky, sitting next to him, said, "It's not, you hayseed. It's the cartoon. Bugs Bunny. Now shut it."

Darkness. It had blinded Tommy for a moment, so that he bumped into the girl in front of him. He saw her shadow move into a row and he followed. Three boys, girl, girl, him, all of them laughing as if the wascally wabbit was who they were waiting for all along.

Geronimoooooooooooo. How often had they hollered that name from toboggans and trees and sliding boards. Geronimo. To the others it was just a battle cry. To Tommy it meant much more. The thing about Geronimo was how they always called him "the last." The last renegade, the last hold-out against the supremacy of the white man, the last Indian warrior to surrender, but only after evading the entire U.S. Sixth Cavalry and Mexican posses for twenty years. Geronimo was a phantom, raiding and plundering, commanding allegiance and respect, defeating the odds. By knowing the Arizona territory better than anyone, he and his thirty-six braves turned two armies into Keystone cops. But the real theme of what he was watching was not bravery. The real theme was betrayal. For Geronimo, nothing was worse. When he met it, he met it squarely, with cunning and aggression. He didn't need two excuses to kill a Mexican.

After the show, Joyce invited them to the Brigadoon. "Free milkshakes.

It's a perk of it being my Dad's restaurant."

"Not me. You guys wanna go play cowboys and Indians?" said Archie.

Jimmy Dog answered for the group. "We don't do that anymore, Bobo. That's kids stuff. I'm going for the free milkshake. No question." Jacky agreed.

"Come on, that's sissy," Archie argued.

Tommy walked away groaning. "I'll play with you, Bobo. Come on."

Archie said, "I want to be the Indian. I'm Geronimo. Called it!"

"That's stupid," answered Jimmy Dog. "You can't be an Indian, you can only pretend to be an Indian. Like Chuck Connors."

"Let's go, Archie. You be Geronimo. I'll be Mingas. I don't care."

"We can't both be Indians."

Apaches were used to defying the odds, not ambushing imaginary prey. With no cavalry to evade or attack, Geronimo and Mingas soon lost interest in the game. They laid down their weapons, walked home in silence, and parted ways at the kitchen. In his bedroom, Tommy unwrapped a gone-too-silent tomahawk from the hockey sweater that hid it from prying eyes. Abed, he closed his eyes and clutched the talisman to his chest. But as tight as he held it, no power could he feel there. It was as the Unseen Spirit had told him, *"You will not see me again until you return the stone of this tomahawk to where it was given to you."*

"Look at it like a birthday present for her," Hector said. "She wants both you and Sister Catherine there to celebrate with her."

"A week before her birthday?" Lucky asked. "Is it an emergency celebration? Is she not doing very well?"

"Oh," said Hector brightly. "The baby is due in a month, then they can start treating her for the other thing. I expect you'll see her back on her feet in no time."

"Is that what the doctors are saying or is that just you talking?"

"Once the decision was made to keep the baby, the doctors have always said the same thing. Wait and see. They're keeping her strong, making sure she eats, giving her blood transfusions when they need to. They may induce the baby early if they need to start the radiation sooner. But Bridget, of course, she's saying she wants the baby to go to term."

The drive from Frenchvale to Findrinny took four hours with all the visits Hector had arranged. A war buddy in Christmas Island who had some lobsters for them to bring home, a Caffrey cousin married to an Iona MacNeil, an ancient uncle in Whycocomagh, and not a drink offered by one of them. Tea, biscuits, cheese, oatcakes, but not a taste of whiskey, rum, or beer. Good, thought Lucky, Hector put the word out with all of them. I need all the help I can get. But as Father Webb told him at the end of every one of his twenty-six weeks of sobriety, "When you're back in the world, Lucky, booze is waiting for you around every corner. You have to learn to say no, not once, not twice, but every time."

All the friends and relatives asked Hector about Bridget. Never once was the C-word mentioned. We all have our crosses to bear. We are praying for her. We will be up to visit. Hector accepted the platitudes sincerely as though each repeated blessing came straight from the saints themselves, like they meant something. Even a sober and pessimistic Lucky felt hopeful as he watched the interior of Cape Breton roll on by the Strato-Chief's big windows and listened to fiddle music and forecasts on the radio.

Perhaps nothing could have prepared him for the sight of Bridget. But Sister Catherine tried. She met him at the hospital room door, her eyes red, her voice pitched to breaking. "Brace yourself, Lucky, she doesn't look good. No one warned me and I had to leave the room as soon as I saw her. I don't want you to be unprepared. It's like all the good of her is going into the baby. They say she's lost weight these last three months, but the baby is doing fine. Oh, Lucky. Try to hold it together. I couldn't. Come on now, she'll be wondering why you're not coming in."

"Lucky!" cried Bridget. "Get over here. Let me get a look at you." And when she pulled him down to kiss his cheek, he could feel the weakness of her arms before he saw that they had turned to mere sticks of their former selves. "It is so good to see you. You look so good, My God, so handsome, so healthy. Doesn't he, Hector? Doesn't he just."

"Well, well, Bridget, it is so good to see you too. How are you feeling?"

"As well as can be expected, I suppose. But what about you? My God, what's it been, five months? Thank you for all the letters. You are so good to write and keep me posted on what you and the other men are doing there in Frenchvale. I'm sorry I couldn't answer every one of them. With all the time on my hands, you'd think I could muster more than I have."

"What are you talking about? I was the one with time on my hands. Time and dirt from all the gardening and stonework Father Webb has us doing."

"What is it you wrote that he always says? Work provides a sense of pride. Well, that's just great Lucky. I hope you can stick with it. You'll be coming back to Findrinny to stay, won't you? Coming back to Mary and Jimmy. They need you, you know."

"I don't know, sis. I don't think it's them that need me. You know how it is. I've taken the pledge, but I haven't been out on my own until now. I need all of *you* to help me keep it."

"I know, dear. Now I want to tell you why I asked you to visit me. I am going to ask you to do something and we don't have much time. The election is in sixteen days."

"The election? What does that have to do with anything?"

"In your last letter to me you wrote that you were doing steps eight and nine of the program. I needed to read about them because you didn't say anything more than that. Hector brought me a twelve-step pamphlet. So now I know. How is it going?"

Lucky looked around the room. With the exception of Father Webb, he trusted these two sisters and this brother-in-law more than anyone in the world. At least they tried to stop his drinking. When he did his lists for step eight of the program, he put his wife, his son, and these three people on the top of one of them. Someday he would ask them for forgiveness, but he wasn't ready yet.

"Yes, you need to reach out and mend relationships," said Father Webb. "But don't rush into it. Don't be impulsive. Take time to pray and talk it out first with someone you trust. Don't just make a list of those you need to ask for forgiveness, make a list of those you need to forgive. And don't be surprised if some names appear on both lists. People often get caught in terrible cycles of hurting each other. To break these cycles of resentment, someone has to step up and be willing to forgive."

When Lucky tried to pray for the strength to forgive those who had harmed him, he had to first shake off the feeling that he was being grossly insincere. It was she who harangued him to no end. It was she who kicked him out of his own house. Surprisingly, in time, sincerity did creep into his desire to forgive. And when he wrote about this, when he put these words to paper, Lucky came to be blessed with a miraculous sense of compassion.

"It's going good," he replied to Bridget's question.

"What are you learning?"

"Well, I'm learning to forgive and the next step will be to ask for forgiveness."

"I'm sorry, Lucky, but we are going to have to mess with that timeline."

"Lucky," said Sister Catherine, "There is something that you did more than ten years ago. You know it. Now I know it. For many years, I didn't believe that you tricked the B'laan, even when those in my own congregation told me. I backed you. But I have heard from someone who was in league with you. Someone who has her own reasons for now telling the truth. I think you know who I am talking about. Our outgoing Member of Parliament, Clemmie O'Leary. And we have seen where these deceptions have led—to death and destruction. You've heard about the killing of Juvy Capion and her children?"

Bridget added, "And Jimmy and Tommy are witness to it too. You didn't know that, did you? Don't ask me how they witnessed it, they just did. They knew things about the Capion killings that only the investigators knew. Tell him, Aggie."

"It's true. I was on the team that investigated the murders. Some details were too gruesome to report, but somehow the boys knew about them. And you know what, Lucky, if that big hole had not been dug into the Three Sisters, none of this would have happened. And now, since you know your own sisters have supported you and stood by you through thick and thin, we want to ask you to do something for us. And not just for us, but for a whole tribe of people you have harmed."

Sister Catherine pointed to a reel-to-reel tape recorder. "Listen to this," she said. "It is a testimony from a seventeen-year-old girl named Sabina who survived a massacre in her village. She came to us with her story and my fellow sisters recorded her."

At dawn they came to get him. Sister Catherine and Father McCoy would accompany him on his mission to the Tampakan. Lucky dreaded the trip. He had not been back there in seven drunken years. He remembered his first ride to the back of beyond, as the Findrinnians called it. At the age of sixteen, he had been hired with four of his buddies to work for the findruine cooperative. They slept in the camp with the B'laan, watching their strange ways, imitating their clackety-clack sounds, complaining about the smell of their food. Two of his mates quit the first week. "That's okay," the foreman said. "We only had jobs for three rookies. There's always a couple that will quit early. Indian shock I call it. You'll get to like them though. Just give them a chance." Of the remaining three, Lucky was the best in picking up the dialect. By September, he had enough to tell a joke and to know if he was being teased, which was often.

His rookie job was to weigh the trucks that carried the findruine to the spur line. These were private operators being paid by the co-op. He enforced the weigh rules the drivers had to follow. Overweight loads would only be paid to a proscribed limit. The overweight could be unloaded, but no driver would waste time or energy to do that. A few asked Lucky to be a good fellow and simply remember the overweight then add it to a future load that may come in under the limit. They were delivering that weight, it was being paid for at the other end, so what did it matter if on paper he borrowed from one load to top up another. Lucky opened himself to this arrangement and the camaraderie that came with it. The B'laan drivers never asked for special treatment, only the whites. It was a little thing and no one seemed to notice. On the contrary, by the third summer his prowess with numbers got him promoted to the manager's apprentice. They had him in mind for a white helmet.

Canada declared war in '39. Lucky tarried for a year and six months until the mines shut down, as much from lack of demand as from patriotism. He signed up at the recruitment hall in Sydney and celebrated his twenty-first birthday in Camp Aldershot, Nova Scotia, and his next in Aldershot, England. On November 10, 1943, he and the rest of the Cape Breton Highlanders landed in Naples, a city of rubble and rats and shellshocked survivors. He had his first drink of *vino* on November 11. It tasted dry and bitter but it got the job done. For the next fifteen months, the Highlanders were part of the great push to rid Italy of Germans, from Naples to the River Ariella to the River Melfa, to smashing the Gustav Line and taking Monte Cassino, and then onto Rome and beyond, to Coriano Ridge where they broke the Gothic Line, but by this time the Canadians' work was already being overshadowed and underappreciated. The Normandy landings had opened a second front and Lady Astor had questioned their gumption, to which the poet soldiers sang back at her:

When you look 'round the mountains, through the mud and rain
You'll find the scattered crosses, some which bear no name.
Heartbreak, and toil and suffering gone
The boys beneath them slumber on
They were the D-Day Dodgers, who'll stay in Italy.

It was at the heights of Monte Cassino with German paratroopers raining fire upon them that Lucky first thought he was a goner. In open sight, concussed and barely able to stand or see from an artillery shell that killed the man next to him, Lucky lay still as the corpse. In the quiet after another explosion, Sergeant Major MacDonald picked him up like a sack of potatoes and carried him to safety. That day, MacDonald saved Lucky's life, and again on Coriano Ridge when he protected the entire platoon at the cost of two appendages. Those losses were apparent for all to see, but it cost Lucky plenty too—in misplaced loyalty, in deceptions, in guilt, in finding ways to forget the guilt, in the loss of all self-respect. After the Grand Deception, Italy would seem like an innocent time.

During the next ten days, Lucky toured the Tampakan Ridge from Kiblawan on the south side, up and over to Datal-Alyong in the back of beyond. He made thirty-five speeches on the subject of betrayal, two some days, three, four, up to five on others. He called them his AA talks, AA standing for Abject Admission. They were a surprise feature of the civics seminars being put on by Kalgad, an Indian organization that was working with the university extension department to teach first-time voters their rights and responsibilities.

The group's leader, Erita Sagada, gave Lucky a speech of her own before he gave his first AA talk. "You will speak to us in our language, rusty as you are at it. You will not speak to us as children. You will speak to us as masters of our own destiny."

From every corner of the forest the B'laan walked or rode to the civics seminars. They filled the chapels or meeting halls or gathered under shady trees. They learned what they could expect on election day, where their polling station would be located, what rights and responsibilities they had finally been given, ninety-three years after Confederation. Lucky sat among them, shaking hands, nodding nervous recognition to former employees. They remembered him as a fair boss, an affable raconteur, a white man who learned their language well enough to tell jokes at his own expense, a person they could trust.

For the smaller meetings, he might stand in his place as if he was at an AA meeting. For the larger ones, he went to the front of the room and spoke as loud as a carnival barker. He delivered his last indictment against himself on June 16, just two days before the general election.

Erita introduced him as a former co-op manager who had lived and worked among the B'laan in the findruine days, before the Three Sisters had been scarred with a crater, before the pollution of Miabut Plamu, before the strike that shut down production of findruine but did not stop Archer-Atlas from strip mining their copper. "Mr. Dunphy has come back to the Tampakan to tell a story of treachery, which even now, years later, is having tremendous repercussions for the B'laan. It is important that you hear his story before you cast your ballots on Monday."

"The story I will tell happened ten years ago," Lucky began. "The Findruine Production Co-operative was under pressure to allow an independent operator to mine copper in the Tampakan. Most of the B'laan and all of the Mi'kmaw were against the scheme, so we resisted the pressure.

"In those days a census was taken. The census told the government that there were less than six hundred adult B'laan living on the Ridge. I know. Ridiculous. Since I've started giving my talks, I've spoken to more than two thousand men and women. The census was a fraud. But that was just the first fraud. It was a set-up for an even bigger one. You see, according to the protections put in place by Indian Affairs, to gain mining rights the independent operator needed the consent of half of the people in the affected area. Half of six hundred. They needed just three hundred B'laan living in the mining area to give their consent.

"People have often asked me how we got the people to sign over their rights to mine the Three Sisters. I will tell you the truth. I will tell you how we tricked you out of your land. It might even be a funny story if it had not caused so much death and destruction. This is what we did. We arranged a meeting and invited three hundred of your people. We told them there would be bigshots there, they'd hear a talk on the proposed mine, for information only, no decisions would be made, and then we'd all have a big banquet. We knew you could never resist a free meal and all the good feeling that comes with eating together.

"But we didn't just invite anybody. We specifically asked people who could sign their name but could not read English. Your Chief Enuffathem, may he rest in peace, knew just who to invite, and he received a big new house for his complicity.

"The politicians were there, Mrs. O'Leary, Mr. MacLean, the Indian agent, Mr. McQueen, Chief Enuffathem, and a spokesperson for the independent operator. That spokesperson was Ronald Atlas MacDonald, the man you call Iron Claw. He was a good friend of mine. During the war, he saved my life, not once but twice. Iron Claw told the three hundred guests how many tons of copper would be taken from the Tampakan. He talked about how the company would mine copper their own way, with heavy machinery, stripping the forest cover away and digging from the surface down for greater production, not following seams like the B'laan always did. He talked about putting up a smelter downstream. And then Mrs. O'Leary, the Member of Parliament, got up and did what she had been told to do by Iron Claw. She said there would be jobs for every able-bodied man. There would be gifts for the B'laan—new houses, a clinic, a school, rides to market twice a week."

He called to a man at the back of the room. "Utad, you were there. I remember you got up and said the salmon might be sensitive to the chemicals the smelter would use. You were right, of course. Someone else said we should only use copper for the production of findruine, which was then worth fifty times more than copper. We heard and noted all your concerns, but it didn't matter at that point. You had already signed the consent forms and Iron Claw had already secured his mining permit.

"At the end of the meeting we ate a grand meal—chicken, pork, rice, beans, lots of fruit, homemade wine and beer. And everybody went away happy."

A small sharp-featured man spoke up. "We were never asked to sign a consent form and we never did sign a consent form. I have been saying this for years, but even my own family has never believed me. For the past ten years we have been blamed for something we did not do."

"What Utad says is right. This is what happened. It was my job to secure the three hundred signatures, in whatever way I could. This was my favour to Iron Claw to show my gratitude to him for saving my life. As people began to arrive for the meeting, I made a big deal about the meal we would share afterward. The people could see it being laid out even as they were gathering. I passed around a paper so everyone who wanted to eat could sign up for the meal. You happily signed, didn't you, Utad, and that is why you do not deny your signature on this paper. You know it is yours. What you didn't know was that written in English above your signatures was a legal agreement giving away surface and mineral rights to a mountain's worth of copper and the go-ahead to dig those gigantic pits that now scar the Three Sisters. What Utad and the other two hundred and ninety-nine got for their signatures was a free lunch. And what Iron Claw got was what we in the mining industry call consent. Free, prior, and informed consent."

"Yo! Get off the phone will you. Yo! Jesus Christ. The polls will be reporting any minute."

Yolanda MacDonald hung up. *"Ìosa,* it's just seven o'clock on the dot now. They just closed this second. They won't be reporting absolutely immediately."

A minute later the phone rang. "The first poll is in, sir," said the campaign manager. Poll Number 57, Mull River: MacDonald, Conservative, 26; MacInnis, Liberal, 21. Same as 1958.

Big Ran'l kept an ear to the phone as Bill Beechum fed him the results poll by poll. He questioned the manager only when the vote strayed off kilter. The inconsistencies were usually racked up to a death in the poll, a family moving away, or the Grits giving away more rum. A few votes here, a few votes there, but only one poll changed hands so far. He turned to CBC TV for the bigger picture. Earl Cameron was sure the Conservatives would take the country, as certain as he could be, but he guessed a Tory or two might go down to defeat in Nova Scotia. Big Ran'l grumbled, but Earl Cameron just as quickly assured him. The candidate needn't worry about his own seat. The endangered ridings were all on the mainland. Cape Breton would stay as blue as the sea.

In his wisdom, Ran'l turned to Yolanda. "You see, for longevity in politics you need good organization. Keep the mistakes to a minimum, keep a muzzle on the mavericks, and run a tight ship. It all starts at the top. Then you get your best people working the levers, you see, making sure nothing's going off the rails. They keep me posted on all the major developments, so I make all the big decisions. My minions take on the detail and the leg work. Leave the hard thinking to the top."

"Will we be buying a house in Ottawa?"

"Of course we will. No reason we can't have a home here and another there. Not that I'd want to be in Ottawa in the winter. Cold enough to break the smoke off the chimney. Jesus, what did you say?"

It was the campaign manager. "The university polls, sir. You're not going to like it. All of them have MacInnis ahead. All five of them, three hundred and five votes in the difference from '58."

"What? That's ridiculous. Did you have people working the students or what? That should be a fifty-fifty split at worst. What the hell happened? When was the last time you polled there?"

"A month back, sir. Everything looked as per usual. There are only about four hundred summer students, but almost all of them voted in this riding. They must have gotten permission from their home ridings. Very strange. But not to worry, sir. You're still a safe six hundred-plus ahead with only the new polls to report."

"Jesus. That's still a shock to the system. It was that goddam Indian at the chapel. Her and that Stainless Steel McCoy. Okay, we're leaving Sugarloaf now. I want to get down there and give my acceptance speech. We'll be there in ten minutes. Get the party ready."

MacDonald rose to his full height. "Jesus, Yolanda, the Liberals cut into our majority by three hundred votes. Let's get down to the Celtic Hall and give a speech. The troops need a show."

The bar had been open an hour when the bagpipes sounded. A great cheer went up for the candidate and his lady. Bobbing their placards like bayonets, the Tory mass surged forward so they could touch his garment or shake his hand or hug his wife. They chanted, "At-las, At-las, At-las!" Big Ran'l steered his wife protectively through the mob as slowly and steadily as an icebreaker. All along the one side of the room lay a great buffet—two pineappled and nutmeged hams, two roast beefs, and so many biscuits and sandwiches and squares, you'd think you were at a funeral.

On the opposite wall, lit up like Yankee Stadium, was a blackboard the size of a soccer field. On it in fine square print were displayed the names of the polls from 1 to 155. From Port Hood in the south to the Tampakan in the north, all the tally lines had been completed except the last five—polls 151 to 155, the new polls.

Not much had been said of the Liberal candidate in the 1962 general election. Inverness County had a long run of Liberalism and so there was no reason to think the riding could not someday return to the fold. Indeed, MacInnis was a most interesting newcomer, a professor who left the classroom to take a run at office, a political scientist who specialized in parliamentary procedure. Governments rise and fall on such skills he might bring to the House. Unfortunately, MacInnis ran a weak campaign. His speeches seemed to have been written by a university professor because they were. He kept spewing on about the common good as if he was Jimmy Tompkins reincarnated. When he spoke of the dangers of assertive individualism, he seemed as aloof as the ivory tower he descended from. It didn't matter. The party brass calculated that if he could get his feet wet in the '62 campaign, develop some charisma and get known by the electorate, perhaps next time he would have a shot at winning. He had the hair and the brains for it.

Big Ran'l put his hand out to Bill Beechum. "Should I take the stage?"

"MacInnis hasn't conceded yet."

"I didn't ask that, I said should I take the stage. The crowd is waiting to hear the good news."

"The last polls will be in momentarily, sir. Hang in there. Hang in there right by the stage. The call will come in on this phone. You'll be the first to know. There's just the new polls to report."

"The new polls? What are you talking about, new polls?"

The manager pointed to the chalkboard.

MacDonald screwed his face into disbelief. "What the hell is that? Bad Axe, Big Hole. There are no places around here with those names. Batoche? This is a joke, right? You're having me on. Is everyone here in on it?"

"Those are the names of the new polls, the ones in Indian country, sir. Kalgad asked if they could name the polls and we saw nothing wrong with that. We've briefed you on all this before, sir."

"Kal what?"

"Kalgad, sir," repeated a hefty woman who had drawn close to the candidate. "It's the name of the Indian organization that is teaching them about their voting rights and so on. Civic education, you know, since it's the first time they've been able to vote." It was Mrs. Widesides O'Leary, the incumbent but retiring Member of Parliament for Cape Breton Highlands, come home from Ottawa to help out in any way she could during the last weeks of the race.

"What in hell's flames?" said MacDonald. His great head jerked from campaign manager to wife to O'Leary. "Why did we agree to that? It's enough they have the right to vote, why do we have to educate them, goddam it. Did we even campaign up there?"

"It was in all my reports, sir. You didn't seem very interested in the new polls, so we didn't think it was worth a serious campaign up there. Anyway, there's nothing to worry about. We gerrymandered the riding so that it includes only the western edge of Indian Land, from the Split along the west side of the Findrinny Brook up and over the Tampakan Ridge. This way all the copper and gold will remain in our grasp but most of the B'laan and all of the Mi'kmaw are in the neighbouring riding. The last census said there were only six hundred adults in the five Tampakan polls. Even if they all voted and even if all of them voted for MacInnis, we'd still win by forty votes."

The telephone rang.

"Get up on the stage," someone yelled. "Take the microphone! Let everyone hear the results!" A roar went up and the crowd pressed forward so that Big Ran'l, Yolanda, Mrs. O'Leary, and Bill Beechum were all propelled onto the stage.

"Okay, wait, okay, give it to me now," the campaign manager said into the phone and on the microphone to the whole room. "What is it? Be quiet everybody so I can hear." And he hollered out the results to the crowd.

"Poll number 151, Big Hole: MacInnis, Liberal, 188 votes; MacDonald, Conservative, two votes. What? Jesus, that can't be right. Read that back to me. What? It gets worse? Poll number 152, Bad Axe: MacInnis, Liberal, 270 votes; MacDonald, Conservative, no votes. Are you sure about these? What? Poll number 153, Batoche: MacInnis, Liberal, 173 votes; MacDonald, Conservative, one vote. Jesus, where does that leave us? Poll Number 154, Sand Creek: MacInnis, Liberal, 128 votes; MacDonald, Conservative, two votes. *Ìosa!* Somebody do a tally there. What's that, four? What about the last one? Not in yet?"

It was Widesides Clementine O'Leary, the incumbent who had been forced to resign, who did the math the quickest. She yelled to the candidate, "It looks like you're behind by a hundred and nineteen votes, with one poll left, Wounded Knee. The trends don't look so good, sir."

Yolanda saw the man on the phone shake his head at what he was hearing from Wounded Knee. "It's not possible, is it, Mrs. O'Leary?" gasped Yolanda. "Could we have lost?"

"Don't say we, Yolanda. I didn't lose. Your husband did. For giving up my seat so he could run in my riding, the Chief has already promised me an appointment to the Senate. I have a job for life. I won't even have to give up my house in Ottawa."

AFTER THE RACE

Like an addict reaching for a drug he has not known for many months, Tommy touched his tomahawk. Closing his eyes, he allowed his fingers to glide over it like the table slides on a Ouija board, caressing, conjuring, then gently stroking its shaft. He pictured a four thousand mile river flowing through the harsh unforgiving Sahara. He imagined an eagle high in the desert sky. The great bird swooped low over Lake Victoria to pluck a fish from its waves, then sailed high, high, high to see the entire Dark Continent from Cairo to Cape Town, Tanganyika to Timbuctoo. Swooping again, the eagle flew over Africa's largest lake, eyeing its blue white water rushing over Ripon Falls and down into a marshy pond, then another stream, and plunging through cascades to enter Lake Albert, then meandering a sluggish path for a hundred miles, disappearing, returning as the wild uneven Fola, then breaking free of the hills near Gondokoro. The river continued still, a swampy dreary sop with lazy sluggish animals on its banks, hippos, warthogs, wildebeests. The Blue Nile had not yet met the White Nile. It still had a long way to go.

Tommy snapped his eyes open and knew that his head had filled again with escapist thoughts. He shook away from the great river and the subsurface of his mind and the floating mass of vegetation that covered them both. Tall, naked, black men cleared the sudd away from his cerebellum, cerebrum, and medulla to form floating islands that allowed boats to pass onward to Khartoum and get him out of the room that held him captive. He pulled on his sneakers and raced as far as his feet would carry him into the field, only screeching to a halt a half-mile away, breathing great gasps of air, for he had run too fast and too long. Around him the chirping of crickets and the twittering of sparrows brought him back to earth. He felt wee, timorous, cowerin' like the mouse before the plough. Then again his legs moved faster than he thought possible as he sprinted away from the uncontrollable jumble inside. He shortened his strides and made to jump a fence. Unbalanced by the warclub in his hand, he hooked his foot and tumbled hard to the path.

Ahead of him, a grove of tall elm and maple loomed. The brambles he had crawled through last January while tailing a fugitive bottle picker were now green and lush and fearfully impenetrable. He skirted the bushes and raced along the bank where a belt of hay separated trees from brook. A dogstrangling vine grabbed at his foot and sent him sprawling face first. His tomahawk flew from his hand and disappeared deep into the thick hay. Panting, he rose to his knees and crawled weakly forward, feeling and hearing the trip hammer in his chest. Dry, warm hay receded before his creeping, slowing hands. He came to a bed where a deer had laid to rest. At last he found the talisman and collapsed where he knew no one would ever find him. Here in the high hay darkness, silent and secure, he buried the tomahawk into his chest and his head in the sweet-smelling timothy. His guilt craved relief and so he sobbed, soul and body. He rattled his head and swore that if he could regain his grip, he would cry no more.

From deep in his imagination, he pulled a picture of walkers, thousands of them, pilgrims flowing from all over India. From the Himalayas to the north, Orissa to the south, the Bengal to the east, and Delhi to the west, they descended upon the town of Kashi on the propitious northern sweep of the Ganges. Tommy chose one woman to follow. She was not old, but very sick, wrapped in her best rags, trudging, hollow, dark, redspotted, teeth separated by disease, wearing in her ears and around her wrists, her last and only gold. There, in the presence of Ganga, the swift goer, Tommy saw her receive purification by fire and water. He watched her wrapped in gold-trimmed silk and borne aloft to a sandalwood pyre. Prayers and incantations were offered and her body cremated in an aromatic bonfire. Pungent smoke rose to the sky and the fire burned and crackled until it expired. The ashes were retrieved and returned to their mother, the Ganges, and the sacred river, as incorruptible as motherlove, gladly accepted her sprinkled remains for all eternity.

The sun found a wide patch of pale blue ethereal sky and shone warmly and steadily on Tommy's face and darkened the freckles that lay upon his cheek. A great time had passed when this lifeforce woke the sleeping boy. He, aware of the trickling brook in his ears, lay still a moment longer. In a delicious half-sleep, he conjured words, calmly, joyously.

Babblebrook. Burble below black ice and snow, a torrent angry in April, a trickle gentle by June. Past billowing fields of bright-eyed daisies, bushy-tailed timothy, blue vetch and buttercups, clover white and alfalfa blithe. All bobbing in the breeze or bound into bales. Bubble, burble, twist, and tumble toward the tiny town. Past houses, shops, and churches, under elm branches and sturdy bridges. To where the rivers meet. Where bagpipers blare and bears break branches. Flow on bonnie Findrinny between banks of beech and birch and maple and spruce. Bring forth your autumn offerings, the vital and the brittle, the mature and the mangled, the scarlet and the brown. Leave town and county, sail out to the harbour, to the bay, to the gulf, to the great beyond. Babble on.

He stood then and strolled and was soon lost in the sight, sound, and smell of verdant July. How green the drying floodplain that held the Salt Ponds. Green, green, and lustrous green the island on the far bank of the forks. Green the grass and green and dark and strong the towering two-hundred-year-old elms that rustled and murmured majestically above.

See the flowers of the field and how they grow. They do not toil or spin. But I tell you that not even Solomon in all his wealth was clothed like one of these. If God so clothes the grass in the field, which blooms today and is burned tomorrow, how much more will he clothe you? What little faith you have.

Tommy found himself at a place that in times of yore had confronted three boys as an impassable boundary to western exploration. It was the place where Sambath of the Clan Kat planted two flags. The place where Jimmy Dog had thrown away his old skates and destroyed fragile ice with a bouldering splash, here where the placid sparkling waters of his brook tumbled into the Ani G'nish, the Bong Mal, the Big River.

A man stood motionless at the meeting of the waters, his back to the boy. In one hand he held a two-pronged fishing spear, poised just above the water. His arms were smooth and muscular. He wore a short doeskin vest frayed in narrow strips of brown leather at the waist. A leather girdle around his waist supported a holster and a long loincloth of soft sealskin. His hair black, shiny, and straight, reached halfway down the vest. Tommy had seen the vest's art once before. Snakes swam there, black flat snakes, like those scary ones they catch in the harbour, like the snakes on the vest of Sambath of the Clan Kat.

"Where are you going?" the man called to him without turning.

Tommy's silence betrayed bewilderment.

"Good day for fishing," said the man, jutting his chin toward the shore. Three trout lay on the bank, skewered on a sharpened stick. A half-beached canoe rocked in the rippling water.

"You look as lonely as Mary March."

The boy said nothing.

"You can stay here and fish with me. See these trout, they get this far up the brook, then stop and think, this is not my beautiful brook. In their confusion, they turn and wonder and begin to retreat to the river. This is when I strike. I need this advantage, you know."

With his chin and lips he pointed to the big river. "Or you can go that way to the harbour. Or you can go upstream, all the way to the land of the Mi'kmaw."

Tommy peered up the wide river, following it to where it curled and vanished around an island.

"I know a shortcut if you want to go there," the man continued, his back still turned to the boy. "One time I took old Dan Maroon along the trail to the place where my people live. Three moons along this river. What do you call this river?"

"You mean Ani G'nish? I think it's a Mi'kmaw word."

"How you say it? Annie-ganish. That means nothing."

"We studied it in school. The teacher said it means where bears break branches while looking for some kind of nut. But one time an Indian told me it was named after a guy named Antiochus. He was a saint."

"Who? The Indian?"

"No, Antiochus, of course. There are no Indian saints. That's what my teacher said."

"There aren't? Maybe not in your cult. Who was this Antiochus the Indian told you about?"

"He was a Greek saint that got beheaded and cheese came pouring out of his head instead of brains."

"Hah! Cheese for brains. You sound like the Trickster. You're having fun with me."

"My teacher said we can't believe what Indians tell us."

"Your teacher is just half right. You can believe everything Indians say, you just have to know how to take it. Sometimes we are just having fun with you." He turned to face the boy directly.

Tommy caught his breath at the sight of him. Half his face was grotesque beyond human recognition. A long jagged cicatrix was scrawled from the forehead, through a sliced eyebrow and socket, to end halfway down his cheek, red, raw, and as ugly as mortal sin. Tommy gripped his tomahawk and prayed.

The Indian laughed, grabbed his eyepatch and stretched its rawhide strap around his head. "Lost it years ago. Scary to look at, ain't it? That's good for me. Keeps bad people away. But fishing is harder since I lost my eye. Can't tell how deep the critters are, so I find a pool where they move real slow or a place where they get confused, then I just spear them hard and fast. I don't miss too often."

In a heartbeat of horror Tommy recognized the gruesome socket from his first encounter with a monster laying agash, agush, and awash in the Findrinny Brook. But unlike that first encounter, this time the monster was armed, and he wasn't drunk.

Suddenly the Indian turned into a killer. He thrust his spear at a living thing that swam at his feet. The swiftness of the attack rattled the boy. He uttered a cry of panic and fled into the grove. When he looked back, he saw a glistening speckled fish flapping wildly on the prongs that impaled it. The Indian held it high, yipping like a dog. When its death throes ceased, he stuck it a second time, with brute certainty, on his skewering stick.

"Check this out." The Indian pulled a long knife from a holster, held it glinting in the sun, and spun it from hand to hand like a magician. Then he sliced the fish and tossed its head to the gulls who screeched like banshees over the decapitation. "What do you think of this? Dan Maroon gave me this butcher knife for my scout work. I'm a guide. Anything you whites give me I get from guiding. I don't take nothing else from you. I ain't no welfare case. I'm a professional. Tell me where you want to go and I'll get you there. We'll work out a deal that's good for both of us."

"I know where I'm going. To visit my mother," Tommy said, stepping nervously from his blind.

"Do not be afraid. That's good news. It's good news that you know where you're going. Everybody should know where they're going and how to get there. Now I would like to introduce myself to you, but as the younger of the two, you must first tell me your name. Is that acceptable to you?"

"My name is Tommy Caffrey."

"Pleased to meet you, Master Caffrey. I am familiar with the name. A Caffrey was a companion of my good friend, Dan Maroon. Good man. Your ancestor, perhaps. You can call me Sam Snake like the others of your tribe. I am Mi'kmaw, from the Clan Kat, the Clan of the Eels. You see my vest? These are eels. But your people, do they care? Noooo. For them, they are snakes and I am Sam Snake. It's not the only thing they have wrong. Can you say *Naligitgonietjg?*"

"Nar-tigit-go-nitch?" Tommy tried three times. "What does it mean?"

"It's one of the names for this place. *Naligitgonietjg*—where bears break branches and gather beechnuts. You say it like you've got a biscuit in your mouth and you get Ani G'nish. It's what we used to call this place until you whites arrived. *Naligitgonietjg*. You know how it got the name? They teach you in school, no? An Indian came down here one time to have a shit. He squatted over there in the glen. All of a sudden he looks up and here come three bears walking around a turn in the path, breaking branches and gathering beechnuts as they caper. All three of them stop and look right at the shitter. He was sure they were going to go for his nuts next. He didn't stop running until he arrived in the village screaming, '*Naligitgonietjg, naligitgonietjg, naligitgonietjg*.' We are not likely to forget that."

Tommy furled his lips. "Trickster."

The man turned to look at him. "Nobody is going to sell *you*, Tommy Caffrey."

The boy drew a deep breath, relaxed, and listened. The sound of the brook, the wind moving through the hay in the intervale, faraway noises, bagpipes. Behind him, from beyond the elm grove, people were cheering. "Go, go, go!" they yelled. Tommy pictured a boy running into the outfield chasing a ball that had skittered past and still rolled faster than his feet. The boy chased the ball gallantly and fruitlessly as the batter easily circled the bases to wild cheering, running across homeplate, arms held high. His teammates clapping him on the back as the lonely outfielder heaved the ball mightily, hopelessly, to another who threw it to the shortstop who threw it to the pitcher.

Tommy peeked again in the Indian's direction. Sam Snake stood as motionless as a heron, his feet wide apart, head bent, holding the spear with its tip poised just below the surface of the water.

"You know much about rivers?" Tommy asked. He did not concern himself that the one-eyed Indian did not answer. He focused his gaze on his brook's mouth. Willingly it gave up its waters to the larger river, like the Moselle to the Rhine, like the Darling to the Murray. He could see then that the meeting of the waters did not signify the demise of the brook, but a joining of forces. His babblebrook might give up its waters, but in turn it received from the Big River a bounty of trout.

"Do I know about rivers? I know every fishing hole along the Big River from the harbour to Kitanglad and all the way up this brook too. Used to be the best brook in the valley. There should be plenty trout now. We call it the Strawberry Run. But they don't go up this brook anymore, just as far as this pool and then they turn around and skeedaddle on upstream. Miabut Plamu smells different to them. It is not their common home anymore. How about you? What do you know about rivers?"

Tommy pulled a piece of paper from his pocket, unfolded it, and drawing near again, pointed to the names. Turning it over to reveal the flip side, too, he answered, "I know all these, see. The Nile, Father Nile some people call it. Then there's the St. Lawrence and the Mississippi, the Missouri, the Amazon, the Congo, Yangtze, Ganges, Brahmaputra, MacKenzie, Shenandoah, Ohio, Potomac, Hudson, Euphrates, Tigris, Jordan—"

"All those names. I never knew there were so many."

"I have more than a hundred rivers on this list. And I know something about all of them."

"What can you tell me about that first one?"

Murky images formed in Tommy's mind. The Nile turns to blood and is plagued with amphibians. Frogs leave the river and flood the king's palace, his bedroom, and his bed. Toads jump on the king and his officials and his people, hop into their ovens, and squat in their baking pans. Then the Lord sends gnats, flies, boils, and hail, and swarms of locusts until the ground is black with them. The insects eat everything the hail hasn't killed. Not a green thing is left in all of Egypt. But the Lord makes the king stubborn and he does not let the Israelites go free.

And then the Lord says to Moses: "Raise your hand towards the sky and a great darkness will cover the land of Egypt so that no one will leave their homes lest they run smack into one another." And still the king remains stubborn. And so one night, the Lord kills all the firstborn sons in Egypt, from the king's eldest to the firstborn of the lowest prisoner in his cell, and the oldest male offspring of the dogs, cats, oxen, pigs, sheep, goats, and donkeys. He kills children as young as me, as innocent as Daisy in her crib. Firstborn sons die in their mother's arms and there is a loud cry throughout the land of Egypt.

And an overwhelming sadness fills the boy. And a revulsion for the great hoaryheaded God who embraces His flock from the ceiling of the cathedral, Our Father who art in heaven. What would God decide about firstborn twin boys, Tommy wonders.

"So what does it all mean to you?" asked Sam Snake.

"To me? How can I answer that? I am only a child. They say God the Father is all-powerful and all-wise, but he is all-vengeful too. It is all-beyond me. Incomprehensible."

"They say! Yes, they say a lot of things. But nobody knows the whole truth. We are all discovering the way and must keep on discovering it. And we all make mistakes along the way. Look at my eye. The result of a mistake. A drunk and stupid mistake."

"I've made mistakes too."

"Well, if you've made mistakes, you need to get over them."

"I've made mistakes that hurt other people. I've lied, stolen. I've been a coward."

"Then seek forgiveness if you need to and move on. But don't only seek forgiveness from another, or even from the Great Spirit. What is most important for you, Tommy Caffrey, is that you forgive yourself. This is an essential quality of mercy. I'll ask you again. What do you know?"

Tommy remembered the simple story of two Egyptian children his own age and what the Nile meant to them. "I know that when the Nile passes through Egypt it creates the world's largest oasis," he began. "It brings life-giving water to the people downriver. The Egyptians dig great channels to bring water to the farmland beyond the banks of the river, then smaller canals to branch off from the main ones. They dig irrigation ditches to divert the water into the fields where the crops are planted. If the river were to stop flowing, the crops would soon die of thirst and the people would starve. But Father Nile never does stop flowing. For thousands of years it has brought the people of Egypt the precious gift of water."

"And have the Egyptians made mistakes? And does their father still provide for them? And do they expect their father always will?"

"They say that Father Nile never goes back on them."

"Yes. Father Nile is on an endless journey bringing life to generation after generation. You too are on a journey though you don't know for how long. If you listen to the wisdom of the people of Egypt you will become wise. And if you listen to the wisdom that comes from the Great Spirit you will be wiser still, you will have something to say, my little riverman. Now you have something to do. I will save my goodbye until you do it."

Sam Snake pitched the skewered trout into his canoe. Tommy stared at the brook babbling by with unabated abandon and abundance, churning happily into the larger stream, adding itself, losing its name, joining the more significant movement. At this moment, a powerful peace visited him, a peace that surpassed knowledge as only mystery can. It came from trusting in an unseen power outside himself, a trust born out of desire and achieved through permission that came from within, permission as swift, persuasive, and undeniable as a bolt of lightning. Like a terrific accident on the highway that everyone survives without a scratch. Like a bush bursting into flame. Like a horse throwing its rider. Like a voice in the night.

Tommy turned to watch Sam Snake paddle his canoe round the down-stream bend. He closed his eyes and opened his ears to the sounds of nature. The wind in the willows, birdsong, the babbling burbling bubbling streams joining in a quiet riot of plashy union, and from farther away, the sound of children and bagpipes. He rose blinking and turned to enter the elm grove.

Deep into the wood, on ground heavily shaded by towering trees, the grove opened into a place of wide, winding trails where neither grass nor bush grew. The boy wandered through earthen pathways, circling on himself, recalling when it was that he had found the stone. It was because of the eight fighter airplanes that appeared out of nowhere, swooping and zooming like devils. Tommy escaped to where the Golden Hawks would not hurt him, to the Treaty Tree, though the name was unknown to him then. This is what the Trickster in the forest called it. The old rattler knew where the tomahawk had come from, just as younger Sam Snake knew, just as Sambath of the Clan Kat had known.

It was over a hundred feet high, the granddaddy of the grove. The immense main trunk divided into three leading branches from where it assumed a vase shape that spread high into the sky until it ended in a feathery canopy like the world's widest umbrella. It was in the crotch of the three leading branches that Tommy had found the stone.

What he wished to hold on to most firmly was the feeling of tranquil certainty, the feeling that permeated him when he watched Sam Snake's canoe disappear around the bend, the feeling that he had direction. To this feeling he knew he could return again and again. Confidence welled up within him at the exhilarating thought. At this brimming moment, he plucked the inspiration, polished it like a pearl, and allowed its smooth perfect glow to seep in and through him.

Tommy became aware that the sunless areas of the grove, while smooth and safe, would not lead him to the cheering children. He had lingered long on the secluded pathways and would soon need to attack the bushes encircling the grove. He banished all doubt and let the pearl grow in size and lustre. Then, satisfied that he could retrieve it when uncertainty, confusion, or temptation led him astray, he gave up his tomahawk.

Well done, good and faithful servant.

Navigating by the sound of cheering children and blaring bagpipers, Tommy stepped from a tangle of wild rose into the vast openness of Columba's Field deep in the throes of the Findrinny Highland Games. He climbed high into the bleachers. Behind him a tug-of-war team was talking tough. On the infield, wee Highland dancers hopped, highcut, sword danced, and did the *Seann Triubhas*. A band of small blond girls in a sea of MacMillan yellow attacked their bagpipes as if in mortal combat.

The caller for the track events took the microphone: "Final call for the fourteen-and-under girls' one hundred-yard dash. Get on your mark! Ladies and gentlemen, representing the Findrinny Highland Society team in this race, having qualified with the third fastest time in the three heats, is Katie Beaton. It is Katie's first final in front of a Findrinny audience, so let's give her a big hand."

She was in the near track. Across her chest she wore the letters FHS. The Venerable Bede stood at trackside, leaning into her ear. "You go, girlie, get on your mark."

"Get ready!" called the announcer.

Katie spread her fingers on the cinder track, stretched her right leg behind.

"Come on girlie, get set," said her coach.

"Get set!"

Katie looked up now, her intense stare straight ahead to where the track veered in its oval orbit.

"Go!"

She sprang like a cougar, leaving the others two feet behind at the start line. Puffed and pumped, steadily, hands cutting through air, still accelerating, staring straight ahead with every technique she had learned and minus the ponytail she dropped in the garbage can, still accelerating through the finish line, arms held high. She cartwheeled, landed on her feet, did another cartwheel, beamed and waved to her family in the bleachers.

"Good race, Katie!" the coach said. "You ran right through that finish line."

"I know, just like you told me."

"Fastest time yet. Look."

Katie saw the face of the stopwatch and smiled.

For an hour Tommy waited near the fence that divided the stands from the track, keeping an eye on her movements while the Games went on. To his inner coward he said, Don't be afraid! Carry through on your decisions. Be cunning and aggressive in the face of danger.

He simply called out her name because that was, after all, the plan. "Katie!" he sang. The name hung in the air like a clock striking one.

Katie looked at her friends and then towards him. She was still in her running togs, tanned evenly on her legs, arms, and face. Her body was lovely, sleek, and strong. He wanted to touch her because she was perfect and what he said would be from the heart and he could say it if he touched her. Her eyes looked mild but wary. He kept his hands in his pockets.

"It's about last week," he began uneasily.

She was silent, waiting.

"That thing I said in the line-up at the show. I'm sorry for that. I shouldn't have told anyone about that. That was between us, like a secret, only I didn't keep it, did I?"

When he stopped talking, she put a foot on the page wire fence. Tommy wanted to mimic her, to lean against the fence, looking casually out to the field. That's what friends would do. But a more important apology was straining within him like a coiled fist.

"And I'm sorry about the whole bridge thing. It was like I was dead or something. I didn't move a muscle to help you. You could have fell in the water and died. And I just stood there."

"Well, I wanted to say something to you too," Katie began. "I'm sorry you got the strap. Philip MacKenzie told me you weren't even in on it."

"The Goon talked to you?"

"You always do that," said Katie. "Whenever I say some guy talked to me, you act shocked. You did it to Joyce even. What's that about, anyway?"

"I didn't realize you were friends."

“Friends? Hah! He’s more like a bodyguard. Didn’t you notice? He’s always hanging around. Even comes over to the girls’ playground sometimes to check on me. I think I liked it better when he was a bully. Anyway, what happened was that my mother talked to his father and his father said he’d whup him but good if anyone ever laid a finger on me again. Anyone. Philip said he got whupped round the house anyway, but if it happened again he’d be sore for a month of Sundays.

“So what did he say about me.”

“Oh yeah. He said, ‘Tom Ass…’ That’s what he calls you, did you know that? Funny, eh? He’s so funny. He said, ‘Tom Ass was just an innocent bystander. He’s not even part of our gang.’ He said he should have told Mrs. MacDonald that you didn’t deserve to get the strap. Anyway, that’s how come I know you weren’t guilty.”

So, as a coward he was not guilty. He was just an innocent, useless bystander. Useless. And to think that the pronouncements of the imbecilic Goon, protector of damsels in distress, were being quoted like legal judgments. Goon-wisdom was being applied to him. The idea stung like iodine. Tommy knew how Sister Dot would see it. The nun saw right through excuses and alibis. She told the first communicants about sins of commission and sins of omission. Geronimo would agree with her. Cowardice was the paramount sin of omission, a kind of silent betrayal, and worthy of the fate of Mexicans.

“Yeah, well, I deserved the strap anyway for just standing there. I think if it happened again I’d be braver. Least I hope I would.”

It was true, Tommy sadly realized. The nature of heroism required courage and spontaneity. In the woods, Tommyhawk, young Indian brave, would take on all odds, but in the real heat of battle, he froze like a popsicle. The moment to be brave for Katie had slipped past like a twirling maple key. There would be no other. Katie was looking at him when he lifted his eyes to her.

“Don’t worry about that. There won’t be another time. I can outrun those guys if they ever try it again. But you know what, Tommy? I know what everyone says and what you think. But I never told on you. I didn’t mean to fink out anyone. I didn’t even want to tell my mom when I got home. They got it out of me that Philip and Simon were involved, but I didn't even see the rest of them. It was only when I got to school the day after the strapping that I found out all who were involved. I was glad the rest got the strap. They've been bugging me for years. But you were my friend."

"You thought I was in on it?"

"My mother asked Jimmy Dog who was there. I guess she meant what kids had chased me, but he told her everyone who was there. She put all the names in the letter she wrote to Mrs. MacDonald. I was so upset about what they did to me, I didn't want to go back to school. Then my cousin Fiona told me that kids were saying I was a tattletale and that was awful, too, but my God, they deserved to be punished for what they did. It was horrible, horrible, horrible, and oh so humiliating. But my mother said I should put it behind me and forget about it. She said she would speak to the ringleaders' fathers and there would be no more trouble. And then she said, 'Katie, you'll just have to learn to run faster than the boys.' So that's why I joined the track team."

"I know, I saw you race. Congratulations. Pretty amazing."

"Coach said he didn't expect me to challenge this year because the other girls are a year older than me. I guess I'm just a fast learner."

As she told her tale, Tommy let her words soak over him like a litany. He observed beyond her superficialities, her absorbing eyes, moving lips, and the hair he once thought so fine. What struck him was her capacity to overcome adversity. The same incident that sent him into paroxysms of guilt had motivated Katie to excel. He had turned into a reclusive bookworm while the real victim of the bridge incident had transformed into a star athlete. How had it happened? There was something in Katie's revelation that defied instant understanding, until it hit him like a slap in the face. She had told people about it. She had good advisers, smart coaches. She made the right choices. Where were his advisors after the bridge incident? Unlike Katie, he hadn't asked anybody for advice. Look what happened when he did ask for advice, as the Unseen spirit had told him to do about the murders in the Tampakan. His mother got Uncalucky involved and she said it changed the outcome of the election. Big Ran'l went down to a surprise defeat. Then Uncalucky went to see the Liberal man who beat Big Ran'l. Now the Liberal man says he wants to do right by the

Mi'kmaw and the B'laan. He wants to shut down the smelter and get back into producing findruine. And he's got Gramma on his side.

"Ugh," Katie squirmed. "It's that awful man."

A red-kilted man had taken over the microphone and was thanking the crowd for their attendance at the ninety-ninth annual Highland Games and insisting that they return next year for the hundredth. He was one of those people who only *thinks* he is good with a microphone.

"You know him?"

"Yes. Joyce and I call him Tartansocks. He tried to close down the Brigadoon. He wanted Joyce's dad to fire my friend Rose who is a waitress there."

Tommy recognized the insulting man who delivered Uncalucky home the night Roger Maris hit the home run that turned the World Series in the Yankees' favour. Katie's tale reminded him of something else. A crazy kitchen party that seemed so long ago. Mommy dancing, Nosey Flynn on the fiddle, Big Ran'l on the Stool of Repentance, Uncalucky singing up a storm and Bobo thinking he was dead of asphyxiaaaaaation, Daddy toasting the other men for the great victory that gave Samwell Hung honorary membership in the Findrinny Highland Society in its centenary year no less. So it was this fool on the stage who made The Cunningham Motion.

"Yeah, I heard about that," he said.

"Katie! Coming?"

"Yeah, just a sec," she sang. "Well, I gotta go. Thanks for wanting to speak to me, Tommy."

"You too. Thanks.

"Maybe you and Jacky and Jimmy Dog will come over and hang out at my house next week. Just don't bring any dead fish."

Katie and her friends receded from view. Tommy stood with his foot on the page wire fence looking out towards Columba's Field. The last tosser had turned the caber. The last dancer had flung. An army of pipers and drummers took to the field marching like Gherkas and playing "Scotland the Brave," his father among them, countermarching now in close confines and trying to avoid crashing drones into one another. Lips pursed around blowpipes, throats bulging like balloons, eyes nearly popping out of their sockets, until suddenly they stopped to face the grandstands and the drum major bellowed, "Massed bands! At the halt! 'The Road to the Isles.'"

The British army had played the tune at the D-Day landings in Normandy. Tommy's father was full of information like that. He said his band played "The Road to the Isles" after the Battle of Coriano Ridge where Big Ran'l lost an arm and a leg and forever tilted to the right. His mother sang it at a ceilidh once. It was all about someone setting sail to their home in the Outer Hebrides and talking about all the places they would pass on their journey.

We are all on a journey, Sam Snake had said. We all have our part to play. The boy could see it clearly now. Both his part and Katie's were played out with unwritten lines. They were both working on mysteries without any clues. It was not the details of Katie's revelations that made him smile, for there was sadness throughout. What brought happiness to his heart was that Katie felt comfortable enough to volunteer the story, leaning against the fence so bonnie and blithe and inviting him to her house to play. With her kindness she had slaked a thirst he assumed unquenchable. He felt the relief of a parched man stumbling toward an oasis. It filled his eyes with tears of joy and his body and soul with the anticipation of renewed life. He dipped and filled his canteen and drank from the precious water of clemency—Katie's gift to him and a gift he finally accepted unto himself. A glorious feeling he allowed to seep into his every dried and dying tissue. Forgiveness.

The blue islands are pullin' me away
Their laughter puts the leap upon the lame
The blue islands from the Skerries to the Lews
Wi' heather honey taste upon each name.

Mrs. Caffrey touched her stomach and watched the second hand sweep around the clock face. When the contractions stopped she looked at the call button, two feet out of reach. Getting to it would be a chore. Every change of position required her to prime her body towards movement with rocking or heaving motions. She crawled her elbows behind her back, hoisted herself into a sitting position, pivoting on her bum, and swung her legs over the bedside. The effort brought beads of sweat to her brow. She laid aside her rosary and pressed for the nurse.

The family poured in before the nurse. Hector in the lead with five chickens following. She hugged them all in turn and thought, my darlin' lively Molly with your curly curls dangling like hanging ivy, and my tough little Bobo so frank and funny, and my dear Jacky growing so tall and strong, and Cissy oh Cissy will he spousify you when I'm gone?

"Tommy, are you coming over to hug me?"

"I will later, I just want to sit here for now."

The reunion was interrupted by a burly nurse who pulled the curtains around them and spoke as if the patient was half deaf. "It lasted how long? Forty seconds? Okay. And twenty minutes since the last one? Has your water broke? No? Let's get you lying down again shall we. Oh my my. Your bum is red Mrs. Caffrey. Is it sore? We'll have to put some cream on that. Are you still having diarrhea?"

She answered in a hushed, barely audible voice, not because she was so weak, but to encourage the nurse to follow suit. The children were three feet away.

"When the contractions get closer, we'll move you into the birthing room. I'll come back with some cream for that bum."

"It's okay for now. The children are here. I'll visit with them first, if I can."

A commotion in the corridor, and in swept Jimmy Dog, followed by his parents. In his arms, Uncalucky carried little Daisy whose head was buried in his shoulder and her little palms covered her peepers.

"Okay," he beckoned. "You can open your eyes now, little Daisy."

The girl blinked, struggled to be let down, then toddled straight toward the sitting boy. "Whoopsie Daisy," she called happily stretching her arms to him.

"She wants you to pick her up, Tommy, and play with her," said Mrs. Caffrey.

"Come see Mommy, Daisy," Tommy said, taking her by the hand and lifting her to the bed.

"Down!" commanded Daisy. She stuck two fingers in her mouth, toddled to Uncalucky and grasped the leg of his pants.

"Getting used to me already, I guess," said the uncle with a shrug that couldn't hide his pleasure.

"She loves her new room," Mary said, "Lucky painted it a sunny yellow and hung a mobile from the ceiling over where her crib will be."

"Come here, Jimmy," Bridget said to the pale brute. "How have you been since your last visit? I've thought about you and Tommy many times since then."

When it came to visions of the supernatural kind, discretion was essential. A few would believe—the gullible, the miraclephiles. There might always be doubt in the others. Were you medicated? What drugs were they giving you? I wouldn't mention this to anyone else. But not these two lads, my brave Tommy and tough Jimmy Dog, a survivor if there ever was one. Left in a basket on Mary and Lucky's doorstep. A childless couple chosen by an abandoning mother, a childless couple who would want and would bring up a babe the mother could not care for out of immaturity, poverty, or affliction.

And look at Lucky. You wouldn't know he was the same person who passed out in a field and woke up covered with snow, who step-danced on tables and stoves and any surface that would hold him, who tumbled down the stairs at the Celtic Hall and let flee a fart at the bishop. It's a miracle he's still alive with all the accidents and incidents and shenanigans, not to mention the war. Don't mention the war, whatever you do. And now they will have two more babies to bring up. Babies of their blood.

She felt them again, the signs of labour, the pain that told her that her uterus was positioning her seventh and final baby to press through her ravaged cervix—from the birth canal and into the world. She breathed into the contractions, as her children watched with awe.

Mary, as much in awe said, "Don't worry my dearies, it just means the baby will be coming soon."

Hector sat on the bed beside Bridget, arm around her shoulder. A nurse entered and was about to speak when Hector broke into a lullaby.

Ho ro, mo nigh'n donn bhoidheach,
Hi ri, mo nigh'n donn bhoidhech
Mo chaileag laghach, bhoidheach,
Cha phos mi ach tu

"We'll now be taking Mrs. Caffrey to the birthing room," said the nurse matter-of-factly. Not a miracle, but part of a process. "It's time for everyone to leave."

Hector said, *"A fhi a fath anish.* It won't be long now. We have to go, my darlings. Mommy will be wheeled away soon."

"I want to talk to Mommy alone."

"It's okay, Hector. I think Tommy has something important to tell me. Please just wait outside for him." She hugged them all again and as the last of them left the room, touched her stomach, closed her eyes, and breathed softly, deeply. "Okay, Tommy, we can be alone now for a little while. I hope you are not too sad about Daisy living with Uncalucky and Auntie Mary."

"I want to tell you the baby's name," he answered. "I'll whisper it to you, but you can't say it out loud until after the baby is born. Promise?"

"A promise is a funny thing," said Bridget Caffrey after considering the bargain in front of her. "Once I've said something in trust, whether it's 'I promise' or 'I love you,' it means forever. An oath like that can't be broken even by time. I would never promise something I didn't mean to keep. So you see you're putting me in a difficult position. I think we should talk about the name first, don't you?"

"Did you know me when I was born?"

"Well, yes."

"No, you didn't. You didn't know how I'd be. I could have had no arms. I could have been a mean kid, no matter what you and Daddy did to stop me."

She began to say that she would have loved him regardless, when he interrupted.

"You didn't know me but you had already decided to love me. You promised to love me even before I was born. Same with all your kids."

"Maybe I was just lucky to have good kids," she laughed.

"Okay, so it's luck, that's all," he said hotly. "If that's all it is, then trust me to think of the right name for the baby. Maybe you'll get lucky."

She felt like someone being forced to jump from a cliff. She spoke in a staring way, expressionless, soft, and rambling. She touched again her bulging stomach as she spoke, as much to herself as to Tommy.

"Seems I'm always having to let other people do for me what I've always done for myself. Make my supper. Change my bed. Bathe me. Take care of the kids. Now I can't even name my own baby. I'm always having to accept incapacity. Like I'm delivering verdicts against my former self."

"This is different, better."

She smiled pleadingly before continuing. "Worse! You want me to accept a name without knowing what it is. And doesn't Daddy have some say? Tommy, can't you see—"

"I'll tell you why I chose the name," Tommy said more forcefully. "I chose it because it makes me think about how awful life can be, but also about how special life can be. It makes me think of you and Daddy and how much you love each other, but also about how much you have given up. It makes me feel that no matter how bleak life seems, there may be shining waters further upstream. There may be answers, not only questions. There may be hope and forgiveness." His voice quavered too soon to say all he wished to say, but after a breath of reinforcement he added with finality, "It makes me think of heaven and earth."

She waited through another contraction then said, "Okay, Tommy, I promise." Then she leaned forward and allowed the boy to whisper the name of her last child.

A WAKE

Languid light on the drive home, crystals in the air, not quite snow, falling to the streets and melting away like memories. Good, Gramma's got the fire roaring. Get the coats off, get the boots off, noisy the house, steamy the biscuits, sweet the smell of stew on the stove. My God, look at the food people have dropped off.

Gramma urges them, "We'll eat now. Hector won't be home till late. He's going to Port Hood with the casket. Bridget will be waked at Archie and Kitty Ann's for another two days before the funeral. Sit! Sit, Sister. Sit, Father. Sit, Mary and Lucky. Erita, sit. Sit, Ran'l and Yolanda."

Beef simmered in onion gravy, chunky potatoes, plump carrots, sweet-soft parsnip, green tomato relish, apple pie, ice cream, repetitious avuncular conversation, droning and comforting, steady as she goes. Uncalucky does a Jim Reeves-Patsy Cline duet with Cissy and pats her shoulder and they smile as applause falls like raindrops. Now that he's sober, he's asked to sing everywhere. The kettle whistles. Father McCoy breaks out a bottle. Knock knock, who's there? It's Nosey Flynn at the door, fiddle in hand. It's turning into a regular ceilidh.

Sundown comes too early. The visitors linger singing and telling stories about the deceased. The priest breathes the scent of scotch on the twins and Sister Catherine says mournfully, "You two be brave now. I know you will."

Gramma Caffrey shoos them off. "You too, Tommy, go to bed now."

"Daddy always lets me stay up on Saturday night till the hockey game is over."

And when they all leave, he stays and looks at the television while she rocks, knits a blankie for baby, and listens to even more fiddles on the radio. Clicking her needles in time with the jigs and reels, then slowing to the heartache of Gow's unearthly lament, and quickening again to the ballad of Shannon Anna Livia Jordan.

The oblong box is on the mantle. It hasn't been opened for months. Hi, MacCrimmon, long time no see. Daddy knows the dead soldier who owned the chanter in the war. Private First Class Gordie MacDonald. Seven fingers on seven holes on top and the thumb flicking high A gracenotes on the one high hole below. His left thumb was for that one, the high A. Blow it. Each note clear, crisp, correct, distinct. Slowly and carefully the notes fall in sequence and out comes that tune Daddy sang for him oh so long ago. The first tune. The Hero tune.

To us thou art Hector the Hero,
The chivalrous, dauntless, and true;
The hills and the glens, and the hearts of a nation
Re-echo the wail for you.

And yet there were forces even he was powerless to affect, big and strong and faithful as he was. And the sadness in his eyes was there when he sat them on his queen bed that morning and told them their mother was in heaven.

"Did you see outside, Daddy, the grotto, the shrine, the roses?" Cissy said. She had gone to pray at the statue and when she looked up she saw a bright light coming from the woman in the clawfooted tub. She was awestruck by what she saw next. Slowly there appeared three women. The coloured woman in the middle exposed her abdomen to show irradiated skin, burned blacker than black. In her hands she held bouquets of golden hued tobacco leaves. On her right stood a woman whose skin was golden brown like caramel. She wore coloured beads and bangles of findruine and blood flowed from bullet holes in her chest and leg. The third woman was white as the porcelain tub that held the inscrutable virgin, and like the virgin, a bright halo surrounded her head. The three women held hands and smiled at Cissy and when their light left, the entire grotto was surrounded with the most magnificent mountain of roses, hundreds of them, red as raspberry chocolate.

"I saw them, Cissy. They are beautiful, aren't they? Mommy always said I expected a miracle. It looks like I got one, didn't I."

The long day had finally grown silent except for an unseen brook softly streaming beneath a pie-in-the-sky moon and stars like pinpricks in the black. Light rose, too, from the town and drifted above in a shimmering glow like a protective dome. The radiance enclosed the houses, the university, the single street of stores, the churches, the ever-running brook, and the convent and hospital high on pill hill.

Tommy sat upright on his bed. Through a crack between door and jamb a thin stream of light entered his room, crossed over to the bed, and lit a sharp line on the wallpaper.

Where is that pearl, he thought, the one I found at the river. Inside, deep inside, in a shell so hard to pry, only able if I'm quiet, quiet, quiet. Quiet. Here in my bed, unseen by them all except Mommy who watches over me always, quietly smoothing pain, hers and mine, then smiling and attentive to all.

He breathed a mantra, *Ger-aww-ni-mo,* inhaling serenity, prying with silence the rough pink and cream oyster shell. No thoughts, just quiet, chasing away the pangs and waves of guilt. *Ger-aww-ni-mooo.* Surrender to the quiet opening, relaxing of all that is buried within, trout on a stick, babblebrook, Mother Ganges, Father Nile, Bonnie Barrow, Stinky Clyde, mumbo jumbo god of the Congo will hoodoo you, sink into jungles, break out of mountains, seep out from lakes, all the river names flooding and jamming. But only one combination would do for the baby, for the mother, for the decision she made.

Tommy Caffrey went to sleep, perchance to dream of a day in July when first he laid eyes on his baby sister. He heard the nurse coming, coming, coming swishing in her starched white uniform, coming for to carry her home. To mother. To milk. Here she is, Mrs. Caffrey.

O, you're back. Ohhh. Hello, beautiful. O, look at you. Did she sleep? No, she should not go back to the nursery. She should stay with her mother. I'll call you if I need you. O look, Tommy. See her tight fists, pink and small, the breadth of your little finger between the last knuckle and the fingertip. Small as they are, she waves them crossly at the cool unfamiliar air. Shhhh. Shhhh, sweetie. O, I have another baby. You have another sister. Unique in every way. All unique. Is that a smile? Look at these gums, these perfect lips, the tiny precious nose, these eyes. These eyes are crying. Are you crying, little baby? Oh, is you too cold, little girlie? Is you not so comfy? Is you bellyhungry? Sorry, baby. Why are you crying, little baby? I'm here. Do you have bad memories? Were you too blue and cold? Were you too twisted? Too squashed? It's okay, I'm here. These little eyes, crying eyes, blinking eyes, blinking at the offending light. These eyes. Shhh, I'll cover you, darlin'. There, that's better. Now you're calm. There now. Calm and sure of yourself. Mumbly. Cooing. Lying on my breast.

Searching, drinking. O, how do they know? Instinct. The will to survive. There now, little sweetheart, my little darlin'. Now, you stay with me. I'll sing to you a lullaby. I'll sing you to sleepy-bye. I will softly serenade you swiftly to slumber. Dadadumm dadadumm. Shhh. Shhh. Lulla. Bye. And good night. Go to sleep, my little Shannon. Lullaby and good night, go to sleep, my little girl. Is you happy, my darlin'? I am.